The Crossroads

ALSO BY PAMELA COOK

Blackwattle Lake
Essie's Way
Close to Home

The Crossroads

PAMELA COOK

hachette
AUSTRALIA

Published in Australia and New Zealand in 2016
by Hachette Australia
(an imprint of Hachette Australia Pty Limited)
Level 17, 207 Kent Street, Sydney NSW 2000
www.hachette.com.au

10 9 8 7 6 5 4 3 2 1

National Library of Australia
Cataloguing-in-Publication data

Cook, Pamela, author.
The crossroads/Pamela Cook.

ISBN: 978 0 7336 3685 1 (pbk)

Families – Fiction.
Family secrets – Fiction.
Romance fiction, Australian.

A823.4

Cover design by Christabella Designs
Cover images courtesy of Getty Images and Bella Rose Photography
Author photo courtesy April Boughton
Text design by Bookhouse, Sydney
Typeset in 12/17.25 pt Sabon LT Pro by Bookhouse, Sydney
Printed and bound in Great Britain by Clays Ltd, St Ives plc

MIX
Paper from
responsible sources
FSC
www.fsc.org FSC® C104740

For John,
forever and always

Chapter One

Rose

SOME DAYS THE DUST WAS LIKE A SECOND SKIN. EVEN HERE, in town. A thick, red, gritty skin that clung so stubbornly to her arms and legs that when she brushed a hand across her limbs the stain on her fingertips was a surprise. Today was one of those days. Eleven o'clock in the morning and already twenty-nine degrees. Ridiculous for this time of year.

Rose O'Shea stared at her upturned palm, fascinated by the strange pattern the red particles had formed. She traced an arc from the base of her index finger to the meaty pad of flesh below her thumb. A fortune teller had told her years ago, studying the lines on her hand, that she would live a long, happy, prosperous life. At forty-nine she figured she was more than halfway through it, and while she wasn't destitute, prosperous wasn't a word she'd use to describe her bank balance.

She pulled out the rag tucked into the string of her apron and wiped down the bar as she gazed out through the open door of the pub. Not an awful lot to see – the odd car passing by, a few locals strolling home with their shopping bags trying to dodge the midday heat, Harry Shepherd's cattle dog stretched out on the footpath waiting for his owner to finish his lunchtime schooner before they wandered off home.

A blowfly zoomed by Rose's ear and she swatted it away with the cleaning cloth still clutched in her hand. 'Bugger off.'

'If you say so.' Declan appeared beside her, a beer glass in one hand, the other pulling on the tap, a grin on his face.

She shook her head. 'Don't you even think about it. I've lost enough staff lately. Besides, if anyone apart from that blowie is buggering off it's me.'

Declan lifted the tap and rested the glass of amber liquid on the bar. 'Is that right? And where would you be buggerin' off to this week, Mrs O?'

She looked across the room, out through the open window, but the scene she imagined was far from the one outside. Instead she saw a higgledy-piggledy roofline, a soft opalescent light and bare-branched trees lining the cobbled streets. The Seine ambled below an ancient stone bridge as she sat watching it, sipping dark, bitter coffee and nibbling on a chocolate croissant at an outside seat at a little corner patisserie. All sorts of elegant people bustled by as the afternoon turned to twilight. One by one the street lamps came to life along the Champs-Elysées, and there, presiding over the city, was the Eiffel Tower.

'Paris,' she sighed, coming back to reality.

The bartender delivered the drink to Harry and returned. 'Really? I never pegged you for a romantic,' Declan teased. 'And who would you be takin' along with you?'

He had the same lilt to his voice as Mick. She wouldn't usually fraternise so casually with her backpacker staff; she preferred to eavesdrop on their tales, hear about all the places they'd been, store the information away for possible future reference. But Declan . . . well, she could chat to him all day. She stared back out at the quiet street, the asphalt so hot she could almost see the vapour rising into the air, the row of shops huddled in the shade beneath a tin awning. One day she'd pack a suitcase and buy that round-the-world ticket she'd always dreamed about, but it wasn't going to be any time soon.

She considered his question. 'Not a soul.' She rubbed at a stain on the polished surface in front of her and dumped the cleaning cloth into a plastic bag by her feet.

'Argh now, as someone who has been there I can assure you it's called the City of Love for a reason.'

Rose smiled in spite herself. 'You are going to make some girl very lucky one of these days, my friend.'

'I'm up for it if you are.' He wiggled his eyebrows.

Rose gave a hearty laugh. 'Back to work.' She forced a scowl and nodded towards the other end of the bar where a grey-headed couple perched on stools. 'The nomads up there look like they could do with a drink.' Harry, now that he was on his second schooner, was chewing off the couple's ears about the local sights. Next week it would be a different couple he'd be boring to tears. Different people, same old story.

'That they do.' Declan shot her a wink before turning to greet the customers.

Cheeky bugger. Completely full of himself but still a breath of fresh air, especially after that last bloke she'd employed. Up and left without giving a scrap of notice, but not before he'd stuck his fingers in the till and fleeced her dry. She'd sworn she would hire a woman the next time, steer away from the bedraggled young men who landed on her doorstep looking for cash to fund the rest of their adventures. But then Declan had appeared with his Gaelic charm. True, she did have a soft spot for his accent, but he was neat and clean and easy on the eye. Damned efficient too. Hiring the backpackers was so much better then employing locals. It was the gossip factor; stickybeaks poking their noses into her business were the last thing she wanted. Given the rate things was falling apart around here, her bank manager would no doubt prefer it if she were a one-woman show, but there was only so far she could stretch herself.

Meryl the postie strode through the door, the height of fashion in her fluoro orange vest and silver bike helmet, waving an envelope about. 'Only one for you today.'

Rose thanked her and grabbed the letter, peering over the top of her glasses to study the fine print in the top corner: Wills Shire Council. Hopefully they'd be more amenable than the Department of Environment and Heritage Protection and actually help her out with the funds to repair the place. It could certainly do with it. Her face fell as she took a minute to really look at the broken window sashes, the dry rot spreading through the timbers, the bare patches of thread in the ancient carpet. And that was only what she could see from where she was standing. Parts of the roof had rusted away, and you took your life in your hands venturing out onto the upstairs verandah. Termites. Voracious little bastards. The airconditioning had even carked it a few weeks back. She looked up at the fan whirring beneath the pressed-tin waratahs on the ceiling and thanked God for small mercies. With a bit of luck she'd be able to make a start on some of the renovations this month. If The Crossroads wasn't heritage listed she could get away with doing it on the cheap, but the number of rules and regulations she had to follow was mind-boggling. She slipped her pinkie under the envelope's seal to rip the thing open, but a voice boomed through the doorway, stopping her in her tracks.

'Rosie Barnes, you haven't changed a bit.'

She stared at the man, frowning. He seemed to know her but she didn't have a clue about him. It took another long, hard look before she worked it out. The face was more lined, the hair above it greyer and thinner, but there was no doubt in her mind about the identity of her visitor.

The envelope slid from Rose's hand, dragging her out of her stupor. She bent down behind the bar and picked it up, then slowly folded it into the back pocket of her jeans, took a breath.

After all these years . . .

'David Ryan.' She cleared her throat to rid her voice of its tremor as she stood. 'What are you doing back in town?'

'Thought I'd come out and see how a few of my old mates were doing. Start with my favourite girl.'

Mates. Not exactly a term she would have used to describe their relationship. Or rather, lack of relationship.

He took a seat across from her at the bar. Age hadn't diminished his height although it had added an extra few kilos to his middle where his navy polo shirt wrinkled across his belly. The unruly blond mop was gone, replaced by a respectable crew cut, but his eyes were still the same striking shade of blue.

'You're looking good, Rosie. Hair's a bit redder than I remember, but it suits you.'

What else do you remember?

'Thanks. You too.' And why the hell was she choking on her words like a nervous preschooler?

Get a grip, Rose.

'You look good too, I mean. How are you?'

'Older, and a bit on the bald side.' He ran a hand over the top of his head. 'Bald is sexy these days, so they tell me.'

'So they tell you or so you tell yourself?'

The man shrugged and gave a quiet laugh. 'Either or. You, my dear Rosie, haven't aged a day.' His smile was lopsided. That same old smile . . .

'Well, since I was seventeen when we last saw each other I know for a fact that you're full of crap.' Seventeen and climbing out of his station wagon pulling on her knickers, but that didn't bear thinking about. She rubbed the sweat from her palms onto her apron.

Dave snorted. 'Same old Rosie. You always did say exactly what you thought. Have you got time for a chat? You can fill me in on what you've been doing for the past thirty years.'

It was actually thirty-two years, but she didn't correct him. The bar top had been buffed to a brilliant shine. She picked up a knife and a lemon from the bowl under the counter and started to cut it into wedges. You could never be too prepared. 'I'm a bit busy right now, Dave.'

'Could have fooled me,' he said.

She looked around the almost empty bar. The nomad couple and Harry were the only customers and their eyes were currently glued to Declan, who was busy spinning them a yarn.

'Come on, Rosie, you're the boss, aren't you? I'm sure you can take a break.'

She was cornered. But curious. Now that the shock of seeing him again was wearing off, she wanted to know more about where he'd been all these years – and what he was doing back here. 'I suppose I can spare a few minutes.' She signalled to Declan, who made his way towards them. 'Dec, can you grab us a couple of light beers?'

'Not for me thanks, Rosie,' Dave held his hands up in a stop-right-there gesture. 'Bit early in the day. I'll have a lemonade thanks, mate.'

'A beer and a lemonade coming right up.'

Rose brushed her fringe back off her face, fluffed up her hair in an effort to hide the greys among the auburn, adjusted her T-shirt – one of her oldest – on her shoulders. What a fright she must look. Not that she needed to impress David Ryan, of all people. She lifted the divider and made her way to a corner table.

Dave sat down beside her. There was a long moment of silence before they both started to talk at once.

'So, when did you—'

'How long have you—'

He laughed. 'Ladies first.'

Declan arrived with their drinks before either of them could try again. 'Here you go. Enjoy.' He gave Rose a wink and a thumbs up as he left.

She shook her head before turning her attention back to her visitor. 'So, I'm not sure where to start.' Certainly not with the last time they'd seen each other. Her stomach fluttered.

'Well, I know you married an Irishman.' He gave her a sympathetic smile. 'And I heard he passed away a few years back.'

She bit down on the soft flesh inside her cheek. 'You've heard a lot.'

'Bush telegraph, Rosie, you know what it's like. I've kept in touch with a few people out here. News travels.'

'Hmm, that it does.' She caught herself fiddling with her wedding ring and dropped her hands.

'I'm sorry about your husband.'

He sounded genuine. But then he always was a genuine sort of bloke. 'Thanks, Dave. How about you?' She'd heard, of course, that he'd married and moved to Brisbane, but that was about as far as it went.

'I lost Kay eighteen months ago.'

'Sorry to hear that.' She really was. Grief was a torture she wouldn't wish on anyone.

Dave screwed up his face and stared out the window. 'You'd know better than most how hard it is. I keep thinking I'll see her walk through the door but then . . .'

His voice trailed off and Rose followed his gaze to the life-sized statue across the street. An Ichthyosaurus. Itchy to his friends. Farms in the district were dying, shop fronts were boarded up all over town but the local tourism scene was alive and kicking thanks to the dinosaur trail. Itchy and his prehistoric mates. Poor buggers, stranded in that inland sea, never to escape, stuck in the middle of nowhere. She looked back at the man seated opposite her at the table, his brow furrowed, hands clasped and resting in his lap. He'd got away and she'd never really expected to see him again.

'So, what brings you out this way after all these years?'

Dave pursed his lips, tapping the pads of his thumbs together. He leaned back in his seat and when he turned his head Rose was shocked by the glassy sheen in his eyes. 'Taking a few weeks, visiting all the old haunts, seeing a few people. I'm thinking about moving here again.'

A strangled noise slipped from her throat before she had time to choke it back.

If he heard it he didn't bat an eyelid. 'The city's not for me, Rosie. It was Kay who wanted to move in the first place. We had a good life, but my kids have their own families now and

I'm at a bit of a loose end. Unit living is so claustrophobic. There's no space. Nothing to look at. I miss the dirt.'

She gave a manic laugh. 'Are you crazy? Some days I think if I see one more speck of the stuff I'll scream.'

'Probably am crazy. I don't know.' He was on a roll and there was no stopping him. 'My daughter, Mel, thinks I'm still grieving, but it's not just that. Of course I miss Kay, but it's more. I miss the land. And the people.' Dave picked up his glass and guzzled down his lemonade.

Was this actually happening? Was David Ryan really sitting across from her pouring his heart out? The last thing she needed was him back in town – a constant reminder of the past she'd left well and truly behind. Her hands had tightened themselves into fists beneath the table. She uncurled them and picked up her glass, suddenly wishing she'd ordered something stronger, a little Dutch courage was what she needed. Since there wasn't any of that to be had she mustered up the real thing.

'Coming back might not be as easy as you think.'

'*You* left. Couldn't wait to get out of the place, if I remember rightly.' He waved a hand towards the bar. 'Doesn't seem like coming back did you any harm.'

An angry heat built in her chest and rose to scald her cheeks. *If you only knew.*

She looked away, ran her eyes around the collection of faces smiling out from the frames on the walls. People she and Mick had met over the years, right here in this pub. David was right, of course. She had made a life for herself back in Birralong and yes, it had been a good one. 'That was a long time ago. And I was gone for less than a year. Things have changed a lot since then.'

'Place still looks the same to me.' He narrowed his eyes a little, pinned them on her. 'Weren't you heading off on a big adventure when you left here, travelling the world? Doesn't sound like you got very far.'

He laughed quietly and it took everything she had not to reach across the table and slug him. She plastered a smile onto her face instead. 'I was a kid. Homesick.' Not entirely the truth but not a straight-out lie.

'My point exactly. You were born and bred in Birralong, like me. It's in our blood.'

'What would you do? If you came back?'

'Oh, I don't know, buy myself a bit of land. Try my hand at being a farmer.'

A sudden laugh burst from Rose's lips. 'You do know we're in the middle of a drought?' Hectares and hectares of dry earth stretched for thousands of kilometres in every direction. What cattle was left had to be fed on food trucked in at higher prices than most people could afford. Life on the land had never been easy, but right now it was harder than ever. And David Ryan, who had never farmed a day in his life, thought he could just waltz on in and become some sort of cattle baron.

'I know, I know, probably not the best timing.'

Now there was an understatement. And her chance to convince him that moving back was a very bad idea. 'There's barely been a drop of rain in the past three years. A heap of people have up and left.' Rose studied the bubbles foaming around the rim of her glass as she waited for her words to take effect. 'Awful state of affairs. The roo problem's getting out of hand again too. Thousands of them. It's like a plague. Even with the cull they're completely out of control. Strathmore is riddled with them.'

'Strathmore? Bernie Bailey's place?'

Rose nodded. 'My daughter married Bernie's son. They're running it now.'

'A daughter, eh?'

'Yes.' Her spine stiffened. Was she really having this conversation? The best she could do now was try to steer it back on track and then get the hell out of it. 'Just the one. Stephanie. She's twenty-seven. And a grandson. Jake. He's almost five.'

Dave shook his head, huffed out a smile. 'Hard to believe we're both grandparents. I still feel like I'm a teenager half the time.'

She stood up and twisted the edges of her mouth into what she hoped was some sort of apology. 'Well, I'd better get back to work.'

Dave frowned briefly before standing. He placed a hand on her shoulder. 'Is everything all right, Rosie?'

'Yes, yes, everything's fine. I just have a few things I need to get done.'

'Of course.' He took a step forward and kissed her cheek. 'It's good to see you again. Been way too long. I'm housesitting for the Tinsdales so I'll pop in and have dinner one night. We can have a proper catch-up.' He turned to leave but pivoted back. 'Or I could come and try my hand at being a barman.'

She gave some sort of half-hearted laugh as she watched him leave, her knees shaking, her hands gripping the edge of the table. David Ryan. One of the town's most eligible bachelors in his day. Two years above her at school. She'd melted every time he said hello to her back then – all the girls had, but she'd taken her crush one step too far. He'd already left town with Kay by the time she'd come running back from Sydney with her tail between her legs.

All these years later and she'd almost managed to convince herself he'd never existed.

She picked up the two glasses and returned them to the bar. Declan had scuttled off to the storeroom to see what needed to be ordered. The nomads were gone, along with Harry, and the place was deserted. A sudden emptiness took hold of her as she looked around the room that had been both work and home for the past twenty-five years. There were days when she'd give anything to get out of the place, to do what she'd planned as a teenager, to travel. Seeing Dave again had dredged up that old urge to flee, but she wasn't seventeen anymore. She had a life here, responsibilities, promises to uphold. And a pub to run. The past was no more than a story – a story she'd never told anyone.

A secret that was hers to keep.

Stephanie

SCONES. YOU COULDN'T GET ANY MORE CLICHÉD WHEN IT came to country cooking than a batch of scones, which was exactly why Stephanie was sliding the final tray into the oven. She banged the door closed and set the timer. Grandma Barnes's famous scones were always a hit, and Stephanie hoped that today would be no different.

Hope. It was about the only thing she had an abundance of right now.

She gave a soft sigh and glanced skywards through the kitchen window. Brilliant blue as far as the eye could see. Her heart hurt just looking at it. Even after three years of solid drought she woke every day hoping that when she parted the curtains heavy grey clouds would be looming. Hoping that the rain would come and their property – and their livelihood – would no longer be under threat.

Hoping that life would get back to what it was before.

She dropped the dishcloth into the sink. Everything was just about ready. The first two batches of scones were lined up on the wire cooler, golden brown pillows of dough that smelled like Sundays. It reminded her of afternoon teas after a big lamb roast for lunch. Of damper and the old cast-iron kettle heating in the fireplace. Her dad and grandpa sharing a couple of long necks later on the verandah, yabbering about the price of wool and how many shearers would be in town next week and how good that would be for business – both the pub and the property – while the sun turned the horizon to tangerine.

So much had changed.

There was no use wallowing in misery, though. There'd been worse droughts and the generations before had all survived them. This land had been passed down to them to take care of – well, to Bryce really, but she was his wife and they were in it together. Gritting their teeth and staying positive was their only option, which was exactly why a busload of tourists was about to descend on Strathmore. She checked the clock above the sink: 10.18.

Twelve minutes to arrival time.

She reached around to untie her apron, folded it in half and half again and returned it to the bottom drawer. It was far too hot for denim but she wanted to look the part, and jeans and western boots were her standard uniform. She undid the cuffs on her shirt and rolled the sleeves up a little. The pink checks contrasted nicely with her tanned forearms and the collar made it dressier than her usual singlet top. All she needed was a hat to complete the look. She plucked her favourite from the hall-stand, the one with the feathered band around the brim, popped it on and took a look in the mirror. Not too bad. A bit of make-up probably wouldn't have gone astray. She pulled a tube of pale pink gloss from her back pocket and ran it over her lips. A smudge of dough had somehow found its way to her eyebrow and she wiped it away before assessing the final result. The woman looking back at her wasn't exactly model material but she was good enough – certainly good enough to play host to a busload of sightseers.

The anticipation of it all was making her giddy. As much as she loved Strathmore, there were times when she missed the happy chaos of The Crossroads, people coming and going, the stories and laughter and noise. One day on the farm could so easily roll into the next, especially now with the stock so run down and not as much physical labour to be done. Bryce hadn't exactly been great company lately, either. He'd shrunk so far inside his shell that any form of real adult conversation was pretty much non-existent. And as much as she adored Jake, there was only so much you could talk about to a preschooler – or a horse, for that matter. Her mood flattened. She needed to make sure Bryce was psyched up for their visitors and she had a pretty good idea where to find him.

Walking down the hall towards the office, she practised moulding her expression into something resembling calm. What was that saying her grandmother had about pouring water on oil? Or was it the other way around? Anyway, it wasn't like she wanted strangers traipsing through their house and across their land either, but if the extra income was going to help pay their weekly grocery bills they both needed to suck it up. She paused at the door of the office. There he was, right where she knew he'd be. Even from behind he oozed tension, his shoulders hunched, his hands clenched into fists on either side of the computer. She angled her head to catch a glimpse of the screen. The weather channel. Same as always. Couldn't he find a better way to spend his day than scanning the internet? You only had to look outside to see that there wasn't any rain on the way any time soon. She took a few more seconds to shake away her irritation and smooth out the frown she could feel on her brow before stepping into the room.

'Hey, babe,' she said. Pouring oil on troubled waters, that was it, and she hoped she was doing it now. 'Almost ten-thirty. The bus will be here soon.'

Nothing.

'Bryce?'

One hand dropped to his thigh and he shifted slightly in the chair but made no effort to turn around. 'I heard you.'

'Okay. I'll go find Jake and we'll see you outside?'

Nothing.

'Okay?'

Was it that hard to answer a simple question?

'I said I heard you, didn't I?' He swivelled the chair towards her. She drew in a sharp breath at the flash of lightning in his eyes.

It stirred her own thunder. 'You could show a bit more interest in this whole thing.'

'In what?' He scowled at her, a crimson stain colouring his cheeks. 'Friggin' stickybeaks dropping by to feast on our misery? This was your brain child, not mine.'

'Do you think I like it any more than you do? I'm doing this – no, *we're* doing this – to bring in some extra money, not for the entertainment value. At least it's something practical.' She waved a hand in the direction of the computer. 'Beats sitting on that thing for hours every day.'

'What's that supposed to mean?' He stood, hands splayed at his waist. His faded work jeans sat low on his hips and his grey shirt hung loose. Couldn't he wear a belt? Make an effort to look presentable?

'I'm saying that checking the weather reports every half-hour isn't going to make it rain. There's plenty of other stuff to be done around here.'

He huffed. 'Like tend to the three sheep and fifty-two cows we have left?'

A vision of the herds that once crowded the station filled Stephanie's head. Thousands of sheep feeding on land that used to be ripe for grazing. Better days. Days that *would* return.

'Look, let's not do this again.' She took a step forward, reached out and held his arm, ran her thumb over his bicep. 'I know it's not ideal. But it's temporary, okay?' She forced a small smile onto her face as she leaned towards him, slipping her hand into his when he nodded and sighed.

A bell chimed. 'That's the last lot of scones.' She turned and made her way back towards the kitchen, a spring returning to her step now that it was almost time. Bryce followed, a few paces behind. Fingers crossed they would get through the morning with him at least pretending to be pleasant. He had to be.

'Where's Jake?' he asked.

She flicked the oven off and eased the tray onto the bench. 'I think he's playing with his trucks out the front. He's pretty excited about our visitors.'

'At least someone is.' So much for pleasant. It was going to be up to her to pull them through. She abandoned the tea towels and closed the short distance between them, looping her hands at the back of his neck.

'It's not forever. Let's just see how it goes.'

Bryce nodded. His palms were solid and warm against the small of her back as he brushed a kiss to her forehead. His skin had that same earthy scent she'd always loved, but the spark that used to light his eyes was gone. It had been missing for a while now. The only thing that would bring it back was rain. Not the paltry showers that fell briefly with the grumbling afternoon storms they sometimes had but days and days of a good solid drenching.

A motor hummed in the driveway and they turned together, looking through the window to see a minibus pulling up not far from the house. A small figure ran towards it, waving to Narelle, the bus driver cum local tourism officer. Stephanie smiled. Her beautiful curly-headed boy, a smaller version of her husband. Nearly five and almost ready for school. She pulled her hands away from Bryce and adjusted her hat. Scones and akubras. Was it all a bit much? Oh well, too late now. 'You ready?'

'No. But it looks like we're doing this anyway.'

She shook her head and made her way towards the door. 'Come on,' she said, jollying him along, 'it won't be that bad.'

There was no response, just the fall of her husband's boots on the timber floorboards. Whether he liked it or not, Strathmore was now a local tourist attraction, at least for the time being, and Stephanie was determined to show their guests a good time.

'Do you have any dinosaur bones?'

'How hot does it get in summer?

'When was the last time it rained?'

'What do you do when the tanks run dry?'

The questions were endless. Stephanie answered each one with a smile, trying to be as informative as possible. No, the dinosaur skeletons were further north. Very hot in summer, usually in the forties for weeks on end. The last decent rainfall was in March 2012. When the tank runs dry we buy water – and try not to shower too often. Her feeble attempt at humour raised a smattering of polite laughter from the women in her group as they inspected the miracle that was her vegetable garden. Most of the men had elected to follow Bryce on a tour of the machinery sheds. She glanced over to see how they were doing. Not too well, judging by the look on her husband's face, which was growing increasingly darker. He wasn't one to suffer fools – not that these people were fools but, given their lack of farming experience, in his current frame of mind Bryce might not be able to hold his tongue.

Please just keep it together, Bryce.

Perhaps it was time to mix up the party.

'So, who's ready for some morning tea?' she said, leading the women in the direction of the house. The table on the porch was already set, Grandma's old china tea cups and saucers laid out on the white lace cloth, cake plates and milk jugs waiting to be filled.

As murmurings of 'Yes, please' and 'Ooh, lovely' followed her invitation, she waved a hand in Bryce's direction. He nodded curtly before saying something to his group that she couldn't make out and they all turned and began the walk back up. Bryce walked a few steps behind, head down, as Jake chattered away. Like the women, most of the men seemed to be in their sixties and seventies. A few, sporting the evidence of a life well lived around their waistlines, were red faced and mopping their brows with handkerchiefs. Fortunately she'd remembered to switch on the aircon. It was a luxury they usually didn't allow themselves, but the last thing they needed was one of their visitors keeling over. Inside she offered everyone a seat and ducked into the kitchen to boil the kettle and warm the scones, politely refusing offers of help. Bryce had stayed outside, and when she poked her head out the door he was nowhere to be seen.

She excused his absence with a fence that urgently needed fixing, and the next half-hour flashed by in a blur of tea drinking, scone devouring and question asking, the tourists obviously determined to get their money's worth. She managed the whole thing on her own, quite professionally too, if she did say so herself. Jake kept everyone entertained with stories about their kelpie, Peppie, who had come out briefly to say hello and then hidden herself back under the house in the shade. When Narelle announced it was time to head off, Stephanie waved them all goodbye, not entirely sorry the morning was over but pleased with how it had gone. Pleased with herself. Only one aspect of it had bugged her and it was only after the guests had closed the doors of the minibus and driven away that she allowed the anger simmering away inside her to come to a boil.

Jake was standing next to her finishing off a scone he'd managed to sneak outside, cream and jam smeared across his chin. She pulled a tissue from her pocket, reached down and cleaned him up.

'Where's Dad?' she asked.

He shrugged. 'That was fun,' he said, licking his lips. 'I'm going to play.' He skipped back towards the house where his trucks and cars were arranged in a circle in the dirt beside the garden.

Oh, to be a child again. She squared her shoulders and turned her eyes to the shed. So much for Bryce being on board. He'd done the absolute minimum and then vanished. Would it have killed him to come inside and be sociable? Give her a hand?

Her quarter horse, Bandit, whinnied at her but made no move to leave the shade of the tree he was standing under as she passed his paddock. His bay coat was dull with dust and his black mane tangled with burrs. Poor thing, he was definitely in need of a bath. Maisie, his mother, had taken shelter under the tin roof of her stable and looked thoroughly bored. Both of them loved getting out and about, doing the show circuit in their blingy saddles and bridles, but the entry costs and the petrol were unnecessary expenses.

Or so Bryce had decided.

All was quiet as she stepped inside the shed, the warm air even thicker than it was out in the open, if that were possible. She sucked in a breath and waited for her eyes to adjust to the dimmer light. A potpourri of chaff and oil and petrol filled her nostrils and she twitched her nose, fighting the urge to sneeze. Bales of hay were piled almost to the roof along part of the back wall. The tractor and excavator, neither of which had been used for months, were garaged in here along with a couple of quad bikes and an old paddock-basher ute. Shelves of tools, all neatly stored, lined the walls. Higher up was a padlocked metal cabinet and inside it, stored safely away, were two rifles. At the far end was an office, separated from the rest of the space by a timber partition, and sitting there at his father's old oak desk, his back to her, was Bryce.

Stephanie started towards him but then stopped. Something was wrong. She watched him carefully, took in his posture. He was leaning forward, his arms on his knees so that his body was hunched, his head lowered, almost touching the desk. Creeping closer, she could see now the way his shoulders heaved. Her own lungs were rising and falling like a pair of bellows. She braced her hands against her thighs, trying to steady herself as she stood, rooted to the spot. And then she heard a noise – a dry, raw rasp. Something primal and unsettling.

Bryce.

A cold finger of ice traced its way up her spine. She drew in a sharp breath. He spun around and for a few long, slow seconds they stared at each other. Even from this distance she could see the rims of his eyes were blood-red, his cheeks wet. He moved quickly then, swiped his palms across his face, and looked away. 'I'll be up in a minute.'

'Bryce?' She took a tentative step in his direction, the swish of her boot on the concrete floor echoing through the shed. Then another step. 'Bryce?' His name was all she could manage.

'I said, I'll be out in a minute.' This time it was a growl.

Get out. That's what he meant. *Get out and leave me alone.*

She left him, still sitting at the desk, still facing away from her.

Outside the sunlight and the heat were like a punch to the gut – another one – and she blinked deliberately as she stumbled back to the house. Vaguely she registered a whinny from the paddock and the faint, far-off caw of a crow but she kept her focus on the door, vacantly noticing Jake from the corner of her eye as she passed him playing in the dirt with his toys.

She pulled open the door, made a bee-line for her bedroom and sank onto the mattress.

Her husband was sitting out there alone, in the shed, and he was crying.

In the ten years they had been together not once, not even when his parents had died, not when they were married, or when his son was born, or after the bust-up with his brother, not once had she ever seen him cry.

Faith

KEVIN BACON FLOPPED ONTO THE STRAW COVERING HIS PEN, closed his whiskery eyes and groaned. The pig was clearly disgruntled.

'I know exactly how you feel.' Faith Montgomery pivoted a stilettoed heel and headed past the animal enclosures into the main area of the cafe. The Grounds was a bee-hive as usual, bearded guys in chequered shirts downing fresh rose lemonades, silky-skinned women in ripped jeans and designer T-shirts chuckling into their chai lattes. She scanned the tables arranged below the wooden pergola, covered by a vine of star jasmine in full bloom. A smile sprang to her lips at the sight of her friend seated at a yellow-tiled table beneath a garden of hanging plants. De-briefing with her best bud was definitely going to make her feel better.

Poppy pushed her chair back to stand, drawing her into a hug. 'Hey, you.'

'It's been way too long.' Faith threw an arm around Poppy's shoulder and kissed her cheek. Straightening back up, she took in the baby bump beneath the ruched khaki top. It was teamed with a multi-coloured scarf, black leggings and knee-high boots. No frumpy maternity wear for Pops. 'And look at you! My God, you look like you have a basketball in there.' She dropped her hands to the swell of Poppy's stomach. 'Feels like it too.'

'Lucky I like you.' Her dark eyes glinted as she raised a perfectly sculpted eyebrow. 'There's not too many people I let get away with that.' She covered Faith's hands with her own. 'But you're right. And I'm loving it.'

'Well, it suits you. That thing they say about pregnant women glowing? You definitely are.'

Poppy tucked a strand of shiny black hair behind her ear and sat back down. 'Can you believe it's only a year since we were here for the wedding?'

Faith looked around the paved courtyard. It didn't seem that long since the champagne glasses had been clinking over the long, food-laden tables. Poppy had been the picture-perfect bride in her figure-hugging Vera Wang lace gown. Faith herself had felt like a princess in silver silk, presuming she would be the next one to take the plunge as she gazed at Lukas looking like some sort of Greek god in charcoal Armani beside her. Her face slipped into a frown at that particular picture, but she forced a perky grin. 'I know. Hard to believe – where has that gone?'

Poppy screwed up her face. 'I guess that night's not such a great memory for you, huh?'

'Oh, don't be silly, of course it is. And will you stop with this whole guilt thing? I told you when Lukas and I first started dating that no matter what happened it wasn't going to affect our friendship – and I meant it. Just because he's your brother doesn't mean you have to feel responsible for him breaking up with me.' She reached out and grabbed Poppy's hand. 'Really.'

'I know. I just . . . it's sort of weird, you know? I had this whole vision of you guys getting married and being my baby's godparents and the four of us all playing happy families together.' She cringed. 'Sorry. Probably not helping.'

'I told you, Pops, I've moved on. I'm fine with it.' Faith sighed. 'Besides, I have more current bad news to relate.'

A waiter appeared beside them, a cheery smile beneath his neatly trimmed goatee. He placed the cups and a plate of coconut bread on the table in front of them with a flourish.

Poppy grinned at her. 'I knew you'd be here on time, so I ordered when I arrived.' She reached for the peppermint tea. 'The first thing I'm doing once this baby's out is ordering a double-shot espresso. But enough about me – what's wrong? And why aren't you at work on a Monday?'

'Dominic fired me. Sorry,' Faith raised her fingers into air quotes, '"Let me go."'

Poppy's mouth fell open. 'You're kidding.'

Faith looked at her friend, straight faced, and gave her head a light shake.

'Why?' Poppy said.

'The company isn't doing as well as he'd expected, so he's downsizing. Keeping only essential personnel.'

'But surely he'd consider you essential? He headhunted you, for God's sake.'

'Apparently Nikita has a better skill set,' she said bitterly.

'Really?' Poppy didn't sound convinced.

'Hmm. She might have a better *set*, but it's got nothing to do with skills.'

'No!'

'Seems so. She was hanging off him like a leech after the staff meeting.'

Poppy snorted. 'So, what are you going to do?'

'No idea. Try to find something else, I guess. Start sending my résumé out to a few of the other events companies around the place,' she said gloomily. The thought of job hunting made the contents of her stomach curdle.

'You know what?' Poppy sparked up. 'This might be a good thing. You can take some time and have a think about what you want to do next. I know the holiday's been forced, but why not enjoy it?'

'True, I've just never been out of work before.' Faith sipped at her coffee, licked the foam from her lips. 'Jobs have always come to me.'

'Like everything else in your life,' Poppy said slyly. Her eyes brightened. 'Maybe it's a sign.'

'A sign of what? That I'm over thirty, terminally single and, as of yesterday, jobless.'

'No,' she reached out and touched Faith's hand. 'Maybe it's a sign that you should do something completely different. Travel, study, start your own business. What did Stella and Brian say?'

Her parents. The eternal worriers. 'Nothing. They're overseas. I haven't told them yet. No point spoiling their holiday – you know what they're like.'

'Well, at least that gives you some time to sort out what you want to do, right?'

Faith nodded. She knew Poppy hadn't really finished that sentence – *sort out what you want to do without them interfering*. 'They mean well, they just get a bit carried away sometimes.'

'Yeah, like that time they called the cops to look for you when we went to the Year Twelve after-party and you weren't home by midnight.'

'I was so embarrassed.' She squirmed just thinking about it, even after all these years. 'The joys of having older parents. And being an only child.'

'You know, they're lucky you never really rebelled. No way could I have handled the cotton-wool treatment.'

'What? It's not like your parents were exactly liberated.'

'Yes, but mine are Greek,' Poppy pointed out, 'and I was much better at sneaking out than you.'

Her friend, as usual, was right.

'You know what you should do now you have some spare time?' Poppy didn't wait for an answer, just went straight on in and provided one herself. 'Get onto Tinder and find yourself a man.'

Faith almost spluttered out her last mouthful of coffee. 'Yeah, because that's going to solve all my problems. There is no way I am going to go out with anyone I meet online. You do know those sites are pretty much just fronts for casual hook-ups, don't you?' She caught her friend's blank expression. 'Of course you don't – you've been happily taken for years. I'm telling you, Pops, there just aren't that many solid guys around to even date.'

Poppy snagged the last slice of coconut bread and sat chewing thoughtfully. She pressed a napkin to her lips, folded it in two and dropped it onto the plate. 'Don't take this the wrong way, hon, but you really need to think outside the box a little more. Be open to a few different options.'

'What, so you're saying I should date anybody who'll have me now that I'm approaching my thirty-first birthday?'

'No, I'm not saying that at all. You're the one who had this thing about wanting to be married by the time you were thirty. Plenty of women are still single at our age.'

'Name one of our friends,' Faith challenged.

Poppy stared across the courtyard. 'Alicia.'

Faith shook her head. 'As soon as they legalise gay marriage she and Danielle will be signing the certificate.'

Her friend was mute.

'See what I mean?'

'All right. But that's just our immediate circle. I'm sure you know plenty of people in the events world who are in their thirties and single. I'm just saying, Faith, you're picky. It wouldn't hurt to branch out a little. Take a chance on someone completely different.'

There was no point arguing. Poppy was a sweetheart but she was like a dog with a bone when she got going. Easier to just agree. 'Maybe.'

A phone hummed from the depths of her new Burberry handbag. It had cost a bomb but it was worth every cent. She rummaged around, whipped out her phone and saw her mother's face lighting up the screen. She turned it towards Poppy. 'Her ears must have been on fire.'

'Hi Mum,' she said breezily. 'How are you doing?'

'Not good, darling, I'm afraid.' Her mother sounded flustered. 'We've had our passports stolen. Some street urchin in Rome just grabbed the bag off your father's shoulder and ran off with it before we even knew what was happening.'

'Oh, no.'

'And we're supposed to be boarding the cruise ship tomorrow and I can't find the copies of the passports I made anywhere in our suitcases and apparently we need them to cross borders or something. I went to the Australian Consulate and they said if I can get a copy scanned and emailed to our hotel they can provide us with temporary ones.'

'Okay.' Faith rolled her eyes at Poppy, who was staring at her from across the table. 'So, what can I do?'

'Well, I made another copy of each, just to be on the safe side. I'm pretty sure they're in the document folder in the top drawer of the filing cabinet. After you finish work could you go and have a look and see if you can find them?'

'I'm not working today.' The words just tumbled out. Her mother had this strange ability to wheedle the truth out of her even when she tried desperately to say nothing at all. Hence her adolescent groundings.

'Are you sick?'

'No, not sick. I'm . . .' She scrambled for a plausible story as she looked across at Poppy, who was now giving her a wicked grin. 'The boss gave a few of us a day off in lieu of all the hours we did on the last project.' Technically it wasn't a lie, more like an over-exaggerated truth. After all, Dominic had praised her for the hours she'd put into the Jump Into Spring event. Right before he lowered the guillotine.

'Oh, that's wonderful, darling. If it wouldn't be too much trouble.'

'Of course not. Text me the details of your hotel and I should be able to email them through in the next couple of hours. Are you having a good time? Other than the passport issue?'

'Time of our lives! We should have done this years ago.'

'Good for you. Talk soon, Mum. Say hi to Dad.'

'Bye, darling.'

She finished the call and gave Poppy an apologetic smile. 'Looks like I'm taking a trip to the southern suburbs.'

'I heard.'

'Guess you did. Sorry, Pops, I better get onto it.'

They stood and gave each other a side-ways hug. 'No problem. Have a think about what I said, *please*.' Poppy held her by the arms.

'About Tinder?' Faith smirked.

'About all of it. The job, dating, life. You just need to get out of your comfort zone a little more, Monty.'

'You'd know all about that, I suppose.' Faith patted her friend's tummy again and picked up her bag.

'Don't be cheeky. See you soon. Hope you sort out the passport drama.'

'Me too.'

She took a different exit on the way out – seeing those animals locked up in their pens was too depressing. All she wanted to do was go home, climb into bed and drag the covers over her head. It was always good to see her best friend, but today's conversation hadn't exactly been uplifting. Still, Poppy was probably right. Her life could do with a shake-up. Once this speed-hump in her parents' travel plans was sorted she'd sit down and brainstorm ideas to make it happen. After she'd taken a nap.

———

The trip from Alexandria to her parents' place in Cronulla took just over forty minutes. En route, she fielded another couple of phone calls from her mother asking if she'd found the papers yet. She probably shouldn't have been so curt with her that last time, but really, she didn't have wings and Sydney traffic was, well . . . Sydney traffic.

The sea air nipped at her cheeks as she climbed out of the car. Stella and Brian's townhouse was brand new, had ocean views from the second-floor balcony and was within walking distance of the beach. The place was a lot smaller than the family home in Burwood. Once Faith had moved out they hadn't needed the extra space and the low maintenance suited their new jet-setting, retiree lifestyle. It made sense, but that didn't stop Faith's disappointment as she stepped inside the door. This wasn't home. Not her home anyway, not the old rambling federation cottage where she'd grown up, its huge backyard filled with old-fashioned roses, a wide green lawn and the tyre swing her dad had made for her hanging from the gigantic jacaranda, its purple petals scattered across the ground like a magic carpet.

This place was all neat edges and crisp white surfaces, much like her own.

She slipped off her heels and padded down the hallway. Spotless as usual, not a mote of dust in sight. Faith got that – she was pretty anal about cleanliness herself. When she'd first moved out it had been liberating to drop her clothes on the floor and leave her dishes in the sink, but after just a few days the novelty had worn off and she'd discovered that she was, after all, her mother's daughter. She'd whipped around and tidied up, then hired a weekly cleaning service to keep her apartment immaculate. Some things were just part of your DNA.

Now she headed upstairs to the filing cabinet.

Pulling open the drawer, she flicked through the tabs on the files, until she reached T, and slipped out the one labelled Travel. Insurance papers, brochures on various European locations, hotel information, but no passport copies. Her mother was usually so organised about this sort of thing, but she had been a bit ruffled about going away for so long. Faith rifled through the rest of the drawer, and the one below, but no luck.

Her feet sank into the soft charcoal plush-pile as she made her way down the hall, pausing at the door to the spare room. A barely used double bed complete with a nautical-themed quilt cover sat beneath one of her mother's original seascapes. Faith's room. Only it wasn't. A pang of childish longing prickled at the back of her eyes but she blinked it away.

Oh, get over yourself, Faith.

The main bedroom was a little further along. She reached the doorway and scanned the space, considering possibilities. The walk-in wardrobe was enormous but not a likely place to keep documents. She opened the drawers in both bedside cabinets, moving the contents around cautiously. This was her parents' bedroom, after all, and some things a girl really doesn't need to know. No surprises, thank God.

'Well, Mum, I don't know what you're on about, but the copies aren't here.'

There was one more possibility. Crouching down, she lifted the white broderie valance and lay flat on her stomach, stretching out her arms to retrieve a small suitcase from beneath the centre of the bed. It was a long shot, but worth a try. She clicked open the catches and sifted through the contents – old birthday cards, paintings from Faith's preschool days, school reports, awards – memorabilia her mother had collected over the years. Faith had seen them all before, had laughed with her mother as they'd read through the badly rhymed poems inside the birthday cards, but that had been years ago. She swallowed the lump in her throat. Stella had always been sentimental but she was also a neat freak, so the fact that these childhood souvenirs had survived the big move made Faith irrationally grateful.

Come on, what is wrong with you today?

At the bottom of the case was a mustard A4 envelope. It was addressed to her – her name pencilled across the front in her mother's handwriting – but she'd never seen it before. She flipped it over, ran her index finger over the seam of the sealed flap and then, before she could think better of it, tore it open. Inside was a single folded sheet of paper. When she slid it out, something fell into her lap: a small white plastic band she immediately recognised as a hospital ID bracelet. She picked it up and studied the faded handwriting: *Eliza*. There was another word or two, then the surname *Barnes*.

Eliza Barnes. Not a name she knew. She unfolded the paper to find a wallet-sized photo of a baby, and on the back was the same name: *Eliza, Crown Street, 27/10/84*.

'My birthday.' The whispered words bounced around in the space between the bedroom walls.

She turned the photo over and studied the tiny face. Her parents had never been great at the whole photography thing, but this baby was younger than the pictures she'd seen of herself. She didn't have much experience with newborns, but this one had that red-faced, squinty-eyed look that suggested she was only recently arrived. Maybe it was a relative, or a friend?

With the same birth date.

A strange tingling sensation rippled beneath her skin. Picking up the piece of paper again, she saw that the writing was flowery, like calligraphy. Nothing like her mother's.

She read the first line.

Eliza, my sweet baby girl.

Her eyes flicked to the image of the baby, and then back to what she now realised was a letter.

You are the most beautiful thing I have ever seen. I wish I could keep you. But I need to do what's best for you, make sure you have a good home with parents who can give you everything you deserve.

Please know that I love you, now and always.
Your mother,
Rosemary.

Rosemary?

Her own middle name. Faith Rosemary Montgomery.

She lifted her head and stared out into the vacant hallway. As a child she'd asked her mother where her middle name had come from, as children do. Was she named after someone? A relative, or a friend? Was it a family name? Her mother's response had been annoyingly vague: *It belonged to someone very special.* But when pushed for more information Stella had changed the subject. When Faith had asked her about it again, years later, the story had changed: *Your father and I both liked it.* The shift had been confusing. She'd shrugged it off as one of her mother's memory lapses.

Was this the Rosemary she was named after? Everything inside her tightened, from the skin on her scalp to the sinews in her shoulders, to the hollow space below her diaphragm.

She gazed back down at the photo. The baby had dark hair, nothing like her own, and the eyes were the murky blue of all new arrivals. There was nothing at all familiar about her.

She re-read the words. *I need to do what's best for you, make sure you have a good home with parents who can give you everything you deserve.*

Something wasn't right. Her heart began to race as she turned the photo over again and fixed her eyes on the date. Her knuckles paled as she clutched at the piece of paper, narrowing it down to the most telling details.

Rosemary.

Eliza.

27/10/84.

She stared at the baby swaddled in a pink hospital blanket, a cold sweat creeping across her forehead. The room began to spin. Faster and faster, her head spinning with it, the walls blurring. The floor dropped. Everything fell away until there was only a black hole, and her stranded in the middle of it numbly beginning to fathom what she held in her hand.

Chapter Two

Rose

THE OLD SUZUKI BUMPED ACROSS THE DRIED-OUT CREEK bed, jolting her about so much that Rose had to clench her teeth to stop them from rattling. But even that couldn't wipe the smile from her face. Her weekly visit to Clementine Downs was the highlight of an often monotonous series of days. If anyone could make her laugh it was her oldest friend, Cleo. And right now she could use a laugh. The council had not only knocked back her funding application – the mongrels – but they'd warned her that the work had to be done asap or they'd slap a derelict notice on her. Her blood boiled just thinking about it. Now the tourist season was well and truly over there wasn't a whole lot of cash filling the till. Then, of course, there was yesterday's visit from a certain person.

But she wasn't going to think about any of that now.

Squinting through the moth-spattered windscreen, she manoeuvred the car carefully across the sandy surface of the road. Sliding head first into a tree was a pleasure she could do without. A bunch of ragged-looking cattle, ribs protruding, heads hung low, watched her pass. Their coats dull and their eyes vacant, they looked like residents of some bovine concentration camp. Rose gave a quiet groan and turned away.

A short distance further and she pulled up and climbed out of the cool of the car into what felt like an outdoor oven. Cleo's old mare, Suzie Q, whinnied at her from behind the wire fence. Her sidekick, Bob, a caramel-and-white Shetland with a Tina Turner mane, came trotting out from the shelter of a pepper tree. Not a scrap of grass anywhere. No wonder the poor creatures were glad to see her.

'Hello, you two oddballs. Don't worry, I didn't forget.' Lifting the boot of the car, she pulled out an enormous bag, ripped open the plastic and tugged out a fistful of carrots. Hauling out a second bag filled with groceries – it was safer to bring lunch than enter the minefield that was Cleo's fridge – she made her way over to the tumbledown pen. Suzie had been named because of her badass attitude and her shaggy black forelock. Time had done little to tame either, but her bravado had never fooled Rose. She held a carrot out in her flattened palm. 'Be nice and leave my fingers attached or it'll be the last one you get.' Suzie took the warning seriously, nuzzling at the carrot before pulling it gently between her teeth and chomping down most politely. 'That's the girl.' Rose gave the horse a scratch behind the ear. 'Your turn, Bobby.'

A door banged and there was Cleo, marching across her battleground of a yard. Her thick bottle-blonde hair had been dragged back into a ponytail and she was wearing her usual garb of workmen's overalls, rolled up to the knee, a black singlet top and a pair of hole-ridden work boots. 'Always know who the favourites are around here,' she grumbled.

Rose pulled another carrot from the bag, the biggest one she could find, and held it up as a peace offering. 'You can have one too, if you like.'

Cleo chuckled. 'Too bloody healthy for my liking. But might come in handy for something else.' She lifted her eyebrows and let out a raucous cackle.

Rose couldn't help but join in. 'Cleo Swayne, you are wicked.'

'What? Cheaper than a vibrator. And a prettier colour.'

'I'm sure you're right. But let's not go there.'

Cleo relieved her of one of the bags and they made their way towards the house, stopping at a wooden pen where an enormous black pig was flat out on its side beneath a corrugated iron shelter. At the sight of the visitor – or, more likely, the bag she was carrying – he heaved himself upright to waddle through a puddle of mud, poked his nose through the fence and gave a loud grunt.

'Right on cue, Tiddles.' Rose dug out yet another carrot. 'Doesn't look like you're getting any slimmer, my friend. There's a nice lot of flesh on those ribs. Would go very nicely with some of my special barbecue sauce.'

Cleo whacked her arm. 'Over my dead body.'

'I was thinking more of his.'

'Well, think again.'

It was their usual way of conversing, a dash of argy-bargy, a sprinkle of innuendo all lightly seasoned with a generous dollop of giggles.

The house was in its customary state of chaos, old machinery parts strewn from one end of the place to the other – Cleo was a great believer in recycling. And hoarding. A blue cattle dog appeared and wriggled round Rose's legs. His older, slower companion, a shaggy cream wolfhound-cross, stood and waited in the shade. 'Clever boy, Sherlock.' She patted the larger dog's head. 'Best place to be on a day like today.'

'G'day, Aunty Rose,' Tim called out from the worn-out couch on the verandah.

'Hi there, Tim, how goes it?'

All she could see of Cleo's son was his ginger buzz cut and his enormous hands resting on his knees. He was head down, studying pieces of what looked like a motor sprawled out on the cement in front of him. 'Trying to fix this generator I found in the shed. The one we've got's on its last legs.'

'Well, if anyone can do it you can, Timbo.'

The boy – more of a man-child, really – bent over the engine parts, lifted one corner of his mouth, but didn't reply.

'Kills me that he even has to do that. Kid should be at school finishing his HSC.' Cleo opened the door and Rose followed her into the house.

Inside was as shambolic as out. Nothing had changed. Rose was itching to get her hands on the magazines and papers piled up around the walls of the lounge room, the stack of plates – clean or dirty, it was hard to tell – on the kitchen bench and the overflowing clothes basket of odd socks that seemed to have multiplied since her last visit, but she knew that Cleo would shoo her out the door with a broom if she even tried. She dropped the bags on the floor by the sink. 'Have you talked to him about going back to school?'

'Refuses point blank. Thinks this place will fall apart without him.' Cleo snorted. 'He's probably right. Hate seeing him waste his brains, though.'

Rose rested a hand on her friend's shoulder. 'He's a smart kid. He'll work it out. Once things improve around here he can get back on track.' She nodded when Cleo held up the kettle. 'How's it going, anyway?'

'Same old, same old. Had the bloody bank manager out here again last week. Putting the screws on us.' Cleo laughed, a sharp cackle that caught in her throat.

Rose understood exactly what Cleo meant. Thank God Mick had decided to become a publican rather than a grazier, otherwise it could be her out here on one of these farms holding her breath until the drought broke. As bad as business was right now she should probably count her blessings. Poor Cleo was doing it tougher than most. If that loser of a husband of hers hadn't left her in the lurch things would have been a whole lot easier. Financially, anyway. Rose glanced across at her as she poured the tea, took in the lines that creased her brow, the dark pouches of skin beneath her eyes.

'I wish I could do something to help.' She took the mug Cleo offered and pulled out a chair.

'You are. You're here. Now, tell me what's happening with you.'

'Dave Ryan's back in town.'

Really? Where did that even come from?

Cleo pursed her lips and narrowed her eyes at Rose. 'Is he now?'

'Yes, he is.' She chose to ignore Cleo's suggestive tone and ploughed on with her story. 'Do you remember the girl he married, Kay Williams? She passed away. He's talking about moving back here. He's house sitting for the Tinsdales.'

'Interesting that you started with that bit of news. You were sweet on him back in the day.'

Rose almost gagged on her mouthful of tea. Cleo didn't know the half of it. 'Yes I was, when I was sixteen years old, along with half the school! He's a fifty-one-year-old man, for God's sake.'

'A fifty-one-year-old *single* man. And you're a forty-nine-year-old single woman. It's been five years since Mick passed. Maybe it's about time you got yourself a bloke.'

Rose widened her eyes and banged her cup a little too forcefully onto the table. 'Am I the only one seeing the irony here?'

'What?'

'The irony – *you* telling *me* I need a man. Seems to me you could do with one yourself.'

'Last thing on my mind,' Cleo laughed. 'More bloody trouble than they're worth. I've sworn off 'em for good. But you should think about it, Rosie.' She slurped from her mug. 'How's the old mate looking, anyway?'

'Dave? Not as good as when he was nineteen, let me tell you. Bit of a paunch around the middle, not quite as much hair as he used to have but not completely bald, which is more than a lot of men his age can boast.'

'For someone who's not interested you seem pretty keen on him.'

'Keen? Where did you get that from? You asked me what he looked like and I'm telling you.' Rose shrugged. 'Anyway, enough about him.'

And me.

Cleo eyed her curiously but took the hint. 'What else is happening? How's the old witch going?'

Rose sighed. Witch was the perfect word to describe her mother-in-law. 'Same as always. Roosting in her recliner like a broody hen in front of the TV every time I go there. Hardly says a word.'

'I really don't know why you put up with it, Rosie.' Cleo shook her head. 'I know, I know, Mick wanted you to look after her, but surely even he wouldn't be happy with the way she treats you.'

'Probably not, but we all have our crosses to bear.'

A loud thud had Cleo standing abruptly. 'And that's mine! If that friggin' man has fallen out of bed again I am going to scream.' She stood, almost knocking the chair to the floor and yelled out the door to Tim before turning back to Rose. 'Stubborn old bugger refuses to call anyone for help and ends up on his arse every time.' Rose followed her to a bedroom at the back of the house to find Tim manhandling his grandfather to his feet. Her hand flew to cover her nose as an acrid smell hit.

Cleo winced. 'Sorry, it's the bed sores again.'

Rose dropped her hand immediately but her eyes watered. 'No, that's okay, can't be helped. Is there anything I can do?' She hovered in the doorway.

'Dad, how many times do I have to tell you, if you need the loo you should call someone.'

The older man, now positioned back in the bed, looked at his daughter through red-rimmed eyes and mumbled something indistinguishable.

'You right with him, Tim?' Cleo looked across at her son, who'd fetched a bed pan and was shuffling awkwardly.

'Yep, all good.'

Cleo spun around and headed back down the hall, through the kitchen and out the back door, Rose following hot on her heels.

She waited until Cleo was settled on the back step before she spoke quietly, sympathetic rather than accusatory. 'He's getting worse.'

'Do ya think?'

Rose knew she had to tread carefully. 'How long has he had those bed sores?'

'A week, maybe more. Came out of nowhere.' Cleo wiped at her eyes. 'Look at those poor bloody beasts out there.' Cleo was taking a tangent but probably best to just go with it. Rose looked past the tangle of passionfruit and pumpkin vines, gigantic tomato plants and a cucumber patch to a small bunch of cattle gathered under a tin shelter. The largest of them, a charcoal-coloured Brahman bull with horns that could definitely do some damage if he were so inclined, stared straight back at her.

'They don't look too bad,' Rose said softly. 'Still got some meat on them.'

'Not much, and even keeping that amount on them is costing me the earth. I'm almost out of lick and there's barely enough hay in the shed to keep them going until the end of the month. And there's Dad on top of all that.' She turned to her friend. 'I don't know how much longer we can keep it up, Rosie.'

The look on her friend's face was beyond despair. Rose took a moment to steady herself. 'No one would think any less of you if you decided it was time for a nursing home.'

'That is *not* going to happen.' Cleo gritted her teeth. 'I promised I wouldn't do it to him.'

'I know, I know. But is it really fair on any of you, going on like this? He needs more care than you and Tim can give him now. He would be better off and you two could concentrate on what needs to be done around here.'

Cleo wrapped her hands around her knees, swaying slightly from side to side. 'I suppose I could try to get him into respite for a while,' she said quietly. 'Give us some breathing space.'

Rose leaned back, hands on her hips in mock surprise. 'Cleo Swayne, are you actually agreeing with me?'

The smallest of smiles crept onto her friend's face. 'Maybe.' She sniffed and nudged Rose with her elbow. 'But don't go getting too used to it.'

'Judging by the smell of those bed sores I think you need to do it sooner rather than later.'

Cleo nodded. 'I will.'

Rose pulled her phone from her pocket and clicked on her contacts, finding the local doctor's number and handing it across. 'There's no time like the present. Call Doctor Peterson now while I go fix us some lunch.' She stood before Cleo could start to argue.

'My God, woman, you are bossy.'

'I learned from the best,' Rose threw back as she disappeared into the kitchen. She stopped beside the door and waited until she heard Cleo, composed again now, speaking to the doctor's secretary.

Finding some space on the cluttered bench top was more than a challenge, but she managed to clear enough room for a bread board and went about making some sandwiches. Hammering sounded from outside – Tim had returned to his project. From what she could overhear of Cleo's phone conversation the chances of getting Cliff into respite soon were good. Rose had always had a knack for helping other people sort out their lives. Spent hours at the bar giving free advice and counselling sessions. If only she were as good at sorting out her own problems. She cut into a ripe red tomato and arranged the slices on a piece of freshly cut, buttered bread, smothering them with salt and pepper. At the end of the day, she and Cleo had the same problem: properties that were bleeding them dry. Once the rains came – and they would – things would start to look up for Cleo, especially if she could sort out some proper care for her father. But a good downpour wasn't going to fix the termite infestation or the broken windows or the rusted roof or any of the other issues plaguing The Crossroads. Nothing short of robbing a bank was going to help with that. And it certainly wasn't going to make David Ryan disappear.

She plonked the sandwiches on a plate and headed back outside, putting on a happy face for Cleo's sake. Today was all about being here for her friend. Her own assortment of problems would have to wait.

Stephanie

IT WAS GETTING HARDER AND HARDER TO KEEP THE SHINE in Bandit's coat. Even after a solid twenty-minute brush, specks of dirt still clung to the hair, thickened his mane and added weight to his already hefty tail. It was one of the things she loved most about him: his thick, black tail. He swished it in her direction now as she lifted his left hind foot to scrape the dirt from his hoof.

'Thanks for that.' She grinned, not put off for a second by the horse's not so subtle suggestion that she leave him in peace with his biscuit of hay. He'd be fine once he was saddled up and moving. Sometimes he seemed to enjoy the outing more than she did. There was definitely something to be said for getting away from it all, and at the moment he was her best option when it came to company. How sad was that? The truth of it tugged at the knot that had formed in her stomach yesterday afternoon. Since the 'incident' Bryce had kept to himself, barely spoken a word. Last night he stayed up late at the computer claiming to be 'researching a new brand of cattle feed', and the sheets on his side of the bed were cold when she woke. He'd sent her a text to say he was checking the fences on the northern side of the property and would likely be gone most of the day. Texting her when they lived under the same roof. What did that say about the state of their marriage?

Usually she'd hang around in town on Jake's days at pre-school but today she'd made the round trip, needed to ride. She raised the back of her hand, the one holding the hoof-pick, and swiped it across her forehead, Bandit's foot sitting heavily in the other. A fly hovered around her nose and she twitched it away. The horse snorted and tried to stamp his front right foot as if in support.

'Only leaves you two to stand on, matey,' she laughed at him. 'They're not that bad. Get over yourself.' He was such a wimp when it came to flies. All it took was one of the little pests to land somewhere on his body to send him into a frenzy of head shaking, which was particularly annoying when she was riding him and attempting to get him to listen. She picked up the bottle of Fly-Gone to give him his usual lathering but instead of a spray the remains of the citronella-scented liquid dribbled down the plastic bottle onto her trigger finger. 'Sorry, Band. We're just going to have to tough it out today.' Bandit kept up his protest while she finished cleaning out all four of his feet before giving him a thorough neck massage. He sank into the pressure, eyes almost closing, and groaned.

Such a sweetie. 'Good boy.'

She threw a worn navy pad across his back before reaching for the saddle, its tan patterned leather already hot from the mid-morning sun, but the sound of tyres on dirt drew her eyes towards the driveway. A black four-wheel drive was cruising towards the house. It wasn't one she recognised. Maybe someone for Bryce. She hoisted the saddle off the fence and settled it on Bandit's back, threading the strap though the girth and giving it a good yank to make sure it was secure. He shook his head wildly at another fly as the car slowed to a stop.

As the driver climbed out and pushed his sunglasses onto his head, settling them into the waves of his light brown hair, Stephanie felt the colour drain from her cheeks. It had been two – no, three – years now since she'd seen him and the memory of their last meeting had every muscle in her body tightening in defence.

'Cameron.' The sound of his name was as foreign as the man's presence.

'Hi, Steph.' He stood beside the car, arms casually folded, the sleeves on his light denim shirt rolled up above the elbows, making no attempt to close the distance between them.

'What are you doing here?'

'I still own half of this place. No need to ask for an invitation.' His tone was hard to read, matter of fact but perhaps a touch scornful.

She dropped her head, kicked away a rock. 'Still as arrogant as ever.'

Cameron laughed, a brief, rough sound that made her bristle. 'Now there's an irony. Where is my little brother, anyway?'

'Not that it's any of your business,' she said, raising her head to look at him directly, 'but he's out checking the fences.' Then she added curtly, '*Somebody* has to do it.'

'I see you haven't changed. Loyal as ever.'

'Of course I am,' she said, knowing she was taking the bait but unable to stop herself. 'He's my husband.' She spun away from him and pulled at Bandit's girth, testing. 'You didn't answer my question. Why are you here? I assume it's not for a family reunion.'

'No, that ball is in Bryce's court. I wanted to have a chat with him, though, see how things are going.'

Stephanie's hands dropped to her hips and her mouth fell open as she turned back to face him. 'What, so you can find out if he's prepared to sell? If that's why you're here you may as well turn around and leave right now. Hell will freeze over before that happens.'

Cameron took a step towards her, his stance matching her own. 'That's not entirely your call to make.' He pivoted, scanning the paddocks. 'No rain lately, I take it.'

'You know damn well there's been no rain. That's why you're here, circling like a vulture.'

'Oh, come on, Steph, you're making me sound like some sort of predator.'

'If the shoe fits.'

He shook his head, as if she were a child who had just said something silly and amusing.

She held back the urge to slap him, wipe the smirk well and truly off his face. 'I'm kind of busy. Bryce isn't here. So, it's probably better if you leave. Now.'

He pulled a folded envelope from his back pocket but made no attempt to hand it across. 'I have a business proposition.'

'You seriously think he'd be interested in any proposition from you?'

'This one doesn't involve selling the farm.'

Her eyes flicked to the envelope.

'And it's not addressed just to Bryce,' he said smoothly. 'I thought you two were partners in this place.'

That's what I thought too.

She curled her fingers around the bridle and let a few quick breaths out through her nose to steady her voice. 'We're not interested.'

'You don't even know what it is.' He tapped the envelope on the back of his hand before holding it out towards her. 'Would it hurt to take a look?'

Bandit stamped his foot. Patience had never been one of his virtues, and while it was normally one of hers, Cameron was testing it. 'You're wasting your time,' she said bluntly. 'And mine.' She picked up the bridle and held the bit to the horse's mouth. He took it without fussing and she slipped the leather headpiece over his ears, drawing the reins over his head before positioning her foot in the stirrup and swinging herself up. She settled into the saddle, glad to be looking down on her brother-in-law. 'There's nothing to consider.'

He tucked the envelope into a gap between the fence post and rail. 'We'll see.'

She pressed her heel against the horse's flank and turned him in the opposite direction.

'Say hi to Bryce for me,' she heard as she trotted away, but she didn't bother turning around to say goodbye.

———

Pushing Bandit straight into a canter, she rode without looking back, focusing completely on the see-sawing movement as she and Bandit fell into their accustomed rhythm. Riding was the only way she had ever been able to clear her head. It took her full concentration – a horse could tell if your mind was somewhere else – and even though she had ridden all her life and it was as automatic as breathing, Stephanie knew it was important to keep her wits about her if she wanted to stay safe. Especially out here.

Eventually she eased their pace back to a walk. Perspiration beaded her forehead and she slanted her hat a little further back on her head. She loosened the reins and let the horse pick his way through the scattered boulders, black basalt remnants of the volcano that had erupted millions of years ago and spewed its contents far and wide. Some parts of Strathmore were so littered with them it looked like another planet, but here the rocks were more spread out, as if they'd been tossed across the dark red soil in some sort of weird abstract artwork. She let out a long, deep sigh and let the tension she'd been storing since the conversation with her surprise visitor dissolve. Bandit slowed in response. She rubbed a hand across his withers and rested the reins in her right hand, moving the other to sit loosely in her lap.

What the hell had Cameron been doing here? Three years and not a word from him. No phone calls or texts at Christmas or birthdays – not even for Jake. But then that hadn't all been his doing. Bryce had made it clear that he wasn't welcome on the place, that if he didn't want to help out and share the workload he could bugger off. It was like a scene from one of those old western movies, only the brawl had been right here on the property.

'This place is sucking us both dry, Bryce!' Cam had yelled. 'And not just financially. We need to get out now while there's still something to salvage. Something worth selling.'

Bryce had been scarlet with rage. Before Stephanie knew what was happening, he'd clenched his fist and knocked his brother to the ground.

'Stop it, Bryce!' she'd screamed. 'Stop it, both of you.'

The air around them quivered, the two men eye-balling each other; Cam from where he lay on the ground, propped up by one elbow, blood dripping one drop at a time onto the dirt outside the barn; Bryce, his chest heaving, his body braced for battle, standing over his older brother.

Stephanie held Jake tightly in her arms, her palm against his cheek, and waited.

Without a word Cameron hauled himself to his feet and wiped at his bloodied nose before bending to pick up his hat from the ground. He dusted the dirt from the brim, placed it back on his head, turned and walked away. And that had been the last they'd seen or heard from him.

Until now.

He looked older, the lines on his forehead perhaps a little deeper, but he still had that same soft light in his grey eyes, the same determined jut of his squared jaw – the one thing the brothers had in common. In every other way they were different, each a replica of one of their parents. Bryce had his father's dark curls, his milky-brown eyes and solid build. Cameron was taller, wiry, with his mother's fairer hair and complexion. If you didn't know them, you'd never pick them as brothers. Brothers who had once been inseparable and were now bitter enemies.

All because of this place.

She pulled Bandit up beneath the shade of a gidgee tree and looked down the gully into the dry creek bed. Rocks, sand and scrub. She closed her eyes and tried to remember when it was last in full flow – the sound of water rushing through the gorge, tumbling over boulders, the cool dark green swirl of it between the gully walls, the sharpness of the breath it dragged from her as she dived into the depths of the waterhole. The memory was there, but faint, like a weakened pulse.

Overhead was nothing but blue. Only a few scattered wisps of cloud, like skeins of white fairy floss. It was strange how the sight of so much blue could dampen her spirits. There were plenty of places where clear skies and sunshine brought smiles to people's faces, and there had been a few times – only a very few – in Stephanie's own life when she'd prayed for the rain to stop. When the paddocks were submerged beneath blankets of water; when the river became a wild beast dragging trees, cattle and even people from its banks. But that hadn't happened now for a very long time. Jake could barely remember rain – apart from the few odd drops that fell with the wild storms that barrelled in from the northwest raising dust and ripping tree limbs from their trunks. Eleven millimetres. The most they'd had in the past few years on any one day, hardly enough to wet the surface of the soil. And no amount of staring at the weather forecast was going to make it rain. The only serious cloud hanging over them was Bryce's terminally bad mood, and lately she had the feeling it was about to burst.

I thought you two were partners in this place.

Cam's words had hit a nerve.

They had been a team. *Partners.* But lately it felt like she was always the one having to make the effort, that it was her job to hold things together. The prospect of telling Bryce that Cam had set foot back on Strathmore left the warm skin of her arms rough with goose pimples. Whatever was in that envelope could only mean trouble. It was addressed to both of them, so there was no reason she couldn't open it first, and then, if it was something Bryce would definitely not go for, she could get rid of it without saying a word. Technically it wasn't going behind his back, it was . . . protecting his interests. Everybody's interests.

She checked her watch. As much as she would love to stay out all day it was time to be heading home. Bandit moved at the pressure of her leg and they turned to make their way back. He side-stepped the remains of a bull, once a huge muscular beast that had produced a multitude of fine offspring; all that was left of him now was a few shreds of rotting flesh and some sun-bleached bones pecked clean by crows and other scavengers. A small mob of cattle had followed them along the track and stood under an ironbark, watching. A young cream-coloured heifer darted away when Stephanie came closer, sheltering behind its mother. There was still a good coverage on this lot, their ribs well hidden behind a thick wall of flesh, but it was slim pickings out here and the lick they were being fed wasn't going to sustain them for long.

'It'll rain soon,' she told them as she ambled past. 'Really,' she told herself, 'it will.'

A solitary kookaburra cackled from where it sat at the top of the tree. Normally the birds' laughter brought a smile to her face but today it sounded more evil than raucous and it left her shivering. She pushed Bandit on, urging him back into a canter, suddenly craving the peach-coloured walls and enclosed comfort of home.

Faith

This cannot be happening.

Only yesterday she'd driven to her parents' house as one person and left feeling like someone else entirely. Somehow, she'd managed to find the passport copies downstairs in the kitchen drawer, scan them and email them to her parents with a note saying she hoped they were having a nice time and their document issues could be sorted in a hurry so they could get on with their holiday. Nothing about the other discovery she'd made. Nothing about her stomach-churning suspicion that they weren't in actual fact her parents.

Fuck!

Twenty-four hours later, she was sitting at her kitchen bench, the contents of the envelope laid out in front of her like pieces of a puzzle, feeling like some imposter had taken over her life, someone whose real identity could only be found by examining the evidence over and over again. She picked up the photo for what must be the hundredth time, pinching the edge between her thumb and index finger, and brought it to eye level.

'Eliza.'

Hair – black. Not white-blonde like her own. Eye colour – probably blue but too hard to tell. Face shape – round and podgy. She held a palm to her jawline, moved it up to her cheek. More angular than podgy, but then a lot can change in thirty-one years. She looked back at the baby – there was something unnerving about her rosebud mouth, the soft arch of her upper lip.

And then there was the letter.

There could be a perfectly simple explanation why her name was written on this envelope, why she and this baby had the same date of birth, why she shared a name with this child's mother. Just as there could be a perfectly simple reason why her parents had always fudged when she'd asked them anything about her birth. She'd assumed it had been because they didn't like to talk about 'that sort of thing', but perhaps there was another reason.

Perhaps they'd baulked because they didn't want her to
know the truth.

Every time the ludicrous idea surfaced she pushed it away
and returned to the reality that was her life. Surely if she'd been
adopted her parents would have told her. That's what people
did these days, wasn't it? Asking them straight out wasn't an
option. They were on holidays and what if she was way off
track with this? How stupid would she sound?

Google was the font of all wisdom. She reached for her
laptop, flipped it open and banged at the keys, typing 'Finding
your birth mother' into the search bar. The mere action of
typing the phrase gave her that same dizzy sensation that
had almost caused her to pass out in her parents' bedroom.
Breathing through it as the list of alternatives appeared, she
chose the link to Jigsaw, an agency dealing with adoption and
clicked on 'How Do I Begin?' Accessing her birth information
was as simple as filling in a form. She had most of the details
they needed – mother's name, date of birth, place of birth and
adoptive parents' particulars, and then the information had to
be printed, completed and posted. Really? Who did snail mail
these days? She'd also need two pieces of her own ID signed
by a doctor, police officer, justice of the peace or solicitor.
Lukas was a solicitor. Urgh! Her smooth, so-together ex who
was shacked up with his current girlfriend only a few blocks
down the road. Could she really go around there and ask him
for a favour after the dressing down she'd given him when
he broke up with her? Not to mention the drunken late-night
texts she'd sent on more than one occasion and lived to regret
the next morning.

But there was someone else she could ask – someone who
worked with Lukas, and her best friend just happened to

be married to him. Faith stared at the screen, then back at the 'evidence'.

This is crazy. I'm not *adopted. Am I?*

Right there on the front of the envelope, written clearly in upper case in her mother's writing, was her name: Faith. She could just shove everything back inside, return it to the suitcase, or throw it in the garbage and forget the whole thing. But something niggled deep down inside her, told her she couldn't walk away without knowing for sure, couldn't leave the question unanswered. All the air went out of her. She slid her eyes back to the screen, shifted her fingers to the keyboard and typed her name into the blank space on the form. When she was done, it stared back at her, each letter lined up one after the other in Times New Roman. The idea that she was not Faith Montgomery stuck in the back of her throat like a piece of gristle and she fought the urge to gag.

If she sent this form, if what she suspected was actually true, then her whole life had been a lie.

———

A bone-chilling wind – ridiculous for October – whipped her hair across her face as she pressed a finger to the doorbell. The footsteps inside grew louder until Nick threw open the door and ushered her inside. 'Come in, come in, it's like the bloody Arctic out there.'

'You're not wrong.' She wriggled the corners of her mouth into some sort of smile. 'Where's Pops?'

'On her way down. She's been wallowing in the bath.'

'Wallowing implies fat and lazy, and I'm neither of the two.' Her friend appeared on the stairs, clinging to the rail while she negotiated the steep descent.

'No, you're definitely not.' Faith hugged her when she made it to the bottom. 'But I wish you weren't pregnant right now and could knock off a bottle of red with me. I am seriously in need of a drink.'

'Well, you've come to the right place.' Nick picked up a bottle from the wine rack nestled inside the empty fireplace. 'I've lost my drinking buddy for the time being.' He smiled at his wife and kissed her temple before heading into the kitchen.

'I could tell by your text something was wrong.' Poppy placed a hand on Faith's arm. 'What's happened?'

Faith's hand flew to her mouth as she smothered a quiet sob.

'Come on. Come and sit down.' Poppy led her through to the kitchen, waving a hand towards the glass her husband was already filling. 'Make it a big one, Nick.'

Faith pulled the well-thumbed envelope out of her bag, tipped its contents onto the table and told her friends about the discovery, as if she were talking about something that happened to someone else, like it was some weird post she'd read on Facebook. Poppy picked up the letter and read it quietly, her husband leaning over her shoulder to do the same. One at a time they studied the bracelet and the photo. She didn't miss the knowing look they exchanged.

'I hate to say it, but this does all seem pretty conclusive,' said Poppy.

'Yeah, it does.' She cleared her throat to ward off the traitorous croak in her voice.

Nick stroked the hollow between his wife's shoulder blades. 'Have you asked your mum and dad about it?'

Faith shook her head. 'I can't.' She took a swig of wine from the fishbowl-sized glass he'd poured for her. 'I mean, why would they lie to me about being adopted in the first place? Why not just tell me about it from when I was a kid like normal people do? Isn't that what happens now? Not keeping it a deep, dark secret?'

Poppy swivelled the bracelet around her middle finger. 'Maybe your mum meant to tell you? Maybe that's why your name was on the envelope and she had it stored with all your old bits and pieces?'

'Then why the hell didn't she just tell me?' It came out a lot louder than Faith had anticipated, startling all three of them.

'There's one way to find out,' Nick offered.

'Yeah, I'll just call them up in the middle of their round-the-world trip and ask them: by the way, am I adopted?'

'Just a suggestion.'

Her rage died at his defeated tone. 'Sorry, Nicko. I know you're trying to help. I just . . . I really don't want to talk to them at all right now. I'm totally pissed off, to tell you the honest truth, and I think if they admitted to it I'd rip them to shreds. They must have had their reasons for lying to me for all these years but I'm not interested. There's no excuse.' If someone had told her she would ever feel this level of wrath towards her parents she would never have believed them. Even as a teenager, when they'd been over-the-top-strict about where she could go and whom she could see, she'd never been this angry.

Poppy placed a hand on hers. 'So, what *are* you going to do?'

She pulled the completed form and identification copies from her bag and pushed them across the table. Two confused faces looked blankly back at her. 'Find out for myself. I'm lodging an application to try to find my birth mother – Rosemary Barnes.'

'Presuming she *is* your birth mother,' Nick corrected.

'Presuming she is.'

'What if she goes by a different name now?' asked Poppy.

Faith shrugged. 'Don't know. I guess if she's changed her name since then – married or something – then there'd be some way of tracking her. There are agencies that help you find people.'

'It's a big step, Monty.' Poppy hesitated, shooting a look at Nick. 'I mean, I can't even imagine giving up my baby, but people have good reasons why they do it I suppose. Wouldn't your mother – your birth mother, if you find out you have one – wouldn't she have tracked you down if she really wanted to find you?'

'Both of you have to be on the register before either party can make contact.' She re-hashed the lines on the Jigsaw website. 'Obviously I'm not on it since I didn't even know I'd been adopted out—'

'*If* you were adopted out,' Nicko interjected.

'If I was adopted out.' She wasn't on a bloody witness stand, but she let the cross-examination go and continued. 'But she, Rosemary, could be on there.'

There was a communal sigh as they all assessed the situation. Poppy failed to catch a yawn.

Faith shuffled the papers in front of her. 'I've kept you guys up late enough. Nick, these need to be signed by a solicitor. Could you do it for me?'

'Of course.' He picked up the pen, let it hover as he caught her eye. 'If you're sure this is what you want to do?'

Faith nodded. She turned the documents over and pointed to where she'd written the words specified on the website. Nick scrawled his signature and handed her back the papers. She smiled him her thanks, momentarily unable to speak.

Pushing the papers back into her bag, she stood. Her knees were shaking and she held onto the island bench for support.

'Well, I'd better get going,' she said, far too cheerily. 'Thanks guys. I'm just . . .' Her chin quivered. 'I don't really know what I am.'

Or who.

'You're not going anywhere,' Poppy said. She was already mastering the maternal do-what-I-say-or-else tone. 'It's late, you've had wine and you're upset. The spare bed is made up and it's yours for the night.'

'I'm fine, really.'

'This is me you're talking to, Monty. You don't have to pretend. And you *are* staying.'

Faith chewed at the inside of her mouth: go back to her empty apartment on her own, or stay here with people she loved. Easy. She threw her arms around Poppy in a rush of gratitude. 'Thanks, Pops. You too, Nicko.'

'No need to thank us. You're part of our family. We'll see you in the morning.' He took his wife's hand and left Faith leaning against the table nursing the remainder of her wine.

Funny. Once upon a time she thought she really would be part of their family. Their real family. Funnier still, she thought she was already part of a real family of her own but that was looking like it could be just a big fat joke. A joke that was definitely not funny.

Her parents had lied to her. She didn't need to get this form back to know it was true. Was the lie why she'd always felt like something was missing, even though she'd been given everything a girl could ever want? Was it why she'd been so willing to accept Lukas's obvious lack of commitment to her all that time? Why she was jobless and alone?

She poured what was left of her wine down the drain. It was all catching up with her. She was so dog-tired she couldn't be bothered trudging up the stairs to the bedroom, which was now a nursery, filled with toys and baby gear. More than she could deal with tonight. She kicked off her shoes, curled up on the sofa in the lounge room, pulled the grey velour throw loosely over herself and closed her eyes.

An image of a black-haired baby was the last thing she saw before she fell into a restless, dreamless sleep.

Chapter Three

Rose

ROSE CLICKED THE SEND BUTTON AND PAID THE LAST OF THE bills. For now. Thank God for internet banking – for the internet in general, come to think of it. If she had to run around and do all her errands in person as well as organise bookings, order supplies and cook the meals, there was no way she would ever be able to spend as much time in the kitchen. Food was her thing: creating new dishes, combining flavours, making an artwork of the plate. It might be a pub in a small outback town, but none of her customers walked out of the dining room without a delicious meal in their belly and a zing in their tastebuds.

She opened the Menus file and began to browse. This week's dinner special was supposed to be salmon poached in white wine with a side of asparagus and dukka-crusted spuds, but the fish the local grocer had brought in hadn't been up to scratch. Maybe she could replace it with the chilli linguine that had been so popular the last time. Some of the locals – including her own daughter – scoffed at her elaborate concoctions, but it was a way of keeping life interesting and she liked to see the smiles on people's faces as they dabbed a napkin to their lips and beamed down at their empty plates. It was a small thing, but it mattered.

Shifting the mouse to the Favourites bar at the top of the screen, she scrolled down the list and clicked on the folder marked Italian. The Wordly Women site jumped out. Not really what she'd been looking for, but now that the page was open there was no harm browsing. Again.

Wordly Women cooking holidays cater to women who want something different from their travels. Organised as small group adventures, our tours suit all ages and are designed to bring women together for a positive, life-affirming experience. Come alone or with a friend or two and join us as we soak up the scenery, learn from culinary masters and get in a little retail therapy. This is the perfect way to see the sights of Italy in a creative, mouth-watering way. Highlights of the tour include sailing along the glorious Amalfi coast, taking in the crystal waters of Capri, cooking with three generations of Italian women in their own family kitchen in the hills of Tuscany and taking in the culture, fashion and breathtaking cities of Rome, Florence and Venice. If you are looking for a holiday that will inspire and excite you, this is it.

Her mind wandered to the rocky terraces of the Cinque Terre, the turquoise waters of Sicily, the painted ceilings of the Sistine Chapel. She could almost smell the rich aromas of the homemade pasta sauces, the garlic, the spices, the garden-fresh herbs.

'Argh, there you are.'

Her eyes flew open and she slammed the lid of the laptop shut. 'Jeez, Declan, do you have to creep up on me like that?' She could feel the flush in her cheeks, hoped he didn't notice.

'I didn't exactly creep.' He came a little closer and gave her a quizzical look. 'Didn't catch you looking at anything naughty, did I?'

'What are you talking about?'

He quirked an eyebrow. 'Plenty of it on the net.'

Did he seriously think she was sitting here looking at porn in the middle of the afternoon? 'I was doing no such thing.'

'Don't get your knickers in a twist, boss, we all have to get our jollies somewhere.'

'If I wanted to get my – jollies – I wouldn't be doing it online.' She shuffled the papers on the desk into a neat pile.

Declan sidled up to her chair. 'No, I don't imagine you would. That fella that came in a couple of weeks ago might be a better option.'

'What fella?'

'That old friend of yours. I saw him giving you the eye. You could do worse.'

Rose twigged to what he was talking about. 'David Ryan and I have known each other since high school and there is no way I would even think about . . . about getting my *jollies* with *him*.' That was ancient history. She stood and pushed the roller chair away from the desk, her arms firmly folded across her chest. 'And why am I even discussing this with you?'

Declan smiled. 'Because you know I'm right.'

'Is that why you were looking for me? To make inappropriate suggestions about my love life?'

Not that I have one.

He shifted from one foot to the other and shoved his hands into his pockets. 'Well, there's something I have to talk to you about, boss. Something you're not going to like.'

Rose's mind scrolled through the possibilities – a customer complaint, the bar balance down again, money missing. Judging by the worried look on Declan's face and the way he was jiggling his knee it could even be worse. She waved a hand signalling for him to explain.

'Do you remember Jana?'

'The pretty little Swedish girl you couldn't keep your hands off when she worked here?'

'That's the one. She's picked up some work on Great Keppel Island and says they're looking for a barman. Suggested I send them an email.'

'And did you?' Rose had a fair idea now where he was going with this but she was enjoying watching him squirm. Tit for tat.

'I did.' His smile faded. 'They um . . . offered me a job. Full board and lodgings and pretty good wages to boot. I'd be a fool not to accept. After all, I did come here to see the country and that's a part of it I haven't made it to yet.'

Rose gave him a knowing glare. 'And I suppose the prospect of getting *jolly* with Jana again makes the idea even more agreeable.'

'Argh, now come on, you know that's not . . . well, all right, there is that. Sewing my wild oats and all.' He dipped his head and scratched the back of his neck. 'I'm really sorry, boss, I don't want to leave you in the lurch or anything, but . . .'

'But you're going to.' She had to hand it to the kid, he had a way of softening her up, even when she wanted to wrap her hands around his throat and throttle him. 'When do they want you there?'

'As soon as possible.' He looked coy. 'But I did say I had to check with you first.' He added a dramatic pause. 'I did hear Dave say he was up for some bar work when he left the other day.'

'Say one more word about David fucking Ryan,' she exploded, 'and I will kick your arse out of here before you even have time to pack your bag.'

He looked at her, eyes wide, standing to attention. Being a casual employee, he could leave whenever he liked. There was no point riling him up and having him walk out before she could find a replacement. 'If you can stay until the end of the week I'd appreciate it. I'll put an ad up on the web and see who I can find.'

'Excellent. And I am sorry, boss. I've had a ball here, I really have.'

'Well, my loss is Great Keppel's gain. Just don't go getting yourself – or Jana, or any other girls you manage to charm over there – into trouble.'

'I'll be on my best behaviour. Promise.' Declan bounced on his toes, gave her his best schoolboy grin and went to leave.

'Declan,' she said, lowering her voice and waiting for him to turn back around. 'I mean it.'

'Okay.' He looked puzzled and then immensely relieved when a bell rang from out in the bar. 'I'd better get that.'

Rose heaved out a sigh and drummed her fingers on the closed lid of her laptop for a moment before opening it again and placing a notice on the pub's website: 'Bar staff wanted urgently.' There were always kids out there looking for work – she was generally turning them away. With a bit of luck she'd find a suitable applicant in a hurry. The prospect of running the bar, the kitchen and trying to come up with some way to keep the doors open was not really one she wanted to contemplate. But if she had to do it, she would.

It was one more complication she could well do without. The conversation with Declan had rattled her for reasons other than his resignation. She switched off the computer and went to shift out of her chair when something crunched beneath her foot. Paper. The envelope she'd folded and shoved into her back pocket two weeks ago and then tossed onto her desk in lieu of throwing it in the bin. She picked it up and smoothed it out, fighting the urge to turn it into confetti.

Immature behaviour, Rosemary.

Her mother's words, always reprimanding.

She dragged open the letter, her ire disintegrating into panic as she reached the final paragraph once again.

Please find overleaf a list of the works needed at The Crossroads in order for it to meet the requirements of the Heritage Act, *as determined by our assessor.*

Also note that for insurance purposes the work will need to be carried out at your earliest convenience.

Unfortunately we are unable to provide any financial assistance to you for the building repairs at this time.

Regards,

Elliot Bligh
Flinders District Council
Environment and Planning Department

A skilled procrastinator, she'd only made it as far as page one last time before she poked the letter back in the envelope.

This time she peeled away the first page and she drew a long, slow breath before she skimmed down to the amount totalled at the bottom of the estimated expenses column. When her eyes landed on it she slumped back into her chair. That couldn't be right, could it? She held the document out at arm's length as if the distance might adjust the numbers. But no matter how hard or how long she looked they weren't going to change. The council wasn't going to chip in a cent even though they had told her on the phone to send in a funding application, given her the impression that the paperwork was a mere formality. Now they were virtually threatening to close the place down unless she had the repairs done straight away.

'You've really dumped me in it, Michael O'Shea.'

Her eyes fell shut and there he was lying in the hospital bed, stick-thin between the stiff white sheets. 'The Crossroads is all yours now, Rosie,' he'd said. 'Make sure you look after her for me.'

'Of course I will.'

Easier said than done, though, as it had turned out. Opening her eyes once more, she folded the pages in her hand roughly and filed them in the top drawer of her desk. She stood and pulled up the blind, blinking at the bright light that spilled in through the window as she weighed her options. Paying for the repairs herself wasn't even remotely possible – the coffers were empty – but she'd made a promise and she was going to keep it. If Mr Elliot Bligh thought he'd heard the last of this he was sorely mistaken. Rose O'Shea would be on his doorstep bright and early to appeal to his community spirit, and if that failed she wouldn't go down without a fight.

Stephanie

'WHERE THE HELL DID THIS COME FROM?' SHE WAS BARELY inside the door when Bryce bailed her up, waving a piece of paper in her face.

It took a few seconds for her to register what he was talking about. Until she saw what was in his hand. 'How did you find that?'

'I was looking for a receipt for the last lot of hay we ordered.'

In the concertina file in the pantry. He never looked in there. What had she been thinking leaving it anywhere he could lay his hands on it?

'Where did it come from?'

She stared at her husband, his eyes like pools of hot tar, frown lines carved like ruts between his brows. Where was the kind, gentle man she'd married six years ago? More than ten years they'd been together now, high-school sweethearts, soul mates she had once believed. But the bickering they'd done over the past year and a half had blown that idea to pieces. All of those arguments had been about the property, or had at least started there. And this one would be worse than the rest. Tears itched at the back of her eyes.

'I asked you a question. Who left this here? Was it him?'

Him. He couldn't even say his brother's name.

'Yes.'

'When?'

'Two weeks ago.'

Still holding the papers, he let his hand fall away. 'He was here two weeks ago and you didn't think it would be a good idea to tell me?' He was quieter now. So much hatred in his face, so much resentment. Stephanie pushed past him, marching down the hall and into the kitchen, some of the beans she'd picked falling out from the folds of her T-shirt and scattering onto the floor as she went.

'Did you speak to him?' He was there, at her back. He tossed the papers onto the table as if they were contaminated.

She dumped the beans into a colander and braced herself against the sink. 'Yes. I did speak to him. Briefly but—'

'What did he say?'

'If you let me finish, I'll tell you.' She folded her arms, matched his glare. He gave a brief nod before she continued. 'He didn't say much at all. Asked how you were, made some comment about the place. And then I told him to leave.'

'What did he say about Strathmore?'

'I don't know. Nothing really. Just that it looked empty or something.'

'But he gave you this?'

'No. I was on Bandit, about to go for a ride. He shoved it in the fence post and then left. So did I.' She signalled to the document on the table. 'I brought it inside when I got back. I was just waiting for the right time to give it to you.' A time they both knew was never going to come.

'And you read it.'

'Yes, I read it.' She pointed toward the table, where the letter sat. 'It has both our names on it, in case you didn't notice.'

Bryce dragged out a chair and dropped into it. The fury was still there, his body stiff with it, but at least he was calmer now. She sat opposite him and reached for the papers, running her eyes over the first page, reading it again.

'Energy 21,' Bryce said. 'A mining company. Unbelievable. What a Judas.'

She shuffled through the pages, finding the handwritten one, her brother-in-law's name scrawled across the bottom line, followed by his job title – Land Access Officer. Cam, it seemed, was now responsible for finding properties in the centre and west of the state that would be willing to work with the company, allow surveys to be done with a view to setting up infrastructure to mine coal seam gas. Strathmore was one of the many in the area he was approaching.

'Did you see what he said at the end?' Bryce huffed. 'Is he completely demented?'

Stephanie zoned in on the last few sentences and read them out loud. *'This is a great opportunity and you would be crazy not to at least consider it. I'm going to be in the area for a while. Give me a call and we can talk about it over a beer.'*

You had to admire his optimism. 'From what I've heard, the surveys other companies have done in this area have found nothing.' She folded the pages and slipped them back into the envelope. 'Are you going to call him?'

'Call him?' He stood and started a slow march up and down the kitchen. 'Are you joking? If he thinks I'm going to meet up with him and have a friendly chat about turning our family's land over to be hacked up and pissed on he can go screw himself. He knows where I stand. I knew he was low, but working for the bloody mining company. Is that a joke?'

'I guess with his experience it sort of makes sense. He's a logical choice for a scout,' she said, trying to stay objective. 'He knows the land, knows the area and the people, and he's an engineer so—'

'He used to be a farmer.'

She shook her head. 'Cam was never a farmer. Not like you. It's in your blood, Bryce, but it's not in his.'

'Sometimes I wonder how we were even born into the same family.'

'Why? Because he doesn't want what you want?'

He stopped pacing and fixed her with a glare. 'Whose side are you on?'

'Yours. Of course I'm on your side. I'm just saying that life on the land isn't for everyone.'

'It's how we were brought up. This place has been in our family for generations. It was left to us to carry on the tradition.'

'That's fine for you, you were happy with that, but Cam wanted – wants – a different life.'

'Yeah, he does – his wallet stuffed with money.' He shook his head. 'I can't believe you're defending him.'

'I'm not. I'm not, Bryce. But we all have a right to live our life our own way. Make our own choices. What if Jake decides the land isn't for him?'

'He won't. I'll bring him up to love it the way I do. He already does.'

'We'll bring him up to love it,' she corrected. 'But you and Cameron were brought up the same way and he chose to leave.'

'Chose to leave me hanging, walk away from his responsibilities. From his heritage.'

She let out a weary sigh. Sometimes her husband's bull-headed, old-fashioned ways made her wonder what she'd ever seen in him. True, it was his gentlemanly courting that won her over in the first place – the flowers he left outside her school locker, the way he insisted on picking her up and dropping her home by curfew on each date, even the way he refused to 'go all the way' with her in his car because he wanted their first time to be special – but the flip side to all that chivalry was the patriarchal chauvinism he'd inherited from his father. There was no point arguing with him when he was in this mood. 'So, what are you going to do?'

'Not a bloody thing. And if he shows up here again he'll be met with the same hospitality he got last time.'

'Because punching someone in the head is a great solution. Really mature, Bryce.'

He didn't reply in words but shoved the chair in hard, rattling the vase of daisies in the centre of the table. 'I'm going to check the fences out by the gorge.'

'I checked them this morning.'

'Well, I'll check them again. Properly.' And then he was gone.

She listened to the sound of his boots clomping down the hallway, the front door whining open and then clanging shut, her heart hammering beneath her ribs. *Properly*. He was going to check the fences *properly*. Not the tardy way she would have checked them. She growled, biting at her bottom lip to stop it becoming a roar. He was just trying to get back at her for what he perceived as a lack of support; he knew her soft spot and he was applying just enough pressure to make it hurt. So what if she hadn't actually grown up on the land? She'd spent half of her childhood on her grandparents' property, helping Pa with the sheep – drenching, branding and shearing. Her parents ran the pub and she might have been considered a townie, but that wasn't who she was. She loved the land, loved farming. She'd even joined Bryce doing an Ag Science degree and they'd planned their future together from an early age – working the land, developing new farming practices, living sustainably. None of that seemed to matter when it came to the crunch. Deep down Bryce still thought of Strathmore as his – she was just an interloper, a tardy farm hand who didn't do things *properly*.

She unhooked her knuckles from the chair, rolled her shoulders to get the blood circulating again. Maybe Cam was right – maybe doing a deal with the mining company wasn't so bad. At least then they could have a life that was more than dust and dying cattle. Would it hurt to find out what the company had in mind?

Running a hand across her forehead she looked up to check the clock on the wall. Jake would be coming out of kindy soon – she needed to get moving. But even as she showered, the tepid water going some way to soothe the turmoil Bryce had left in his wake, the idea of finding out more about Cameron's proposal stayed lodged her mind, a splinter in a festering wound.

Faith

'IT'S A STUPID PLAN.' POPPY FELL BACK INTO HER CHAIR AND shook her head dismissively.

'Thanks for the support, Pops.' Faith crossed her arms, sulking. That was mean and she knew it. Poppy had been nothing but supportive. In the two weeks since the 'discovery' she'd called every day to see if there'd been any news, and today she'd hopped straight in the car after their brief phone conversation. But Faith wasn't exactly feeling like Miss Congeniality.

'Well, what do you expect me to say? You can't just jump on a plane to Queensland on some hare-brained spy mission to stalk your birth mother.'

'Why not?'

'You know nothing about this person other than her name, age and where she currently lives.' She waved her hands around like she was conducting a choir. 'She could be a total nutter. You could get there and decide you don't want to have a relationship with her anyway. Then you've opened a can of worms you might not be able to seal back up.'

'Which is exactly why I'm not going to let her know who I really am.'

Poppy pulled herself upright again. 'What? So, you're using an alias?'

'No. I don't need to. Her name isn't on the contact register and neither is mine. There's no way she can track me down, even if she wanted to, which she clearly hasn't up until now. I can use my own name and she won't have any idea who I am.'

'Hang on. How do you even know this woman you found on Facebook is her? There must be a thousand Rosemary Barneses out there.'

Poppy was being exasperatingly rational. It wasn't as if Faith hadn't thought this through. She'd done nothing but think about it over the past twenty-four hours, since the documents containing her birth details had arrived, surprisingly quickly, in her mailbox. When her suspicions had been confirmed her entire breakfast had ended up in the toilet, but once she waded through the weedy forest of her emotions she'd launched herself onto the mercy of the internet. She held up a finger and reached for her laptop. 'Just a sec.' She shifted the computer so it sat between them.

'Birralong,' she said, pointing at the image of a series of buildings silhouetted against a sunset, a windmill in the foreground. 'Population, eight hundred and seventy-nine. Situated in Central Queensland. Home of the giant ichthyosaurus.'

'Ichthy . . . what?' Poppy pulled the screen forward and peered at the giant statue on the screen. 'That looks like a mutant dolphin.'

'A prehistoric dolphin. Or, to be more precise, a fish-lizard. And that –' she pointed at the two-storey building at the back of the sculpture, 'is the pub owned and managed by Rosemary O'Shea.' She paused, her gaze falling on Poppy, her voice a hum. 'Nee Barnes.'

'How do you know?'

She clicked on another tab and opened a Facebook page headed The Crossroads Hotel. The same pub appeared in the cover photo. It was a typical country-style pub, double storey, verandahs all the way around on both levels and a wrought-iron balustrade around the top deck. Painted on the silver roof in a vibrant green, matching the timber poles below, was a sprig of clover, each individual leaf shaped like a heart, all three joined by a single stem. The building itself was a deep salmon colour. She let Poppy take it in before clicking on the About heading and reading aloud: 'The Crossroads Hotel was taken over more than twenty-five years ago by the now late Michael O'Shea and his wife Rosemary. Rosemary, who still manages the pub, grew up in Birralong, her family, the Barneses, are descendants of early European settlers in the area. A stay at The Crossroads is an outback experience you don't want to miss.' She watched Poppy's face, could see she was still confused. 'My original birth certificate has Birralong listed as the place of birth for Rosemary Barnes.'

'Oh.'

They stared at the screen, dumbly.

'Is there a photo of her?' Poppy asked finally.

Faith shook her head. 'She's a ghost. No personal Facebook page and nothing else I can find online.'

'Runs a pub in Queensland,' Poppy stated blankly.

Anyone would think it was Poppy who had just found out she was adopted. 'Yep. And it just so happens they're in need of a new bartender.'

Poppy swivelled around, fixed two black eyes on Faith. 'You're not seriously thinking of applying?'

'Already have. Rosemary was very impressed with my CV and offered me the job pretty much immediately. I start on Friday. I'm booked on a flight to Townsville tonight and then a Rex plane out to Birralong tomorrow.'

'You can't be serious.' Her friend's face twisted with horror.

'Completely.'

'But you've never worked in a pub in your life. You hate manual labour. What are you thinking?'

Faith huffed. 'You're the one who said I should expand my horizons, try something different. *Get out of your comfort zone*, I believe were your exact words.' She gave Poppy a sly grin. 'So, that's what I'm doing. Anyway, what have I got to lose?'

Poppy fell quiet. A deathly, horrible quiet. If Faith were honest she wasn't so sure it was a great idea either, now that the dust had settled. When she'd found the ad for new bar staff on the hotel website she'd sent off an application immediately. And when the response had come back within the hour offering her the job, she'd accepted, hopped online and booked the airfares before she could properly think the whole thing through. She'd packed her bag and sat down beside it on the bed last night, almost in awe of her uncharacteristically impulsive behaviour.

'I don't know, Monty,' Poppy said. 'Sneaking around like this, it's deceitful, it's just not your style.'

'Well, you know what? Maybe it's not my usual style, but I've been lied to my whole life. So now it's my turn.' She glared at the computer, aware of the rise and fall of her chest, the red rash dimpling her neck. If she didn't understand her own screwed-up feelings about this whole mess, how could she possibly explain them clearly to someone else? She kept her watery eyes fixed on the clover leaf on the computer screen.

'I know I'm not a mother yet.' Poppy's voice was soft, like a shower of rain on a summer's day. 'But I do know that I already love this baby and I can't imagine what would ever bring me to give him – or her – up. And I can't imagine what it would have been like if Nick and I had been told we would never be able to have kids.'

Faith frowned, confused.

'What I'm saying is, there are other people involved here, Monty. This isn't just about you.'

The tears that had been brimming began to fall.

Who else is it about, then?

'*Just* about you,' Poppy continued. 'This involves your parents and the woman who had to make that horrible decision, so I'm not sure that doing this behind all of their backs is the way to go.'

'I can't talk to my parents about this while they're away, and I need to act on this now.'

'I get it, Faith, I do, but wouldn't you be better off just writing to this woman,' she pointed to the computer, 'to Rosemary, telling her what you've discovered and getting some idea of what she's like, before you go traipsing up to Queensland – into what's virtually a desert, and can I just remind you, you hate the heat – and attempting some fraudulent scheme that could totally backfire?'

'It won't backfire. This way I get to see what she's really like before I take the next step.'

'And if you don't like her? If she turns out *not* to be the person you want her to be?'

Faith had no idea what sort of person she wanted her biological mother to be. Until a couple of weeks ago she'd only had one mother, the woman she'd always assumed had given birth to her and whom she had loved unwaveringly. Discovering it was all a lie had thrown her life – and her loyalties – into chaos. 'I don't know,' she said, more to herself than to Poppy. 'I'll work that out later.' She stared at the image of the pub, her soon-to-be workplace. 'It'll be fine, Pops. Really.'

They sat quietly once more, letting the finality of her decision sink in. There was a lot at stake here, but there was no rule book for adults who discovered completely out of the blue that they were adopted.

Poppy moved closer and wrapped her arm around Faith's shoulder. 'I'd better take you to the airport, then.' A smile slid onto her face. 'After we eat.'

'Is that an invitation to lunch?'

'Yep. Thai, my shout. I have a craving for Pad See Ew.'

'Wasn't that last week's craving?' Faith closed her computer and slid off the stool before helping Poppy down from the one beside her.

'Yeah, it was, along with oranges and Vegemite.'

'Thai sounds good.' She headed into the lounge room to collect her already packed bags. The past week had been a rollercoaster of emotions – surprise, shock, anger, sadness, disillusionment, just to name a few – but thanks to her bestie she'd never felt alone. Poppy might not completely agree with the plan, but she was still in Faith's corner. 'We can wash it down with a Margarita,' she grinned, meeting her at the door, 'a virgin one for you.'

'Tease.'

Faith locked up her apartment and took her friend's arm. As they stepped into the elevator she couldn't shake off the feeling that life as she knew it was about to change.

Drastically.

Chapter Four

Rose

ROSE SCANNED THE ADDRESS BOARD IN THE FOYER OF THE Wills Shire Council building. There he was. Third floor. Normally she would take the stairs, get in a bit of incidental exercise, but she didn't want to arrive at Elliot Bligh's office puffing her head off. The lift would give her time to make sure she was cool, calm and collected.

She pressed the button and waited. The building was new. Stark white walls and shiny grey-tiled floors. They obviously had plenty of money to spend on their own offices, but not enough to share around the community. Rose wrinkled her nose at a faint, lurking odour of disinfectant, no doubt left by an over-zealous cleaner. A young woman dressed in a smart two-piece business suit stepped out of the elevator and they shared polite smiles before Rose hopped in and rode up two floors to the Office of Environmental Planning. She dropped her shoulders, straightened her neck and pushed open the door, but she was soon disappointed to see the reception desk was vacant. Before she could take a seat, a man of about her height but a decidedly rounder body barrelled into the waiting room.

'Mrs O'Shea? I'm Elliot Bligh,' he announced. 'Come on in.' Seemed welcoming enough as he gestured toward the door of his office.

'Thank you.'

Rose took a seat as Mr Bligh positioned himself behind his desk and laced his fingers together. He had deep-set eyes overhung by brows that needed a serious trim. Serious did, in fact, sum up the man. He launched into his spiel looking through Rose rather than at her. 'So, I've pulled out your heritage grant paperwork for The Crossroads.' He motioned to a file sitting beside his computer. It reminded Rose of those actors on a late-night infomercial. 'Unfortunately we were unable to support the application.'

'Which is why I'm here,' Rose replied.

Mr Bligh looked puzzled for a moment. 'Ah, I see.' He gave her a slow, knowing nod. 'I'm afraid you've wasted your time if you've come here to lodge an appeal, Mrs O'Shea. Once a grant is refused, there is no possibility of the decision being reversed.'

'As I stated in my application, Mr Bligh, The Crossroads is a heritage-listed building, the only one of its kind in the shire. Surely the council would want to make sure such an important local icon is preserved.'

He slid the file towards himself, opened it, pulled out the top page with a theatrical flourish and ran his eyes over the print before placing it back down and returning his attention to Rose. She made sure to keep eye contact, watched as he rested his elbows on the table and pressed his now steepled fingers to the cleft above his chin. 'You've certainly let the place run down.'

Her stomach plummeted. Who the hell did this man think he was? He was a government lackey, and a minor one at that. Her eyes burned but she wasn't going to let this idiot get the better of her. 'Running a hotel is a costly business.' Keeping her voice steady and civil was a challenge. 'And things have been a little slow, especially with the drought.'

He looked at the piece of paper. 'There was an application applied for and granted only two years ago, if I'm not mistaken.'

'That's right. And those repairs were done. But with a building like this there's always something else.'

'I presume you knew the costs involved when you began the business?'

'Of course we did.' He was really starting to get on her goat. 'But we – my late husband and I – bought it more than twenty-five years ago, so of course it's deteriorated since then. As I said, I've kept up with the repairs as best as I can but—'

'And as *I* said,' he interrupted, 'and as was stated in the letter we sent, the council is not in a position to approve further funding at this time.'

She could feel a film of perspiration on her upper lip. She wanted to dab at it with a tissue but she didn't want to give Elliot Blight any idea she was conceding defeat.

'Mr Bligh,' Rose shifted closer in her chair, deliberately relaxing the corners of her mouth. 'As I said, there has been a drought for a number of years now.' She held up her hand as he went to speak. 'And while that obviously affects those on the land most severely, it does damage to businesses as well. When people don't make any money they have less to spend, so service providers – like The Crossroads – also suffer. I fixed

the things that absolutely had to be fixed for the place to func-
tion last time but I wasn't able to do it all, and since then . . .'
A mental picture of those greedy bloody termites chewing their
way through her woodwork made her pause. 'Since then there's
been a termite issue.'

Elliot Bligh looked totally bored sitting there behind his
desk. He gave a heavy sigh, clearly convinced he was dealing
with an imbecile. 'I am aware of that, but it doesn't change
the fact that the council cannot grant you any more money.'

That, it seemed, was that. Rose let her eyes drift to the
framed portrait on the desk. A polished-looking family dressed
entirely in white with cheesy summer smiles, Mr Bligh included,
looked back at her. The man must have a heart but he certainly
didn't bring it to work with him.

'I presume you are aware that termites and rotting boards in
a commercial building could constitute an O-H-and-S issue?'

'Yes, I am.'

'So, you would also be aware that they need to be attended
to immediately.' He'd set up his target and now he was going
in for the kill.

A fire flared in Rose's cheeks. Blood pulsed at her temples.
She'd had enough of this man's bullshit. 'Well, they're not going
to be. I just do not have the money and that's all there is to it.'
She placed her hands on her legs, hooking her fingers around
her kneecap and squeezing hard. The plan to be business-like
had just flown out the window.

Elliot Bligh let out a small snigger. In that case,' he said, his
voice patronisingly slow, 'you may need to look at alternatives.'

'Such as?'

'A bank loan perhaps? You do have collateral.'

'I've already looked into that possibility. The banks won't lend me any more money, not in the current climate.'

'I see. In that case the only other option you would have is to sell the property to someone who can afford to carry out the designated repairs and maintain it properly.'

'That is not an option.'

'Well, as I said, and as the letter states, Mrs O'Shea, we are unable to be of assistance at this point in time. How you deal with the repairs is your business.' He pushed himself up from his chair signalling the end of their meeting.

Rose stood and as he rounded the desk she took a step sideways putting herself between him and the door. 'So, that's it, is it?'

'I'm afraid so.' He flicked his eyes to his watch. 'I have another appointment.'

Mr Elliot Bligh was dismissing her. Rose picked up her bag and moved towards the door he was now holding open. 'This is nothing personal, Mrs O'Shea. The council has a limited budget and you have already been privy to a portion of it.'

Rose stopped and faced him. He had the smug look of a cat that had just swallowed a mouse. Whole. Prior to their meeting she was just a name on a piece of paper. She'd come here with the intention of putting a face to her name, showing this was about more than dollars and cents, bricks and mortar, but she'd been well and truly stone-walled. He was just doing his job, but that fact did nothing to even out the erratic pounding of her heartbeat.

She sashayed out the door without bidding him goodbye, keeping her lips clamped tightly together until she reached the ground floor and stepped out into a blindingly bright day. She fished around in her bag for her sunglasses and pushed them on with a little too much oomph, jarring the bridge of her nose and making her eyes water. At least that would have been her story if anyone asked. But there was no one there to bother asking. She was on her own.

Damn you, Mick O'Shea.

She made her way back to the car.

Couldn't you have bought a normal bloody hotel, not one that was going to cost me a friggin' fortune when you shuffled off?

He'd left her with a lifetime of wonderful memories, but he'd also left her with a noose around her neck just waiting for the hangman to pull on the rope. He had left her with something else to look after too – or at least someone else. Someone who might be able to bail her out.

It was a long shot, but it was worth a try.

Stephanie

THE HOT METAL OF THE BUMPER BAR STUNG THE BACK OF her calves as she hoisted herself up onto the bonnet. She twisted her hair into a bun to get it off her neck and let the breeze that hushed through the old willow cool her skin. Her boots rested lightly against the grill. They needed a clean. Shorts and RMs weren't the best look, but it beat sweltering in jeans, and besides, Bryce had always said her legs were her best asset. Not that he'd taken much notice of them lately.

Anyway, this wasn't a business appointment; it was more like a reconnaissance mission. Meeting here, away from prying eyes, did have an underhanded feel about it, but there was no way Bryce could find out. A squadron of moths was doing death spirals inside her stomach. Flipping her phone over, she checked the messages. None. It calmed her a little, although seeing her last message to 'Corey' on the screen sent the fighter pilots back into a spin. Giving Cameron an alias had been a spur-of-the-moment thing. Not that Bryce would ever check her contact list. Not really. There was just no need to create more drama, which was exactly why she'd waited until he was a long way from home before pulling the crumpled letter from the garbage and retrieving Cam's number.

Meeting here at the old swimming hole – Cam's idea – was perfect. Well, officially it was a swimming hole. Right now it was nothing more than a dust bowl bordered with chunks of granite. The rope they'd used to swing from was still there, frayed and weathered but intact, hanging from the branch of the gum tree, its trunk a smooth shade of white where strips of bark had peeled away to litter the dried-up pool below.

The hum of a car. Cameron. The same black LandCruiser but from this angle it was obviously a company car, *Energy 21* scrolled in silver lettering on the driver's-side door. He walked over and joined her, back against the ute, arms folded, giving no more than a slight rise of his eyebrows in greeting. Up close he seemed more like the Cam she remembered, the same solid shoulders and angular jaw, and now she could see them, the same ghost-gum eyes beneath the expensive ray bans.

'Not sure I've ever seen it this dry,' he said, his voice jarring in the morning quiet.

'Me either.'

They sat in silence for a minute. She knew she should prob-ably start some sort of conversation since she was the one who'd called him, but sitting here not saying anything was strangely comfortable.

'Had some fun here, didn't we?' He turned his body towards her then and there it was, the one thing he and Bryce shared – that heart-melting smile. 'Remember that time we all camped out and Todd Harper climbed into his sleeping bag with the black snake? I've never seen anyone move so fast in all my life.'

Stephanie laughed with him at the memory. Todd had bolted into the bushes, his usual tough-man swagger somewhere down around his ankles with his boxers. 'Not sure who was more scared, him or the snake.'

'The thing slithered away damned quick. Todd pretty much walked on water as I recall.' *This* was Cam, *their* Cam, the man she'd loved like her own brother before everything went haywire.

They'd all hung out here together back in the day, a whole bunch of them, first as kids when their parents would drop them off, then as teens when they'd drive out themselves, pitch tents, camp in swags under the stars, cook damper and charcoal spuds in an open fire, skinny dip after the cask wine went straight to their heads, the couples trying a few more adventurous moves when the opportunity arose. It was where she'd first slept with Bryce, where they'd lost their virginity together when sharing the same sleeping bag became more than they could stand, both of them seventeen and over the moon for each other. She drew in a long wistful breath, the pungent scent of bush mint swamping the even headier perfume of sweat and sun lotion and sex.

'I gather you read the letter,' Cam said, bringing her well and truly back to the present.

'Yeah, I did. Before Bryce screwed it up and threw it in the bin.'

He tipped his head back, raised his eyes to the gnarly branch hovering above them and shook his head. 'I knew it was a long shot – especially after the reception you gave me at Strathmore last week – but . . . it was worth a try.'

'You didn't really expect us to welcome you with open arms.' It was more a statement than a question, but she waited for his response anyway.

'I guess not,' he said wearily, 'but I'm not the monster he seems to think I am, Steph. I'm just here doing my job and – whether he, or you, believes this – I think this would be a great opportunity, for both of you. The technology we're using is state of the art. It has minimal impact on the environment and could bring in big dollars for the place in the future.'

'Giving me the sales pitch already?'

'Isn't that why you're here?'

She shrugged. Of course it was, but she wasn't ready to admit it.

'I take it my brother doesn't know where you are?'

'Correct.' She snorted. 'He'd hit the roof.' A flush of shame warmed her neck. She'd never gone behind Bryce's back before – for anything, let alone anything to do with the farm – but then again, he'd never behaved the way he had been lately either. She ran her tongue over the dry patch of skin on her bottom lip, squinted at the bank opposite where a skink had taken up residence at the base of a dead tree. 'I've done my research, Cam, like everyone else around here. Coal seam gas has more than—' she curled her fingers around the words, '*minimal impact*. I've seen pictures of the set-ups, the scars it leaves on the land. It's not exactly environmentally friendly.'

He stared across at the lizard that was now darting after a march fly. She could see him weighing up her words. He'd always been a thinker and usually what he said made sense. As hard as it was she waited him out. 'There's a lot of media bullshit out there,' he said finally.

'What, so the pictures of the pipes snaking all over people's land and the methane bubbles turning the rivers into dirty spa baths are forgeries? Come on, Cam, you might be working for the mining company but even you have to admit that sort of evidence speaks for itself.'

He dropped his arms, rested his hands beside him on the car and tapped his fingers. 'Some of it does. But there are ways to go about it that aren't as damaging. You do know that the state owns the rights to anything that's down there?'

She nodded. 'But as far as we know, there isn't anything. They've already done surveys out here. So, I don't get why you're even looking?'

'New technologies are coming through all the time, Steph, new prospecting methods and new mining techniques. If they did find anything you'd be more than compensated. It's something to consider, with the drought and all.'

And there was the crux of it, her Achilles heel, the reason she'd contacted Cam in the first place. 'Bryce has already made up his mind. You know as well as I do he's never going to agree to Strathmore being carved up.'

'And what about you? From what I recall you put just as much hard yakka into the place as he does.' He straightened, hooked his thumbs into the tabs of his jeans, and looked down at the furrow he was making in the stony earth with the toe of his boot. 'You do have a say in what happens.'

'Unlike you,' she shot back.

'That's not quite right,' he said pointedly. 'I know I gave up my claim to what happens at Strathmore when I opted out of farming. It might be Bryce's baby now, but technically I'm still half-owner.'

She gave him a wry smile. 'So, we're pulling that card now, are we?'

'No,' he sighed, 'we're not.'

Not yet. But if it came to that, he could. They were getting nowhere fast. 'It's just not a good time right now, Cam.'

He narrowed his eyes at her.

'Bryce is . . . he hasn't been himself lately.'

'What do you mean, not himself?' he asked, frowning.

She cleared her throat. 'He's been sullen, angry.'

'Exactly how he was the last time I saw him, then.'

'No, it's more than that.' She shouldn't even be here speaking to Cam and now she was discussing Bryce's state of mind with him. What sort of wife was she? A desperate one. That's what she was. Desperate. And Bryce was . . . the word was there, lurking, the word she hadn't dared utter, even to herself. 'Depressed.' She looked straight at him then, knowing it was true now that she'd said it aloud. 'He's depressed.' It was like a ten-tonne weight being lifted from her shoulders and then dumped straight back down again.

He sat a little taller, his gaze still fixed on her. 'As in, you think he's suffering from depression?'

'I don't know. Possibly.'

'But you haven't asked him about it directly?'

Stephanie's laugh seemed to echo even through the open space around them. 'This is Bryce we're talking about. But I did look up a website – beyondblue – and he has a lot of the symptoms listed there – withdrawing from people, being unreasonably irritable, not wanting to go out, being tired, sleeping a lot. He's just not himself anymore.' She pictured her husband sobbing in the shed, but it was too much to share with anyone, even his estranged sibling.

'Things are always tough in drought times, you know that.'

Her temper flared. 'Of course I know that. But I also know *him*.' This was pointless. What did she want Cameron to do about it, anyway? She'd come here looking for a solution, but she was looking in the wrong place.

'If there is anything down there,' he said guardedly, 'it could take the pressure off. Financially, I mean.'

'Not everything is about money, Cam. Things might be tight, but we've survived through tough times before and we will again.'

He lifted a shoulder ever so slightly. 'I guess so.' He reached into his back pocket and pulled out his wallet and handed her his business card. 'But take a look at this website. It's all outlined here in black and white. There are also some case studies and testimonials. Let me know if you change your mind.' He stared up into the tree overhead where a cockatoo was stripping leaves from a reedy branch. 'I can put Strathmore at the bottom of my list. But sooner or later someone will come calling.'

She smiled. 'The devil you know.'

'Something like that.'

He began to walk away but stopped. 'I know it must have taken a lot for you to call me,' he said. 'It's been good to see you, Steph.'

'You too,' she said. He turned and made his way back to the car, disappearing behind the black-tinted windows and driving away, leaving a cloud of dust blossoming in the air.

She climbed back behind the wheel of her own car and reached down to take a swig from the bottle in the console. Ugh! Too hot. She turned the key in the ignition and let the engine idle. What had just happened? She'd come here to find out more about the mining thing from Cam and ended up talking herself – and him – out of it. Or maybe she'd just come to see Cam. She missed him, missed the family banter the boys had always carried on with, the camaraderie that came with growing up together, being part of a gang. And deep down she was sure that Bryce missed his brother too. She slipped the business card into the side pocket of her wallet. Despite her guilt, the meeting had been a good thing. Cam would back off now but he was probably right. It was only a matter of time before either this company or somebody else wanted to find out what was beneath Strathmore's soil. Knowledge is power, her old English teacher, Mr Sutton, used to say. It was time to find out more about what their future could possibly look like, and that included doing something positive about Bryce's depression. If she could come up with a plan to give him hope again everything would be better. She drove back along the track to the main road, lighter than she'd been in weeks, like a pigeon that had been flapping around in circles and had suddenly found the direction home.

Faith

THE RUSH OF AIR WAS LIKE A HOT, HARD SLAP AS SHE STEPPED off the plane. Townsville had been muggy and sticky, but at least the sea breeze had cooled her clammy skin as she'd walked along The Strand. She squinted as she crossed the tarmac and slid her sunglasses down over her eyes. They might be retro but fortunately they were also functional.

She glanced back over her shoulder – she was the only one getting off the plane and by the time she reached the gate her suitcase was already waiting for her on the luggage trolley beneath a sign that read 'Welcome to Birralong'. The carpark – more like a parking space – was deserted except for a mud-splattered four-wheel drive. As the plane roared back to life behind her the attendant disappeared inside the oversized man-shed masquerading as a terminal. She hauled her bag down from the trolley – it had only been used once and there were definitely new scratches on the shiny, champagne shell. Regional airlines, what could you expect?

At least the wheels were still intact. She righted it and manoeuvred it across the gravel in search of a taxi rank. Her phone was still on airplane mode, so she switched it back on. SOS only. Great. Now what was she supposed to do?

'You right there, love? Got someone picking you up?'

She bit her tongue. Now was probably not the time to quibble about patronising labels. 'Ah, I was just going to call a cab but I don't seem to have a signal.'

The man closed the door of the 'terminal', locking it with a key, and then came towards her. 'Only signal you'll get here is Telstra.'

'I'm with Optus,' she said faintly.

'Won't be making any calls, then, not from that phone, and you won't be calling any cabs. None of them around here either.'

She shoved her laptop bag under her arm with a loud grunt.

'I'm heading into town now,' the man said. 'Can give you a lift, if you like?'

Get into a car with a man she'd never seen before? Was this guy kidding? She twisted her head in the direction she assumed was town. 'How far is it?'

'Ten k. It's no trouble. I'm going anyway.'

Ten kilometres. Too far to walk in this heat, especially dragging the hard-case. She peeked through her dark green lenses at the man. He was tall and broad shouldered, probably in his mid-forties, neatly dressed in jeans and a short-sleeved cotton shirt, clean shaven too although it was hard to see his eyes in the shadow of his hat brim. Still, what choice did she have? 'Okay. If you don't mind.'

'Not a problem. Name's Darren. Everyone calls me Daz,' he said giving a broad grin. He reached out and shook her hand, his palm a little too moist for her liking, but his grip was firm.

'Faith.' She followed behind as he made his way towards a battered silver LandCruiser with the biggest bullbar she'd ever seen and opened the boot.

'Nice name.'

'Thanks.'

Darren – Daz – lifted her bag into his boot. 'Got all your worldly possessions in there, have you?'

She looked dumbly back at him.

'Your suitcase.' He closed the back door. 'Heavy. Especially for someone as petite as you.'

Petite? She was five foot ten, hardly petite. Why was he even commenting on her size? Maybe she shouldn't be getting in the car with this guy. He could be some kind of crazy axe murderer, this place a real life Wolf Creek. A twinge of panic stopped her in her tracks, standing on the passenger side, contemplating the door handle. The window slid down and Daz lowered his head so she was in his line of vision.

'You getting in?'

Too late now. 'Oh, yeah, sorry.' She pulled the door open and edged into the seat beside the stranger, the headline flashing before her eyes: *Woman's Body Found In Outback Queensland.* A blast of airconditioning hit her face as the window closed.

'Better belt up, love. The local copper's got eyes like a hawk.'

She pulled the seatbelt across her shoulder and clicked it into place, keeping her eyes firmly planted on a lump of mud plastered to the glass right in front of her.

'Where you heading?'

She bit back her nerves as the car turned out onto the road. 'The Crossroads. Do you know it?'

Daz chuckled. 'Rosie's place? Everybody knows it. You out here on a holiday or planning to work?'

Rosie. Rosemary. O'Shea nee Barnes. 'Yes.'

Daz gave her a strange look, tipped his hat further back on his head. Sweat marks darkened the brim.

Oh. She hadn't answered his question. 'I'm starting work there on Friday.'

'Funny,' he said, scratching at a mole on the side of his neck. 'Most of the packies who work out here bus in. You look sort of posh to be working at a pub.'

She looked down at her clothes: Guess cut-offs and crisp white Converse teamed with a navy-and-white striped tee. Not exactly backpacker garb. 'Looks can be deceiving,' she said, borrowing one of her mother's quips. Except in this case, they weren't. 'What's a packie?'

Daz sniffed. 'Local lingo for a backpacker. Some of them come and don't want to leave. One girl – she was working at Rosie's place – met a local fella and ended up getting married.'

He turned to her and winked. 'You never know what might happen.'

'You never know,' she murmured.

They hit the outskirts of town without passing a car in the opposite direction. Daz slowed down and eased the LandCruiser over a hump. A sign announced the Wills River but as far as she could see it was just a dried-out bed of sand. 'Is that a river?'

'Yep, that's her.'

'Wow. It really is dry out here.' There were always reports on the news about the drought but she'd never taken much notice.

'You said it, love. She looks a whole lot better with some water in her. In a good year she comes up pretty high.' Daz pointed to a ridge below a steel windmill that marked the entrance to the town.

'Hard to imagine.'

'Well, if you stick around, with a bit of luck you'll get to see it for yourself.' He turned left at the next corner past a neat-as-a-pin post office, a dazzling white with red trim, into what looked like the main street. A row of cars were parked beneath an awning in the centre of the road, which was twice the width of Sydney streets. She peered through the dirt at a row of shops – a cafe, a bank, what looked like a second-hand store, a Chinese restaurant, some sort of clothing store. The car slowed as Daz made a U-turn and pulled up outside a two-storey building.

The Crossroads.

'And that fella right there is Itchy.' He pointed across the road to the weird amphibious creature whose fossils had been discovered not far from here. In the driving holidays they'd done when she was a kid she'd seen the Big Banana and the Big Merino. Birralong had its very own big . . . thing. 'He may look mean, but he's harmless.' Daz laughed out loud at his joke as he climbed out of the car.

'Thanks for the lift.' She slid up the handle of her bag as her pseudo-chauffeur reached out a hand for her to shake. Again.

'Not a problem. Good luck with the job – and don't worry, Rosie's bark is worse than her bite.' He gave another self-congratulatory chortle and got back in the car, driving off with a beep of his horn as Faith wiped her hands down the sides of her denims.

She looked up at the hotel. That picture she'd seen online was either old or Photoshopped. Rust had devoured parts of the roof and the smoky pink paintwork on the walls and arching porticoes of the verandah was flaking away like bark from a tree. A series of doors, detailed in forest green, opened onto both the upstairs balcony and the verandah below, but some were boarded up and some of the balustrade railings were missing. A meticulously pruned hedge highlighted the sorry state of the pub's facade. Music filtered from somewhere inside.

'Piaf?' Not what she was expecting.

She took a step foward, bracing herself before stepping up to the threshold. A sign above the door read *Michael and Rosemary O'Shea, Proprietors*. This was it. In a few moments she would come face to face with the woman who'd given birth to her. Suddenly hot again, she tugged at the neckline of her T-shirt. Bits of hair, fallen loose from the pony tail she'd tied it into, tickled the nape of her neck. One step forward then she stopped, turned her head in both directions. Not a soul in sight. The entrance was right there in front of her. It was as simple as walking through a door. Daz's words played along in her head to the notes of the music spilling out onto the footpath: *Her bark is worse than her bite*. Faith had hoped for someone warm and fuzzy, someone who might be open to . . . to what? Really, she had no idea what she was hoping for, but there was no point standing on the pavement like a lost puppy. She'd come here for a reason, and that reason was behind those doors. Squaring her shoulders, she sucked in a good lungful of air and stepped inside.

She pushed up her sunnies and let her eyes adjust as she looked around. A beautiful old timber bar, polished to a brilliant shine and bordered by black-and-white floor tiles, dominated the centre of the room. Vintage musical instruments – old guitars, violins, piano accordions and even a harp – lined the shelf above and the walls were decorated with a series of framed photos. Small tables and chairs – all of them vacant – were positioned at intervals at the front and sides of the bar looking out through the opened windows. It was just before 11am, so not surprising that the place was quiet. A sudden tinkling of glass made her start.

'Hello, there. What can I help you with?' A tall, bearded barman complete with a man-bun greeted her with a disarming grin.

'I'm looking for Rosemary.'

'Are you, now? Well, that's a shame because Mrs O isn't here.' He was Irish, probably in his early twenties, would look mighty fine in a suit. 'Is there anything I can be helping you with?'

Damn. 'I'm starting work here on Friday.' She took a seat on one of the bar stools under a ceiling fan that was doing little more than moving the blanket of warm air from one part of the room to the other.

'You'd be Faith, then. The boss told me she'd found a replacement for me but she never told me it was a gorgeous young woman.'

'So, it's your job I'm taking?'

'Big shoes to fill, if I do say so myself.'

Faith huffed. 'Which you just did.'

He gave a sly grin. 'May as well get the formalities over and done with.' He slid a form and a pen in front of her. 'Fill in your details and I'll grab you a drink. What'll it be?'

She considered a vodka on the rocks – perhaps a little too early in the day. And perhaps better to keep a clear head. 'A lime and soda would be great. Thanks.'

Pen poised over the line where she was supposed to write her name, she froze. What if the woman at Jigsaw was wrong? What if she wrote her real name down here and Rosemary immediately knew who she was? No, the woman had assured her – multiple times – that there was no way her birth mother (BM as she'd started to think of her) could know her name.

'I'm Declan, by the way.' The barman returned, placing a glass in front of her, which Faith immediately picked up and drank in one go.

'Ah, I needed that. Thanks.' She felt better already. 'Hi, I'm Faith.'

'Pleased to make your acquaintance, Faith.' He watched her as she filled in the form. When she finished writing she looked up to see him still standing there, his mouth half-open and a curious look on his face.

'Is everything okay?' she asked.

'Well, I was just thinking,' he said, a glint in his eye, 'since you're already here . . . perhaps you could start work tomorrow.'

Her fingers froze around the pen she was still holding. 'Tomorrow?'

Declan wrinkled his nose and nodded. 'I'm meeting up with my girl over on Great Keppel. Wouldn't mind getting there sooner rather than later.' He paused and leaned in on one elbow, lowering his voice conspiratorially. 'If you know what I mean.'

Tomorrow. Could she really start tomorrow? The whole idea of getting here early was to suss out Rosemary before actually starting the job, thereby leaving open the possibility of making a quick exit. Starting sooner didn't give her much opportunity for reconnaissance.

'It would really be helping me out,' Declan continued, obviously hoping to capitalise on her lack of response. 'And you wouldn't want to stand in the way of true love, would you now?'

She snorted. 'True love?'

'Absolutely.' He drew a cross over his heart.

Picking up a menu to use as a fan – was it stinking hot in here or was it just her? – she studied him while she weighed her options. There didn't seem to be a whole lot to do around this place, unless you wanted to look at fossils, which she didn't, and maybe she'd have a better chance to check out Rosemary once she was actually working for her. 'All right, I guess so.'

Declan's face lit up. 'Ah, you're a gem.'

'Yeah, well, true love can't be denied,' she said, delicately raising one eyebrow.

'I can show you the ropes this afternoon if you like.'

'Fine.' But there was that small issue of her complete lack of bar-tending skills.

'Are you okay?' Declan asked. 'You look a little pale.'

'Yeah, just hot,' she covered, fanning madly. 'Doesn't this place have aircon?'

'Afraid not. It broke down a few weeks back.'

Great.

'And it won't be fixed anytime soon,' a voice growled from the entrance, 'since those bastards at the council won't cough up.'

Faith turned slowly. A woman who looked to be in her late forties strode towards the bar. Her hair, dark auburn on top with tips that looked like they'd been dipped in a pot of honey, framed her face in shaggy layers reaching to her shoulders. She wore faded jeans and a bright orange T-shirt that clung to her trim frame, a string of turquoise beads around her neck, and a pair of purple-framed glasses that rested precariously on the end of her nose.

'If that bloody moron Elliot Bligh had half a brain he'd be dangerous.'

'I take it the meeting didn't go too well, then?' Declan asked, shifting the row of clean glasses from a tray to the shelf above him.

'That's a friggin' understatement.'

She swallowed hard as she watched the fire in the woman's slate-blue eyes burn.

'This is Faith,' Declan jumped in. 'My replacement.'

The woman turned towards her. Faith had never fainted, but now, as her ears began to ring and black spots cartwheeled in front of her eyes, it was a distinct possibility. All she wanted was to jump off the stool and run. Remaining upright was the best she could do. She felt her lips twitch into a watery smile and raised her hand in a paltry, royal sort of wave. 'Pleased . . . to meet you,' she stammered.

Rose looked her up and down, then grunted. 'Well, you sort her out,' she said to Declan. 'I have things to do.' Picking up her folder she disappeared through a doorway at the back of the bar. The door banged shut and a few bottles on the shelf wobbled and clanked.

Declan rested on his elbows, one hand folded on top of the other. 'That,' he whispered, his eyes dancing a jig, 'was your new boss.'

Her insides flipped inside out and back again as she gripped the edge of the bar.

No. That was my mother.

Chapter Five

Rose

ROSE STOPPED DEAD AT THE GATE. THE WEEKLY DROP-INS TO her mother-in-law were torture enough for both of them, but the request she was going to make today left her feet refusing to budge. The house didn't exactly shout 'Welcome, come on in!' either. If she didn't know better she would have sworn it was deserted. Louvres permanently closed and covered in cobwebs, the old wooden door warped and weathered, what was once a lawn now a bed of dried-out prickles and weeds. Even the gnarled old gum tree in the corner of the yard had given up the ghost, its bare branches scratching at the roof like arthritic fingers.

With a bit of luck, it would topple over one day and put the old biddy out of her misery.

Don't be so uncharitable, Rose.

She paused and placed her palm on the metal gate. It resisted with a groan and she had to lean hard against it to force it all the way open. Her feet crunched the short distance to the three front steps, trapping tiny sharp pebbles inside her sandals. When she reached the small porch she shook them out before lifting the tarnished metal knocker and rapping three times, slowly, against the door. It was the same routine she always followed before slipping the key into the lock.

'Hello, it's me,' she called. 'Rosemary.' As if it would be anyone else.

Silence.

And not the good kind. The silence here was the brooding, weighty kind that got you in its clutches and left you suffocating.

She lifted the bag she was carrying onto the kitchen bench. After she loaded the milk, butter and meals she'd prepared into the fridge, she stocked the cupboard above the sink with biscuits, bread and tinned vegetables, then squared her shoulders before heading for the lounge room. Her mother-in-law sat in her usual chair, a worn leather recliner, directly in front of the television, eyes glued to an old black-and-white Hitchcock.

Rose sat down in a chair opposite. 'Hello Letty, how are you?'

'I'm watching a film.'

'I can see that.' Today probably wasn't the day to fight fire with fire. She sweetened her voice. 'Would you like a cup of tea?'

Rose took her grunt as a yes and returned to the kitchen. She stifled yet another sigh as she performed the next part of the ritual. It was the same each time she visited: Letty barely acknowledging her presence, followed by a one-sided conversation and if Rose tried to make any suggestion that the woman actually leave the house for an hour or two, an argument that ended in a screaming match.

That was not what she wanted today. She filled the kettle and set about making the tea. It had been the same for years now, ever since Mick had asked her to take care of his mother just before he died. He'd brought Letty out from Ireland and set her up in a house in town years earlier, but the woman had never been happy, complained constantly about the heat and the flies, and resisted all attempts her son made to ensure her comfort. Nothing had changed in the past five years. If anything, the old bat had only become more cantankerous, more resentful, since her son's death. She flat-out refused to have any maintenance done on the house – 'a waste of good money' – and claimed that she didn't give two hoots about 'bricks and mortar'. Time and again Rose had asked her to move into a room at the hotel but Letty flatly refused, saying she was just fine on her own and to quit pestering her about it. Suggestions that she call a tradesman in to do repairs on the house were met with the same response – that would involve spending money and God forbid Letty should do that. It wasn't because she didn't have any; she'd had her own money squirrelled away before Mick died and then he'd left her a hefty sum in his will, just to make sure she was looked after, which Rose knew for a fact was sitting untouched.

The water bubbled from the kettle into the teapot and Rose covered it with the cosy; heaven help her if it wasn't scalding when it made it to the cup. Letty had always been a creature of habit, but in her twilight years her obsessive nature had hardened. Along with her bitterness. She'd never been soft or motherly. In a fit of anger years ago she'd spat at Rose that it was her fault Mick had never returned to Ireland, and by inference her fault that Letty herself had ended up here. No matter how hard Rose tried, nothing she did was ever good enough. Her calls and emails to Mick's two brothers had been ignored – there'd been no love lost between them and their mother, who had always favoured her eldest son. Even if Letty did agree to return to Ireland now there was no one who wanted her, so she and Rose were stuck with each other.

The tea brewed – three minutes, no more and no less. She set out two cups on the sink, added a dash of milk to each and filled them, being careful to not let any leaves float over the brim of the stainless-steel strainer. She stirred a heaped spoonful of sugar into the one decorated with purple thistles. Sometimes, on the days Letty was being particularly venomous, Rose pretended it was arsenic she was stirring into the cup. But not today. Today she was going to be especially nice. Popping the cups onto their respective saucers, she placed them on a tray with a packet of biscuits and turned towards the doorway.

She stopped briefly and raised her eyes up to the ceiling. 'Wish me luck.'

Letty pounced as soon as Rose entered the room. 'Don't put it there, it'll leave a mark.' Rose resisted the temptation to slam the cup down on the varnished side table beside her mother-in-law's chair. Instead she pulled a coaster from the mantelpiece and placed the cup down gently, sliding a Ginger Snap onto the saucer. She sat quietly and studied her mother-in-law's face. If it was true that the eyes are the window to the soul, then Letty O'Shea's soul must be made of iron. Rusted iron. She let out an involuntary snigger. The older woman flashed her a look that would cut glass and Rose composed her face into a well-practised neutrality.

She sat back in the armchair and waited. They played their habitual game: which of them would be the first to break the silence. It was always Rose, but she generally didn't crack until the end as she was rising to take the drained tea cup and asked whether Letty needed anything else before scampering out the door.

While the *Vertigo* soundtrack rose to an ear-splitting crescendo Rose scanned the room. Nothing ever changed. Old family photos crowded the mantelpiece, faces from home Letty hadn't seen for years and would never see again; tatty lace curtains thick with dust over windows bolted shut; in the corner a round wooden table surrounded by four high-backed chairs that would never be occupied. Sad to think that a woman's life could be so solitary, even if she did only have herself to blame. Some days Rose sat and watched the dust motes float in the sunlight, fancied they were the dandelion tufts she loved to blow on as a child, then follow their path as they wafted in the breeze, the grass itchy against her thighs as she lay in the yard dreaming of far-off places. Back in the days when life was easy and brimming with possibilities. When did that change? When she was a teenager, of course, adrift on an ocean of hormones, when life on the farm was no longer enough. Was that what made her up and leave? Seek the excitement of the city? Not that it really mattered now. It was too long ago. And she'd made a good life for herself when she'd come back. A good life with Mick and their daughter, her friends and customers, and for a while her parents. She'd worked hard to get back to being the good country girl – and woman – she was raised to be and for the most part she'd succeeded.

Letty, though, would try the patience of a saint. Rose had been grief stricken when her own parents had passed away within a year of each other. Even though she'd been in her thirties at the time and a mother herself, she'd felt cheated somehow. Orphaned. It had taken her years to recover and even now the memory left her throat dry and her stomach hollow. When she thought about her mother-in-law no longer being here the word that came to mind was relief. Did that make her a bad person? She looked across at the woman sitting mutely in the chair slurping tea from a chipped cup. There was no one else to take care of her. Rose was it. The cup rattled on the saucer as Letty lowered it to the table and wiped at her chin with a handkerchief before sagging back into the chair. Rose checked her watch – eleven minutes and twenty-three seconds. If there was going to be a conversation she was going to have to be the one to start it. She wriggled forward, avoiding the spring she knew, from previous experience, was poking through the cushion.

'Letty,' Rose zoned in on the almost-heart-shaped mole floating in the sea of wrinkles below her mother-in-law's left cheek bone, 'I have a favour to ask.' Letty's face remained completely blank, eyes glued to the TV.

'Letty?'

'What?' Letty barked. 'What sort of favour?'

This was it, her one and only shot. 'You know The Crossroads is heritage listed,' she began.

'What's that got to do with me?'

'Well, nothing really, but . . . the thing is . . .' Why was this so bloody hard? Why couldn't she just say it?

Letty spun her head around, her mouth gaping wide, exposing her yellowing teeth. That look, right there, was exactly why the words were stuck in Rose's throat.

'The thing is *what*?' Letty scowled and flicked a finger at the TV. 'Can't it wait?'

On the screen Jimmy Stewart was facing directly at the camera, a look of sheer terror on his face. Rose knew exactly how he felt. She probably should have waited for the film to end, but it was too late now.

'Not really,' she ploughed on, stringing the words together quickly so she could get it all out in one go. 'The thing is, the building needs fixing up and because it's listed the repairs have to be done in a particular way. It costs quite a bit. Business hasn't been great the past couple of years and I don't have the money to pay for the renovations. I was wondering if . . . hoping you might . . .'

'You want me to give you the money.' Letty said it blandly, reducing Rose's bumbling question to a hard statement of fact.

'Not give, just loan.'

Letty narrowed her eyes, her mouth shut in a thin, flat line. Rose tried to arrange her own expression into something that was optimistic and friendly but that more likely resembled the one she'd seen Jimmy Stewart wear just a few screenshots ago. Any glimmer of hope she may have harboured when she'd come up with this plan evaporated as soon as the woman opposite began to speak.

'This is why you've been buttering me up all these years, isn't it? So you could get your hands on my money. The money my son left me in good faith so I could look after myself in my old age, and you – who he left more than he should have – you have the nerve to come here and ask me for the little savings I have. I was there when they read his will. I know how much he left you, and if you've squandered it that's your problem.'

Bit by bit the air left Rose's body. She could feel herself physically shrink as the voice droned on through the cloud that had appeared inside her head. How stupid had she been to even think her mother-in-law would have any sympathy for her situation or be prepared to help her out? It had been a move made out of sheer desperation and really, the outcome was no surprise. When the rant ended and the cloud lifted she unknotted her hands and flattened her palms against the chair.

'Well, it was worth a try,' she muttered. She picked up the cups and dumped them back on the tray. 'I've re-stocked the pantry. You know where I am if you need anything.'

Letty huffed and returned her gaze to the television screen.

Back in the kitchen, Rose washed and wiped the china, packed it into the cupboard and collected her bag. She didn't bother to look back into the lounge room or say goodbye. The door clanged behind her as she pulled it closed, a jarring sound that set her teeth on edge. Hard and cold and sour.

Stephanie

'SORRY I'M LATE.' AN ARM APPEARED AROUND EACH SIDE OF Stephanie's shoulders and she was crushed into a bear hug. A musky-vanilla scent swam around her as a cheek caressed her own.

She smiled. 'Hi Mum.'

Rose dropped to the bench beside her. They'd opted for a picnic in the park today, both preferring the freshness of the outdoors to the beery smell of the carpet at the pub or the grease-filled air of the takeaway shop. 'What have you been up to?'

'Visiting your grandmother.'

'Lucky you!'

'Stephanie,' Rose scolded.

'Oh, come on, Mum, we both know you'd rather pluck out your own eyeballs and eat them sautéed on a piece of mouldy bread.'

Rose raised her eyebrows.

'Thank God for Nan and Pa, otherwise I would have dipped out completely in the grandparent lottery.'

They sat side by side for a few moments, visions of Rose's parents swimming in Stephanie's head just as she was sure they were doing in her mother's. As strict as they'd been they'd treated her like a princess. Why were the good ones always taken too early? She watched a duck, one of the green-headed ones Jake loved to feed every time she brought him here, waddle down and plop into the pond.

'True,' Rose said finally. 'So true. But Letty does at least have a soft spot for you.'

Stephanie laughed out loud. 'I guess she does, in her own warped sort of way.'

Her mother didn't reply but reached down into the cooler bag she'd brought with her and pulled out two foil-wrapped packages. 'A ham-and-pickle sandwich for you,' she said, rambling off the words written in black texta. 'And a turkey-cranberry-and-sundried-tomato focaccia for me.'

'Thanks, Mum.' She ripped the foil from the sandwich in double time. When had she got so hungry?

'My pleasure, squirt.'

'Muuum.'

'I'm sorry, sometimes it just pops out. I don't know why it bothers you so much. Jake has a nickname.'

True, he did. Bear. From the Old Bear stories she'd read him when he was a baby, and even he was starting to baulk at it being used in public now he'd almost reached the wise old age of five. 'Yes, but he's not twenty-seven years old.' She took another bite of her sandwich and finished chewing. 'So, you didn't tell me how your favourite mother-in-law is?'

Rose gave a long, slow sigh.

'Let me guess, she was watching a DVD.'

Rose nodded. '*Vertigo*.'

'Oh God, not again. Maybe she should watch less Hitchcock and go for something sweeter. It might rub off on her.'

'Hell would freeze over first.'

Stephanie looked at her mother, heard the venom in her voice. She always preached about not speaking ill of the elderly but she wasn't exactly being Mother Theresa herself.

Quiet fell as they ate their lunch. Was there anything as good on earth as home-made pickles? Her dad could devour an entire loaf of crusty bread and a whole jar of them in one sitting, with a little help from his offsider. It was him she could thank for the nickname. A sharp pang of grief pierced her chest. Even after all this time she missed him.

'How's Jakey boy?'

'Good.' She took another bite. 'Couldn't get into kindy fast enough this morning. His turn for show and tell.'

Rose laughed. 'Funny little fella. I thought he was a little quiet the last time I saw him. Not his usual sparky self.'

'Really?' The last time Jake had visited her mother was a couple of weeks ago, after the tourist visit, after the 'incident' with Bryce, when she'd fled the farm in a panic and come into town for some company. Had Jake been quieter than usual that day? She hadn't noticed, but then she'd been too busy acting like everything was fine. 'He was probably just tired.'

'And how's Bryce?'

'He's okay.' She'd made up her mind to tell her mother all about the visit from Cam and her worries about Bryce, but now ... well, she would probably make a big deal out of it and that wouldn't help the situation. Being an only child had its perks but it also meant way too much scrutiny. Bryce and Rose had always got along well, although her mother hadn't wanted them to marry so young, had wanted her to get out and see the world. But that had been Rose's dream, and Stephanie never wanted to give her mother the chance to say *I told you so*. It was exactly why she didn't want to confide in her about Bryce's behaviour, share her suspicions about his depression.

'Haven't seen him much lately,' Rose said, offhandedly.

'Well, he does have work to do, even when you visit.'

'I know, I know. I just wondered if he was avoiding me for some reason.'

'Not everything's about you, Mum.'

Her mother gave her a look that was half-hurt, half-annoyed. 'I didn't say it was. Where's all this coming from, Stephie?'

Where was it all coming from? She'd been trying so hard to sound normal, upbeat even, but now she'd let her mother's niggling get the better of her.

She screwed the foil wrapper into a ball and stuffed it into the bag, pulling out a thermos of coffee and two china mugs from the basket her mother had brought along. 'I'm just a bit tired, that's all.' Tired was always a good excuse, but this time it was true. She'd been dragging herself around for the past week trying to resist the temptation to have an afternoon nap. 'Sorry.'

Her mother held the mugs while she poured the milky brew, the delicious coffee aroma already giving her an extra spark.

'That's okay,' Rose said, the shadow crossing her face making a liar of her. 'Make sure you're looking after yourself.'

'I am. How about you? How's everything at the hotel?'

'Declan's leaving,' her mother said gloomily.

'Oh no. When?'

'End of the week.'

It was strange that she hadn't said anything until now. 'What are you going to do?'

'I put an ad on the website as soon as he told me and luckily I got a good applicant straight away, so I snatched her up. Sounds good on paper. Actually, she just arrived this morning but I haven't had a chance to meet her properly yet.'

'We could have cancelled.'

'No, we couldn't,' Rose said, blowing gently across the lip of her mug. 'Our Wednesday lunch date is a firm tradition, and we've missed the last couple.' She patted Stephanie's leg and sipped her coffee. There was something different about her today, something Stephanie couldn't quite pinpoint. Something heavy.

'Is everything all right, Mum?'

'Yes, of course it is.' She almost sang the words, before she looked away and stared out across the park. 'Shall we walk?'

Stephanie knew there was no point picking at her mother for being evasive when she was playing exactly the same game. 'Okay.'

They packed away the mugs and thermos, threw their rubbish into the bin and put the basket into the car. Walking was part of their weekly ritual, usually along the river – or the riverbed as it was now – after their lunch. They fell into a steady rhythm, following the curve of the track as it wound around the bank, the conversation winding along with it as they stuck to lighter topics in some sort of silent mutual agreement. She dropped Rose off at the hotel on her way to collect Jake from kindy, waving her goodbye with a half-smile and a sigh of relief. That had been hard work. She'd come away from the meeting with Cameron charged and ready for action, but after spending a couple of hours with her mother, pretending everything was fine, her brain was completely fried.

Faith

THE ROOM WAS A SHOEBOX. A CLAUSTROPHOBIC SHOEBOX filled with antique reproduction furniture. Great. Pulling a face at the musty smell, she kicked the door shut behind her. She dumped her case by the bed and dug her fingers into the cushion of muscle around her collarbone. Ouch. She twisted her head from side to side, triggering a series of audible cracks at the base of her skull.

Slightly more relaxed, she shifted to the window and pushed it open. Pointless, really. The air outside was even hotter than in here, if that were even possible, although it was fresh. Thank God there were screens to keep the flies out – there seemed to be a zillion of the feral things. Her room was at the back of the building and looked over the yard of the house next door. A cockatoo landed on the top of the paling fence that divided the storage yard of the pub from the neighbour's house, where white sheets flapped on a Hills hoist. The bird took a couple of tentative steps then launched itself onto the dumpster, the lid of which was open, and proceeded to scatter rubbish all over the ground. Someone would have fun cleaning that up later. She turned back to the room, surveying it glumly. It wasn't a hovel, but it wasn't exactly five star, and it was going to be home for however long she worked here. However long it took her to decide whether or not she wanted to fess up about her true identity. Her BM, aka 'boss', hadn't even bothered to make small talk, just palmed her off to be 'dealt with' by the hired help. Maybe Poppy was right, maybe this wasn't such a great plan after all. Maybe Rosemary Barnes wasn't mother material and that's why she'd given her away in the first place. Faith drew in a quick breath to stave off the nauseous wave of uncertainty swelling inside of her.

Well, suck it up, it was your idea.

She slumped onto the bed and pulled out her phone. Still no reception.

SOS was certainly right.

———

Back downstairs, lunch was on and the place was a little more crowded. Well, occupied; a dozen or so people could hardly be called a crowd. Declan was still doing his one-man show behind the bar, busier now with the increase in clientele. Rosemary was nowhere to be seen. Now was as good a time as any to eat – and if the wickedly good aroma of garlic and spices wafting through the room was anything to go by, the food was better than the accommodation.

Settling herself on a stool, she picked up the menu, reading this time instead of fanning. *The best meal you'll get in Birralong.* Quite the claim. Not that there would be a lot of competition, based on the fleeting glimpse she'd had of the place so far. Her mouth began to water at the wide selection of meals.

Declan appeared out of nowhere. 'Crowd should die down around two-thirty,' he said. 'Then I can show you the ropes.'

'Ropes?'

'Show you where everything is,' he clarified. 'Get you up to speed on the place. Since you're starting tomorrow.'

Her appetite vanished.

'That *is* okay, isn't it?'

'I guess so. If it's okay with the boss.'

He drummed his fingers on the bar top. 'Don't you worry yourself about that. Mrs O will be fine with you taking the reins. Raved about how experienced you are. In fact,' he paused, theatrically, 'she almost didn't give you the job because she thought you were over-qualified.'

Oh, God.

She'd probably overdone the whole bar-experience thing in that CV. Should have stuck to the old less-is-more rule. 'Well,' she smiled bravely, 'hopefully I won't disappoint.'

Declan pointed at the menu. 'How about we get you fixed up with some food before we put your neck on the chopping block?'

She felt her smile waver.

'Mrs O is pretty particular about things. She'll let you know loud and clear if you're not up to scratch. But I wouldn't expect you to work on an empty stomach.'

'Oh, right.' Particular. 'In that case I'll have a burger and chips, please.'

'Excellent choice, madam.' She watched him turn to a man seated a few stools away from her. 'Can I get you a drink, my friend?' He was as smooth as silk – but annoyingly likeable.

'Some sort of beer would be great,' the man replied. 'Surprise me.'

She shifted her body ever so slightly, holding the menu in front of her but looking from the corner of her eye towards the newcomer. He was fair haired and olive skinned with a face that looked like it hadn't seen the sharp edge of a razor for a day or two. His broad shoulders were slightly hunched as he stared down at the phone he held in his lap.

'Didn't you already order?' He jerked his head towards her. 'Or are you just extra hungry?'

She jumped at the deep rumble of his voice and dropped the menu to the floor.

'Excuse me?' she said, feigning ignorance.

The man slid off his stool, picked up the menu and handed it back to her. Declan arrived back just in time, placing two beers on the counter. 'Flying Pig,' he announced. 'It's a pale ale. Bloody good drop.' He pushed one in the stranger's direction and shifted the other in front of Faith. 'You can try one, too. Sample the wares.'

'Thanks.' She grabbed the glass and drank, hiding the pink roses blooming in her cheeks.

The man nodded at Declan. 'I'll grab a burger too, thanks mate. Since it's such an excellent choice.'

He was taking the piss out of both of them. If there was one quality she detested in a man it was arrogance. She deposited her glass back on the bar in front of her and watched the tiny foam bubbles rise. Declan was right – it was a nice drop.

'Cheers,' Jerk-face said, but she didn't bother to reciprocate. There were plenty of smart-arse men in Sydney. She had no intention of fraternising with any out here. She ignored him and he left the bar, taking a seat at a table by the window.

The lunch-time rush had grown to what must have been a solid dozen or more. Declan ferried drinks to tables, vanished out back every now and then to collect plates, and served his customers with a friendly ease. Before too long he brought her burger, a mountainous creation with a bamboo skewer pierced through the centre holding it together. 'Get your laughing gear around that,' he said in a faux Aussie accent that made her smile.

She watched his every move, taking note of the way he dealt with the customers, how he poured the drinks, handled the till and kept the whole place running like clockwork. Presumably he wasn't chief cook as well, because there was no way he could be whipping up what looked like solid meals when he was out here fronting the bar and playing waiter. A minute later another body barged through the swing doors balancing two plates – a round, red-faced girl in her early twenties who looked completely frazzled. She delivered one to a corner table before approaching the man by the window.

Faith heard the clunk as the plate hit the table and then the nasally whine of the girl's voice. 'Aren't you Cameron Bailey?'

'Yes.' Nothing else.

'I knew I recognised you,' the girl gabbled. 'You used to hang out with my older brother, Garth Rockman. He runs the produce store now. Got a little girl, Kira, she's a doll. You back in town to see your family?'

Faith crunched on a very tasty hand-cut chip, angling her head ever so slightly.

'Here on business,' the man said eventually.

'Oh, right. That your car out there?' Faith turned just enough to see the girl lift a hand from her hip to point at a black four-wheel drive.

Jerk-face was staring down at his plate. He gave a reluctant nod.

'If that's who you're working for I can't imagine your business going too well.'

'Thanks for the lunch,' he said, completely insincerely, dismissing the girl, who tossed her head and flounced back into the kitchen.

Returning her attention to her lunch, Faith studied the mountain of meat, salad, egg and bun teetering on the plate. There was no hope of it all holding together, so she lifted the lid off the roll, placed it onto her plate and picked up a knife and fork. The burger got better and better with each bite. How could something so good be hidden away in a backwater like this?

'I take it from the look of unadulterated bliss on your face that the food meets with your approval?' Declan reappeared, hanging over the bar towards her, clearly not one to be bothered about maintaining personal space.

Orgasmic was the word that came to mind. She finished her last mouthful and dropped the cutlery onto the plate. 'I honestly think that's the best burger I've ever eaten.'

'I know, I know. How good a cook is she? I keep telling her she should get out of here and share her culinary talents with the world. Staying locked up in Birralong is a crime to humanity.'

'That girl with the plaits? She's the chef?'

'No, no, no. That's Amber,' he scoffed. 'She's the kitchen hand and occasional barmaid.' He lifted a hand to cover his mouth. 'I doubt she could boil an egg. Rose, the boss, is chief chef, publican, accountant, barmaid, waitress – you name it, she's it. Wednesdays are her days off. She prepped the food earlier and Amber and I just put it all together.'

She finished her last mouthful of beer. 'Wow.' So, her BM was a one-woman band.

Declan banged out another tune on the bar top. 'You ready for your first training session?'

'Now?'

'May as well. Won't get busy again until later.'

Her thumb found its way to her bottom lip and she tapped the nail against her teeth. Really, how hard could it be? She was a smart, capable woman. Bar work would be a cinch. 'Okay.' She slipped off her stool and joined Declan behind the bar, listening carefully as he explained where everything was, how Rose liked things done and all about the daily routine.

'Now,' he handed her a schooner glass. 'Let's see how skilled you are at pulling a beer.'

She took the glass, held it under the tap and silently talked herself through the steps she'd read online. *Step 1, tilt the glass at an angle of 45 degrees.* Easy. Or it would be if she didn't have someone breathing down her neck. She gripped the handle of the tap. *Step 2, aim for about midway in the glass.* Did it say to pull hard or slow? Declan was standing right there in her peripheral vision with that cocky grin of his. No pressure. None at all. She dragged the handle down and almost squealed when the amber liquid began running into the glass but her delight turned to something else completely as the band of white foam widened. Before she knew what was happening beer was dribbling onto the floor and the overflowing glass looked more like an explosion of shaving cream than a schooner of ale. 'I'm a bit rusty,' she said, giving Declan a sheepish look.

Declan darted his eyes to the glass. If her face was as red as it felt he'd be reaching for the fire extinguisher any minute. 'A bit rusty, eh?'

She couldn't bring herself to look at him.

'It's a bit like riding a bicycle,' he said, narrowing his eyes at her. 'You know what I mean?'

No need to nod, of course she knew what he meant.

'So, I take it you haven't actually pulled a beer before, then.'

She shook her head this time, grudgingly.

'And I also take it you haven't actually managed a bar.'

If it was possible for an entire body to wince, hers did just that, face scrunching, shoulders lifting and toes curling inside the sensible new black ballet flats she'd bought as part of her bar-tending uniform.

'Okay.' Declan peeked over his shoulder and then took a step closer. The guy had no idea about personal space, but she wasn't in a position to argue. 'I'm not sure why a stunner like you would want to pretend to be a barmaid to get a job in a place like this, but since I want to get out of here as much as you seem to want to stay, I'm going to keep this little piece of information between the two of us and hope you're a bloody fast learner.'

'I am,' she whispered.

'Right,' he took the glass from her hand and nudged her aside with his hip. 'Watch and learn. Slow and steady is the key,' he instructed. 'Tip the glass, ease the tap on and when the glass is just over half-full, ease it back up again. The key word there being *ease*. Got it?'

This time her nod was more enthusiastic. After all, she wasn't an idiot.

'Right. Give it another go, then.'

She wiped her sticky fingers on her sides, stepped back into the spot he vacated for her and followed his instructions, filling the next glass almost to the brim with just the perfect amount of head on top.

'Did you know you poke out your tongue when you're concentrating?' It wasn't Declan's voice this time, but the deeper, gravelly one of the man who'd sat beside her at the bar earlier.

Jerk-face. Was he trying to be funny?

The look she threw at him was definitely not jovial.

'Just an observation,' he said in reply. 'I'd like another beer, please.' He signalled to Declan, holding up his glass. 'Might be better if you do it, mate. Same again.'

'I'm sure I can manage.' Faith dragged out a glass from the clean stack above her head. *Fat Pig,* wasn't it?' she asked.

'Flying Pig.' His lips curled.

As much as she wanted to jam the tap down, over-fill the glass and throw its contents in the guy's face, she managed to keep her cool and follow Declan's directions to the letter. She pushed the finished product across the bar with a smirk of her own. 'That'll be six dollars.'

He looked past her to Declan. 'You might want to chat to your staff about being pleasant to the customers.'

'Oh, I think she's doing just fine.'

Jerk-face took the hint and his glass and retreated back to his table.

Declan gave her a mischievous grin.

'What?' she asked.

'Clearly looks can deceive,' he said. 'I took you for more of the meek-and-mild type, but I see the fella there has ruffled your feathers.'

'I don't like sexist arseholes. But don't worry, I'll keep my comments under control for future customers.'

'Getting it all out of our system with your first one, eh?'

'Yeah, something like that.'

'Well, customer service aside, you did a mighty fine job of serving that beer.' He lowered his volume. 'Even if it was a virginal experience.' He laughed then, obviously enjoying his innuendo. 'Now we just have to teach you everything else that goes with managing a bar. Ready for a crash course?'

She laughed, settling her hands low on her hips as the tension she'd been holding finally left her body. 'Guess I have to be if I'm starting tomorrow.'

'Better get moving, then.' He handed her a notepad and pen. She listened carefully while he ran through the contents of the bar, showed her where everything was kept, how the cash register worked, what days deliveries were made, who the casual staff were – not that there were many of them – and a whole list of other bits of information she would need to know to run the bar efficiently. Thank goodness she had an almost photographic memory. By the time they'd finished the run-down the bar was virtually empty and Declan crooked a finger for her to follow him into a storeroom out back.

She stood behind him as he opened a fresh box of wine and began stacking the bottles onto a shelf, labels to the front. 'So, what do I need to know about Rosemary?'

'First up, don't call her Rosemary,' Declan warned.

'Okay. What does she like to be called?' The word MUM flashed on and off in her brain like a tacky neon sign. She blinked it away.

'Well, she's not one for formalities in general, and she hates me calling her boss. Or Mrs O,' he chuckled. 'But somehow I get away with it.'

Declan, she was sure, got away with quite a bit with most people.

'Most people just call her Rose.'

'What's she like?'

He paused, a bottle of merlot in each hand, lips pinched together, considering her question. 'Tough as old boot leather on the outside,' he said, turning his head in her direction, 'but sweet as apple pie underneath. Her husband passed on a

few years back, from what I've heard. Just the one daughter
– Stephanie.'

A daughter. Who would be my sister – or half-sister. She
ran her tongue across the back of her teeth and swallowed.
'Oh, really?' Declan held out his empty hands and she pulled
two more bottles from the box and passed them to him. 'How
old is she, the daughter?'

His forehead wrinkled. He hummed. 'Not sure, somewhere
in her late twenties, I think. Has a young fella. Jake. Bonza lad.'

'So, she's married?'

'Aye, she is. To one of the local graziers. Old farming family.
Quiet fella but nice enough.'

Stephanie. Rose's daughter. Her other daughter. Faith had
always wanted a sibling, preferably a brother, but a sister would
do. If the girl was in her late twenties, then there wasn't a huge
age gap between them. 'I wonder if we look alike?'

Declan paused, a wine bottle mid-air, and looked back over
his shoulder at her. 'If who looks like you?'

Shit. Did I say that out loud?

'I mean, do they look alike, Rose and her daughter?' Good
save.

There was a look of confusion on Declan's face but he
answered regardless. 'A little. She has hazel eyes, though, long
brown hair. Quite the looker.'

Dark hair, different-coloured eyes, a few years younger. So,
most likely different fathers. Mick O'Shea was presumably
Stephanie's but who was hers?

Declan coughed loudly and pointed to the stack of boxes.
She bent down and tossed aside an empty carton before opening
another. Now was not the time to start pondering her genetic
heritage. Now was, in fact, the perfect time to change the

subject before she roused any suspicions. 'So, what part of Ireland do you come from?'

'Argh, the opportunity to talk about myself. Brilliant!' He rambled on and on about his home town of Kilkenny, how he'd started university but decided to defer his degree in osteopathy and travel while he was young. The stories kept rolling out until the boxes were empty and the shelves fully stacked, and he let her officially clock off.

She grabbed her bag from its hiding place behind the bar, her head whirling with information. 'Thanks for fast-tracking my training and . . . you know, not saying anything.'

'No problem. Works for both of us. You'll be fine.' Declan regarded her carefully. 'Whatever you're looking for out here, Faith, I hope you find it.'

'Thanks,' she smiled. 'Me too.'

Chapter Six

Rose

NO MATTER HOW HARD SHE CRUNCHED THE FIGURES THEY just wouldn't work, and staring at the numbers all day wouldn't change anything. Cutting back on the more gourmet-style items on the menu and reducing the number of dishes would help a little, but the small amount she saved wouldn't eradicate the termites. Reducing the range of liquor she stocked was a possibility, but at the end of the day a pub had to stock more than just tap beer and cheap wine. She pinched the bridge of her nose and massaged her closed eyelids trying to ward off the lurking headache.

Closing the lid on her laptop, she walked to the window and gazed across to the small garden at the end of the delivery area. Buds were starting to form on the roses. Soon they would be a mass of crimson, yellow and apricot blooms. Her mother had loved them; always had a crystal vase full of them sitting on the kitchen table, the scent so strong Rose could smell it as soon as she opened the door and stepped inside. These had been planted the year she and Mick had opened the pub, the same year Stephanie was born; had grown and blossomed for the past twenty-seven years. All that time. The Crossroads had been Mick's life. She had been right there with him every step of the way, worked herself to the bone to get it up and running, but it had always, really, been his. It might have been her home town but he was the one with the big personality, the one who people remembered. Even now most of the locals still called it 'Mick's place'. Everything about it was exactly the same as the day he'd died. It was like a shrine and Rose was the caretaker. Not a very good one, as things had turned out.

Oh, Michael.

She lifted her eyes to the endless, deep blue of the sky, to a single patch of cloud. The shape of a heart. As she watched, thin threads of it began to break away and disappear, each fragile vein dissolving until there was nothing left but a faint idea of what had once existed.

A dream.

When had she given up on her own dreams? She knew the answer before she'd even asked the question: the day she held her newborn daughter against her chest, breathed in the sweet, milky scent of new skin, held her lips against the baby's forehead for one brief moment and whispered goodbye.

The nurse had looked at her with kind eyes before she took the baby, swaddled in a pink hospital blanket, and walked briskly out the door. Rose's heart cracked in two. She had to go home. There was nothing for her in Sydney. No money in her bank account, no job for weeks now while she'd waited for the baby to come. No courage left to set off on her own. Telling her parents had been out of the question. They hadn't wanted her to leave Birralong in the first place but had trusted her, let her go with a guarded blessing. And she had let them down – before she'd even left town. Let herself down. But she would not let her baby down. Her daughter would have a happy, full life with two parents who wanted her and loved her, two parents who could give her everything.

It had been years – decades – since she had allowed herself to dwell on the past so completely. Not a day went by when it didn't flash across her mind but she'd trained herself in the fine art of denial. Learned to push the memories and images away, lock them up and hide the key.

But life was wearing down her defences.

Her feet moved her toward the dresser unbidden. Her hand reached for the drawer and drew it open. She stared down at the tray she plucked her jewellery from each day. Pairs of silver earrings, some she hadn't worn in years; the rose-gold cross her mother had given her the day she left for Sydney; a broken string of mottled pearls that might have been her grandmother's. She breathed in slowly as she lifted the tray and placed it on top of the dresser. She could put it back right now, leave the room and forget about it all over again. But no. Her eyes drifted. And there it was. Tucked away. Right where she'd hidden it all those years ago. In the place she'd never allowed herself to look.

Her fingers crept towards it, almost of their own volition. The cool blue satin of the small pouch was feather light as she picked it up it and held it gingerly between her fingers. The click of the fastener as she popped it open and then, as she hooked a finger around it, the gossamer softness of the single black curl as it lay like a question mark in the hollow of her damp palm. She stumbled backwards, vaguely aware of the outline of her retreating form in the oval mirror as she sank onto the bed, mesmerised by the lock of hair. Her eyes fell closed and it came in a rush: the fluttering of dark lashes against ruddy cheeks, the pouting of pink rosebud lips, the perfect crescent moons of tiny nails. And then the strange, empty space between her arms when her baby was gone.

She slumped forward blood pounding in her ears.

When she looked down it was there still, in her hand.

Real, not a dream.

The one memento her rogue caseworker had allowed her to keep.

She pushed it into the pouch, clipped it shut and put it back into its hiding place, shoving the tray securely on top and jamming the drawer closed. She brushed a knuckled finger beneath each eye, sniffed away her tears and looked at herself, face to face, in the mirror. Really looked. Staring back was a forty-nine-year-old woman with creases around her eyes and enough lines on her forehead to tether a charging bull. As a teenager she'd made the hardest decision of her life, before or since. The one she had to make now came a close second. The Crossroads had been her home for all these years, Mick's legacy, but as hard as she'd tried, there was no saving it. Sometimes, like it or not, you had to admit defeat.

Stephanie

SHE KEPT HER EYES ON THE ROAD WHILE JAKE CHATTERED away like a drunk parrot in the car seat behind her, rattling off one story after the next, all seemingly disconnected. It made her smile to hear him yabbering – soothed the worry triggered by her mother's comment about him being a bit on the quiet side lately. Kids changed from one day to the next and Jake was no different. He was perfectly fine.

She peeked at him in the rear-view mirror as he started in on the potato printing they'd done at preschool, and it struck her again what a mini-Bryce he was – soft brown waves of hair that fell across his forehead, milk-chocolate eyes and the cutest dimples she'd ever laid eyes on. If he had a sister one day would she look the same or would she have the O'Shea genes? Straight hair and hazel eyes? Or maybe a redhead? What was the point? Everything was on hold until the drought broke. Things were too uncertain, Bryce had said, they needed to focus all of their energy on holding the farm together, and throwing a baby into the mix would be stupid. *Stupid.* That was the word he had used. At the time, two years ago, she had agreed. Being bedridden with hypertension for six weeks the last time hadn't exactly been a party – and the doctor had said there was a good chance of history repeating itself. Bryce had too much on his mind to have to look after Jake twenty-four-seven while she lay back in bed and rested. And her mother had enough on her plate trying to keep the pub up and running. But now her son was almost five, and the yearning for a second baby was a constant ache. A little brother or sister for Jake, she didn't care which as long as it was healthy. Growing up as an only child had had its advantages, but it wasn't what she wanted for her son. He needed a playmate, and she didn't want too big an age gap between her children. Even if she fell pregnant now he would already be at school, making his own friends, drifting more and more into being his own person, separate from her and from the family. But then there wasn't much chance of her falling pregnant anyway, unless it was an immaculate conception. She and Bryce had barely spoken let alone touched each other these past few weeks. The drought had extended to their bedroom, their once active sex life all but evaporating.

'Mummy, we're here.' He was right. The swimming pool car park, into which she had driven while her mind was busy somewhere else.

'Right. So we are. Let's get to it, then.' She jumped out the door, unbuckled his seatbelt and pulled his swimmers from the bag on the floor. Jake snatched them from her hand and ran ahead straight through the open gate and into the change rooms. He could never get into the pool quick enough. She smiled and grabbed the rest of his gear from the car.

'Hi Clarissa,' she waved to the pool attendant who doubled as the swimming instructor. A few kids were already in the water, some with floaties on their skinny little arms, heads high, and others bobbing under the water, aid-free, like hungry ducklings.

'Got my goggles, Mum?' Jake ran up to her, his voice high-pitched with excitement.

Goggles. Did she put them in? She scrounged around in the bag, pulling out the towel and clean underwear she'd packed. No goggles. She must have left them at home in the rush to get out the door. She looked back at Jake cautiously. 'Sorry matey, I think I left them at home.'

'But Mum, my eyes will sting.' The high pitch was turning to a whine. A major meltdown was about twenty seconds away.

A pair of bright pink goggles appeared between them. 'I know they're not your colour, Jakey, but at least that way you get to swim.'

Stephanie held her breath, eyes flicking from her son to her friend, Holly, who had the goggles swinging like a pendulum from her index finger.

'Okay.' Jake jumped forward, plucked the goggles from Holly's hand and was off, his small feet slapping against the hot concrete pavement.

'Hey, manners,' Stephanie called after him.

He turned with a mischievous grin, still running. 'Thanks, Holly.'

'You, my friend, are a life saver.'

'You can thank me tomorrow night with a glass of wine.' Holly started towards the shelter where the contents of her bag lay spread across the grass.

Stephanie followed. It was only the two of them watching the lesson today it seemed, a good chance for Holly and her to have a catch-up. She placed a towel over the hot aluminium seat. 'Tomorrow night?'

'Don't tell me you've forgotten.' Holly wound her thick sandy hair into a bird's-nest sort of arrangement on top of her head. 'Rocco's birthday bash in at the pub.' She gave Stephanie a piercing look. 'You and Bryce are still coming, aren't you?'

She looked past Holly to where the kids were motoring through the water, arms flapping. Baby birds learning to fly. 'Not sure,' she mumbled.

'Oh, come on, Stephie, you haven't been out with the gang for ages. It's Rocco's thirtieth. Everyone will be there. And you can't use having no babysitter as an excuse. My mum's already volunteered to mind him and Kira.'

'Yeah, I know, it's just . . . we've got a lot going on.'

'Like what?'

'Farm stuff, things to do around the house.'

God, how pathetic do I sound?

Holly stretched her legs out in front, crossed her ankles and rested her hands on her hips. 'Stephanie Bailey, you are the most efficient woman I know. Do not tell me you can't do all your usual chores and handle a night out. That's a load of crap and you know it.'

Stephanie sighed. 'We'll try and get there,' she said meekly.

'Which means you won't.'

'No, it means we *will* be there if we can.'

Holly flicked her eyes across to the pool, where her daughter was about to dive. They watched her belly flop into the water. 'Good job, Kira,' Holly called out, giving the thumbs-up signal, before turning back to the conversation. 'Steph, you know you can talk to me if you have a problem, don't you?' Her voice was soft, any hint of irritation gone. 'About anything.'

Stephanie smiled briefly. 'I know, but there's nothing wrong. Honestly. Bryce is a little stressed about the drought, no different to anyone else around the place. I promise, if we can get there we will, okay?'

'Okay.'

They shared a smile. Holly was an upfront sort of person but she knew when to stop pushing. There'd been times when Stephanie had confided in her – about arguments with her mother, issues with other friends that cropped up from time to time, girl stuff – but she'd never really opened up about problems in her marriage. Until recently there hadn't been any. She and Bryce had always been solid. And as far as the town knew, that's the way it was going to stay.

Now all she had to do was convince Bryce that a night out was a good idea. About as much chance of that happening as good old Itchy being resurrected from the dead.

Probably less.

Faith

BEING A BARMAID WASN'T SO BAD. PEOPLE HERE WERE generally friendly and she was hardly run off her feet. In fact, her first few hours had been pretty cruisey. Ambling down the street towards the library, she was more than pleased with her new-found skills. Rose had eased her into it with a short shift after Declan had hopped on a lunchtime bus out of town. She'd been basically left to her own devices, her 'boss' busy with paperwork and whatever else she did in that office of hers and, thankfully, business had been exceptionally slow. Their conversations had been brief and work related, and somehow Faith had managed to keep her nerves under control, but it was early days.

She pulled her phone out of her pocket feeling faintly optimistic, only to have her hopes dashed. The internet at the library had better work, because there was certainly no wifi at the hotel and she was having major withdrawals. How did people survive out here?

The automatic door slid open and she stepped into a rush of blissfully cool air.

A woman popped her head up from behind the counter. 'Hi there, can I help you?' she chirped.

'Hi. Are you Suzy?'

'Sure am.'

'Declan from the pub said you have internet here.'

'We sure do.' She spun around in her chair and emerged into the open lounge area bordered by neatly stocked shelves. Kids' drawings were strung across the room, and Suzy ducked her head as she made for a row of computers. 'There's a three-dollar-per-hour fee,' she said, switching on the one furthest from the desk. 'You staying at the pub, are you?'

'Hmm-hmm.'

'Lovely. In town long?'

People were certainly curious around here.

'Not sure yet.'

'Righto, there you go. Give me a shout if you need any help.'

Her fingers hit the keyboard. She typed in her email password, buzzing with pleasure. Yes! Civilisation. Her inbox was mostly filled with spam that had snuck past her junk filters, but midway down the page was a message from her parents' joint account. The subject line read 'Cruising The Mediterranean'. It would just be another of their travel tales, the latest update on their jolly European adventure. Her eyes shifted to the right, her index finger moving in the same direction but she stopped short of hitting delete and kept scrolling. A few lines down was one from Poppy. She opened it: *Faith, where the hell are you? I've tried calling. Why haven't you rung me??? Get in touch asap.*

Shit. Poor Poppy would be worried out of her mind. Faith clicked reply, spilled everything that had happened since her arrival onto the page – finding the hotel, meeting her mother (but not actually meeting her mother), being thrown into the deep end at the bar – finishing off with some lines of reassurance. *Don't worry, everything is fine.* She paused, staring at the final sentence. If only that were true. Poppy didn't need to know that she was living in a hotter-than-hell building that looked like it was ready for demolition and that her 'mother' was the boss from said hell. No, Poppy definitely didn't need the fine print.

Faith hit the send button and returned to her inbox. 'Cruising the Mediterranean' still niggled. She clicked it open and skimmed through the contents but didn't bother replying. There was enough going on here in Birralong. Dealing with her parents – and her anger with them – could wait. She deleted her junk mail, closed the browser and made her way back across to the central area of the library. Suzy had vanished. Her desk was neatly organised, a stack of paper beside the computer and a small piles of books waiting to be processed. A collection of owls of varying shapes, sizes and materials watched over the place from a shelf on the back wall. It seemed like everybody was into owls. Faith wasn't a collector of anything – brought up to respect a clean shiny surface – but she could see the appeal. Owls were cute but wise, demure with a spark of lunacy.

'That's my favourite.' A voice pulled her out of her avian musings and she looked down to see a small boy pointing to the flock. 'That big one there with the googly eyes.'

She followed his gaze to a large fluffy thing that looked more like a Furby, its eyes attached to springs so that they wobbled around making the bird look demented. 'Suzy always lets me play with him when I come in for reading time.'

A woman stepped up beside him. 'Well, Suzy isn't here right now and I told you we're not staying, just returning the books we borrowed.'

'But you said we could borrow some more.'

'We can, straight after little school pick-up tomorrow.' She took her son's hand but he pulled it out of her grip and moved closer to the counter.

He stomped a foot. 'But I won't have anything to read tonight.'

'One night without a new book won't kill you. You have plenty of your own. Now, get moving or you will be heading straight to time-out when you get home – without your cars.' His mother shook her head as she looked at Faith. 'Sorry, he's a bit tired and cranky after his swimming lesson.'

Faith gave back a quick smile. 'No problem.' The threatened time-out seemed to have subdued the boy but he was still pouting as the pair turned towards the door. 'Do you know where the librarian is, by any chance?'

The woman halted. 'Suzy? Probably ducked out for coffee and ran into someone at the cafe. Loves a chat.' Her smile was warm and soft, her hair pulled into a pony tail and she was wearing a cap which she pushed back as she spoke.

'And she just leaves the place open?'

The woman nodded. 'Yep. Everyone knows everyone else here. There's plenty of eyes. Besides, Suzy's hubby's a cop, so no one would be game to nick anything.'

'Wow. Wouldn't happen in Sydney.'

'Well, country life has its down sides but security isn't generally one of them. Is there something you needed help with?'

'Ah, yeah, there is actually. I arrived in town yesterday and I only have Optus. Is there a phone shop or anything like that around?'

'There's a place across the road, two doors down from the Salvos. Talk to Guy. He should be able to sort you out with something.'

'Okay, thanks.'

While they'd been talking the boy had slipped out the door and was now twirling around the rail of the access ramp, upside down, feet to the sky. 'Come on, Jake,' his mother said, helping him right way up, before turning around. 'See you. Good luck.'

'Thanks.'

As they walked down the street hand in hand, Faith's brain re-wound itself to yesterday's conversation with Declan.

Jake. Bonza lad.

She watched the woman get into the car, take off her cap and throw it onto the back seat, her long brown hair spilling down her back.

Dark hair and hazel eyes.

Faith moved towards the door, pressed her hand against the cool glass and pushed it open as the grey HiLux pull out from the kerb. The woman lowered her head and waved as she drove by. Killer smile. Declan had referred to Rose's daughter – her other daughter – as a 'looker'. It all added up.

It was Stephanie.

Her sister.

Chapter Seven

Rose

SHE PULLED OPEN THE OVEN DOOR AND WHIPPED OUT THE tray of steaming hot pastries, replacing it with another before sliding an egg lift under each bite-sized golden morsel and leaving them on the rack to cool. They were all equally sized, the edges evenly crimped. Not bad at all. She nodded to herself as she turned to survey the carnage – an open jar of flour, scraps of leftover dough, a discarded butter wrapper, the chopped-off ends of a couple of bunches of shallots and bits of semi-dried tomatoes scattered across the bench – which would have to be dealt with before she started on the desserts.

'Amber's arrived.' The new girl poked her head through the door. 'Anything I can do to help in here?'

'You could clean up this lot while I start on something else. Everything you'll need is under the sink.'

'No problem. Smells delicious.' The girl smiled as she set about packing up the cutlery and stacking the bowls and plates. Rose had been so preoccupied the past couple of days she'd hardly had a chance to speak to Faith. She was actually quite striking. Tall and lithe with a peaches-and-cream complexion and the most gorgeous head of shiny blonde hair. Not made for the outdoors.

Rose scanned the shelves of the fridge, pulling out the ingredients she needed for the next course. 'I hope Declan gave you the rundown on everything before he scooted off.'

'Yes, he did. Quite charming, isn't he?'

'That's one word for it. Excellent worker, though. I'm sorry to lose him.'

They each fell to the task at hand, Faith scrubbing away at the mixing bowl in the sink, Rose filling a board full of mini pavlova shells with cream and fruit. There was still a cake to ice before double checking everything was sorted out up front.

'So, have you owned the place long?' Faith's question dragged Rose's mind back to the pavs.

'Only twenty-seven years.' She gave an ironic laugh. 'More than half my lifetime.' She sliced a kiwi, cutting each piece in two and positioning the pieces like wings in the centre of each dessert. 'About as long as you are old, I expect.' The girl's age had probably been in her CV, but it wasn't a detail Rose had retained.

'I'm a little older.' Faith blew at a piece of hair that had fallen across her face before brushing it back with her gloved hand. 'Long time to be in one place.'

'I suppose it is.' There was a sense of relief now that the decision to sell had been made, but it wasn't a topic she wanted to dwell on. 'How about you? Have you always lived in Sydney?'

'Yes. I have.'

Rose piped tiny buds of whipped cream around the edges of the pavs, concentrating on getting each one exactly the same size.

'Have you been there?' Faith paused. 'To Sydney?'

The girl was still at the sink, her back to the table where Rose was working. 'A long time ago,' Rose said, feigning a lack of interest, picking up the sifter and sending a snow shower of icing sugar over the pavs.

'Did you like it?'

Rose stopped sifting. Sydney was like another planet – the small flat in Glebe with the rickety staircase she'd shared with two of the other barmaids at the Lord Nelson, the hustle and bustle of George Street, the ferries and boats scooting about on the harbour. Oh, and the curved, ivory sails of the Opera House shining in the morning sun. Nothing could beat it. 'Yes. Yes, I did,' she said softly, and then, shaking herself out of her daydream, 'but I wasn't there long.' She neatened the filled cases into three rows of six, tore off a sheet of greaseproof paper and wrapped it loosely around the tray. 'How about you? I take it you haven't been out this way before?'

'No.' Faith had finished the washing up and was drying the cutlery.

'Strange sort of place for a girl like you to come for a job.'

'A girl like me?'

There was a defensive, almost alarmed tone to Faith's question. 'Well, you're young, attractive, obviously intelligent. Just strikes me as a little odd you wanting to work in a bar all the way out here. Most of my workers are backpackers.'

'Oh well, you know, something different.'

'What did you say your usual line of work was?'

'Events. Events management. The company I was working for closed down. It was a boutique place but unfortunately the owner spent more than he made, so he ended up going bankrupt.'

'I know the feeling,' Rose grumbled.

'Sorry?' Faith turned. Her eyes were more mauve than blue, just like that doll Rose had loved when she was a kid. Wide and violet and piercing.

She'd opened her big fat mouth and put her foot well and truly in it. 'About being in dire straits,' she said breezily, as if it was the most ordinary thing in the world. She slid the tray onto the bottom shelf of the fridge before closing the door and resting against it while she dusted her hands down the front of her apron. 'Running a business is no picnic.'

'I guess not. You must be good at it, though, after doing it for all this time.'

'You'd think so, wouldn't you?' Rose said, unable to hold back a shallow laugh. 'I'm sure you've noticed this place isn't exactly the Hilton. It's been falling apart around me for years.'

Faith, finished at the sink, scrunched the wet tea towel into a ball. 'Declan said the pub is heritage listed.'

Rose nodded. She'd already said too much. Once the news got out that she was putting the place on the market all hell would break loose. She didn't even know how to go about selling, but surely there was someone out there who would be interested. The local real-estate agent should be able to put her on the right track, but first Stephanie had to be told, when the time was right.

'How about doing a fundraiser?'

'A fundraiser?'

'Yeah. I mean, this is the only pub in town, isn't it? I'm sure everyone around here would rally behind it, especially when you've been here for so long. We did one for a listed place in Surry Hills once. It was great. All the locals got right behind the cause.'

'Well, folks out this way aren't exactly rolling in dough.' The very idea of her neighbours taking pity on her and gossiping behind her back about what a botch she'd made of things was definitely not appealing. Rose rattled her head, as if she had water stuck in her ears. 'And I am *not* a charity case.'

'Oh no, no, I didn't mean anything like that.'

'Anyway, right now I'm more concerned with getting tonight's bash over and done with, so if you don't mind meeting me in the bar once you're done there, we can double check the liquor stock and make sure everything is ready to go.'

Faith gave her a faint smile. 'Sure,' she said turning away and wiping over the sink one more time.

Rose knew she'd been unnecessarily brusque, but, really, what was the girl thinking suggesting she air her dirty laundry for the whole damned town to see. The required repairs ran into tens of thousands of dollars – there was no way she was going to get down on her hands and knees and beg her friends and family for help. Not in a million years.

Once Faith had retreated back to the bar Rose wrenched the bag from the garbage, dumped it onto the floor and snagged it with a tie before heaving it out the door and into the yard. The girl had only been trying to help; she shouldn't have snapped at her like that. Rose had made up her mind to sell – it was the best, the only, decision – but it was all still raw. Serve herself right for getting chummy with the bar staff. One day she'd learn her lesson. She let the door bang behind her as went back inside, the timer on the oven chiming to remind her the last of the empanadas were ready.

The mouth-watering smell of steaming hot pastry filled the kitchen as she opened the oven. Her stomach gurgled, reminding her she hadn't eaten since breakfast. Breaking one of her own rules, she snitched an empanada from the tray and popped it into her mouth, huffing loudly when it burned her tongue. She waited a few seconds before she bit down and chewed. Hmm, that was damned good – just the right amount of shallot to offset the creaminess of the cheese and the tang of the tomato. And the pastry – her mother's recipe – was to die for.

Baking was definitely her forte, even if she wasn't so good at cooking the books.

Stephanie

It will be nice to have a night out together.

Rocco's your mate, you can't let him down.

Jake's all excited about his sleepover.

Stephanie wasn't sure which of the arguments had worked. Not that it mattered now they were on their way. Sitting in the car beside him, silence as thick as a bucket of molasses between them, she was pretty sure Bryce had only come out of obligation. But, she hoped, once he warmed up, once they got inside and met their friends, he would be fine.

She hoped. There was that word again.

She turned towards the driver's seat, where he sat, eyes fixed firmly on the road ahead. Dusk wasn't the best time to drive out here, but so far there'd only been a few roos in the distance, none trying to turn themselves into roadkill. 'It'll be good to see the old crew,' she said lightly.

'Yeah.'

'I think Rocco's out for a big night. Did I tell you Holly bought him a gift voucher for a ride on a Harley? It's a whole-day thing.'

'Did she? How much did that cost?'

'Not sure.' She could tell by the tone in his voice that however much it cost was too much. An extravagance. 'You only turn thirty once, I suppose.'

He gave a sniff of disapproval. He wasn't one to squander his hard-earned dollars.

'Mum said it's fine for us to stay at the pub tonight. We can have a few drinks, make a night of it since we don't have to worry about Jake.'

'We have stuff to do back at the farm in the morning, Stephanie.'

Stephanie. Her full name. The one that meant she was in trouble. 'Like what?'

'What do you mean *like what*?' His jaw hardened as he turned to her. 'The same things we need to do every other bloody day.'

Oh no. Not now. Please do not do this now.

She reached out and touched his arm, the first physical contact they'd had in weeks. His skin was warm, his bicep firm beneath the sleeve of his shirt. 'Exactly. It will still be there when we get home, babe. There's nothing urgent.'

He gave a slight shake of his head and his face softened. 'You're right. We probably should make a night of it. Don't get out all that often.' Whether it was the touch of her hand or the gentleness of her voice she wasn't sure, but one or both seemed to have done the trick.

He smiled at her and she could feel herself melting. He looked so damned hot in that crimson polo, freshly shaven, the scent of his cologne suddenly intoxicating. It made her brave and she dropped her hand to the top of his leg and gave it a squeeze. 'No, we don't get to do *it* that often.' She leaned closer, almost whispering. 'Maybe we can do *that* tonight too.'

He looked over at her, his eyes dark and shining. 'Why, Stephanie Bailey, are you propositioning me?'

'I do believe I am,' she purred.

He laid his hand over hers, lacing their fingers. 'Sounds like an offer too good to refuse.'

'So, we'll stay in town?'

He nodded and turned his attention back to the road. Stephanie relaxed back into her seat, their hands still clasped.

———

Holly wasn't wrong when she'd said the whole town had been invited to the celebration. The bar was already crowded, noise spilling out onto the footpath as the juke box pumped out 'Dirty Deeds'.

Stephanie rolled her eyes. 'Let's hope Rocco hasn't programmed in every single Accadacca song.'

'Good chance.' Bryce took her hand as she stepped out of the car.

The night air quivered with heat. The temperature had only dropped a few notches from the thirty-six degrees it had peaked at earlier in the day. She was glad she'd worn something cool and strappy. It was good to get dressed up for a change – she'd even dragged out her new western boots, the ones with the pink trim. Her bare arms were already tanned from days spent riding in the spring sunshine. Not exactly sun safe, but it made her feel healthy. Sexy even. She shot a glance at Bryce as they headed inside and he gave her a wink. Yep, it was going to be a good night, all right.

'You made it!' An ear-piercing squeal greeted them. Holly smudged a kiss against Stephanie's cheek before moving on to Bryce. 'Rocco is going to be so happy to see you, Brycie.

He's over the back there with the rest of the boys. They've got some jugs set up already. I'm going to steal your wife and get her some champers.' She gave Bryce a slap on the back and grabbed Stephanie's arm. 'Come on, girl, party time.'

The back bar was only slightly less raucous, filled with bunches of women who waved at them as they lined up for a drink. It was like a typical backyard barbie, men in one corner and women in the other, at least until the booze kicked in later in the night. But that was exactly how she wanted it – a catch-up with her friends and she was on a promise for later.

'What's got you all smiley?' Holly asked.

Caught. 'Nothing. Just happy to be out and about.' She scanned the back of the bar. 'Where's Mum?'

'She was here a minute ago,' Holly said. 'Ah, over there.'

Stephanie looked to where Holly was pointing and saw her mum chatting to a tall, greying man she didn't recognise. 'Who's that?'

'David Ryan. One of the Ryans who used to own the motel. He's housesitting for the Tinsdales. What rock have you been hiding under, Steph?' She gave her a crazy-eyed frown before turning her attention back to the other side of the room. 'Think he has the hots for your mum.'

'That's ridiculous.'

'Why? They're both single. I hear he's around for a while, so your mum might see some action.' Holly laughed.

'Oh, don't be gross, Holly.'

'What? They're not exactly ancient. She might be your mum but she still deserves to get a bit every now and then.'

'I'm not even going there.'

'Can I help you?' A voice from behind the bar interrupted their conversation before any more wild images could form in her head.

'A bottle of the pink bubbles, thanks,' Holly replied to the barmaid, who nodded and left to fill the order. It was the girl from the library. 'You didn't tell me your mum had hired more staff.'

'Declan did a runner. Headed out to one of the islands or something.'

'Oh really? That's a shame. He was great. Good eye candy too.'

A bottle and two glasses appeared on the bar in front of them. 'Cheers.' The new girl smiled.

'Faith, this is Rose's daughter,' Holly said as she picked up the bottle. 'Stephanie, meet Faith.'

'Hi, nice to meet you,' the girl gave a stiff smile.

Stephanie picked up the two glasses. 'Hope you got your phone sorted.'

'I did. Thanks,' Faith said before turning to Raelene Jennings, who was tapping her very long glittery nails on the bar.

'Imagine having to serve this lot on your second day on the job.' Holly called back over her shoulder as she made a bee-line for the courtyard.

'Stephieeeeeee!'

'Here she is!'

'About time!'

A chorus of shrieks erupted as she and Holly joined their gang. It was warm out here – but not as stuffy as inside – and the music was, thankfully, not quite so deafening. Holly popped the cork and filled their glasses while the girls all talked over the top of each other. 'Cheers. Here's to us.'

They all raised their glasses and clinked. 'To us.'

The champagne tickled her nose. She licked the sweetness from her lips after taking a few good sips. Being with the girls again was just like old times. It would be the same for the boys. Bryce would be sharing a few drinks and stories with them all, laughing, relaxing. The troubles of day-to-day life on the farm, the visit from Cam, the tension that had built up between them over the past few months – it would all vanish. It would be just like old times, at least for one night.

———

A few champagnes, a delicious meal and some very funny speeches later it was starting to feel like things were just warming up. Bryce had been hanging with the boys, but that was okay; they had the whole night to spend together, and he was having such a great time with his mates. Her mother had been racing around like a mad woman all night organising the food, making sure everyone had enough to drink, chatting with the guests. Anyone would think it was her party. Stephanie kept on eye on David Ryan who, in turn, did seem to be keeping an eye on Rose. Whether or not it was reciprocated was hard to tell. The woman wasn't exactly an open book. The thought of her mother with another man made her a little queasy. Of course Rose deserved to be happy, but it was impossible for Stephanie to picture her with anyone other than her dad. A part of her she couldn't quite identify, somewhere deep inside her, bottomed out whenever she stopped long enough to really think about him. Which was why she couldn't think about any of that right now. Her glass was empty, Holly's too no doubt, and it was time to crack open another bottle.

Where was that shouting coming from? It had to be shouting for it to be audible over the thrumming of the music and the shenanigans of the gathering. As she moved closer to the bar the voices grew louder. She stood still and strained to decipher them, and within seconds she zeroed in on one. Bryce. She looked around the courtyard. Her friends had all stopped talking, were holding their drinks in their hands, their ears trained towards the sounds coming from inside.

A few of them flicked their eyes towards her as Holly approached. 'Is that—'

Stephanie cut her off before she finished the question. 'Sounds like it.'

The next voice she heard was Rocco's. 'Mate, just leave it.'

She pushed her way through the crowd to the other side of the room just in time to see Bryce shoving someone up against the wall. His shoulders lifted as he drew his right elbow back. And there, sprawled against the wall, Bryce's left hand pinning him down, was Cam. Their eyes were locked. For a few thick seconds the room fell quiet as Bryce angled slightly to the side, his chest puffed, his hand reaching for the collar of Cam's shirt. An eerie sense of déjà vu had Stephanie watching the action along with everybody else, until she saw her husband close his hand into a fist.

'No. Stop, Bryce!' Her shout broke the spell the room seemed to have fallen under. Bryce froze and turned, just long enough for Rocco and a couple of others to grab him from behind and pull him away. He shot her a look, his eyes fierce. She had the sudden image of a fighting dog being dragged from its kill. She rushed at him, ready for a fight of her own. 'What are you doing?' she hissed at him as he shrugged out of his friends' grip. From the corner of her eye she could see Cam smoothing out his shirt, composing himself, but right now he wasn't her concern. It was Bryce she'd witnessed being the aggressor, Bryce who needed to explain himself. She was dimly aware of the crowd around her reassembling itself, mumbled voices, awkward staring as he stood, mute, anger dripping from every pore.

'What's going on?' Rose appeared, her hands on her hips.

'Nothing,' Cam said roughly. 'Nothing's going on.' He nodded briefly. 'I was just leaving.' Without even a glimpse at his brother he pivoted and headed out the main door. Before Stephanie could quiz him further, Bryce shoved past her and stormed away in the opposite direction, past the bar and out through the courtyard.

Rose turned to her, her voice low. 'You don't think he's going after Cameron, do you?'

She pursed her lips, shook her head and turned to Rocco. 'What happened?'

'M'not sure.' His eyes were bloodshot but he wasn't completely totalled. He frowned. 'One minute we were all here listening to TJ's story about his fishing trip and the next minute Brycie's about to take a swing . . .'

'Why was Cam here?'

Rocco looked a little sheepish. 'Ran into him yesterday and asked him along. I didn't even think about it being a problem.'

The look Stephanie gave him was enough to launch him into a longer explanation. 'Well,' he said, dropping his eyes to the half-full beer glass in his hand. 'I thought it might be a good chance for the two of them to bury the hatchet, have a drink and a laugh.' He peered at her, as if trying to get her into focus. 'Not such a great idea.'

'No. It really wasn't.' She patted him gently on the arm. 'But it's not your fault, Rocco. Sorry about your birthday celebration being hijacked.'

Holly had made her way into the thick of things at some time during the commotion. 'Do you want me to come find him with you?' she asked, stumbling over the words.

'Thanks, Holls. Best if it's just me.'

A hand gripped her arm and she turned towards her mother, who was clearly not happy. 'It's okay, Mum, I'll sort it.' Rose didn't tolerate any kind of violence in her hotel. If the boys hadn't both left when they did they would have been turfed out on their ears regardless of the family connection. Stephanie made her way out through the back of the bar in the direction Bryce had fled, ignoring the concerned looks from her friends, focused only on tracking him down and finding out what the hell had just happened.

———

The reek of stale beer and rotting garbage pulled her up short. It was dark out here. The music and noise of the pub thudded behind her like a muffled heartbeat. A tin can fell from the top of one of the bins lined up by the fence and she flinched, the hairs on the back of her neck prickling. Slinky, the neighbourhood cat, jumped from the bin to the ground, his black coat melding with the night, to nudge at the can. He flashed his gold eyes at her before getting on with his scavenging. Otherwise, no sign of life. The temperature had dropped slightly now it was almost midnight and she took a moment to let the cooler air wash over her bare arms. Her palms were clammy. She wiped them over the flimsy fabric of her dress.

'Bryce?' she called his name and waited.

No reply.

She made her way around the corner of the building and along the driveway. Surely he was out here somewhere. The heels of her boots clacked on the asphalt as she approached the side street. A blister was starting to form on her heel but she pushed the burn aside as a figure came into view, slumped against the last post of the fence, left leg bent at the knee, the sole of his foot butted up against the palings. One hand was in his pocket and in the other . . . was that . . . She zoomed in on the arm dangling by his side, watched as he raised his hand to his mouth, saw the orange tip of the cigarette pulsing in the dark.

Other than with a slight twitch of his jaw, he didn't bother acknowledging her approach.

'When did you start smoking again?' She could hear the reprimand in her voice but she hardly cared.

Looking away from her towards the street, he blew out a slow stream of smoke. 'I don't know,' he said vaguely. 'A month or two ago.'

'I thought you'd given up for good.'

'I had. I just . . . why are we talking about this right now?' He turned to her then, but his face was hidden in the shadows. 'Don't you have something more important to have a go at me about?'

Stephanie pounced. 'And why shouldn't I? What happened in there?'

'Cameron.' He spat his brother's name as if that was all the answer she needed. He brought the cigarette to his lips again and inhaled. Stepping forward in a rush, she ripped it from his hand, dropped it to the ground and crushed it beneath her the sole of her boot. The shock of it forced him upright. He hooked his thumbs through the tabs of his jeans and straightened his shoulders. She didn't need to see his face – everything about his stance was confrontational. If it was a fight he wanted she was more than ready to give him one.

'Is that it? That's the only explanation I get? What is going on with you, Bryce? We came here to have a nice night out,' she paused, letting the vision hang, 'but you decide to turn the place into a fucking boxing ring.'

'He had no right to be here.'

'Rocco invited him.'

'Bullshit.'

'Go and ask him yourself if you don't believe me. He hoped you two might be able to suck up your differences and act like brothers again. But he was obviously deluded.'

'I'm not the one who walked away from his family.'

'Oh, get over yourself, Bryce,' she chided. 'When are you going to get off your bloody soapbox about loyalty and heritage? Cam lives his life the way he wants and so do you. Just because those two lives happen to be different doesn't mean you have to be enemies.'

'You don't get it—' he started but she cut him off.

'No, you're right, I don't get it. I've tried and tried but I just do not get why you can't live and let live.'

'Then there's no point having this conversation with you. No point at all.' He pulled something from his pocket, car keys, and started to walk up the street away from her.

'Bryce.' She watched him head towards the main street, to where their car was parked. 'Don't be an idiot, you've had too much to drink.' Something ploughed into her temple. A beetle, she batted it away, a rising sense of panic pushing her feet to move, to follow. She watched him cross the road, saw the lights of the ute flash, saw him reach for the handle and open the door. 'Bryce,' she called again, louder this time. Sharp. But the sound of her voice was drowned out by the screeching of the car as he did a U-turn and sped off up the street, the smell of burning rubber lingering in a cloud of smoke.

She raked her hands through her hair, bracing her head between her palms as she watched the tail lights of the car fade. A sob stuck in her throat as the night replayed itself: her hand in his as they talked in the car; the wink of his eye when she'd whispered a promise in his ear; the sickening glare he'd given her as he strode out of the bar.

So much for a nice night out.

She wrapped her arms around herself against the shiver that had nothing to do with the temperature. Footsteps and voices came from somewhere behind her as she stood on the corner beneath the streetlight trying to compose herself, trying to ignore the message behind Bryce's last words.

No point at all, he'd said.

No point at all.

Faith

THIS WAS SO UNFAIR. DECLAN'S ASSURANCE THAT WORKING at the pub would be a breeze was starting to show itself for what it was: a big, fat lie. Pretty much everyone in town – not to mention the rest of the district – was at tonight's birthday bash and she was running from customer to customer to keep them all well hydrated. Amber, on the other hand, believed that bar-tending was a euphemism for gossiping. No wonder

Rose preferred not to hire locals. The only good thing about the event was that her 'boss' had been so preoccupied that the two of them had hardly been in the same room for more than a few minutes at a time. Tonight, with a wall-to-wall crowd, Rose was stationed in the kitchen doing the food with a couple of friends she'd called in to help out. The lack of contact gave her the chance to observe her BM from a distance, get a handle on her personality. So far her list of traits was fairly positive:

Well respected.

Organised.

A do-er.

No-nonsense.

The only other word she could come up with was scary – there was something about Rose's feisty, say-exactly-what-you-think attitude that was, well, intimidating. And very un-mother-like. Stella was all smiles and pleases and thank-yous, all about niceties and not rocking anyone's boat. Maybe it had been her fear of rocking her daughter's boat that had stopped her from telling her the truth. But Rose was nothing like that – the complete opposite, in fact.

'I'll have another schooner of New, thanks love.' She looked up and there was Daz, her friendly chauffeur.

'Sure.' She grabbed a glass and began to fill it – she was a beer-pouring pro. That smart arse who'd been in here the other day would be grinning on the other side of his conceited – albeit very handsome – face if he could see her now. 'Having a good night?' she asked, passing Daz his drink.

'A beauty.' He took a sip of his beer. His face was more flushed than when she'd met him, probably a result of him making the most of the bar tab. 'How's the job going?'

'Great.' Another customer was waiting and she side-stepped to her left but Daz was not to be deterred.

'If you need a tour guide, someone to show you the local sights,' he winked, 'you let me know.' There was a noticeable slur to his voice and his ring finger, Faith noticed was bare.

'Thanks,' she mumbled. Before she could take the next order a ruckus on the other side of the room had all heads turning.

Peering through the crowd, she was just able to see what looked like the beginnings of a brawl. Two men were fronting up to each other – one had his back to her, the other was obscured by the mob of people. The circle around them seemed to instinctively expand as the argument began and then, when they realised it was escalating, sucked itself back in again.

'What the—' Rose rushed out from the kitchen, stretching up like a ballerina on the tips of her toes. 'What's going on?'

'Your girl's bloke,' Daz leaned over, giving a commentary, 'and his brother, about to go at it hammer and tongs.' He looked like he'd just won the raffle.

'Like hell they are.' Rose flipped open the partition and pushed her way through the throng. Daz followed suit. The taller of the two men was now pinned against the wall, his face clearly visible – the guy who'd made her feel like such an idiot in front of Declan.

Oh well, karma's a bitch.

Your girl's bloke, Daz had said. Had he meant Rose's girl as in Stephanie? She bent her head, trying to get a better look just in time to see Cameron Bailey – she remembered his name (although Jerk-face suited him better) – push his way past the bystanders and out into the night. His brother, who appeared to be the instigator of the whole thing, looked less than contrite as Rose and Stephanie gave him the third degree. He shoved past them both, and his mates, and stormed away, leaving via the back door. An uneasy quiet had fallen while the room held its breath, but now it lifted and the party-goers got back to business, guardedly at first and then, as if trying to compensate for what was surely a downer on the evening, became even louder than before. Within a few minutes the whole thing was forgotten, at least by the revellers. Rose stalked to the kitchen looking seriously stormy, muttering something about 'bloody testosterone'.

———

By midnight everyone's enthusiasm seemed to have waned. Copious amounts of alcohol had been drunk and the evening began to draw to a close. Guests left in groups of twos or threes and within half an hour there were only a handful left.

'Come on, you lot, Narelle lent me the minibus. I'll drive you all home.' Rose rounded up the leftover drinkers, who included the birthday boy, his wife and two other couples. 'Has anyone seen Stephanie?' she called out, to no one in particular.

'Didn't she go home with Bryce?' Holly, the wife, was staggering more than a little, a half-full glass of champagne in one hand and her bag swinging from the other. Her eyes were bleary and the neat up-do her hair had been in on arrival had morphed into a tattered mess.

'They're staying here tonight,' Rose said, scanning the room. 'At least they were. If I find out he's driven home with that amount of booze in his blood I'll wring his neck.'

Faith collected the last of the glasses, wiping the tables for a little longer than necessary. It couldn't be classed as eavesdropping if she was just doing her job. This was honestly better than a night at the movies.

Rocco shifted from foot to foot, looking like he needed the bathroom. He took some time composing his next sentence. 'Ah, actually, he did drive himself home. I mean, I'm guessing that's where he went. He drove off after . . . well, you know . . . but Steph wasn't with him.'

Rose scowled. 'She's probably gone to bed. Which is where you lot need to be. Come on.'

The group followed obediently behind her like rodents stumbling after the pied piper, a couple of the women with their arms around each other, declaring the night totally awesome.

Amber rushed from behind the bar, bag hitched over her shoulder. 'Can I grab a lift too, Mrs O?'

Rose searched Faith out. 'You okay to finish up?'

'Yeah, that's fine.'

'Vacuum's in the cupboard under the stairs, if you could run it over once you're done with the rest of the clean-up?'

It wasn't really a question and it wasn't really fine, but what could she do? 'Sure.'

Faith stacked the last of the empties onto a tray and dumped them on the bar, ready for the dishwasher. Stale beer was all she could smell and it was making her feel ill – it seemed to have leached into her pores despite the perspiration that was seeping out. A shower was definitely on the agenda before bed. But the night wasn't over yet.

Vacuuming. How she loathed it – which was why she paid a cleaner at home. She wrestled the dreaded machine, an upright hoover that looked like it had come out of the ark, from the cupboard. Thank God this barmaid thing wasn't permanent. She plugged the monster into the powerpoint beside the juke box. Maybe a little accompaniment while she performed the last of her slave duties for the day might help soothe the pain.

Vac in hand, she scanned the categories. *Eighties Rock, Heavy Metal, Pop Princesses, Karaoke Favourites.* Tempting. You could never beat a good karaoke, and it just so happened to have one her favourite sing-a-long power ballads. She hit the button and pumped up the volume.

Humming along to the verse, she let her mind drift over the swirls of green carpet. This song had hit the charts well before she was born, but it was an age-old classic at the drinking sessions she sometimes indulged in on a Friday night in Chinatown after a long week at the office. It was one of the few times she managed to totally chill and hang out with her friends. Colleagues really, rather than friends – she hadn't heard from a single one of them since she'd been given the flick. Misery plumped itself up and started to get comfortable but the chorus began just in time. She belted it out, feeling every bit of Bonnie Tyler's angst, knowing exactly what she meant about her heart having a total eclipse. She negotiated the vacuum around a bar stool until her eyes landed on a pair of rich brown leather boots. The singing came to an abrupt end.

'Don't mind me, I was enjoying your performance.'

Him again. Jerk-face. What the hell was he doing back?

'We're closed.' In case you hadn't noticed. 'Sorry.'

'You don't sound sorry.' His rolled-up shirt sleeves had fallen down below his elbows. He pushed them up one at a time and reclined against the bar. 'Look, I was probably a bit rude to you the other day when we met. I'd just been . . . well, let's just say my visit here got off on a bad foot and I wasn't in a great mood. I apologise.' He held out his hand. 'I'm Cam.'

Was he taking the piss? It was hard to tell. His voice had lost that sarcastic edge and there was a distinct smile in his eyes. Still, he had no business being here.

She lifted her hand to his and felt the warm, sure grip of his fingers. Nothing like Daz's sweaty grasp. 'Faith,' she warily. 'And you're right, you were rude.' His smile became a full-blown laugh that was frustratingly contagious. 'But apology accepted. Doesn't change the fact that we're closed, though. The doors are only open because the aircon's not working.'

'I noticed,' he said, as if that was the point of the conversation. 'Those ceiling fans don't really cut the mustard.'

Now that the room had emptied, the temperature inside had dropped and the fresher air drifting in from outside was pure heaven. She unplugged the vacuum and wheeled it back into its den before making her way back to the bar. 'I did notice you through the crowd tonight.' That did not come out at all as she'd intended. 'I mean, I saw that you had some trouble with—'

'With my brother.' His gaze fell to a particularly stained patch of carpet. 'Yeah, I thought it was better that I be the one to leave given that the publican is his mother-in-law.'

'Where have you been since then?' She knew it wasn't any of her business, but it had been well over an hour since the almost-punch-up.

'Walking around. Thinking,' he said quietly. 'I was on my way back to my motel and saw everyone had left. Hoped I might be able to persuade Rose to serve me a nightcap.'

'She's not here. Driving the night owls home in the minibus.'

He gave her a look somewhere between forlorn and pathetic. 'I could really use a drink. And since it's after hours I can buy you one too. A peace offering?'

She studied him for a moment. The image of him being manhandled by his brother, his patronising gruffness the first time they'd met – none of it fitted with the meek, almost rueful man sitting in front of her. The contrast made her curious. And she had worked up a thirst. 'Well, I guess one drink wouldn't hurt.' She ducked behind the bar. 'What'll it be?'

'A scotch on the rocks with a beer chaser, thanks.'

'*One* drink?'

'Well, technically it is one. Since you drink them together.'

'Technically,' she corrected him, 'it's two.' She held up a beer glass. 'One.' Then a smaller tumbler. 'Two. Two glasses equals two drinks.'

He smiled again. An open, genuine thing that lit up his face, crinkled the faint lines around his eyes. 'Okay. You win. It's two. But who's counting?'

As hard as she tried to remain straight faced, she knew her lips were betraying her as she tonged a few chunks of ice into the smaller glass and added a couple of slugs of scotch before filling the schooner glass, leaving only a thin layer of froth on the top.

'I see your beer pouring skills have improved.'

'Yes.' She made sure not to meet his eyes as she filled a second glass.

'Cheers.' He lifted the glass. 'Nice to meet you, Faith. What brings you to Birralong?'

Now, there was a question. The truth slid its way onto the tip of her tongue. She gulped at her beer. This whole lying thing was tougher than she'd anticipated. Stella's insistence on honesty had left Faith with a vehement dislike of liars – and now here she was lying to every single person she met. She needed to stick to the story so she didn't trip herself up.

'I saw there was a job here and I applied. Simple.'

'You don't really look like the barmaid type.'

'Is that right? What type do I look like?'

'Oh, I don't know exactly, but something more sophisticated, something less . . . domestic.'

Really? Was she that transparent? 'Well, I'm just taking a break from my normal life, reassessing,' she shrugged, 'you know.'

Cam narrowed his eyes. 'Strange sort of place to come to do that.'

'Not really,' Faith countered, warming to her own fiction. 'I've never seen this part of Australia and it seemed as good as anywhere else. How about you?' she asked. Deflection was always a good tactic. 'I heard you're actually a local.'

He laughed again, but this time it was shallow and tinny. 'Not sure I qualify as one anymore. It's like leaving the priest-hood: once you're gone there's no going back. But yeah, I used to live here. It's still home, I guess.'

They sipped their drinks. Bonnie's anguish had been followed by Adele lamenting the loss of her lover. Faith had a sudden flash-back to singing – no, howling – along to the song just after her break-up with Harry, tears smearing ugly black trails down her cheeks, her friends doing a heartfelt back-up. A shudder caught her unawares.

'You okay?' Cam asked.

'I just had a horrible vision of me doing a rendition of this song in a club one night when I was very, very drunk.'

'Happens to the best of us.' He twirled his glass around on the coaster and stared into his drink. Faith left him to his reverie and went to switch off the juke box. The ceiling fans whirred overhead but otherwise the place was unusually quiet. She closed the door but left the windows open and returned to take a seat beside Cam, who was so lost in his thoughts he didn't seem to notice her.

'What was all that about with your brother?'

He looked across at her then. 'Straight for the jugular, eh?'

She frowned. He was good at asking the questions, not so good at answering. 'I'm an upfront sort of person.' Well, usually anyway.

'Let's just say we have a long-running disagreement and he took exception to me being here.'

'So, what *were* you doing here?'

He shrugged. 'The birthday boy invited me. Not that it made any difference to Bryce – my brother. He thinks I should be black-listed by the whole town just because he and I don't see eye to eye. Stubborn as a bull.'

Faith nodded, unsure where to go next. She shouldn't really be interrogating him even though she was dying to know more. And not just more about him – although there was that – but more about her brother-in-law, about the family situation, the mysterious job Amber made reference to before she walked off in a huff when she delivered his lunch the other day. Her glass was just about empty and as tempted as she was to have a refill it was getting late. A yawn slipped out.

'I'd better let you get to bed.' He finished the last mouthful of his drink and hopped off the stool, which left him standing awfully close. She breathed in the faint scent of his aftershave – something peppery and woodsy – as she stood to say goodbye. If she'd been wearing heels they'd be about the same height, but in her practical work flats she had to tip her head back slightly to meet his eyes. Up close, they were a haunting, smoky shade of grey.

'Nice meeting you, Faith,' he crooned. 'Again. I hope we get to chat some more. Thanks for the drink.'

She clasped her hands in front of her. 'Yeah. Same. I mean, nice meeting you too. Enjoy your visit – or whatever it is.'

God, I am such an idiot.

He gave a soft chuckle as he turned to leave. Faith watched the rhythmic jaunt of his shoulder blades before her eyes dropped lower. It was only when he'd disappeared from sight that she caught herself blushing and she wriggled herself back to the here and now. There was still no sign of Rose, or Stephanie for that matter. Maybe she'd taken herself off to bed after her husband's dramatic exit. Her new 'family' was nothing if not interesting.

She locked up and climbed the stairs. The whole thing with Cam was bizarre. He was so different tonight from how he'd been that first day; restrained, even a bit dejected. After the night's events it wasn't really surprising. Whatever had happened between the two brothers had obviously caused a very deep rift. And judging by tonight's little show the rift wasn't going to be mended anytime soon. Clicking the bedroom door closed, she rested against its old timbers. Everything about her was clammy, from her hairline to the hollow at the base of her spine to the soft patch of skin behind her knee. As inviting as the bed looked, the thought of climbing in between the sheets in this state made her cringe. She peeled off her shirt and unbuttoned her jeans and as she turned on the shower and stepped beneath a steady flow of tepid water she remembered those silvery eyes and those strong, tanned arms peeking out from beneath the chequered shirt and, despite herself, couldn't help but smile.

Chapter Eight

Rose

'JESUS, MARY AND JOSEPH!' ROSE BANGED HER HEAD – FOR the third time – as she attempted a backwards crawl out of the cupboard under the kitchen sink. Mick had been fond of spluttering the phrase whenever something went wrong. She shuffled her way back, shifter in hand. Hopefully the damned leak was fixed.

'That's a sight for sore eyes.'

She was still on all fours, backside to the door, when the voice made her turn awkwardly. David friggin' Ryan. 'Have you ever heard of knocking?'

'I did,' Dave said, motioning towards the doorway, 'but you mustn't have heard me. Need a hand with anything?'

Rose pushed herself upright and tossed the shifter onto the table. 'No, thanks. Nothing I haven't done before. What are you doing here?'

'Came to shout you a coffee over at FJ's. Before opening.'

She glanced up at the clock. The pub didn't open until 11am on a Saturday. Most of the food was prepared and Faith had done a pretty good job on the clean-up last night. After the paltry few hours of sleep she'd had a good dose of caffeine would go down a treat. Even if it did mean making small talk with David Ryan. Even if it meant pretending he was nothing more than an old mate. 'All right,' she said, eyes down as she flattened out the wrinkles in her shirt, 'but I don't have long.' She ran her hands through her hair and pulled her wallet from the drawer.

'Someone a bit grumpy this morning?'

'Hmm, lack of sleep will do that to you.' They left the hotel and stepped out onto the footpath. Rose could feel the heat of the cement through the bottoms of her old runners. She probably should have spruced herself up a bit before venturing out, but what the hell. A few cars were parked under the shade shelter in the centre of the street but otherwise the place was pretty much deserted. The town was sleeping off its hangover.

As Dave stepped forward and opened the cafe door Rose suppressed a smile; he'd matured into quite the gentleman. FJ's was as empty as the street outside. Thank God. The last thing she needed was a bunch of busybodies jumping to conclusions about her love life. She nodded hello to Sally, who was already eyeing her and Dave carefully from behind the counter, and made a dash for a corner table beneath the front fender of a sky-blue 1950s Holden. It wasn't often Rose got the chance to be a customer. A framed poster of Elvis, onstage in black leather being ogled by a bunch of adoring women in the audience, sat beneath the bumper bar and the walls were plastered with old 45s, cabinets filled with model cars and a whole lot more fifties memorabilia. Sally and Tom had done a good job on the place, there was no doubt about it, and it was certainly a hit with the tourists. Dave ordered the coffees and then settled into a chair beside Rose.

'So, a bit of excitement last night, eh?'

Rose groaned. 'Could have done without it.'

'How's your daughter?'

'No idea. She'd gone to bed by the time I went looking for her last night and she'd already left by the time I got up this morning at six. Left me a note saying she was taking my car and would give me a ring later. I tried calling her but she's not picking up.' Stephanie was skilled at avoidance. After all, she'd had a good teacher. 'Did you see what happened?'

Dave shook his head. 'Not really. I was having a chin wag with Rupert Quinn over at the bar. The next thing I know there's a whole lot of shouting and some bloke about to get his head knocked off.'

Sally delivered their coffees, making no attempt to hide her interest in their conversation. 'I heard about that brawl. Such a shame. Terrible to see brothers come to blows like that.'

'It wasn't a brawl and there were no blows,' Rose snarled. It was bad enough that Sally had 'heard about it', let alone that it was Rose's son-in-law who appeared to be the guilty party.

Sally gave her an if-you-say-so glare and sauntered back to the counter.

'Sorry, Dave.' Rose poured a stream of sugar from the glass jar into her cappuccino and gave it a stir. 'I just hate the bloody gossip that goes on around here.'

He laughed. 'You should be used to it by now, Rosie.'

'Yeah, you'd think so.' The fact was, her business was everybody else's business. That's what she'd loved about the city: she could be anyone she wanted to be among all those thousands and thousands of people. Dress the way she wanted without anyone commenting or judging or telling her how she should or shouldn't behave. Being seventeen and pregnant in Sydney had certainly got her a few looks, but nowhere near what she would have got if she'd come back here to Birralong after she'd got herself into trouble.

Got myself into trouble. Who am I? My mother?

She shuddered.

'Rose?'

She looked up, and there was the man responsible. Well, the man who was once the boy who had been responsible. 'Sorry?'

He looked at her like she might be ready for committal to a lunatic asylum. 'I said, what's the problem between those two boys, anyway? Rupert tells me they're brothers.'

She refocused. 'They are. It's such a shame. It all started when Cameron went off to uni and decided he didn't want to work the farm anymore. He made noises about selling up when Bernie passed away, but Bryce wouldn't have a bar of it. He's like a son to me, Bryce, but he has these outdated notions that he just can't seem to let go of. And to add insult to injury Cameron's now working for a mining company, scouting for properties.'

'Shit. That's not good.'

'No,' Rose agreed. 'Him showing up now is the last thing Stephanie needs. Things are already hard enough.' She pressed her hand across her mouth. She'd said far too much. 'What are you up to for the rest of the day?'

'Not much,' he said. 'Just heading back out to do a few jobs around Glen and Deb's.'

Rose's ears pricked up. 'They're out past Strathmore.'

Dave nodded. 'Sure are.'

All the talk about Stephanie and Bryce had her worried. And she did need to get her car back. Chatting to Dave wasn't as awkward as she'd expected. After all, they were both adults now and what had happened between them was a long time ago. He had no idea what the consequences of their backseat tryst had been and she . . . well, she had no intention of ever telling him. They were two different people now and there was no harm in them being friends. 'Would you mind giving me a lift out to pick up my car?'

'I'd love to,' he grinned.

————

They drove in amiable silence soaking up the airconditioned chill of Dave's brand new Range Rover. Whatever he did for a crust, he must be doing it well. Rose made the trip out here once a week, if she could get away from the hotel, but being in the passenger seat was a completely different experience. Strathmore was in the opposite direction out of town to Cleo's place, Clementine Downs, and the landscapes couldn't be more different. The dry, red soil still dominated the scenery but the country was rockier out here. Wilder. Huge granite boulders littered the paddocks and in the distance the remnants of what was once a volcano sliced a solid grey line across the horizon.

From the shade of a pepper tree a herd of knobbly-kneed camels eyed the car as it passed, the ground at their feet covered in clumps of grass so dry it looked petrified. It was a miracle that any animal could survive out here really, but somehow even these alien creatures – this particular group 'adopted' by the local vet when it looked like the drought had well and truly numbered their days – managed to find something to sustain them. Not for the first time Rose was grateful she'd opted for life in town rather than hanging onto her parents' property. Her brother had been happy to sell up, used the money to expand his own property. The two of them had been as different as chalk and cheese. For Steven, the remoter and rougher the better, hence his migration to the Territory. While Rose could appreciate the raw, rough beauty of the land, farming life was too unpredictable. Too much hardship, too much struggle. There were definitely easier ways to make a living.

Or maybe not.

'I know I've already said it, but jeez I miss this place.' Dave was wallowing in nostalgia.

Rose rolled her eyes. 'You may have mentioned it once or twice.' She looked across and saw the pained expression on his face, the droop of his mouth. *Sarcasm is the lowest form of wit, Rosemary.* 'Have you been back to your folks' old place?' she asked, adopting a kinder tone.

Dave nodded but only barely. 'Just to the front gates. I tried to muster up the nerve to ask the owners if I could go in and take a look but couldn't bring myself to do it. Stupid, I know.'

'Not stupid at all.' Rose felt a rush of sympathy for him, for the loose moorings he seemed to have, which only compounded his grief for his wife. She hadn't really considered what she would do once The Crossroads was sold – how she would feel or where she would live. Leaving behind her life with Mick would be hard, but the possibility of doing something new was like a small bubble of excitement bouncing around her innards. 'You're just like your grandmother,' her own mother had told her when she was a restless young girl with itchy feet, 'gypsy in your soul.' Her mother had said it like it was a bad thing, but Rose had tingled with pride.

'You seem to be off with the pixies today,' Dave said as he turned the car off the bitumen and approached the entrance to Strathmore.

'Sorry, a few things on my mind.'

He reached out and patted her hand, which was fine, but then he wrapped his fingers around hers, holding on a little longer than necessary.

She sat up with a jolt. 'Here we are,' she said loudly. Dave returned his hand to the steering wheel and Rose kept her gaze focused directly ahead between the two towering gums that marked the border of the property. Silver branches kissed against a backdrop of deep, dark blue, framing a rust-coloured road that stretched to a paler sky. The whole effect was three-dimensional and entirely breathtaking. Sometimes the beauty of the place made her head spin.

It was still a good ten minutes' drive to reach the house from the main road through paddocks that a few years ago would have been occupied by hundreds of robust cattle. Dave shook his head, muttering something about it all being such a bloody shame. Rose, as always, fell speechless.

The homestead came into view, with the neat gardens and small patch of lawn that Stephanie had mollycoddled into an oasis. Maternal pride swelled in Rose's chest. That girl of hers was really something, she could turn her hand to anything when she made up her mind. Pride turned to jitters, though, as Rose looked towards the house. There was no telling what state of mind Stephanie would be in today – there were very few people in the world who intimidated Rose, but her daughter, when she was in a mood, was one of them.

She turned to Dave and forced a smile. 'Come on in.'

'I can wait in the car if you like.' He looked as nervous as she felt.

'No,' she said in a tone that brokered no argument, 'you can come in.' She was already out and making her way to the door.

The house was quiet. Rose peered through the fly-screen. 'Knock, knock, anyone home?' She waited, listened. Bryce's ute was in the carport beside Steph's smaller town car. She turned to Dave and shrugged, pulled open the door and stepped inside. 'Stephanie?'

It was cooler than outside, here on the screened porch, and everything looked normal – placemats arranged on the wooden table, some of Jake's books and a packet of coloured pencils piled at one end, cushions plumped on the old floral lounge at the end of the room. Rose peered through the alcove that opened into the kitchen. Water dripped from a tap into the sink. After the success of her own plumbing work this morning she could probably fix that leak for Stephanie too.

'Mum?' Her daughter's voice called from the other end of the house before the sound of footsteps and then she appeared in the doorway. 'What are you doing here?'

Her cheeks were pale and dark circles ringed her eyes. But better not to comment on that.

'Dave drove me out to get my car.' She said it casually, hoping to keep the conversation civil.

Stephanie, seemingly, had no such intention. 'I *said* I'd drop it back this afternoon.'

'Your note said you would see me some time today,' Rose corrected. Ugh, there it was, that snarky tone she wanted so badly not to use. 'Dave was coming out this way, so I grabbed a lift.'

Stephanie crossed her arms but didn't reply. If Dave wasn't here it would probably be a different story.

'Where's Bryce?' Rose asked.

'Out on the bike somewhere.'

'How's he feeling this morning?'

'Fine.' She lifted one eyebrow. 'As far as I know.'

'And how are you?'

Stephanie's arms fell to her sides as she came down the two steps to the verandah to stand in front of her mother. Up close Rose could see that the lids of her daughter's eyes were puffy and red. The question answered itself. 'Look, Mum, if you've come here to give me a lecture on my husband's behaviour last night, I can do without it.'

'Of course I didn't come here to give you a lecture. I just wanted to see if you were okay, see if there was anything I could do.'

'Well, you weren't exactly supportive last night.'

'Supportive?' Rose gave her head a rattle and blinked at Stephanie. 'Of who? Bryce?'

'Yes, of Bryce. I know he made a scene, but he *is* my husband and it might have been nice if you hadn't humiliated him in front of all his friends.'

Okay. This was not the way Rose had anticipated the conversation playing out. Bryce was the one who had caused the trouble but now she was the scapegoat. *It wasn't on.* 'I think he did an excellent job of making a fool of himself without any help from me, Stephanie. He was out of order and you know it. And, as I recall, you did a pretty good job of calling him out on it yourself!'

Stephanie's eyes flashed. 'He's my husband.'

'And it's my pub.'

'Oh yes, and that's all you care about, isn't it? That your precious reputation might be smirched.'

What the hell was going on here? How had she become the villain?

'Steph, in your mum's defence . . .' Dave joined in from somewhere behind her. Rose scowled at him and he stopped.

She took a step towards Stephanie and made a conscious effort to soften her voice. 'I know you must be embarrassed about last night, darl, but Bryce was out of line. You told him so yourself. And driving off like that when he was way over the limit was totally irresponsible.'

'Not that it's any of *your* business.' Bryce's rough-throated growl startled them all. They turned simultaneously to stare at him, standing in the doorway, one foot inside the house and one foot out.

'Bryce,' Stephanie said, her tone at once reprimanding and cautious.

Rose stepped out from behind Dave, who was the proverbial pig in the middle. 'It *is* my business, actually.' She addressed her son-in-law exclusively now. If he wanted to play hardball, she was more than capable of bouncing it right back. 'You acted like a total thug in my hotel, in front of the whole town. You're lucky Patterson wasn't doing road patrol or you'd have been arrested. I know you and your brother don't see eye to eye, but fighting in public is not the way to deal with the situation.'

Bryce pushed the door behind him open, keeping his eyes pinned to Rose. 'Like I said. It's none of your business.' He shot a fiery look at Dave. 'None of anyone's business. Now I'd appreciate it if you leave.'

'So, that's it?' Rose asked, incredulous. 'No apology, no explanation?' The man was stubborn, always had been, but she'd never seen him this belligerent, and certainly never witnessed him being aggressive the way he'd been last night.

Stephanie rushed forward and stood beside Bryce. 'I think it's best if you go, Mum.' There was a tremor in her voice but a determination in her eyes that told Rose there was no point pursuing the conversation. That was Stephanie, always putting him first. As much as Rose didn't like it, for the time being she would have to walk away. 'The keys are in the car,' Stephanie added, eyes on the floor.

Rose shook her head, flashed her eyes at Dave and walked past her daughter and son-in-law out into the heat of the day.

Jake, who had followed his father up from the shed, skipped across the yard and wrapped his arms around Rose's legs. She gave him a quick hug before striding to the car, already opening the door as Dave came up behind her. 'What the hell was that all about?'

'I have no idea,' she said, slipping in and lowering the window. 'Thanks for bringing me out here.'

Dave, clearly perplexed, returned to his Range Rover.

Rose reversed out and started back down the road. Suddenly she wanted nothing more than to be away from the place. She could strangle that son-in-law of hers – and Stephanie along with him. Why did her daughter have to be so damned cloak-and-dagger about everything? Why couldn't she just say straight out what was going on, confide in her mother for once?

An apple never falls far from the tree.

And even as Rose turned the steering wheel and headed for home she knew it was true: her daughter was more like her then she had ever realised. Maybe it was time they both stopped hiding the truth – from themselves and from each other.

Stephanie

'DADDY, ARE YOU COMING BACK OUT?' JAKE CALLED FROM outside. Bryce, still standing at the door, turned to look at his son.

It was the first time Stephanie had seen him since she and Jake had arrived home just after nine. Jake had sulked all the way home after she'd picked him up early from the sleepover, begged her to come back for him later. As eager as she'd been to get home and make sure Bryce was okay, seeing him again filled her with dread. Using Jake as a buffer wasn't one of her proudest moments, but now they were here she wasn't sorry.

Bryce had been working on the tractor when she'd pulled up in the drive, only his ankles and boots visible beneath the bulk of the machine. Jake had jumped straight out of the car and gone into helper mode, following instructions to the letter, giggling at whatever his dad said, beaming with satisfaction when he handed over the right tool. She'd heeded the warning glare Bryce had given her and kept her distance. At least one relationship in the family seemed to be solid.

The ache inside her temples deepened as she watched Bryce now, teetering on the threshold.

He looked a little rough up close, hardly surprising after last night's events, and his eyes smouldered from her mother's ill-timed visit. She made a move towards him.

'Dad?'

They could talk about this now and risk being interrupted by Jake – risk Jake catching them in the middle of another blazing row – or . . . 'Go,' she said quietly, making the decision for them both.

His face softened a little, relief, as he stepped back outside. The door banged shut behind him and she winced.

'Coming, mate,' she heard him say. Through the window she watched them make their way back to the tractor, saw Jake jump up and down then dive into the tool box.

Nausea rippled at the edges of her stomach and she worked hard to keep it down there. It had been a while since she'd been out for a few drinks and okay, she'd had a few champagnes, but the Panadol she'd taken had done nothing to ease the sickly sensation. No doubt the tension didn't help. She needed to keep busy, keep her mind occupied. Normally hanging out with Bandit would do the trick, but she was feeling too fragile to brave the heat. Housework was suitably mind-numbing and there was always washing to be done.

In the laundry a pile of musty towels lay on the floor beside a basket half-full of Bryce's dirty work clothes. Plenty to do here. She opened the machine and started to fill it when her insides rolled again, saliva pooling in her mouth, a cold sweat breaking out across her forehead.

Oh, no.

She moved quickly into the bathroom and flipped up the toilet seat just in time for the dry heaving to begin. Bile and remnants of last night's finger food reappeared, her belly clenching, as she vomited over and over again into the bowl. When it was done she closed the lid and rested her cheek against the cool plastic. It took a few minutes for things to settle, until she could open her eyes and breathe normally.

I am seriously never drinking again.

She pushed herself up to rest against the tiled wall. She hadn't been this sick since she was pregnant with Jake.

Oh, God. How long has it been?

She'd never had the most reliable menstrual cycle, so a late period wasn't unusual, but . . . she counted the weeks off with her fingers. Two. She was two weeks late.

But when was the last time we . . .

She stared hard at the wall. The last time she and Bryce had had sex was about a month ago, the night Jake had stayed with her mother after the school fete. It had been fast and perfunctory, and she'd suspected Bryce would have preferred to be watching the movie she'd dragged him away from. For once he hadn't claimed to be too tired, and she remembered more clearly now how she'd batted at his hand as he fumbled around for a condom and he hadn't even argued. She hadn't given it a thought, even later, as they lay side by side in the dark, so relieved had she been to release some of the tension not just between the two of them but in her own body. She'd fallen asleep, quietly rejoicing in the almost foreign wetness between her thighs and the lingering scent of sex on her sheets.

She gagged again and lunged back into position. This time, though, there was nothing left to bring up, just the same dry retching repeating itself until her eyes watered and she managed to sit upright. Standing was an effort but she managed it, turned on the tap to splash her face and rinse the acidy taste from her mouth. Grabbing a hand towel, she wiped it across her chin and looked blearily in the mirror. Her skin was sallow and her cheeks were the colour of bleached bones.

She lifted a hand to the curve of her breast beneath her shirt. Definitely tender. And she had been feeling more tired than usual too. A lot more. Her instincts told her that the vomiting was not caused by a hangover.

It had taken them months and months of trying to get pregnant with Jake; could it really happen this time around without them even thinking about it? She knelt and rummaged around in the cupboard under the sink for the pregnancy test kit she'd bought a year or so ago when her hopes had been raised but quickly dashed. Sliding a foil packet from the box, a rancid taste scorching her tongue, she peeled open one end and stared down at the slim, plastic stick. For years now she had played this moment on repeat over and over in her mind. She wanted to feel elated at the idea of being pregnant again, but instead of the anticipated euphoria there was apprehension, and one terrifying question.

What will Bryce say?

Faith

HER THIRD DAY ON THE JOB AND FAITH WAS LEFT TENDING the bar alone – again. Only just shy of 10am there'd been a knock on the door and she'd opened it to find Rose, looking less than happy, requesting that she swap her afternoon shift to the morning. So much for recovering from last night's late finish. And so much for surreptitiously getting to know her BM, who had disappeared without a trace. She'd showered – this time trying to wash the cobwebs from her eyes – made herself presentable and opened up the bar at eleven o'clock. Thankfully it was quiet, the town still in recovery mode.

Harry wandered in for his lunchtime schooner as she pottered around behind the bar; his dog, Cricket, waited faithfully outside under the shade of the verandah.

'The usual, Harry?'

'Yes, please, my dear. Rosie not in today?'

'She'll be in later. I think. She had something to do this morning.'

He gave her a fatherly smile as she placed his beer on a coaster. 'Here's looking at ya,' he said, lifting the drink to his lips and downing a good few mouthfuls before coming up for air. 'Medicinal, you know.' He winked and settled himself in for the day. 'How are you liking the place so far?'

'I haven't seen that much of it, to be honest. I've been here four days and I've been working for three of them.' Sightseeing hadn't been high on her agenda, but she had to admit that cabin fever was starting to set in.

'That's a shame. You want to make sure you get out to the gorge and take yourself up to Mount Eliza and watch the sunset.'

'Mount Eliza.' She repeated the name robotically, the two words leaving a chalky taste on her tongue. The connection between the name on her original birth certificate and the landmark made her pale.

Harry didn't seem to notice. 'That's right,' he continued. 'Just north out of town. Doesn't look that high from down here but you get a beaut view from up there. Take a camera if you have one.'

'Yeah, I do. I will. Enjoy your beer, Harry. Let me know when you're ready for lunch.' The old boy had a standing order of a cheese-and-ham toastie followed by a bowl of vanilla ice cream smothered in strawberry syrup. Despite Rose's efforts to persuade him to try something more adventurous from the menu, Harry liked what he liked, and what he liked was to eat the same thing every day.

Mount Eliza.

That could not be a coincidence. If things went smoothly and Rose was back in the early afternoon, Faith would get off in time to take up Harry's suggestion, see some local attractions including the one she was probably named after. Outside the sun was blaring down, as usual, so walking wasn't a great idea, unless she was after a dose of heat-stroke, but it would still be good to get out – a change of scenery might help clear her head, formulate a plan as to when she would tell Rose why she was really here. This whole subterfuge thing was becoming way too stressful.

A few more customers arrived, and Harry wasted no time wandering off to do some rumour mongering. Last night's drama was the talk of the town. Phrases like 'Not sure who threw the first punch' and 'He could barely stand he was so pissed' floated around the lounge. Never let the truth get in the way of a good story, as her dad always said. Harry certainly wasn't. Nor was she, for that matter – she'd spun the tale about why she was here so many times now she was almost starting to believe it was true.

'Couldn't Rose give you the morning off after your herculean efforts last night?'

Cam. Annoyingly buff in a pale blue T-shirt. She bit down hard on her bottom lip as he took a seat at the bar, busied herself tidying some bottles. Everybody was staring – it was hardly a surprise when the subject of their conversation had just appeared in the flesh. 'You know they're all talking about you,' she said.

'Yep.'

'It doesn't bother you?'

'Won't last long.'

He was clean shaven this morning, fresh, no sign of last night's melancholy. 'Would you like a drink?' Finally, she met his eyes. 'Perhaps a Flying Pig?'

He laughed. 'Why not?'

Harry sauntered back as she poured the beer. 'I hear you and your brother got into a bit of biff last night.'

The sexy grin Cam had been sporting dwindled to a death stare. 'Rather not talk about it, Harry, if you don't mind.'

Direct but polite. Nice.

'Fair enough. Had my own share of family bullshit over the years, so I know where you're coming from.'

She pushed the filled glass towards her customer, taking the money he offered and giving him a look that she hoped was supportive.

Harry kept on talking. 'I was telling young Faith here about the local sights. Told her she should get on up to the Mount to see the sunset.' He slurped at his beer. 'Can't beat the view from up there.'

'No, you can't.'

'If I still had me car I'd take her up there meself. Bastard of a thing not having a licence anymore.'

'Thanks, Harry, that's sweet,' she said, butting in. 'I'm sure I'll get up there soon.'

Cam flicked his eyes from Harry back to her, amused. A customer waved at her from the far end of the bar. By the time she returned Harry had finished his drink, said his fare-wells and toddled off home for his afternoon nap.

'You've finally escaped, I see.'

He gave his ear an exaggerated rub. 'Man, he can talk.'

'Seems harmless enough.'

'He is. Most of the time.'

'At least he backed off the whole family thing.'

Cam nodded. He was drinking that beer awfully slowly.

'Isn't this the last place you'd want to be today?'

'A man's not a camel,' he said wryly, holding up his glass, but then shook his head. 'Actually, I wanted to drop by and apologise to Rose for last night.'

'Apologise? But it wasn't your fault, was it?'

'Well, technically no, it wasn't. But . . .' His voice ebbed away to a murmur. 'I should have known better than to set foot in the place. There was no way Bryce was going to take it on the chin.'

From what she'd seen Cam was definitely not the aggressor. 'You weren't to know.'

'Thanks.' He looked up at her and smiled. 'So is the boss lady here?'

She shook her head. 'Out somewhere. She just asked me to do the morning shift instead of the afternoon. I guess she'll be back soonish.'

'So, you'll be off duty this evening?' His mouth was hidden by his glass as he peeked at her over the rim.

Oh God, those eyes of his could be her undoing – the colour he was wearing made them look positively ethereal. 'Hmm.'

'Any plans?'

She did have plans. Of a sort. A long, solitary walk and some good hard thinking. 'Nothing much. Just taking a bit of a look around town.'

'I'd be happy to play tour guide,' he said. 'I mean, I know Harry would be your first preference, but since he doesn't drive anymore, I can step in as chauffeur. And on the plus side,' he added, 'I have twenty–twenty vision.'

She'd been polishing the bar as they spoke, round and round in a circular motion, anything to keep herself distracted. She could feel him watching her, and her body was doing this tingling thing she really wished it wouldn't. Yes, they'd had a nice time chatting the night before, but she did not come here to date, not that this was a date, just a friendly gesture from someone who knew his way around town. She lifted her palm to her chin and pressed her fingers against her lips. And there were those eyes again, gum grey, pinning her down.

'Okay,' she said, surprising herself. 'I finish at four.'

'Great. I'll swing by about four-thirty and pick you up.'

The smile he gave her as he turned to leave sent a hot shiver skipping all the way down to the tips of her polished toes. Was this the same guy she'd labelled a sexist pig a few days ago? Her mother had always told her not to judge a book by its cover. Checking out his arse as he walked out the door, she wholeheartedly believed that Stella, as usual, was right.

———

Hair blow-dried, face freshly exfoliated, she bounced downstairs ready for her tour. Rose had let her off early so she'd had ample time to prepare for her not-a-date. She'd kept the make-up low-key – tinted moisturiser, a single coat of mascara and a light brush of lip gloss. The outfit had been more of a dilemma – it needed to make an impression without looking like she was trying too hard. After a couple of changes she'd opted for a white linen shirt, knee-length denims rolled up a notch or two and her trusty Converse.

Cam and Rose were deep in conversation at the far end of the bar. He gave her a wave, said what she presumed was a quick goodbye and came up to meet her. It was impossible not to notice the way his eyes roamed her body, although the ogling was definitely mutual.

'Hi. Ready to go?'

'Is this okay?' She gestured to her clothes. 'I didn't know if we would be walking far or . . .'

'It's fine. You look great,' he said, signalling for her to go first as they stepped outside.

She dipped her head, hiding her smile. When was the last time anyone had told her that?

'I can't guarantee those shoes are going to look like that when we get back, but hey, nothing a good bleaching won't fix.'

'I didn't really bring any other walking shoes.'

'Don't worry, we're not going too far.'

He opened the door of his car, a black four-wheel drive with what she assumed was his company logo on the side panel, and she sank into the plush leather. When he joined her and started the engine she actually giggled at the surge of cold air.

'You have no idea how much I miss airconditioning.'

Cam laughed. 'I can imagine. Can't believe Rose hasn't had hers fixed.'

'She'll get round to it, I guess.' She didn't know her well, but Rose was obviously a very proud, independent woman who wouldn't appreciate her problems being bandied about. 'So, where are we off to?'

'I can give you the rundown on the town centre and then drive up to Mount Eliza, as per Harry's instructions. He wasn't wrong. It is a must-see. I've got a few nibbles and something to wash them down.' He hooked his thumb towards the backseat. 'Hope you like champers.'

She looked over her shoulder to see a box filled with crackers, nuts and an assortment of savoury snacks alongside a cooler bag, a gold-topped bottle poking from its almost zipped-up lid. So, maybe this was a date? She lit up from the inside out. 'I love it.'

As they cruised around the streets Cam pointed out the points of interest and gave her a commentary: the swimming pool complete with a stunning mural of black cockatoos and gum trees (done by a local artist), the old railway siding, a string of rusted carts sitting motionless on the tracks as if someone had forgotten to pick them up, the bakery (sausage rolls to die for) and a few of the not-so-savoury landmarks such as the local recycling facility (aka tip) and the police station (which he hoped she wouldn't be visiting). She bombarded him with questions and he answered them all with a casual flair.

'Well, we'd better start heading up to the old girl or we'll miss the show,' he said as they drove across the bridge spanning the riverbed.

'Old girl?'

'Mount Eliza.' He wiggled his brows. 'It's a term of endearment.'

'Oh, right.'

Eliza.

Had Rose chosen that name hoping to infuse some of herself, some of her home, into her baby? She looked out her window at the endless expanse of dry dirt. It had a unique, barren sort of beauty she'd never seen anywhere else. This is where she would have grown up if Rose had made a different decision. Who would she have been then? How would her life have unfolded? There would have been no fancy private school, no designer clothes, no deposit given to her when she bought her apartment. She would have had other things, of course, possibly a sibling, a more insular and perhaps more interesting existence, one she could still hardly fathom even now that she was here. Poppy had said she couldn't imagine what it would be like to give up your child. Why had Rose? And what role had her father played in the whole scenario?

'Look.' Cam slowed the car, pointing to the opposite side of the road. 'Brolgas.'

Two elegant birds, as tall as the fence post they were standing beside, danced across the ground on legs that looked like giant chopsticks. They were the colour of melting snow, with only a faint splash of scarlet on their feathery scalps. Stretching themselves out, they slanted their heads into the breeze and rose from the ground, floating higher and higher, the dark slate of their wing tips kneading the sky like metallic fingers.

'Wow,' she sighed, as they grew smaller and smaller.

'Pretty amazing, aren't they?'

She didn't have any words. Cam didn't speak again either, and she was grateful for the silence.

This would have been my life.

She gazed out the window as they continued on the straight, flat, road towards Mount Eliza.

This would have been my life, and it wouldn't have been all that bad.

Chapter Nine

Rose

'BIT QUIETER THAN LAST NIGHT.'

'Thank heavens,' Rose mumbled. She looked out from behind the bar, where Dave had taken up residence on a stool. He wasn't wrong. After the wall-to-wall crowd for Rocco's birthday bash the place was a veritable graveyard. Saturday nights in the off season were typically slow, but this one was morbid. Only a handful of regulars had come in for dinner and an even smaller number had popped in for drinks. Faith had disappeared on some sort of sightseeing trip with Cameron Bailey, of all people, and it was so quiet Rose had given Amber the night off. Even though it wasn't great for business the lack of customers was a relief after the chaos of the past twenty-four hours.

She busied herself behind the bar while Dave sipped at his beer. The awkwardness she'd felt around him earlier in the day had eased. There were more important things to worry about. She reached up and ferreted around on the shelf above the sink to retrieve her phone.

'Any news from your daughter?' Dave asked.

She frowned as she typed in her password. 'No, she hasn't returned my call or texted me back. But I do have a missed call from my mother-in-law.'

'That's never a good thing.' He chortled at his attempted joke, but his face fell flat when he saw Rose wasn't amused. 'Everything all right?'

Rose looked up as she dialled Letty's number. 'I couldn't tell you the last time she actually called me.'

'Did she leave a message?'

She shook her head as she held the phone to her ear, waiting until it rang out and dialled again. No answer. Letty had probably gone to bed – it was well after ten – but the fact that she'd rung at all was unsettling. There'd only been a handful of times over the years, and most of those had been when something was wrong – a blackout, the television not working, the fridge going bung. If that was the case, though, she would have called back. And back. 'I think I'm going to have to close up and go check on her.'

Dave sprang to life. 'I can hold the fort if you like?'

'Would you mind?' Explaining to the handful of regulars settled in at the pool table why she had to close early was a drama she could do without. But Dave . . .

'Of course not.' He'd already made his way through to the service side of the bar. He tipped his head towards the door. 'Off you go.'

'Thanks. She's just around the corner in Turner Street.' She smiled stiffly, not one hundred per cent convinced it was a great idea. 'I won't be long.'

She pushed her phone into her back pocket and headed out. The night air was a little chillier than it had been for the past week and she shivered. A jacket probably wouldn't go astray and she had half a mind to head back and get one, but the memory of that missed call made her decide against it. She picked up her pace to keep herself warm, rubbing her hands up her bare arms as she walked. Families! You couldn't live without them, as the saying went, but sometimes they were damned hard to manage. Her mother had never missed an opportunity to remind Rose that being part of a family meant taking the good with the bad, but when it came to Mick's mother there hadn't been a whole lot of good.

She stopped at the corner to cross the road, taking it at a diagonal, her footsteps loud on the hard surface. Not that anyone was around to hear; she could fire a gun out here right now and nobody would notice. Little green men could land in a space ship and whisk her away never to be seen again and not a soul would know. Mind you, that was probably preferable to the reception she was about to receive from Letty when she barged into her house in the middle of the night. No doubt she'd get a good telling-off for not having replied to the call sooner.

The gate gave its usual complaint as she pushed it open. No lights on, but that didn't mean much; Letty was a miser and usually only had a lamp on once the sun went down. By this time of night she would most likely be in bed anyway. Rose pushed the key into the lock and turned on the light.

'Letty,' she called quietly.

No reply.

'Letty?' A little louder this time. 'Are you awake?'

A faint glow shone from the lounge room but there was no sound from the television. Rose rounded the corner to see Letty's slippered feet poking out from the base of the arm chair. Katharine Hepburn, a large hat secured to her head with a scarf tied beneath her chin, was frozen on the screen, her hands suspended mid-air in front of her like a wind-up doll. *African Queen.* Rose peered into the gloom. 'Letty?'

Nothing.

Her stomach twisted itself into a knot. The skin on the back of her neck prickled.

Something was wrong. Four steps. That was all it would take to find out what.

She took them in a rush and came face to face with Katharine, in all her black-and-white glory. The only sound was her own heart, clattering away inside her chest like a lobster thrashing in a pot of boiling water. She lifted both her hands and pressed them, one over the other, to her sternum. From the corner of her eye she could see a figure sitting in the chair. She turned, her heart in her mouth. And there was Letty, perfectly still, head tilted to one side, eyes glazed, jaw hanging open. She looked like one of those creepy ventriloquist dummies waiting for the puppeteer to stick his hand up her back to bring her to life. But as Rose stood, staring, she could see that was not going to happen. She inched forward and touched one of Letty's hands where it rested beside the remote control in her lap. Cold. More than cold. Icy. Rose snatched her hand away as if she'd been given an electric shock. She pulled out her phone and re-checked the time of Letty's missed call. 8.14. More than two hours ago.

She must have called for help.

And now she was dead.

Fuuucckk!

Fuck fuck fuck fuck fuck.

What should she do? Call someone. But who? Stephanie was an hour away. So was Cleo. She needed someone here asap.

Dave. He was just around the corner. She dialled the main line to the pub as she crept out into the kitchen. Somehow it didn't seem right to have the conversation in front of Letty. She waited in the dark as the phone rang. Once, twice, three times. And then—

'She's dead.' She blurted it out as soon as she heard Dave's voice.

'What? Rose, is that you?'

'Letty. My mother-in-law. She's dead. In front of the television. In the lounge chair.'

'Shit.' Rose imagined Dave running a hand over his thinning hair, his blue eyes darting like pinballs around the bar. 'Righto. I'll kick everyone out and lock up. Be there in ten.'

'Number eight.' She hung up, tipped her head back against the wall and let her eyes close. 'Oh, Mick, I'm so sorry.' She heaved a long, slow breath out into the silence. Five years ago he'd asked her to look after his mother. Practically begged. Those last days in the hospital had been hell. Her happy-go-lucky larrikin of a husband had turned to skin and bone almost before her eyes, the cancer they'd detected too late eating him away from the inside. Letty had fallen to pieces, wept like a baby, and Rose's heart bled for her, at how unbearable it must be to bury a child. She knew what it was to lose a child, of course. But that had been a choice and as far as she knew – or hoped – her daughter was still alive. There was nothing she could do to help Mick other than hold his hand and honour his wishes. Caring for Letty hadn't been easy but she'd ignored the barbs, had persevered even on the toughest of days because she'd made that promise. What must he think of her now?

Her mind was running rampant. She needed to focus. Get busy. She flicked on the light and bustled around the kitchen, wiping down the bench that was already clean and putting away the cups that were already dry in the rack on the sink. Anything other than go back into that room. It seemed more like hours rather than minutes but finally there was a tap on the door and Dave let himself in. She was so relieved to see him she could have thrown her arms around his neck and kissed him.

'She's in here,' she said instead, and led the way into the lounge room. Braver now that she had company, she picked up the remote from where it lay in the folds of Letty's tracksuit top and turned off the television.

'What happened?' Dave asked, his eyes flicking from Rose to Letty and back again.

'She died.'

'I can see that.'

They looked at each other and burst into peals of riotous laughter. Rose's eyes watered and she put a hand over her mouth to try to control herself. What sort of horrible person laughs about someone dying? Dave looked equally mortified with himself.

'What do we do?'

'Technically, it's a bit late for the doctor,' Dave said, failing to curb his gallows humour. 'But they'll need to organise a death certificate, so we do need to ring one. And the police.'

'Police?'

'It's protocol when anyone dies alone.' Dave was suddenly serious. 'I'll put the kettle on.'

Thank God somebody else was taking charge. Rose made the necessary phone calls while Dave pottered around in the kitchen. The next couple of hours passed in a blur as Letty was officially declared dead and Doc Fisher organised an ambulance to take her body to the hospital. It was well past the witching hour by the time they arrived back at the hotel.

'I don't know about you, but I need a stiff drink after all that.' Rose opened up and headed straight to the bar.

'Me too,' Dave agreed. 'The stiffer the better.'

She grabbed a couple of tumblers, filled them with ice, set them beside a bottle of premium whiskey and pulled up a stool beside Dave. They drank their nightcaps quietly, both staring vacantly into their glasses. It wasn't until she'd refilled them that Dave broke the silence.

'Funny thing, death,' he said. 'Reminds you how bloody short life is.'

Rose nodded, taking a sip and swishing the liquid briefly across her tongue before letting it trickle down her throat. The burn was good. 'Not that Letty's was short,' she said, finally. Her mother-in-law had reached the ripe old age of eighty-six, a pretty good innings.

'No, but . . .'

'I know what you mean. Every time you're confronted with it you think about your own mortality.'

'Exactly,' said Dave, 'and about the ones you've lost.'

'I should have checked my phone earlier. If I'd got there sooner . . .'

'If you got there sooner it wouldn't have made a difference. You heard the doctor, it was most likely a massive heart attack. It was a wonder she was even able to make the call before it took her.'

Rose sighed. 'Probably wanted to give me a piece of her mind one last time.'

Dave smiled. He'd always had a nice smile. Warm. Comfortable.

'Do you believe there's something else?' she said. 'Life after death?'

He pursed his lips, pondered his drink. 'I never used to, not until Kay passed. But then I could feel her with me, you know, her hand on my shoulder, a kiss on my cheek when I was falling asleep. I don't know, maybe it was just wishful thinking, but after that I had this feeling she was there.' He paused and looked across at Rose. 'Sounds crazy.'

'Not at all. I used to spend hours talking to my husband at night. Telling him about Stephanie, then about Jake. He was only a tiny baby when Mick died. He never really got to be a granddad. Not sure if he could hear me, but it made me feel better.'

'Do you still chat to him?'

'Not as much,' Rose admitted, only just realising it herself. 'Only the odd whinge about his mother. Guess I won't be doing that anymore.' She picked up the bottle and poured herself another generous glass, and then did the same again when Dave nodded his agreement. Neither of them was a big drinker and yet here they were downing the stuff like there was no tomorrow. 'Certainly numbs the pain,' she grinned, holding her glass up.

'I got a little too fond of it for a while there,' Dave confessed. 'I wouldn't say I was an alcoholic or anything, but the occasional nightcaps started turning into longer sessions. Drinking alone is never a great idea. I woke up one day and found I'd polished off a lot more than I should have. Tipped what was in the liquor cabinet down the sink and haven't drunk alone since.'

'Very wise.' Rose had never been more than a light drinker – a two-glass screamer, Mick used to tease. Being around the stuff day in and day out probably had something to do with it, not to mention watching some of her customers pour too much down their throats and then lose control. Exhibit A, her son-in-law just twenty-four hours ago. Still, there were times when a medicinal glass or two were definitely called for. Exhibit B – finding your mother-in-law dead in the middle of the night. She poured them both a third – or was it a fourth – glass. The medicine seemed to be doing the trick. The heaviness she'd felt after the ambulance had vanished into the dark was gone. In its place was a light, airy feeling, like floating through clouds.

'Do you ever get lonely?' Dave's question pulled her back to earth.

'Sometimes.' It was true. 'Most of the time I'm busy enough that I don't notice. You?'

'Yeah, I sure do.' He looked at her with eyes that were soft and gentle and full of sorrow. She leaned forward and rested her hand on his leg. There was no harm consoling the man. He placed his hand over hers and they sat quietly together for a few moments until Rose turned her palm over and their fingers laced. Their bodies drifted towards each other, until their lips met, hesitantly at first, but then something much needier and insistent. He tasted of scotch, of course, but of more than that: life. It wasn't just the alcohol making her buzz. It was something she hadn't felt in years. Desire. She sat back, opening her eyes and searching Dave's. He answered the silent question with an ever so slight nod of his head and followed her up the stairs to her bedroom.

Stephanie

THE TELEVISION DRONED, UNWATCHED, IN THE LOUNGE ROOM. Sitting alone at the kitchen table Stephanie let the background chatter soothe her nerves. Thankfully her stomach had settled, although if her last pregnancy was anything to go by, the nausea would resume first thing in the morning and last well into the afternoon. That particular issue was on the back burner. Even though she knew now that it was true there was no point raising Bryce's hackles. Not when they had something more important to discuss.

She slid the booklet – pages she'd printed from the beyondblue website – out from under a pile of newspapers. According to this information she was a carer and it was her responsibility to help the person who was suffering. Flicking through, she stopped at page nine and skimmed over the section headed 'Beginning The Conversation'. Talk sensitively and quietly, it said, use 'I' statements, no accusations. Stay calm. She checked her body language. Her shoulders were arched, her muscles as taut as fence wire. She rolled her neck one way and then the other, running over what she was going to say, once again, in her head.

Footsteps rounded the corner. She fidgeted in her chair and looked up to see Bryce. His eyes were downcast and he had that same half-annoyed, half-lost expression he'd been sporting for weeks. Or if she really counted back, probably months.

She picked up the papers and covered the booklet.

'Off to sleep?' she asked.

'Out like a light.' He stood in the doorway, arms crossed. 'I've got a bit of work to do on the computer.'

'Can it wait?' She made sure she was smiling. He edged out into the hallway. 'I'd like to talk to you.' Good, she'd remembered the 'I' thing. 'Please, Bryce.'

There was an audible sigh as he came in and took a seat opposite her at the table. 'If this is about last night . . .'

'It's not.' Not entirely, anyway.

'I had too much to drink. I shouldn't have left you there like that.'

True, but agreeing would only get his back up.

Stay calm.

'Do you remember when we went on our honeymoon?' she asked.

He frowned. 'Of course.'

'Remember when we were sitting on the beach, watching the sunset that first night and we promised that no matter what happened, no matter what life threw at us, we would always talk about it.'

Recognition flickered in his eyes.

A deep breath. 'I'm worried about you, babe. You're not sleeping well, you seem to have lost your appetite, your moods are—'

'Running this place isn't exactly a picnic.'

Stay calm.

'I know.' He'd folded his arms up high across his chest, tucked his hands tight against his sides. She reached out and cupped his elbow. 'But you're not alone, Bryce,' she said. 'I'm here.' Her heart rapped against her ribs as she pulled the printed booklet out once again and ran her fingers down the edges of the sheets.

'What's that?'

Here we go. 'Some information I printed from the beyond-blue website.'

His brows furrowed, deeper this time.

She looked at him, imploring him silently to meet her eyes, but he kept his gaze fixed on the papers in front of her. 'It's an organisation that helps people who have depression,' she said softly.

His Adam's apple jumped. 'And that's what you think my problem is, do you?'

Stay calm, stay calm, stay calm.

'Yes, I do.' She kept her eyes on the booklet and pushed it across the table towards him. 'You have a lot of the symptoms listed in here.'

'Is that right?'

'You haven't been yourself for a while now, Bryce, and I feel . . .' That's it, focus on your reaction, not his actions. 'I feel it would help you if you went to speak to someone, a doctor or a counsellor.'

He dropped his head, shaking it from side to side. 'This is unbelievable. You are unbelievable. I don't need to speak to anyone, Stephanie, because I don't have fucking depression, all right? What I do have is a property that's going to the dogs because of this fucking drought, a bank balance that's shrinking faster than the dam in the top paddock and a brother . . .' He flattened his mouth into a razor sharp line. 'A brother who is hell bent on destroying the place.'

'It's not his fault.'

'Are you defending that prick again?'

'No. But you can't keep blaming him for everything. All he's done is offer us an opportunity. Maybe we should look into it. It might be a way for us to stay afloat, make us less reliant on the cattle. Cam said the environmental impact isn't as severe as the lobby groups make out.'

She heard herself and stopped. Nerves had got the better of her, made her lose focus, go off script. She hazarded a glimpse at Bryce's face and straight away wished she hadn't. The stranger she'd seen more and more lately, the one who was always there lurking in the shadows, stepped out into the light. Ice in his eyes, teeth clenched, he angled his head towards her, speaking almost in a hiss. 'You told me you didn't speak to him other than to tell him to leave.'

Bile slithered up her throat. If she lied to him now things would only get worse. 'I didn't. Not that day.'

'You've seen him again?'

'I called him. Asked if we could meet.'

He sprang to his feet, sending the chair crashing to the floor. 'What the fuck sort of game are you playing, Stephanie?' Hands on hips, he paced the kitchen floor. He had the wild-eyed look of a fox caught in a trap. She'd never been afraid of him, not physically, but a cornered animal could be dangerous.

'I'm not playing games, Bryce,' she said. 'Okay. I did arrange to meet Cam, but only to try to find out more about his offer, to see if it might help. I was worried about you. I am worried.'

'Help? How could it *help*?' he yelled. 'You don't have to worry about me, Stephanie.' He flailed his hands about in the air and stomped back to the table. 'I am not depressed. The only problem I've got is that my wife, who is supposed to be supporting me, supposed to be standing with me, has lost track of her loyalties.'

She checked the door. 'Bryce, keep your voice down.'

'Don't tell me what I can and can't do in my own home!' he shouted.

'Stop right there.' Her palms came down hard against the table. Enough was enough. 'This is my home too,' she corrected him. '*Our* home. Yours and mine.' She waved a pointed a finger between them. 'We're in this together, Bryce. I am supporting you, but you need to get rid of this battlefield mentality and open your eyes. Things have been tough. People who have been in this game longer than us have gone under. There's no shame in getting help. You seem to have some prehistoric idea that you're the man of the house and have to shoulder the burden alone. But you don't.' Her voice began to quiver. 'I want to help you. I want to fix whatever is wrong.'

'How many times do I have to tell you there is nothing wrong.' He picked up a mug from the table and hurled it across the room. She lifted her hands to her ears as it connected with the edge of the bench-top, sending shards of china splintering across the floor. In the seconds of quiet that followed all she was conscious of was the rapid rise and fall of her chest as her lungs scrambled for air.

'Mummy?' A small voice pulled them both from their stupor.

Jake hovered, his fingers curled around the timber architrave, hair mussed and eyes screwed up against the light.

'Bear,' she said, standing and moving towards him.

'I heard a noise.'

Bryce stood by the sink, his back to them, arms spread out on either side, shoulders heaving.

'Daddy just dropped a cup.' She forced herself to speak quietly, didn't look at Bryce as she clutched the curve of Jake's shoulder. How small it was beneath her hand. 'Come on, I'll take you back to bed.'

Walking down the hall without a backward glance, she tucked him in and kissed his forehead, watched his eyes close as she smoothed back his curls. By the time she returned to the kitchen Bryce had gone.

The chair was still upended. Broken china littered the floor and there was something else lying there too. Scraps of paper. The pages she had printed and stapled together had been ripped into shreds. She kneeled and scooped up a few pieces, gathering them together like a hand of cards.

She rose wearily, utterly drained. Laying the pieces she had collected out in front of her, the advice she had memorised but failed to follow fell into a ragged jigsaw.

Stay. Calm.

A shrill laugh spilled from her lips. She needed time to think. Maybe Bryce did too. Perhaps some time apart would do them both good, give them some breathing space. It would mean admitting to her mother, and everyone else in town no doubt, that they were having problems, but right now that was the least of her worries. There was Jake to consider in all of this too, and whether her husband liked it or not, a new baby.

If she was going to save her marriage she needed to do something decisive. And she needed to do it now.

Faith

THE SUN WAS SINKING BY THE TIME THEY SET OUT THE nibbles on the picnic table and popped the cork on the champagne. As dusk approached, a final splash of daylight brightened the sky. Threads of mauve cloud were looped across the horizon. The day became translucent. Faith let the bubbles settle before lifting the glass – a real glass champagne flute, not plastic – to her lips, but the ones on the inside continued to fizz. This was most definitely a date.

'Cheers.' Cam clinked his glass against hers.

'Cheers.'

They settled onto the wooden bench, backs to the table, their bodies angled slightly towards each other.

'So.'

'So,' she echoed. 'This is nice.' The swarm of flies currently trying to use her face as a landing pad, however, wasn't. She waved a hand wildly to shoo them away, but it did about as much good as the repellent they'd doused themselves in.

'Sorry, didn't think they'd be this bad,' Cam said.

'Not your fault. Although Aerogard isn't exactly my signature scent.'

'I imagine not.'

'What do you imagine it would be?' she asked. There was something about the stillness up here, about the way the champagne (Moët, another detail that had caught her attention) was already going to her head that was making her a little reckless.

Cam studied her face for a moment. 'Something sweet.'

Faith groaned. 'Really?' She was so not sugary.

'I hadn't finished.' He tutted, and she nodded for him to continue. 'Something sweet but with an undercurrent of spice.' Her mouth crept up at the corners. 'Am I right?'

'Spot on.' She met his gaze and they shared a knowing smile. She took another mouthful of champagne and flicked her eyes away. Above and around them the day had deepened to indigo. In the distance a ball of white sank from the sky, the orange aura surrounding it gradually fading away, washing the flat plain beyond the mountain into a sea of darkness. A row of skeletal trees guarded the rim of the picnic area. A single bird call punctuated the quiet. She heard the intake of a breath and turned to see a look of awe on Cam's face.

'Never gets old,' he said.

Sunsets never did. Her albums and laptop were full of images just like this one. 'Shit! I completely forgot to take a photo.'

Cam laughed. 'Oh well, you'll just have to come back.'

'Guess so.'

They turned at the same time to grab a cracker from the cheese plate but it was a seething mass of miniscule black wings and legs. 'Hope you weren't hungry,' he said, apologetically.

'I'll live.' She took another sip of champagne, the alcohol filtering into her veins making her bold. 'So, tell me, what's the real deal with you and your brother?'

He looked back out to the thin line of light still visible beyond the charcoaled sky. 'We jointly inherited Strathmore when my parents passed away,' he said wistfully. 'My mum died first, my dad not long after.'

'I'm sorry.' It always seemed like such a banal thing to say, but he looked so sad, and she was truly sorry.

He nodded briefly. 'I was halfway through my final year at uni in Brisbane. Bryce was working back on the farm after finishing up his ag science degree. I took a semester off and came home to help him sort things out then went back to uni. When I came home again I tried to convince myself I could forget about being an engineer, but it was never going to work. Bryce and I had different ideas. We argued. I was miserable anyway. So I told him I was leaving but he saw it as a betrayal, said I was deserting him, deserting Strathmore, said our parents would be rolling in their graves.'

'That's a bit rough. Are you still partners in the place?'

'Only on paper.' He paused for a moment. It was too dim to see his face clearly, but she could tell he was struggling. She moved closer and without thinking twice hooked her arm though his. 'I offered to help them out,' he continued on, as if the physical contact she'd made was completely normal, 'financially if they needed it, but I think that only made things worse. When the company asked me to come out here scouting for properties as potential investment sites I thought it would be a good way for him to keep working the place but have a buffer.' He shook his head. 'Bryce is pig headed, like our father. I should have known better.'

'I take it the answer was no.'

'You got it.'

They sat silently for a good long minute watching the day disappear. Faith could feel the gentle expansion and contraction of his abs against the back of her hand as he breathed. She felt comfortable sitting here beside him. Comfortable and brave. 'What's Stephanie like?'

'Stephanie is great,' he said, with no hesitation. 'Those two were made for each other. She's like a little sister to me. I really miss her – more than I miss Bryce sometimes. She's gentle and kind – not a pushover though, can stand up for herself. Although when it comes to my brother her glasses are pretty rosey.'

'What do you mean?'

'Bryce can do no wrong as far as she's concerned.'

'Understandable, I guess.'

'True, and she's loyal, I'll give her that. She's put her heart and soul into that place. She might not have been born into the family but she's part of it and I'm not sure he gives her enough credit.'

This whole family connection was getting weirder by the minute. Cam thought of Stephanie, her half-sister, as his own sibling. It almost made being on a date with him a little creepy.

'She came to see me the other day,' he said, 'to find out about the mining possibilities. Bryce would have a fit if he knew.' He stopped again and she heard him swallow. 'She said she thinks he might be depressed.'

'Really?' She'd heard stories on the news about farmers taking their lives because of the drought. It was pretty heavy stuff. 'Do you think he would be?'

'Who knows? I haven't seen enough of him lately to be able to judge. But I respect Steph's opinion enough to think she might be right.' He hummed out a sigh. 'Anyways, enough about my family dramas. Tell me about yours.'

She was glad night had fallen and he wouldn't be able to see her eyes. 'I don't have any really.'

'Oh come on, every family has its share of crap going on.'

'Not mine. Normal suburban family. Mum, Dad and one kid.'

'No brothers or sisters?'

'Just me.'

'And you've run away to the outback because?'

She batted her free hand against his arm. 'I haven't run away. I'm just trying something different while I decide what I want to do with the rest of my life.'

'No boyfriend?'

'No,' she mumbled, 'not anymore.'

'Ah, but there was.'

'Yes. He was my best friend's brother.' She laughed. 'Still is, just not my partner anymore.'

'Is that tricky?'

'Not really. Poppy and I had a much stronger relationship, as it turned out.'

'Good for you.'

A chill skipped up her arms. She rubbed her hands over the dimpled skin.

'It still gets cool at night here in spring. Do you want to get going?'

She didn't want to get going if it meant returning to her suffocating room, the noise from downstairs throbbing like a migraine.

'We could grab a pizza and take it back to my hotel,' he said. 'Wash it down with another bottle?'

'I'd like that.'

'Me too.' He shoved the fly-bitten remnants of their snacks into a plastic bag along with the empty bottle, and hopped down from the table. He held out his hand and Faith reached for it, arcing her fingers around the edge of his palm. This was not what she was supposed to be doing, but it felt good – and hadn't Poppy told her she needed to 'be open to different options'? Well, Cam was certainly different from the guys she'd dated in the city. And after all, wasn't meeting new people all part of the outback experience?

———

Pizza demolished and another three-quarters of a bottle of champagne drunk, she nestled in on the lounge, one leg tucked beneath her, the other stretched out towards where Cam sat at the other end. She rested an elbow on the back of the cushion beside her, aware of the goofy smile on her face. Dinner had been casual but nice. More than nice. They'd laughed their way through slice after slice of a super supreme while Cam told her crazy stories about growing up on the farm.

'Do you miss it?' she asked, picking up the echo of their conversation.

'Yeah, I do.' His easy smile dissolved into something more melancholy.

Faith picked up the glass she'd deposited on the floor and took a sip, let the bubbles dry on her tongue before she spoke again. 'So, why did you leave and go into engineering in the first place?'

'I guess I just wanted more.' Cam looked down at his socked feet and wriggled his toes. 'And I'm happy with my decision. It's a hard life.' He shrugged. 'Maybe I was just too lazy.'

'What you're doing now, talking to farmers about mining for gas, I'm gathering it's not winning you many friends.'

'You'd be surprised.' He raised his head, the fine lines across his forehead deepening. Faith fought back the urge to reach out and smooth them away. 'There are *some* people who listen to common sense,' he said. 'Things have to change. Life doesn't just stand still.'

'You're not wrong there,' she said tartly. She drained her glass and placed it back on the floor beside the lounge.

He narrowed his eyes at her. 'Why do I get the feeling you're not telling me something?'

The drinks had loosened her tongue. She pushed her toes into Cam's thigh. It seemed they'd loosened her inhibitions too. 'I'm not hiding anything, I just . . .' He was watching her closely, his eyes fixed intently on hers. They looked darker tonight, smokier. She was tired of talking. She moved towards him, kneeling on the couch, lifted her hands to his face and pressed her mouth against his. Her eyes fell shut as she relaxed into the kiss, let him pull her closer until she was sitting in his lap, fizzing with more than just champagne. He dropped his hand, trailed it down the side of her breast. A moan tripped up her throat and she pushed herself closer, even more aware now of the steely line of muscles spanning his abdomen, and the firm bulge between his thighs. They kissed gently at first, then more hungrily until they finally came up for air. She rested her forehead against his, lowering her eyes as he lifted the hem of her T-shirt. His lashes flickered against hers as he raised his chin, giving his eyebrows the lightest of quirks. If she nodded her assent, said yes to him peeling off her top, she would be saying yes to so much more. Her nipples hardened inside the white lace of her bra. For five years there'd only been Lukas, nobody in the year since, and only a few casual flings before. Cam's hands were solid against her hipbones. Her chest rose and fell, keeping time with the rapid thump of her heart. Finding a man was not the reason she'd come to Birralong, but the heat of his body as she straddled him was so damned inviting, so enticing.

'Hmm-hmm.' She smiled, and lifted her arms above her head. Cam removed her shirt and then, starting at the top, she unbuttoned his, each breath she took getting shallower so that when they kissed again her head swam. His skin was so warm against her palms and the blood hurtling through her veins made her own deliciously hot. Making out on a motel lounge, a gorgeous man pinned beneath her, was not one of the images that had flashed through her mind as she'd sat on the plane peering out the window at the endless carpet of red dust. It was almost as if she was a different person from the one she'd left behind in Sydney, and in some sense she had been ever since she'd opened that envelope. When Cam wrapped his arms around her and stood, she coiled her legs around his hips and let him carry her to the bedroom. This might not have been what she'd planned when she arrived, but she was pretty sure it was going to be something to remember when she left.

Chapter Ten

Rose

SUNLIGHT SCREAMED THROUGH THE WINDOW. SINCE WHEN did she go to bed without closing the blinds? She screwed her eyes tighter and rolled over, the sheet scraping against her breast. Her breast? Since when did she sleep naked? She was a top-and-bottom girl when it came to pyjamas, liked having all her bits covered. A gurgling sound came from somewhere behind her. Somewhere close. Somewhere very close. Cracking one eyelid open she peeked back over her shoulder to find the source of the horrendous noise.

David Ryan! What the—

She opened both her eyes and lifted a shaking hand to each side of her head. Oh, that hurt. It was all coming back to her. Letty. Dave coming to her rescue. A drink at the bar. More drinks. The kiss and then . . . she squirmed a little and felt the unmistakeable ache between her legs. Not surprising considering how long it had been. A rush of heat warmed her cheeks as she turned back to the comatose form beside her. Dave's face was slack with sleep, his mouth half-open, his chest rising and falling in time with his snores. Slipping out from between the sheets, she tiptoed to the bathroom door, gripped the handle, twisting it as quietly and carefully as she could, and dived inside.

'Holy mother of God, Rosemary O'Shea, what the hell were you thinking?' she muttered into the mirror. The face staring back looked dumbfounded. Her hair looked like she'd been dragged backwards through a wind tunnel, a panda had nothing on her as far as the mascara went, and the bags beneath her eyes were packed for a round-the-world trip. But her appearance was the least of her problems. Out there in her bed was a man. And not just any man. David Ryan – the first man she'd ever . . . ugh!

She grabbed a towel and dragged it roughly around her very naked body. The hours after Letty's death were a blur, but as she forced herself to think back the fog started to thin. It had all been very hurried once they'd reached the bedroom, each of them fumbling at their clothes like teenagers in a rush to get laid. It hadn't been unpleasant. In fact, it all came back to her more clearly now, it had been quite the opposite. An unexpected tingle in her nether regions made her jiggle on the spot. Apparently her body had missed sex, even if she'd told herself she hadn't, because judging by the way the two of them had gone at it, the whole event had been quite enjoyable. But that didn't make the current scenario any less awkward.

This was not something she had time to process. Her mother-in-law was laid out on a trolley at the local morgue and things needed to be organised. Stephanie had to be told, for one, and funeral arrangements made, but she certainly couldn't go anywhere looking like this. Dropping the towel, she stepped into the shower and turned it on as hard and as hot as she could stand. She stayed there until her skin turned a mottled shade of pink and was just in the throes of drying herself off when a squeal followed by muffled voices had her reaching for the door knob. It only took an instant for her to take in the scene. There, in the middle of the room, mouth open almost as wide as the door behind her, was Stephanie. Dave, propping himself up on his elbows, hairy chest exposed as the sheets slid down across his belly, looked as if he'd just been caught stealing from a lolly jar. His head spun from Stephanie to Rose and back again as he began to stammer. 'I . . . um . . .'

'Mum, what the hell is going on?' Stephanie lifted her hands to her hips.

'Well, I think that's fairly obvious.' Rose surprised herself with her calm tone, behind which she was sucking back an inappropriate fit of the giggles. She wondered vaguely if she'd completely lost her marbles. 'But there is something I do have to tell you.'

'If it's the fact that my grandmother is dead, don't bother.' Stephanie looked at her, tight-lipped. 'The news is already out.'

'Right,' Rose said. Of course it was. It would be common knowledge by now.

'It would have been nice to find out from you, though, instead of hearing about it on the town grapevine.' Stephanie turned her attention back to Dave, who was leaning over the side of the bed ferreting around on the floor for his clothes, revealing far too much bare flesh. He sat back up, pulling on his shirt. The poor thing looked completely flummoxed. 'But you were *obviously* too busy,' she added.

'It wasn't like that—' Rose began.

'Save it, Mum.' She left, closing the door with a bang.

Rose heaved out a long, slow sigh.

'I'm so sorry, Rosie,' Dave said, out of the bed now, climbing into his underwear and jeans.

'Not your fault. There's two of us here, remember.' A trickle of water ran down her shin reminding her she was still sopping wet, wearing nothing but a towel. She hitched a thumb back over her shoulder. 'I'll just . . .'

'Probably best if I go.'

She gave him a weak smile before retreating back into the bathroom. When she came out again he was gone. Really, she wasn't sure how she felt about that particular situation, but like it or not she needed to go downstairs and face the music.

Stephanie

'WATCH THIS, MUMMY!' JAKE CALLED FROM THE PLAY equipment in the corner of the hotel courtyard. He flipped himself over the monkey bar and hung upside down, his hair flapping in the breeze his body made as he swung forward and back. It reminded Stephanie of the corellas she used to watch as a kid, twirling on the telegraph wires, their spiky combs vibrating in the wind.

'Very clever,' she called back. The sun glinted off the silver metal of the swing chain and she held a hand to her forehead to shield her eyes as she tried to focus on her son. Anything to take her mind off the scene she'd just walked in on in her mother's bedroom. When had that started? Holly had made noises about it the other night, but she'd laughed and told her she was being ridiculous.

Apparently not.

Still, no more ridiculous than the events of the past two days. A couple of hours before she'd tossed an overnight bag into her car, strapped a yawning Jake into his seat and told him they were going on a little holiday to help Nanny at the hotel. Her stomach had been doing backflips ever since she'd forced her eyes open but since Bryce had chosen to sleep in the spare room she'd been able to race to the toilet without him being any the wiser. She'd been unbundling Jake from the car when Beverley Wilson, walking past in her fluoro pink runners and lycra pants, told her how sorry she was to hear about her grandmother. She'd thanked her dumbly before putting two and two together. Bev's partner, Graham, was the local undertaker. That was when she'd set Jake up in the kitchen with a bowl of Weet-Bix and headed upstairs to see her mother. Big mistake.

She closed her eyes, waiting for the next wave to pass, barely registering the sound of footsteps on the path. Once it was safe she looked across to see her mother positioned on the bench seat beside her.

'Hi Nanny.' Jake was in the sandpit now, building a fort, no doubt to house a crew of his Avengers figurines.

'Hi matey.'

Rose was gazing straight ahead so that Stephanie saw her in profile, saw her probably for the first time in her life as a woman rather than as her mother. The lines around her eyes were more noticeable from this angle, especially without her glasses, and the creases on her throat more pronounced. But even without make-up she was striking for a woman of her age, her wet hair curled back around her ears, her mouth plump and full. It made perfect sense that a man would find her attractive.

'Sorry for barging in like that,' she apologised. 'Bad timing.'

'You can say that again.'

They sat for a minute, watching Jake, both equally unsure how to proceed.

Stephanie suddenly remembered why she'd stormed into her mother's room in the first place. 'What happened to Letty?'

'I had a missed call from her last night, so I went around to check on her.' Her mother's voice was uncharacteristically timid. 'She was gone. The doctor thinks she'd been there like that for a good couple of hours.'

'What time did she call?'

'Quarter past eight. I was working and . . . they said it was most likely a massive heart attack and nothing could've been done, but if I'd got there earlier . . .'

'Oh Mum. It doesn't sound like it would have made any difference.'

'Still . . . your father.' Rose's head drooped as she gave in to a small tremor of despair.

Stephanie couldn't remember the last time she'd seen her mother cry. When her dad had passed away Rose had been as solid as a concrete shed in a cyclone, taking over the running of the pub and helping Stephanie with the baby while she dealt with her own grief. She'd even seemed a little cold about it. But maybe it hadn't been that at all. She put an arm around Rose's shoulder. 'Don't beat yourself up, Mum. You've looked after her for years. She wasn't an easy woman.'

Rose huffed.

'I should have done more to help you.' It was true. She had tried in the early days, but Letty wasn't a baby person, and Jake got on her nerves. When had she last seen her grand-mother? Her birthday probably, when Stephanie had called around, sans Jake, to deliver a box of toffees and a bunch of chrysanthemums. It had been a short visit, neither of them having very much to say, and Stephanie had been more than relieved when she'd stepped out of the dank mausoleum of a house into the spring sunshine.

'You've had more than enough on your plate,' Rose said, patting her hand.

And there was the window she needed. 'About that . . .' she said cautiously, looking across at Jake who was making vrooming noises as he pushed a truck through the sand. 'Is it okay if we stay with you for a few days?'

Her arm was still slung loosely around Rose's shoulder. They twisted towards each other and their knees bumped.

'Of course.' Rose reached across to pull her into a hug. Stephanie rested her forehead in the crook of her mother's neck as the first of the tears began to flow. A hand patted her spine as her body gave in and started to shake. How had it come to this? Sitting in her mother's garden, a bag full of clothes on the back seat of the car, her husband not even caring enough to call and check in on his family. Rose said nothing, and she was grateful. What she needed right now was time to think. To sort out her next move. Work out how to fix things.

'Do you want to talk about it?' Rose asked as Stephanie sat herself upright and dabbed at her cheek.

'No,' she said. Even if she did want to talk about it she wasn't quite sure where to start. Telling her mother about her pregnancy before telling Bryce seemed like too much of a betrayal. Once he'd had a little space, time to think about things, he would realise she was only trying to help him and everything would get back to normal.

Time and space, that's all they needed.

Faith

SHE HITCHED HER BAG OVER HER SHOULDER AND ADJUSTED her sunglasses as she pushed open the back gate. She wasn't exactly hung over, but perhaps one or two fewer glasses of champagne would have been wiser considering she had to work this morning. Cam had dropped her in the side street early enough for her to have time to change out of yesterday's clothes – retrieved from various places around his motel room – and make herself respectable. Hmm. There was a loaded word. Sleeping with a guy on a first date was hardly respectable.

Neither was deception.

Voices from the garden filtered through to her foggy brain. She peeked around the hedge. Stephanie and Rose were seated on a bench seat, the younger woman's arm around her mother's shoulder. She watched Rose turn and hug her daughter. Had Rose ever actually held *her* when she was a baby? Or had she been whisked away before her mother could even say goodbye? An inexplicable sadness overwhelmed Faith, an unexpected sense of loss that left her eyes stinging. She had read an article about cellular memory once, about how bodies hold onto events, especially stressful or traumatic ones. Perhaps her body was remembering. She blinked back the tears but a sob escaped before she could catch it.

Stephanie turned and spotted her.

Rose too. 'Good morning,' she called. 'Doing the walk of shame, are we?'

This was exactly why she'd been trying to creep inside. She faked a cough to cover the tortured sound that had given her away. 'Guess so.' She fought the urge to flee – it would only make her look more idiotic.

'Faith, have you met my daughter, Stephanie?' The two women were facing her now. Nothing to do but go with the flow.

'Yes, we met the other night. Hi.'

'Hi.' Stephanie gave a tight smile.

'Faith had a date with Cameron last night,' Rose continued. 'Showing her the local sights, I believe.'

Oh God, could this get any more embarrassing?

'Cameron?' Stephanie asked. 'As in, Cameron my brother-in-law?'

Rose nodded and pinched her lips together. 'One and the same.' She stood then, adjusting her top and folding her arms. 'I take it the date went well?' she asked Faith, pointedly.

'Yes. Thank you.' A hole opening up in the pavers and devouring her right about now would be the best thing ever. 'I'd better get moving,' she said, inching towards the door. 'Shower and all that sort of thing, before my shift starts.'

Stephanie was staring at her, eyes like saucers.

'Righty-o,' Rose said. 'Oh, and just so you know, my mother-in-law died last night. I'll be a bit busy with the arrangements over the next couple of days. Hope you won't mind picking up the slack.'

'Oh, I'm so sorry,' Faith said, quickly adding, 'I'm happy to help out.' She'd agree to pilot the next shuttle to Mars if it meant she could get away.

'I'll be around, too,' Stephanie said. 'Haven't pulled a beer for a while but I'm sure you can keep me on track.'

'I'll just . . .' She waved a hand towards the door.

'Yes, go, go,' Rose said.

It was a struggle not to run.

'Must have been something in the air last night,' she heard Stephanie mutter, as she left.

Safely inside her room, she walked straight to the window and looked down to where the two women were still talking in the garden. Most likely about her. In the past ten minutes her feelings had kaleidoscoped from guilt to grief to paralysing embarrassment. Her straightforward plan was becoming far too confusing. The guy she'd just slept with was her half-sister's estranged brother-in-law, and her BM's mother-in-law had just died. Stephanie's husband was depressed and Rose was virtu- ally bankrupt. These people had lives and problems of their own. When she'd decided to stalk Rosemary Barnes she hadn't allowed for the matter of additional family and she certainly hadn't foreseen any romantic liaisons.

This isn't just about you.

Poppy's words rang out loud and clear inside her head.

She'd got herself into a situation that was far more complex than she'd ever imagined.

The question now was, how was she going to get out?

Chapter Eleven

Rose

PEN IN HAND, ROSE SAT BY THE WINDOW OF THE FRONT BAR trying to conjure up a list of names. So far there was herself, Stephanie, a couple of women Letty used to play Bingo with at the bowlo before she became a recluse, and . . . well, that was probably the sum of it. How sad to get to the end of your life and have so few people to mourn your passing? Mick's brother, Collin, had sounded annoyed rather than grief stricken on the phone as he gave insincere apologies for both himself and Ned. His response had hardly been a surprise.

And of course, the old girl had remained difficult until the end. Dying at home on your own in the middle of the night meant a whole lot of complications. Since there'd been no prior illness a post mortem had to be done before a death certificate could be issued. The funeral would probably be Friday at the earliest. Not that there was much to organise.

She tossed the pen onto the table and glanced down at her watch. There was a meeting scheduled with the priest and then

Cleo was coming in to help her sort a few things out at Letty's. Going back into that house alone gave her the heebie-jeebies.

A brassy laugh from the other end of the room made her turn. Harry and the boys, already settled in for the day, were cracking their usual jokes and Faith was smiling along politely. The girl was certainly fitting right in. They hadn't had much time to chat over the past few days. Rose made a mental note to check in with her, see if everything was all right, especially in light of the surprising hook-up with Cameron.

Her eyes fell back to the very short list of funeral invitees on the table.

'Hi there, Rosie.'

At the sound of David Ryan's all too familiar voice her stomach plummeted all the way down to her toes. Her eyes fell shut at the memory of his euphoric groans as the two of them writhed between her sheets. Anyone with half a brain would have known not to make the same mistake twice.

'Dave,' she said, forcing herself to look up. The happy-go-lucky man she'd met again a fortnight ago – spent the night with just two days ago – now looked more like a schoolboy whose dog had eaten his homework. His hands were shoved deep into his pockets, giving him a hunched, uneasy posture. 'What are you doing here?' It came out harsher than Rose intended and she wished instantly that she could take it back.

He bobbed his head from side to side. 'Well, I wanted to see how you were, but if you're busy . . .' He started to walk away.

'Dave, wait.' She gestured to the empty seat at her table. 'Come and sit down.'

'Another scorcher,' he said, almost managing a smile as he pulled out a chair.

The weather was always a good buffer. Rose looked out the window. 'It is,' was all she could manage.

'Funeral invites?'

She nodded. 'At least the wake's not going to cost much.' Her shallow attempt at a joke didn't raise a laugh from either of them. They sat quietly, the murmur of voices behind them, the whirring of fans overhead. Finally, Rose mustered up enough courage to speak. 'Thanks for helping me out the other night.' And that was the clanger that broke the proverbial ice. Dave spluttered out a laugh and, once she realised what she had said, Rose did the same. It took her a good, long minute to get herself under control. 'With Letty, was what I meant.'

'My pleasure,' Dave grinned. 'On both fronts.'

This was the point at which she needed to address the very large elephant sitting at the table between them. 'About that,' she began slowly.

'Rosie . . .'

'Dave, please, let me speak.' She waited until he nodded his agreement before continuing. 'I don't really know what happened the other night. Maybe it was the scotch or the fact we'd both just been confronted with a dead body or—' she slowed the pace of her words as she realised the truth of what she was about to say. 'Or that we are two lonely people who needed some comfort.'

Dave nodded.

'The thing is, I'm not really looking for any kind of romantic relationship.'

'Thank God.' The stiffness in Dave's face and posture vanished as he relaxed back against the chair.

'Oh.'

'Don't get me wrong, Rosie,' he lowered his voice, leaned forward conspiratorially. 'It was great. Even better than I remembered.' He paused and held her gaze.

A strange, sickly sensation overcame Rose at his reference to their ill-fated liason all those years ago and she felt her body start to sway.

If only you knew.

She blinked and drew in a shallow breath.

Dave carried on, oblivious. 'But I'm still grieving and I'm not in a position to get into a relationship either.'

'Well, that's a relief.' On both counts. No elaborating on their teenage antics and no attempt to turn their one night stand into something more. Rose captured her smile and schooled her features to mirror Dave's serious expression.

'I know this sounds corny,' Dave said tentatively, 'but I hope we can still be mates.'

'Haven't heard that line in a while.' Rose chuckled. 'Of course. You can never have too many mates.' He smiled back, a soft genuine thing that sparked a sudden urge in her to confess the truth. Surely he had a right to know he had another child out there somewhere?

'How about I shout us both a lemon squash to seal the deal.'

The corners of Rose's mouth twitched as the moment passed. This wasn't the time or place. 'As long as you don't buy me a scotch, I'm in.'

He gave her a wink and went to stand as a couple of car doors banged outside. Two men dressed in smart jeans and matching polo shirts walked into the pub. One carried a folder under his arm and the other a clipboard. Stopping in the doorway, they looked around, obviously checking the place out.

'What's with Bill and Ben?' Dave asked.

'Not sure,' Rose said. But as she started towards the two men she had a sickening memory of having booked a property valuation and then, in the light of everything that had happened since, promptly forgotten about it. 'Can I help you?'

'Yeah, we're looking for a . . .' The man with the clipboard looked down at it. 'Rosemary O'Shea.'

'Well, you've found her,' Rose replied. 'What can I do for you?'

'We're here to do the valuation.'

Oh, great. She cringed at the man's overly loud voice. What a way to announce she was selling. 'It's not a convenient time right now.'

The man she'd decided was 'Bill' held the clipboard up and pointed a stumpy finger. 'Says here you made an appointment.' 'Ben' pulled a sheet of paper from his folder and handed it to Rose. She read the scrolled lettering heading the page: *RJ Rasmussen Property Valuations Specialising in Heritage Homes and Buildings, Brisbane.*

Dave walked up behind her. 'What's all this about, Rosie?'

A dozen eyes were boring into the back of her head, ears pricked, waiting.

These two characters had driven a long way to do their job but she needed to break the news first. 'I'm afraid I'm in the middle of something right now,' she said, sweetly. 'Could we possibly reschedule.'

The two men looked at each other. *We've got a nutter here*, she could see them thinking. 'Sorry, madam,' Bill said, sounding anything but, 'you booked the valuation and we will be charging you for our time whether we do it or not.'

The events of the last few weeks were bubbling inside her like molten lava. She had a dead mother-in-law, a daughter whose marriage seemed to be in dire straits, an awkward situation with an ex-lover who was currently loitering at her shoulder and she was desperately trying to rustle up attendees for a funeral even she didn't want to attend. The last thing she needed to deal with was her virtually derelict hotel and her decision to sell it.

'Well, you will just have to *unbook* it and send me the bill,' she waved a hand towards the door and shooed the men away.

'Bill' scowled, holding up the board as if it was a trophy he'd just won. He turned to leave with 'Ben' following hot on his heels. Rose loomed in the entrance, arms folded across her chest, well aware that everyone in the bar – including her daughter – had heard the exchange.

How had such a screw-up happened? She'd always prided herself on being such an efficient manager, logged every appointment in her diary, but with everything else that had been going on this one had completely slipped through the cracks. She spun around, girding herself to face the onslaught of questions.

'You sent them packing. Good on yer, Rosie,' Harry Shepherd called, raising his glass high before downing another mouthful. He obviously had no clue what was going on.

Dave leaned towards her. 'I think you just got dumped in it,' he said quietly.

Stephanie frowned. 'What's going on Mum?'

Blood pumping furiously, making her head spin, Rose made her way to the bar. Was this what it felt like to have a heart attack? 'I think I will have something stronger than lemon squash. Faith, pour me a gin-and-tonic, please. A double.'

Dave sidled up and perched himself on the seat beside her while Stephanie, standing opposite, stared her down.

'Right, Mum, spill the beans.'

Rose shot a glare at Harry and his mate, Ernie, who were hovering like a pair of expectant seagulls. 'This is a private conversation, if you don't mind, gents.'

Harry tipped his hat and the two of them shifted down to the end of the bar, no doubt trying to nut out what they could about the kerfuffle. Faith returned with Rose's drink, placing it down and then making to leave. 'No, you can stay,' Rose said. 'It's nothing you don't already know.' She ignored the pointed look her daughter shot at the barmaid and took a deep breath before launching into her story.

'As you might have overheard, they were property valuers. The Crossroads is in need of a little TLC. More than a little. There's a list as long as my arm of repairs, and since the place is listed, they have to be done to a certain standard. I've been trying to put aside the funds, but,' she hesitated and took another sip of her gin, 'I'm completely skint. I've been pouring more and more money into this place over the years and with business the way it's been, there isn't anything left to do the renos.'

'Mum, why didn't you say anything?' Stephanie looked wounded.

'I didn't want to worry anyone. You've got enough on your plate, and to be honest I was trying not to think about it,' Rose confessed, letting out a laugh that sounded slightly hysterical. 'The bank won't give me any more money – I've already taken out a reverse mortgage, and . . .' She clenched her teeth. Letty was up – or down – there somewhere laughing at her. 'Other options didn't transpire.'

'How much money are we talking?' Stephanie asked.

'The estimate is over forty thousand, and that's conservative. Could be more.'

'I can help you out,' Dave offered.

'No.' Rose jumped at him. 'I mean, that's very kind of you, Dave, but I've never been one to take charity and I'm not about to start now.'

'It's not charity, it would be a loan.'

'I appreciate it, but no thanks. I'd never be able to pay it back.'

'I suggested a fundraising event.' Faith had been standing slightly to one side but moved up to address the group. 'Get the town on board. It wouldn't be that hard.'

'That's a great idea,' Stephanie said, lighting up. 'No one in Birralong would want to see this place close down. We could have it at the Community Centre, get the Council on board.'

'I'm pretty sure we could get some media interest too – you know, the whole drought-brings-businesses-to-its-knees aspect. People love that sort of thing.' Faith was sounding animated, even excited, about the prospect.

'Well, other people might love "that sort of thing",' Rose snapped, 'but I don't. This is my place and it's my responsibility. That's the bottom line.'

Stephanie looked at her, eyes darkening. 'So that's why the property valuers were here,' she said slowly, nodding as the pieces started falling into place.

Rose polished off the rest of her drink and placed the glass carefully on the bar in front of her. She took a moment to collect herself. 'Yes. I'm putting the place on the market. I've gone over and over the sums, and with the debt I'm already in and the cost of the repairs, there's no way I can ever come back, not without selling.'

'You can't,' Stephanie choked out. 'The Crossroads was Dad's pride and joy, he loved this place. You can't just up and sell it at the drop of a hat.'

Rose looked at her daughter, saw the look of anguish on her face. 'Steph, this isn't something I'm doing lightly. It's been coming for a while now.' She took Stephanie's hand. 'I know your father wanted me to hang onto it, but sometimes you just have to face reality.' Nobody spoke. Stephanie pulled her hand away. Rose inhaled sharply, glancing down at her watch. 'Now, if you'll excuse me, I have to go to see a priest about a funeral.'

She walked out the door well aware of the confusion she was leaving in her wake. And yet all she could feel was relief. Squinting into the sunshine as she made her way towards the church, she sucked in a breath of clean, fresh air, holding it for a few seconds before letting it go. She could kick herself for forgetting about the appointment with the property valuers but at least now she didn't have to work out how to broach the subject with Stephanie, and she didn't have to vacillate any longer. The decision had been made, the word was out, the pub would be sold. She'd kept her promise to Mick for as long as she possibly could, but now it was time to let go.

Outside the door of the church, she stopped on the step, and looked skyward.

I did the best I could, Mick.

And as she stepped inside she could have sworn she heard him reply.

I know you did, Rosie. I know.

Stephanie

'DID I HEAR YOUR MOTHER SAY SHE'S SELLING?'

Stephanie kept her eyes firmly on the glasses she was unstacking. Harry Shepherd and his sticky-beaking was the last thing she needed.

Dave, still seated the bar, answered for her. 'Good chance Rose is just letting off steam, Harry,' he said. 'Nothing to worry about.'

She looked up, pushing her hair back off her face, in time to see Harry nod. He didn't look convinced. He ambled off anyway, drink in hand, no doubt to chew on the nice juicy piece of fat her mother had just served up.

'Thanks,' Stephanie said. Dave was sitting looking lost, and an image of him lying bare chested in her mother's bed just hours ago popped into her mind. If only a customer – or ten – would appear right now; she could certainly use the distraction. Working behind the bar had its challenges, but she had to admit she'd missed it. As much as she loved the farm, couldn't get enough of the wide open spaces, the trees and the endless skies, sometimes she craved the people, chatter and noise of town. Even more so since Bryce had become so introverted. A girl could only live on air and water for so long.

'It's a damned shame she has to sell this place,' Dave said, his voice diplomatically low.

She nodded. Just thinking about it made her chest tight. The Crossroads was where she'd grown up – when she wasn't out with her Nan and Pop. It was still home. She looked around the walls, at the dozens of smiling faces beaming out from inside the frames, their time at the pub captured with a single click, each a part of the place's history. Her eyes landed on one face in particular – Michael O'Shea. Sometimes she still couldn't believe he was gone. Right there in that photo he was as large as life, one arm around Rose, and Stephanie herself posing for the camera on the bar beside them. She was about nine in that photo, skinny arms and lanky legs, hair almost to her waist. He had loved her long hair, would brush it for her sometimes, never let her get it cut. Even as an adult, whenever she visited the hairdresser she could hear him saying, 'Only a trim, Stephie, no more than half an inch.' The pub had been his pride and joy, second only to his family. What would he say now if he knew the place was being sold?

She didn't have to think long to come up with an answer: find a way to make sure she doesn't have to sell.

'Everything all right?' Dave asked.

'Oh, yeah. Fine.' She gave her head a quick shake. Her recollections of her father were only adding to the misery that Rose's bombshell had created, but maybe she was on to something.

Resting her elbows on the bar, she inched forward, speaking quietly. 'Dave, what do you think of that fundraising idea of Faith's?'

'I think it's bloody brilliant.'

'Me too.' She sighed. 'But Mum will never go for it. '

'She doesn't necessarily have to know about it, does she?' There was a flicker of mischief in the man's eyes.

'You think we could organise something without her knowing?'

'We could certainly do the groundwork, get enough of it sorted so that it would be impossible to cancel it once she finds out.'

A surge of adrenaline flooded her veins, her mind already filling with possibilities.

'And I meant what I said.' Dave's voice drew her back to the bar. 'About the loan, so if worse comes to worst . . .'

'That's lovely. Really lovely. But we might not need to go that far. Faith seemed keen to help, and I know enough people around the place who would be willing to chip in. I'm pretty sure that between us we'd be able to pull something together.' Now that the idea had settled in it was sounding more and more like a goer. 'The town could do with a bit of a bash anyway, don't you think?'

'Well, if it couldn't, I certainly could.' Dave was sounding as thrilled as she was herself about the prospect of a party. 'You let me know what needs doing and I'll be onto it.'

'Deal.' She looked around. Harry was eyeing her suspiciously, muttering something to his mate. If those two got word of what she and Dave were planning, Rose would hear about it before sunset. She ducked her head and lowered the volume as she returned to the conversation. 'Let's keep it to ourselves for now. I'll talk to Faith and see what we can come up with.'

'Mum's the word.' Dave tapped a finger to the side of his nose but then laughed. 'Or in this instance, it's not the word.'

'Yeah, right.' She attempted a matey laugh. He had a dad-jokey sense of humour – but he meant well. 'I'd better get back there and make sure Jake isn't driving Faith nuts. Would you mind keeping an eye on things out here for a minute?'

'It would be a pleasure.'

She made her way out to the kitchen. He was a good guy – her mother could do a lot worse. But matchmaking wasn't on her radar. Somehow they would find a way to keep The Crossroads open for business and in the family. A project like this was perfect right now. Something she could manage when so many other aspects of her life seemed to be spiralling out of control. The hardest part was going to be keeping it quiet. Another secret she was keeping from her mother, along with the tiny life growing inside her. Her elation faded as she paused at the door, her hand falling to rest on her stomach. Hopefully the outcome – in both cases – would be worth the temporary subterfuge. Voices inside the kitchen caught her ear. Jake was yakking away to Faith as if they were old friends. Her little chatterbox. He could always make her smile.

Faith

JAKE BALANCED ON A STOOL AT THE KITCHEN BENCH, ARMPIT deep in a cloud of soap foam. 'How's this?' He held up a mug, suds dripping from its base onto the floor.

'Looks great.' She'd read somewhere that kids responded to positive feedback. 'Maybe just get it into the rack now so it can dry off.'

He nodded and tipped the mug upside down. 'Mummy showed me how to do it,' he said. 'Like this, so the water all goes away.' He turned around and picked up a plate, dropping it into the sink. A bubble landed on the tip of his nose, sending him into a fit of giggles.

'That's awesome.' She went back to preparing the vegetables for tonight's meals. Since the old woman's death complete chaos had descended, with Rose coming and going, Stephanie moving in – which Faith wasn't entirely convinced had anything to do with the grandmother's departure – and that whole commotion in the bar this morning over the imminent sale of the hotel. Her BM was certainly a force to be reckoned with. The way she'd laid it all on the line out there was pure gold. Faith had felt a small puff of pride as she watched the scene unfold and remembered Rose wasn't merely her boss.

Her phone chimed. She looked down to where it sat on the table beside the chopping board as the green message lit up: *Hey, how's it going? Should be back tonight. Want to have dinner?*

Cam.

He'd been out of town since their night together but had texted her every day and rung her twice. His voice had sent a tingle trickling down her spine, not to mention a few other places, but the prospect of seeing him again, being up close and personal, sent shivers of a different kind scurrying across her scalp. How had she got involved with anyone, let alone her sister's estranged brother-in-law? She needed to keep her distance and concentrate on the reason she'd come to Birralong in the first place.

Whipping off the flimsy disposable gloves – she hated the slimy feel of the things, but they were a hygiene prerequisite – she typed back a quick, non-committal response. *Can't tonight. Have to work.*

Send.

That should keep him out of her hair, at least for the time being. Out of her hair – and her bed. Thinking about their antics the other night was certainly sending her out of her mind. She chopped away at the carrots while Jake hummed the *Play School* theme song. He was a pretty cute kid. Being an only child meant no nieces or nephews, so she'd never had much to do with children. A lot of her friends seemed to have gone into hiding since they'd had babies. Poppy had better not be joining them.

'I'm going back to my place later and I'm going to stay the night and me and my Dad are going to go out on the bikes.' Dad. Home. Bikes. Her brain was having a hard time keeping up with Jake's babble.

'Bikes?'

'Yeah, I've got a pee wee and Dad lets me come around Strathmore with him sometimes. You know, when he's checking the pumps and stuff.'

'Oh right, a pee wee is a motorbike?' Surely a five-year-old was too young for that.

'Yes, silly.' He tugged at the plug, sending suds flying.

'So, your dad is working on the farm this week, right?'

'Yeah, he's always working.' He jumped down from the upturned milk crate. 'Mummy usually is too but she said she wanted to see Nanna, so we're staying in town this week.'

Interesting. 'Do you stay with Nanna a lot?'

'No.' Jake murmured, his eyes downcast. The joy he had radiated while he did the washing-up suddenly evaporated. He looked far more worried than any five-year-old should be. 'But Mummy and Daddy have been yelling at each other a lot. I think that's really why we came here.' He patted his hands on his T-shirt, leaving two wet splotches on the front. 'I like coming to town, but I miss my Dad.'

'Wow, looks like you've made a bit of a mess there, Bear.' Stephanie's voice surprised them both. The knife slipped and nicked the edge of Faith's finger. She'd been caught, gloves off, digging for information.

'Ow.' Blood oozed from the cut. She stuck her finger in her mouth, cringing at both the salty taste and the sting.

'Sorry.' Stephanie looked far from it. 'I didn't mean to sneak up on you.'

'Mummy!' Jake flew towards his mother, twining his arms around her thighs.

'Hey, matey. You've been busy. How about you hop out into the sandpit for a minute while I help Faith clean up in here.'

'Yay.' He raced to the door, letting it bang shut behind him, and vanished into the garden.

'I'll grab you something for that.' Stephanie said, stepping into the pantry and reaching up to the top shelf.

She ran her hand under cold water, wincing as she patted it dry it on a sheet of paper towel. She'd always been such a baby about injuries – the sight of blood made her positively squeamish.

Stephanie unwrapped a band aid and wound it around the cut. She had the whole mother thing down pat. 'Kids,' she said quietly, as she tossed the wrapper into the bin. 'You never know what they're going to say.'

Faith could feel the blood vessels in her cheeks burn. 'No, guess not.'

Stephanie stood at the window, watching Jake. 'Bryce and I have been having a few issues,' she said, hesitantly. 'I've tried to shelter him from it as much as I can, but he hears things, I suppose.'

The dull sound of voices seeped through the wall from the bar, followed by a loud squeal as Amber arrived and greeted her customers. She was doing a few extra shifts this week and by the sound of it was doing more play then work. The silence in the kitchen dragged on. Faith had no idea what to say and Stephanie was making no attempt to leave.

A half carrot sat on the table beside a bowl of slivered beans. 'I'd better get this finished,' Faith said, moving back to the table.

'So,' Stephanie turned around and crossed her arms. 'You're seeing Cam.'

It was more of a statement than a question, but one that required some sort of response. She kept her focus on the cutting-board. One mangled finger was enough. 'We've only had one date.'

'A date that went pretty well, I take it, since you didn't get home until the next morning.'

Ouch. She probably deserved that after grilling the kid. She slid the last of the julienned carrots into a dish. 'You could say that.'

'He's a good guy.' Faith was taken aback by Stephanie's shift from vigilance to sincerity.

'He said the same about you.' This conversation was turning her into a nervous wreck. 'I mean, he said good things about you, too.'

'We had a lot of fun back in the day. I wish things had been different.'

Curiosity got the better of her. 'Different?'

'Between Bryce and Cam. I'm sure you saw the drama the other night. Neither of them is to blame, really. This mining business is just making it worse.' She gave her head a shake. 'Are you seeing him again?'

Wow. Who was doing the interrogating now? 'Ah, I'm not sure.' She covered the bowls of vegetables in cling wrap and stored them in the fridge.

'Well, not that it's any of my business, but from memory Cam falls pretty hard pretty fast. He's not usually into casual flings.'

She was so right – it was none of her business. Faith bristled. 'Neither am I.'

'Good. Then hopefully neither of you will get hurt.'

What does it matter to you anyway? she wanted to ask, but it would come out sounding too bitchy. 'I don't know why you care, given the situation between Cam and Bryce.'

'Family is family,' Stephanie said. 'I know we don't know each other very well, but you seem like a nice person.' She looked back out the window, Jake clearly in her line of vision. 'And I like happy endings.'

Don't we all.

If things had been different, if they'd grown up together like normal sisters, this conversation might have gone in a completely different direction. Faith might have admitted to her feelings for Cam and Stephanie might have played matchmaker. But then if they'd grown up together she and Cam would have known each other for years. Funny, that's how it actually felt. She leant against the table, arms folded and sighed.

Stephanie turned back towards her. 'So, what's this fund-raising idea you mentioned earlier?'

The conversation, thankfully, was moving into more neutral territory. 'It might be a good way to get some support behind the pub, a rally-the-troops sort of thing. But Rose wasn't interested.'

'Of course she wasn't.' Stephanie shook her head. 'That pride of hers will be her undoing. It's a great idea. Maybe you and I can get together tomorrow and have a chat about it? Jake's going to spend the day with his dad and I'll have some time on my hands. I could help you in the bar and we could talk about it then?'

'Yeah, that would be fine. I'll jot down a few ideas tonight.' Event planning trumped vegetable chopping, hands down.

'Great. Well, I'd better go and check on the rascal,' she smiled and made her way outside.

Faith wiggled her shoulders, shaking away the built-up tension. She watched through the window as Stephanie snuck up behind Jake and blew a raspberry on the back of his neck. He doubled over in peals of laughter as his mum sat down beside him in the sand.

You seem like a nice person.

Yeah, a nice person who is lying straight to your face. The two of them came from totally opposite worlds. They had different backgrounds, radically different life experiences. Their conversation had got off to a bad start, but by the end of it they did seem to be on the same page. Was there some sort of genetic bond that helped them connect? Or was she just willing there to be something there when there really wasn't? Either way there was no denying that Stephanie *was* a nice person – kind, thoughtful, caring – and she was going through a hard time. Like her mum.

Our mum.

Faith's phone buzzed. She'd switched it to silent so she wouldn't be tempted to reply to any more messages from Cam, but when her best friend's face showed up on the screen she picked it up immediately.

'Hey you,' she said, 'how's that baby of yours?'

'Hey . . . yourself.'

Was she panting? 'Are you okay, Pops? You're not in labour, are you?'

'God no. Do you think I'd be calling you if I was? The baby's getting bigger, so I'm a bit short of breath. I look like a friggin' heffalump.' Her laughter echoed down the line. 'No, all going according to plan on that front. Six weeks and counting. How's everything going up there?'

Faith snuck a glance over each shoulder. 'Not so good,' she confessed, her voice dropping to a whisper.

'What do you mean?'

'I just . . .' She had no idea where to even begin. 'There's a lot going on here,' she said, leading with a vague summary. 'These people are really nice,' she said, borrowing Stephanie's word. It wasn't exactly the best adjective for Rose, but it worked as a general description. 'I'm not sure I can lie to them anymore.'

There were a few quick puffs before Poppy replied. 'So, what are you going to do?'

How could she tell them the truth now, after she'd so blatantly deceived them all? 'I don't know.'

'Oh Monty,' Poppy went quiet. Faith knew what she was thinking, but she was so grateful she kept it to herself. 'Sorry to complicate things, but I got a call from your mum today.'

'My mum?'

'Stella,' Poppy said, sounding slightly irritated.

'What's she doing calling you?'

'They arrive back tomorrow.'

'Shit.' She jumped up, tightening her grip on the phone. She hadn't checked her emails for a few days. 'I didn't think they got back until next week?'

'They're coming back early so they can surprise you on your birthday. They wanted to make sure you'd be around. I could hardly tell them you're in the outback when they think you're beavering away at work. I can pick them up from the airport and stall them, but I need to know what you want me to say.'

Faith's head was spinning. Her parents always made such a fuss of her birthday. It had been fine when she was younger, but she was an adult, for heaven's sake. Why couldn't they just get on with their own lives like normal parents?

'Okay,' she said, more decisively. She was becoming a master at making things up as she went along. 'I'll email them and say I've headed off on a bit of a soul-searching trip after being retrenched. That'll buy me some time while I work out what to do here. Do you really want to pick them up, Pops? I'm sure you have better things to do.'

'I wish I did,' Poppy groaned. 'If I have to tidy that nursery one more time or go baby shopping with my mother again I think I'll neck myself. It's fine. I'll collect them and elaborate a bit on how you decided to take yourself off on an impromptu adventure.'

'Thanks, Pops, you're an angel.'

Amber stuck her head in the door, grumbling that she didn't get paid enough to run the place on her own.

'I've got to go. Look after yourself. Love to Nick.'

'Let me know what you decide about the other mother situation,' Poppy said. 'Love you.'

'Love you back.'

She hung up the phone, numb with dread. Things were crazy enough without throwing Stella and Brian into the mix. This was all getting too hard. It had been so straightforward when Rosemary Barnes had been nothing more than a name on a piece of paper, when there hadn't been a sister or a nephew or a guy she was trying not to fall for. They were all real people with problems of their own – and feelings she didn't want to hurt.

It was time to bring this whole stupid charade to an end.

Chapter Twelve

Rose

'JEEZ, MY PLACE IS IN A STATE, BUT THIS JOINT LOOKS positively bloody haunted.' Cleo screwed up her nose at the cobwebs and broken windowsill while Rose fiddled with the lock on Letty's door. Again.

'Tell me about it.' She jiggled the key one more time. 'Ah, success.' The two of them stepped inside, Rose trying not to gag at the memory of her last visit to the house.

'So, do you have any ideas for a suitable burial outfit for the old girl?'

'Not really. The undertaker asked me to find something appropriate.'

'What, like a witch's cape and hat?'

Rose gave a reluctant laugh. 'Don't be awful. The woman has passed, Cleo.'

'Yes, I know, but I'm no hypocrite and neither are you, Rosemary O'Shea. She was an old bat and never appreciated anything you did for her.' Cleo followed her into Letty's room.

'And now you have to clean up after her so those scumbag sons can reap the rewards. It's not right.'

It had been a while since Rose had set foot in the bedroom. She watched her friend's face as she gazed, wide-eyed, around the walls. A faded print of the Virgin Mary hung above the bed. She was holding a heart-shaped vessel pierced by a knife, her head slightly bowed, surrounded by a halo of sickly yellow light. The gilt-edged frame was cracking, small flakes of gold peeling away and dusting the pillow beneath. On the opposite wall was a large wooden cross with a ceramic figurine of Jesus nailed onto it, his face contorted with pain, his ribs exposed above the cloth wrapped around his waist. A string of rosary beads hung from a hook screwed into the wall at the base of the crucifix.

'That's disgusting.' Cleo shuddered. 'For a woman who was supposedly so religious, she wasn't exactly a shining light of Christian charity, was she?'

'No, not exactly.' Rose wrinkled her nose at the pungent mix of moth balls and eucalyptus that permeated the room.

'Do you think she'd be up there with Mick?'

'If she is she's no doubt giving him a hard time for leaving me to look after her,' Rose scoffed, then sobered. 'I'm not really sure, to be honest. I mean, if there's a heaven or not. I'd like to think there is, that we'll all see each other again one day when we shuffle off, but then I wonder if it's just something we humans have made up to make ourselves feel better about dying.'

'I don't know either, but I do know if you and I meet again up there after we've carked it,' Cleo pointed towards the ceiling, 'there'll be one helluva party going on. And your mother-in-law will not be invited.'

'And I'll well and truly be wringing Michael O'Shea's neck when I get there.' Bringing Cleo along had been a stroke of genius. Stephanie had gone to drop off Jake, and Dave . . . well, she didn't really want to ask Dave for any more favours at the moment, even though they'd done the post mortem on their one-night stand. She looked at her friend and was tempted to spill the beans, but no, there'd be time for that later. 'Anyway, down to business.'

Pulling open the wardrobe door, she flicked one by one through the hangers. There were a few pairs of slacks, a couple of knitted cardigans, four tweed skirts that looked like they'd come out of the ark and, right at the back, two dresses that could only be described as dowdy.

Rose held up two outfits for Cleo's inspection. 'Looks like it's one of these.' The first was a long-sleeved brown knit that closely resembled a potato sack and the other was a maroon suit, a jacket-and-skirt ensemble that, while obviously ancient, might pass muster. 'What do you think?'

Cleo came closer and eyed the choices. 'Definitely not that,' she said, pointing at the brown number and pulling a face. 'Has she got some sort of blouse to go with the other one?'

Rose shuffled around in the closet and found a cream collared shirt. 'It's got a bit of a stain on the front,' she said, holding it up to the light and peering over the top of her glasses.

'Rosie,' Cleo said, taking her by the arm, 'no one is going to notice it, my lovely. She'll be in a coffin.'

They looked at each other, unable to stifle the inevitable laughter.

'I knew it was a good idea bringing you along,' Rosie said.

'Of course it was. Now, let's see if she has a nice brooch or something to pin on that lapel. And what about her wedding ring? Would she want to be buried in that?'

'Good thought. Yes, she probably would.'

Rose laid the selected outfit on the bed and opened the top drawer of the dressing table to find a hairbrush, an old fob watch and a red velvet ring holder. She picked it up and flipped it open. Inside was what looked like an engagement ring, a small emerald with a diamond on either side set into filigree, and a plain, thin gold band. Simple but stunning. Letty had never worn jewellery as long as Rose had known her, but at some point these rings must have been on her finger. At some point she had been a young, married girl. Had she been happy then? Was it the move to a foreign country and the loss of her beloved son that had turned her into such a cranky, miserable woman?

Cleo had moved to Rose's side. 'What's in this?' she said, picking up a small box, a lacquered image of rolling green hills on the lid. She gave it a rattle.

'No idea,' Rose shrugged. 'Have a look.'

Cleo wriggled the top off to reveal a single sheet of folded paper, which Rose pulled out and opened. She scanned the page. It was Letty's handwriting, which even at the best of times was barely legible, and the date at the top was 5 April 2010. Five years ago, a few months after Mick's death. She lifted a hand to her mouth, holding it firmly against her lips as she read on. The paper in her hand began to flutter. Beside her Cleo's breath hitched. When she got to the end she turned to her friend who, for once in her life, was speechless. 'Do you think this is legal?'

Cleo took the paper from Rose and ran her finger down to the bottom, to where Letty's signature was scrawled above a second name followed by the words *Justice of the Peace*. 'I can't see why not. I mean, it's not from a solicitor or anything but it's signed and witnessed.' She handed it back to Rose.

'Holy shit!'

An arm flew around Rose's shoulder as Cleo wrangled her into a hug. 'Maybe she wasn't such a mean old stick after all.' They fell backwards onto the bed and cackled like a pair of crazed kookaburras.

If the will Rose was holding in her hand was above board, Cleo was right. Letty had fooled them all.

Stephanie

'SO, I'LL COME BACK AND PICK HIM UP IN THE MORNING,' she said stiffly. This whole situation was so weird, so other-worldly. Jake had run straight off to play with Peppie, leaving the two of them standing in the front yard like a couple of kids in the playground on their first day at school. The morning heat was making her feel unsteady. She swayed a little, blinking her eyes and focusing on her breathing.

'You okay?' Bryce asked, frowning.

'Yeah, I'm fine,' she lied.

She looked out across the paddocks. A strange haze shimmered above the earth, making the wide expanse of red dust almost iridescent. A few wayward clouds idled on the horizon. The day was eerily quiet. Everything seemed . . . desolate. How could she be here, face to face with her husband – her best friend, the father of her son and unborn child – and not have a clue what to say next? Neither of them had mentioned her current 'holiday' at The Crossroads. And if Bryce wasn't going to comment on it then she certainly wasn't going to bring it up. She was tired of being the peace-maker. Tired full stop. If he wanted to play the let's-stick-our-heads-in-the-sand game, she wasn't going to spoil his fun.

Bandit ambled over to the fence and whinnied. At least someone was happy to see her. Turning away from Bryce, she walked the length of the yard to meet him, rubbing his cheek and resting her forehead against his. She closed her eyes and inhaled that familiar, horsey scent. Home.

'Hey there, old friend,' she whispered. 'I hope he's looking after you.' Bryce was probably only throwing him and Maisie – too lazy to leave the shelter of the tree – a piece of hay morning and night. They were her babies, not his. Unlike the one she was carrying. 'I'll be home soon,' she said, trying to convince herself as much as the horse.

Jake bolted out from inside, already changed into his bike-riding gear, his little legs protected by the thick leather padding and his helmet stuck under his arm. She watched as he placed it on the ground and ran back into the shed. He was in his element. A biking day with Dad. It would do him good, do both of them good. She made her way back to where Bryce was still standing, hands in his pockets, watching his son. She wanted to reach out and touch him, loop her hand through his arm and rest her chin on his shoulder. But that would be sending the wrong message. He needed to know that she was serious – that she would come home when he was willing to let her in, willing to talk, willing to change.

'I'll leave you to it,' she said.

'Oh, right.' It was as if he'd just remembered she was there.

'See you in the morning.' She didn't bother looking back at him as she made her way over to Jake. The events of the past few weeks had toughened her up, put a steel rod into her previously supple spine. But not where Jake was concerned. 'You have fun, Bear,' she said kneeling down, pulling him into a cuddle and planting a sloppy kiss on his cheek.

He squirmed. 'Urgh, Muuummm.'

When had that started? When had her little boy decided that squishy kisses and Mummy were yuk?

'Just for that . . .' She tickled him and kissed him again. This time he threw his arms around her neck and gave her an eskimo kiss in return.

'That's better. Ride safely. I love you.' Her voice splintered around the words. Why did leaving him here, in his own home, with his father, feel so unsettling?

'Love you too, Mummy,' he said, and then, calling to Bryce, 'Come on, Dad!'

He ran towards his father and grabbed his hand, pulling him into the shed. A shadow fell across her heart as she watched them disappear into the darkness. She had the sudden urge to run after them, take Jake's hand and put him in the car, take him back to The Crossroads. No. She was just being silly. Jake was going to have a lovely time with his dad and, she hoped, vice versa. Maybe Bryce would realise what he was missing. She looked towards the house. She really needed to collect a few more of her things and some extra clothes for Jake, but if she walked back inside right now she wasn't sure she'd be able to leave. No, she needed to be strong. The clothes could wait until tomorrow. Maybe then she wouldn't need them anyway.

As she opened the car door Bandit gave her another urgent whinny. Without looking back at him she turned the key in the ignition, kept her eyes fixed straight ahead and drove away, the road in front of her dissolving in a rust-coloured blur.

Faith

IT WAS THE FIRST CHANCE SHE'D HAD TO PACK HER BAGS. She'd been too exhausted last night and was hard at it behind the bar again first thing this morning. As soon as Rose had returned from whatever she was doing at her mother-in-law's place – in a bizarrely upbeat mood for someone who had just chosen a mourning outfit for a dead relative – Faith had clocked off and practically sprinted up the stairs. For the past forty-eight hours she'd gone over and over the options and kept coming up with the same conclusion: the best thing to do was to leave. She'd come here to meet her birth mother, and she had. Despite her initial grumpiness, Rose had turned out to be a decent woman, a woman who, for whatever reason, had not been able to keep her child. A woman to who Faith might one day be able to reveal her true identity. Springing a long-lost daughter on Rose right now just didn't feel right. The timing was all wrong. Perhaps later, when she'd processed the whole thing, dealt with her own feelings about being adopted, she could get back in contact, but in the meantime she had to get back to her real life.

She pulled the last of her things from the cupboard and laid them on the bed, folding her clothes one item at a time and stacking them into her suitcase. Her champagne-pink, designer suitcase. What had she been thinking bringing that out here? It didn't exactly fit the carefree young traveller image. Admittedly almost everyone had believed her story – everyone except Declan. A smile sprang to her lips as she remembered the wary look he'd given her when she pulled that first beer. Luckily he and Cam had been the only two in the bar that afternoon. Cam, previously known as Jerk-face. Her smile widened. What a tool he'd been when they first met. Hot. But a tool. So different to what he really was, who he was. She picked up her once-white Converse, now dirt stained and shabby from their walk. Their one night together. When she'd felt like a different person, and yet never more like herself.

If they'd met somewhere else, some other time . . .

Tears pooled in the corners of her eyes. She whipped them away with the back of her hand, shoved the shoes into the top of her bag and banged the lid shut. It was stupid. She hardly knew the guy.

A sharp knock had her head whirling towards the door, one hand still on the case, the other flying to her chest. She absolutely did not want to speak to anyone. Whoever was out there would go away if she didn't answer, didn't make any noise. Another knock.

And then a voice. 'Faith? It's me, Cam. Are you in there?'

Shit!

She waited, hunching over – as if lowering her body closer to the floor was going to make a difference.

'I know you're there. Rose told me you'd come upstairs.'

Maybe he was bluffing. She crouched a little lower. If she stayed quiet long enough he'd get the message and go.

'Faith, please, I want to talk to you. Can I come in?'

Her eyes darted to the door knob. It wasn't locked. If he wanted to he could walk right on in. Or she could open the door and act like an adult. Be upfront instead of sneaking away without an explanation. After all, wasn't the whole point of leaving to stop being so deceitful?

'Just a minute.' She straightened herself up, inhaled a lungful of air and took the four short steps to the door. Her hand trembled as she reached out to open it.

'Hi.' Did he have to look so damned freakin' handsome. Every bit as delicious as he had on Saturday night, but definitely not anywhere near as happy. That mouth – *oh, that mouth* – was definitely not smiling.

'You didn't answer my calls or reply to my texts,' he said, hands in his pockets, looking directly into her eyes.

'No.' Best to keep it simple.

'Any particular reason?'

She wasn't sure what to do with her hands. If she had pockets of her own that's where they'd be stuck. She tucked her hair back behind both ears at once, before pinning her arms across her chest.

'Look, can I come in for a minute?'

She took a step back, and let him into the room. He stopped beside the bed, his gaze on the suitcase.

'You going somewhere?'

Crunch time. 'Yes,' she said, and then more forcefully. 'Yes, I am.'

'What, as in you're leaving town?'

She dipped her head. 'I, um, have to get back to Sydney.'

'Why?'

Why? Why did he need to know?

'I got a job offer.'

Cam looked suspicious. 'You said you were taking some time off to think about what you wanted to do next?'

'Yeah, I was. I have. Anyway, this job's come up out of the blue and it's too good an offer to refuse.' What was wrong with her? Was she completely incapable of telling the truth anymore?

'Right.' He moved a step closer. She uncrossed her arms and let them hang as he spoke again. 'Still doesn't explain why you didn't answer my calls.'

He wasn't going to let her off the hook. She ran her tongue across her bottom lip and forced her eyes up. As much as she hated to do it, she didn't have a choice. 'Look, Cam, I had a really nice time with you, but it was just a one-night thing. I thought you knew that.'

He studied her face, as if he was trying to work out a tricky anagram, one that was perhaps missing a letter. 'No,' he said, the crease between his brows deepening. 'No, I didn't know that.'

'You're transient here and so am I, so it was never going to be anything else.' She was on a roll now, almost believing her own bullshit.

'So, it was just a quick fuck.'

She flinched. 'Pretty much.' Quick wasn't really an apt description, but it was better not to quibble.

'Well, there you go.' He shook his head with a mournful sort of laugh. 'I've always considered myself a pretty good judge of character. Looks like this time I was wrong.'

It would have been easier if he'd been pissed off. They could yell at each other and she could kick him out feeling all justified and saintly. But it wasn't anger in his tone – it was disappointment. A lump formed at the base of her throat. She swallowed past it – she was not going to cry. If he didn't get out of here her resolve was going to falter. Not game to risk another look at him, she turned towards the door and pulled it open.

From the corner of her eye she saw him start to make an exit, but then he stopped slap bang in front of her. She looked down at the patch of mud on the front of his boot. The boots he'd been wearing that night he'd snuck into the bar and conned her into giving him a drink. The night she'd floated up to her room feeling like a smitten schoolgirl.

'Bye Faith. It was nice to meet you.' His farewell was strained, barely audible.

She watched the boots walk away, kept her head down until they were out of her line of vision, and waited a few seconds before letting the door click quietly shut.

You've just made a huge mistake, Faith.

The tightness in her stomach and the tears welling in her eyes told her that the voice in her head was most probably right. But it was done now, he was gone. And the sooner she left Birralong, the better.

Chapter Thirteen

Rose

SHE RAN HER HAND ACROSS THE OLD POLISHED TIMBERS ON the bar top, her eyes over the photos cluttering the walls. Dozens of customers smiling, laughing, celebrating. She hoped that whoever bought the place would carry on the tradition, not that there was much room left up there. It was only just starting to sink in: someone else would soon own The Crossroads. Her throat tightened. It seemed impossible. Mick had bought the pub the year he arrived in town with money he'd inherited from his grandfather. It had taken him eighteen months of travelling around the country before he 'hit the jackpot'. That's how he described it afterwards – finding the perfect hotel and meeting Rose, all at the same time. It wasn't quite love at first sight, but not far off. He'd swept her off her feet with his Irish charm, said her red hair reminded him of his mother. God forbid. And then they'd thrown themselves into doing up the building, filling it with people and music. Mick had always been a party person and Rose loved listening to the customers' tales, all the time dreaming that one day it would be the two of them taking to the road. He promised he'd take her back to Ireland one day, when they could afford it, when Stephanie was older, when the business allowed them to escape. But one day never came. Deep down she knew he was only saying it to keep her happy. Birralong might have been his adopted home, but it was one he never really wanted to leave. And then the cancer got its claws into him. Less than two months and he was gone. It all happened so fast, a frenzy of doctors' appointments, visits to Brisbane, specialists' referrals, a token course of chemo, but the medicos had been straight with them from the start: it had spread so far already that there was virtually no hope. Afterwards she'd been numb. She'd stepped into Mick's shoes as the publican, kept his memory alive. It was almost as if he hadn't died. As if he'd just popped down to the cellar and left her to run things for a bit.

Soon it would be someone else standing right here in her place.

Even though she'd made the decision, had made it public, it still hurt.

She rested an elbow on the bar, leant her cheek against her upturned palm and hummed out a sigh but there was no one close enough to hear. A few locals were chatting at the other end of the room, but otherwise it was quiet. Faith was upstairs in her room. Stephanie was due back from dropping off Jake, and Rose was champing at the bit for her to return. At least Letty's legacy was something to be happy about.

And bingo, here was Steph right now, walking through the front door. Rose watched her closely, took in the sag of her shoulders, the pinched, haunted look on her face. People had always commented on what a beautiful girl she was, fresh-faced, her long brown hair as sleek as melted toffee. But today she looked drained, older than her years. There was a shadow over her. One that Rose was about to lift.

'Hello there,' she chirped. 'Get the little fella off all right?'

'Yeah.'

'Took you a while.'

Stephanie pulled up a stool and sank onto it, her body sagging. 'I went for a drive after I dropped him off,' she said drearily.

Rose barely listened. She was too desperate to break the news. 'I have something to tell you.'

'Oh, really?' Steph took off her hat and scratched at a mark on the brim. 'What now?'

She'd been noticeably cool ever since the announcement about The Crossroads, but Rose ignored her snarky tone and continued. 'Cleo and I went around to Letty's to find an outfit for the burial.'

'I know that already, Mum.'

'Stay with me. I'm getting to the good part.' She reached behind a tray of glasses and pulled out the piece of paper she and Cleo had found secreted away in her mother-in-law's dressing table. 'We found this.' She unfolded it, spun it around and placed it in front of Stephanie.

As she read, the look on her daughter's face changed from annoyance to surprise and then to disbelief. 'Is this for real?'

Rose nodded. 'She left you everything, Steph. The house, her savings, the money your father willed to her that she'd hoarded away.' She clapped her hands together. 'The lot of it.'

'But why would she do that? Why wouldn't she leave it to you? You're the one who looked after her all these years. Put up with her crap. I've barely seen her since Jake was born.'

'I know, I know. But I guess, when it comes down to it, you're flesh and blood and I'm not.'

'What about Dad's brothers?'

Rose reached over and took the will from Stephanie. Pulling off her glasses, she ran her index finger along the words as she read them aloud. 'Under no circumstances should any allowance be made for either of my surviving sons, Collin Ray O'Shea and Edward William O'Shea, to receive any of my property or money. Neither of them has contacted me or done anything to assist me in any way at all for the past ten years and it is my decision that my house and the entirety of my savings go directly to my only granddaughter, Stephanie Clare Bailey.' She looked back up at Stephanie. 'I'm no lawyer, but she made what she wanted pretty clear. Even if they did bother to contest it I don't think they'd have a leg to stand on.'

'Wow, that's great,' Stephanie said flatly. Her chin fell to her chest, and she covered her face with her hands.

If Rose could have highjumped across the bar to get to her daughter quicker she would have, but instead she made a dash for the partition, threw it up and was by her side in a matter of seconds. She put an arm around Stephanie's shoulder and kissed the top of her head, just like she used to when she was a little girl. 'Is it Bryce?'

Stephanie nodded.

'Oh, sweetheart, it'll be all right. Everyone has their moments. Lord knows your father and I did, but we got through. You and Bryce are made for each other. Whatever it is, you'll sort it out.'

Stephanie choked on a sob. She lifted her head and wiped at her cheeks. 'He's changed, Mum. I don't even know who he is anymore.'

Rose knew exactly what she meant. Bryce had always been quiet, but lately he'd become flat-out contrary. And rude. Not what Stephanie needed to hear, though. 'He's just got things on his mind, love.'

'He has, I know. But he used to include me in those things, we were a team. Now it's *his* farm and *his* problems. He won't let me in. He seems to resent everything I do.' Her voice cracked. 'We hardly even talk anymore.'

'What's he like with Jake?' Rose asked.

Stephanie fell quiet, looked down to where her hands rested in her lap and prodded at a spot in the middle of her palm. 'Jake's the only person he still seems to want to be around.' She shook her head and flicked her eyes back up to Rose. 'We had this massive fight the other night. I . . . I said he might need to see a counsellor and he went ballistic. Started screaming like a madman, throwing things around. I was really frightened. Jake woke up and came out.'

'And that's why you came into town for a few days,' Rose said, nodding slowly.

'I left him a note saying a bit of space would be good for us. He hasn't even asked me when I'm coming home.'

'But he still wanted to see Jake.'

'Yes.'

'Well, that's a good sign. He hasn't cut himself off completely. How did he seem when you were there this morning?'

'He didn't say much.' She gave a quick shrug. 'I didn't think it was the time to get into it, not with Jake there.'

'Hmm.' Rose drummed her fingers on the bar top. 'How about tomorrow I come out with you and bring Jakey boy back here so you and Bryce can have a proper talk, clear the air. You can tell him about the inheritance – that should spark him up a bit.'

'Maybe.'

Rose gave her shoulder another rub. She'd never wanted Stephanie to tie herself down at such a young age, but the marriage seemed to be a match made in heaven. Until now. No wonder Stephanie had been looking so drawn lately.

A problem shared is a problem halved.

A buzz came from Steph's back pocket and she reached around to fish out her phone. 'It's Bryce.'

Rose moved away to let her take the call. She busied herself checking the snack machine, flicking the odd glance at Stephanie, and trying to zero in on the subject of the conversation. While she couldn't hear the voice on the other end she could see the effect his words were having on her daughter.

'What do you mean he's gone?' Steph's eyes grew larger as she held onto the edge of the bar with her free hand. 'Bryce? Bryce are you there?' She stood slowly, frowning as she listened to her husband on the other end of the line.

Rose returned, laid a hand on Stephanie's arm only to have it brushed away.

'Bryce!' she screamed. 'Bryce, are you there?'

Rose held her breath as Stephanie lowered the phone and looked up. 'There's been an accident,' she said, her voice shaking. 'Bryce is injured.' Her next words were barely loud enough for Rose to hear. 'Jake's missing.'

Stephanie

'STEPHANIE.' HER MOTHER'S VOICE WAS MUFFLED, COMING AT her through a haze. 'Stephanie, what's happened, what's wrong?'

Her hand began to shake and the phone fell with a clunk to the floor. When she leaned down to pick it up, there was Jake smiling at her on the screen saver, snuggling with Peppie, his arms circling the dog's neck. She lifted a hand to her mouth, pressed two trembling fingers against her lips. 'Um, it's . . . it's Jake, he's gone missing.' Saying it again tipped her over the edge. Her body became too heavy for her legs. They bent beneath her like boughs that bowed but refused to break. There was a noise as something fell away from her and crashed and she tipped forward, supporting herself against the bar.

'Steph.' Her mother's arms were around her waist, holding her up. The scent of vanilla. A flash of auburn hair.

'I'll grab a chair.' A different voice, another pair of hands. They lowered her into a seat. She couldn't be here; she couldn't be sitting here like this when her son was out there somewhere on his own. Lost. But everything was spinning and it was taking all her concentration not to throw up.

'Keep your head down for a minute.' Her mother again.

She nodded and closed her eyes.

Stay calm.

The sooner she pulled herself together the sooner she could find Jake.

'Would you like a drink?' A glass appeared in front of her. The other pair of hands. Faith. Her lavender eyes.

She took a few tentative sips. Tiny black dots danced as she looked down into the water. She wiped them away with the back of her hand, blinking a few times as she righted herself. 'I need to go home,' she began slowly, testing to see if she could actually speak. She could probably manage if she took it one phrase at a time. 'Bryce had an accident. On the bike.

He passed out. Jake was on his pee wee. But when Bryce came to, he couldn't find him.'

'How long was Bryce unconscious?'

'I don't know. He sounded strange, slurry.' Was that how she sounded now? 'He didn't have his phone on him. He came back to the house to call me.'

'So, is he going back out to look for Jake?'

She found her mother's eyes. They stared at each other for a few seconds, frozen. 'I think he might have passed out again.'

'Call him.'

'What?'

'Here, give me the phone.' There were people around. Stephanie knew they were there, that they were all gawking, but she watched her mother hold the phone to her ear, listen, hit end and then dial again.

Come on, Bryce. Please. Just answer.

Rose ended the call. 'Right, we need to ring an ambulance. It sounds like Bryce is injured. We need to get out there.'

'Mum,' she choked out.

'It'll be okay, love.' Her mother sounded so sure, so definite. 'It'll be all right,' she said, gently. But as she rounded up the few customers who remained, her voice wasn't gentle at all. 'Young Jake's missing out at Strathmore. We're going to need all hands on deck.'

While Rose bustled around giving instructions Stephanie made herself stand, dragged the car keys from her back pocket and started towards the door. Stepping outside she looked up and the sight that met her eyes caught like a knife in her chest. A bank of angry clouds bruised the horizon growing deeper and darker with each passing second. A sickly yellow light paled the sky. Something growled in the distance. Her mouth began to water and she swallowed hard to stop the acid bubbling inside her belly from creeping its way up her oesophagus.

Thunder.

For the past four years she had gone to bed every night and prayed for rain. Only a very few times had her prayers had been answered.

This time she begged for the complete opposite.

'Not now,' she whispered, 'please not now.'

Please don't let it rain.

Faith

JUST SAY IT. STRAIGHT OUT. WHAT CAN SHE DO? YOU'RE A casual worker. No contract. No obligation. Things happen, circumstances change. Stephanie was here to help, and there was always Amber. She kept up the pep-talk all the way down the stairs trying to convince herself that the story she'd concocted to tell Rose would be met with a smile.

Of course, her time working for the woman suggested otherwise. She ran through her spiel one more time: her parents had been forced to return from overseas because her mother had fallen ill with a weird virus, and Faith had to go home immediately. Who was going to argue with that? Yes, it was yet another lie, but it did include a half-truth. They were coming home, voluntarily and not sick, but those were details she didn't need to broadcast. Besides, what did another lie matter in the whole revolting, sticky web she'd already spun.

She stopped outside the bar and closed her eyes. Her stomach was still reeling from the scene with Cam – now she was going

to do an encore performance with her birth mother. But it was
for the best, for everyone. Taking one last courage-inducing
breath, she rounded the corner – just in time to see a stool
crash to the ground, Stephanie in a state of near collapse and
Rose struggling to hold her upright.

'Shit.'

'I'll get a chair,' she called out, rushing towards them. The
whole room had fallen into a hush. A few customers stood to
help, but Rose flapped them away. Faith's heart began to race.
She'd never been good with emergencies, tended towards total
panic, but with Rose taking charge, talking gently as she stroked
her daughter's arm, Faith had time to get her flibberty-jibbet
nerves under control. Stephanie had turned ghostly white and
looked like she was about to vomit. Water. Wasn't that always
what they offered first? Faith ran behind the bar and filled
a glass. When she returned Stephanie looked up at her, eyes
bleary and distant and took a few small sips. Rose, kneeling
by her side, gave a tight smile and nodded towards the bar.

A customer, one of only three, was standing at the other
end. Could he not see that there was a problem here?

'Schooner of New, thanks,' he said as Faith approached.
She recognised his slick black comb-over but didn't know his
name. 'What's going on with young Stephanie?'

'No idea,' she replied, coolly. 'Not feeling too well, I guess.'

Comb-over man nodded, as if this answer explained everything, took his beer and retreated back to his table. She busied
herself wiping down the already clean counter, keeping one eye
on the other end of the room. Stephanie, still hideously pale,
had come around, and she and Rose were talking frantically to
someone on the phone and to each other. Whatever it was, it
did not look good. Huddled so close together, the similarities

between the two women were obvious – the same oval face, the same softly curving profile. Mother and daughter. A real mother and daughter who had the same history – a history she wasn't a part of and a bond she would never truly share. She and Stella shared a history though, a lifelong history, all bar a few weeks. Wasn't that the important thing in all of this? Longing swamped her like an errant wave, left her giddy and floundering. She huffed out a breath and tried to regroup.

Rose stood swiftly and spun around. She marched towards the boggle-eyed drinkers, waving her arms wildly as if trying to scare off a pack of marauding crows. 'Young Jake's missing out at Strathmore. We're going to need all hands on deck.' The men started to skoll their drinks before Rose even reached their table. They followed her instructions and mumbled their way out the door.

Faith watched Rose approach, a sense of urgency in her stride, a fiery determination in her eyes.

'There's been an accident out at the farm. I have to drive Stephanie home,' she said.

Poor Stephanie. No wonder she'd almost passed out. Faith contained her curiosity and tried to make herself useful. 'I can close up here if you like – or keep the bar open until normal closing time?'

Rose paused for a minute staring at the photo-laden walls, her eyes misty, shifting from image to image. 'No,' she said finally. 'It's better if you come. Jake's somewhere on the property, and it sounds like Bryce is injured. We're going to need all the help we can get.'

She nodded, although she doubted she'd be any help at all. The sight of blood made her want to throw up. She was the person most likely to fall apart if things got ugly, but Rose had asked her and she couldn't refuse. After all, Jake was her nephew, even if she was the only one who knew.

She locked up the till and headed for the stairs. 'I'll just run up and grab my bag,'

'No time for that.'

They were at the ute in a matter of seconds. Stephanie was already belted into the passenger seat. Rose climbed in on the driver's side, and as Faith pulled open the back door a fat drop of rain splashed against her cheek. She looked up to a sky blistering with thick, black clouds, and scuttled into the car. As more drops began to fall, beating out a weird, staccato rhythm against the metal roof, Faith suddenly remembered why she'd come downstairs.

Her plan to leave, it appeared, would have to wait.

Chapter Fourteen

Rose

RAIN POUNDED THE WINDSCREEN. SHEETS OF WATER COVERED the road and Rose's eyes stung as she tried to focus. Thank God it was straight and flat. Twice now the car had planed across the dirt surface and she didn't want to risk it happening again.

The swish of the windscreen wipers was curiously comforting. Inside the car nobody spoke. Stephanie sat slumped in the front passenger seat. Her hair had been pulled back into a loose bun with just a few strands falling around her face. Her body angled slightly towards the window and curled in on itself, she looked smaller. She wore the same lost expression as she had the time her cat, Spider, had been hit by a car. The poor thing had come limping back into the pub, dragging his back leg behind him, and had fallen into the little girl's lap and died. Just like that. Stephanie had looked down at the black-and-white bundle of fur, dry eyed, staring hard, trying to comprehend what had happened. She didn't speak, didn't wail, but purely by her body language – and the look of utter devastation on her face – Rose knew her child's heart was broken. Just like she knew it now. She wanted to reach out and grab Stephanie's hand, tell her it was all going to be okay, but taking one hand off the wheel was too big a risk. That her grandson was out there somewhere in this hideous weather actually beggared belief.

'Stop!' Stephanie's screech was loud even over the deafening noise of the rain. She jumped upright, fingers clutching the dashboard.

'What is it?' Rose hazarded a quick glance at her daughter.

'Stop the car. I think I saw something, back there.'

Hitting the brakes too hard could send them skittering. Rose gently lowered her foot, not bothering to pull to the side of the road. Before the car was even at a standstill Stephanie had launched herself out the door leaving it open behind her, water teeming onto the seat. Rose reached across to try to close it, but her belt jammed and she found herself pinned. 'Shit.'

'I'll get it,' Faith said flinging open her own door and leaping out. Rose had forgotten the girl was even there. Taking a little more time, she released the tension on the seat belt, undid it and climbed out of the car. Her foot sank into a pothole overflowing with water. Lifting it out and sidestepping the hole, she squinted through the rain to see Stephanie standing by the boundary fence, hands raised to cover her eyes, looking out at the water-logged paddocks. From her stance Rose could see she was searching for something – someone.

'What's happening?' Faith's voice was faint as she stepped up beside Rose. The girl's hair was plastered to her scalp.

'Wait here,' Rose said.

She jogged along the road, water streaming down her face and inching beneath the collar of her shirt, calling to Stephanie as she approached. By the time she reached her side the two of them were drenched to the bone.

'What is it, Steph? What did you see?' She put an arm around Stephanie's shoulder and looked out into the distance.

'I saw something move. Over there by that boulder.'

Rose wiped both hands across her eyes to try to clear her vision and looked to where Stephanie was pointing. 'There's nothing there, love. Might have been a kangaroo trying to get to shelter, or your eyes playing tricks.' She waited for the bite back but it never came. Stephanie merely fell against her and hung her head. 'Come on,' Rose said, trying to infuse some oomph into her voice. 'The quicker we get there the quicker we find him.'

Wrapped around each other, heads down, they trudged back to the car in silence. Their boots sloshed through gullies of water on the road, pools Rose knew full well from years of living in the outback could soon become a flood.

And if that happened, the chances of finding her grandson safe were slim.

Stephanie

Please let them be okay. Please.

She repeated the same phrase over and over in her head all the way out to Strathmore. It was the only way she could stop her mind from going somewhere darker. Somewhere with pictures of Bryce lying dead on the kitchen floor, his eyes wide and staring, mouth gaping, the phone lying in the open palm of his outstretched hand. Pictures of Jake, his bike abandoned, curls flattened by the rain, eyes stinging as he tried to find shelter in the hollow of a tree. Calling for her.

Please let them be okay. Please.

Please . . .

Drive faster, she wanted to scream at her mother, even though she knew it was completely irrational, that Rose was getting them there as quickly as she could. If she hadn't made them stop they'd be there by now. She must have fallen into some kind of paralysis when they reached the gate, had just sat there like a sun-drunk skink while Faith jumped out and opened it and Rose drove on through. Now all three of them were soaking wet. But who cared? Getting there and finding both of her boys safe was more important.

She couldn't see anything much out the window, but she knew exactly where they were, knew every bump and rut in the road. As soon as her mother pulled up in the yard she jumped out, dimly registering Bryce's bike, lying on its side by the fence.

Her husband's name stuck in her throat as she vaulted up the steps, yanked open the door and raced into the kitchen. The sight of him lying there motionless wrenched it free. 'Bryce.' He was on his back, Peppie nuzzled into his side. The dog's tail thumped against the tiles as Stephanie's knees hit the floor with a thud. 'Bryce, can you hear me?' She cradled his face with her hands.

He didn't move. Didn't speak.

But his cheeks were warm, that was good wasn't it? Pulse, feel for a pulse. She held two fingers to the inside of his wrist. Shuffling came from somewhere behind her. Footsteps. She lowered her head, bent forward and stayed completely still. There it was, blood flowing through his veins, the swell of it beneath her fingertips. 'He's okay,' she said, emptying the air from her lungs.

Rose kneeled beside her. 'A few cuts and scrapes by the looks of it,' she said.

Stephanie scanned his body, her eyes coming to a quick halt where her mother's hand hovered above his shin. His jeans were ripped below the knee and there was a hump where one shouldn't be. A bone. A wave of nausea rolled through her body.

'Looks like it's broken.' Rose sat back on her haunches, raised her eyes to Stephanie's. 'No wonder he passed out. I can't believe he made it back here.'

'It was the only way he could help Jake.'

'Putting this on might help.' Faith spoke softly as she held out a cloth. 'I'm not much good at first aid, but I've seen them do it in movies.'

'Thanks.' Stephanie took the cool, damp wad of material and placed it on her husband's forehead.

'I'm going to call and see where that bloody ambulance is,' Rose said, pushing herself to her feet. 'And we're going to need the police out here to look for Jake.'

'Cameron.' The idea came to Stephanie in a flash. 'Ring Cameron. He's the only other person who knows this place the way Bryce and I do. We need to get him out here.'

'I can call him,' Faith offered.

She left her mother and Faith to make the calls and turned her attention back to Bryce.

'Please wake up, babe, please. We need you.'

Drops of water fell from her hair onto the cut on Bryce's temple. The blood had congealed on the wound, but the water moistened it again, sending a faint trail down his cheekbone, like a crimson tear. Stephanie bent lower and kissed it away.

His skin was clammy beneath her lips. This was so far from the reunion she had wanted, the one she had imagined. The man she loved was unconscious on the floor and their son was out there somewhere, alone. She wanted them to be a family again, to be happy again, like they were before. They would get through this. They just had to find Jake.

'Bryce,' she whispered, a palm against each of his cheeks, 'can you hear me?' She sat a little more upright, kept her eyes on his face, forced some steel into her voice. 'Where's Jake?'

The sound of his son's name seemed to rouse him. His eyelids flickered. He groaned.

'Jake,' she urged him again. 'Where is he?'

'Don't know,' he mumbled. 'Woke up. Gone.' Bryce's head tipped to one side as he fell back into silence.

Stephanie had no doubt Jake would have gone to get help. He wasn't even five yet but he was smart and sassy and knew his way around the farm.

My boy.

'Cameron's on his way.' Faith hovered, one arm folded across her body, clutching the other to her side. 'He won't be long. Said he was just down the road, at . . . Rivonlea?'

'It's the next property.' Stephanie looked up at her mother. 'Where's the ambulance?' She could hear the pitch of her voice rising but she didn't care.

Rose walked to the window and peered out. 'Thank God. Here they are right now.'

'The police? Where are they?' This was all happening way too slowly. Why weren't there people here to help?

'I called Paul.' Her mother was being ridiculously calm. 'He's out at Maxine and Ted's place, some sort of emergency out there, but he's getting on to the rescue team. They'll have people out here as quickly as possible.'

'How long?'

'I'm not sure. But they'll be here as soon as they can, love.'

'Well it's not soon enough,' she screamed as she pushed herself to her feet. This was her son they were talking about, her son was missing and people were fucking around. She was not going to just sit around here and wait and do nothing while Jake was out there alone.

All three women turned towards a noise as two paramedics rattled a trolley into the kitchen. Stephanie stumbled through what she knew of the afternoon's events as they moved in to do their assessment.

'Concussion,' she heard one of them mumble a few minutes later.

'Broken tibia.'

'Head wound will need stitching.'

Bryce twitched, gave a quiet moan. 'The old windmill.'

Stephanie sank back onto her knees beside him, the voices around her buzzing like white noise in her brain beneath the words that had spewed from Bryce's mouth: *The old windmill.*

'Bryce.' She shook his shoulder but he didn't stir. 'Bryce.' One of the paramedics gave her a glare as he strapped a mask to her husband's face.

She wiped his hair back off his forehead and spoke quietly into his ear so only he could hear. 'I'm going to go find him. He'll be okay. I'll find him and then we'll come see you in the hospital. I love you.' A final kiss to his forehead and she stood again. Bryce was injured, but he was going to be okay. She couldn't just stand around here any longer.

Rose followed her into the hallway. 'Where are you going, love?'

She was already slipping her arms into the sleeves of a Drizabone. 'To look for Jake.' She couldn't focus on anything else right now; not her husband, injured and in pain and about to be taken to hospital, not the baby nestled inside her womb, and not the look of concern darkening her mother's face.

'I'll come with you.' Rose began to pull another coat from the rack.

'No, Mum. It's pouring rain and we only have the two horses. I need one for Cameron.' She didn't have time to waste on this conversation. 'I need you to stay here and coordinate things. Keep the walkie-talkie in the kitchen switched on.'

'Steph, I know you're worried out of your mind.' Rose stepped in front of her and stood in the doorway, blocking her path. 'But we need to wait for the police. Do this properly.'

She plucked a two-way from the shelf by the door, gritted her teeth. 'There's only a couple of hours of daylight left, which is why I need to get out there right now and find him.'

'But you can't go out there alone. At least wait for Cameron. Or some of the others – they'll be here soon.'

'Mum,' she snapped, 'I can't just sit here and do nothing.' Hysteria was making her screech. *Stay calm. Stay calm.* 'I'm going out there and I'm going to scour this place from top to bottom. Bandit knows the place as well as any human. He won't let anything happen to me. Now please, just move out of the way.'

Rose only moved closer, gripped Stephanie's arms and held her tight. 'Be careful.'

She shrugged her mother's hands away. Through the veil of the flyscreen and the curtain of rain beyond she saw something move outside. 'Cam's here.'

Thank God.

'Coming through.' The trolley rolled towards them, an ambo at each end. Bryce, secured firmly in place, looked slightly more comfortable now the gas had taken effect. Stephanie brushed another kiss to his temple before they wheeled him out the door and into the ambulance, which had been positioned as close as possible to the house. When she turned back to Rose she saw tears in her mother's eyes.

'It'll be fine, Mum, I promise. I'll find him.'

Her mother mumbled something she didn't have time to hear.

As the ambulance pulled away she trudged out into the rain towards Cameron. They met in the middle of the yard, Cam reaching out to squeeze her shoulder. The cold fear in his eyes, she knew, mirrored her own. They could do this. Together they would find Jake and bring him home. He would be wet and cold, but he would be alive. Near the old windmill, Bryce had said. It must have been where they'd reached when the accident happened. It wasn't much but it was a starting point.

She made her way across to the horses, Cam close behind. The old windmill was right next to the creek – the creek that for years now had been dry. But the way this rain was falling it wouldn't be long before it broke its banks. They had to find Jake. There was no other option.

Faith

I couldn't bear to lose another child.

They were Rose's exact words. Exact. Stephanie mightn't have heard or understood what her mother said, but Faith certainly did. She couldn't move, couldn't breathe. Muscles rigid, she stood open-mouthed lurking in the hallway. Coming here had been a mistake. The only useful thing she'd done so far was to call Cam. He didn't even have to be asked to come over. As soon as she'd said Jake was missing he'd told her he'd be there right away.

Because that's the sort of guy he is.

Rose was the one she needed to focus on now. Rose standing there looking ... bereft. That was the only one word for it: completely and utterly bereft.

She needed to do something practical, not gawk like a morbid onlooker at a crash site. She licked at her bottom lip before pulling it between her teeth, pushed herself away from the shelter of the wall and walked to the front door.

Through the flyscreen wire she watched the ambulance crawl away and Cam's car pull up in the driveway. Her heart, traitor that it was, skipped a beat as she watched him battle his way through the rain to a wooden shelter where Stephanie was already gearing up the horses.

Rose shuddered.

'Anything I can do?' Faith asked, softly. 'I could go and help them look.' It was a ludicrous idea, but she was really clutching at straws.

Rose turned to her, eyes swollen. 'No,' she said. 'It's too dangerous. We need to wait here for the rescue team.' She shifted her gaze back to Stephanie and Cam. 'At least she's not going out alone.'

'No, Cam will look after her.' Even though she hadn't known him very long, she knew it was true. 'Can I get you a cup of tea?'

Rose nodded. 'Thanks.'

In the kitchen Faith opened and closed cupboards, finding cups and boiling the kettle. She couldn't keep her eyes away from the window. A never-ending stream poured from the sky. The yard was quickly becoming a swamp. She couldn't remember ever seeing rain this torrential – wherever that poor kid was, he'd be drenched. Or worse. How did Stephanie and Cam have a hope in hell of finding him? But they would; they had to. In the meantime, all she could do was be here with Rose. Her birth mother had seemed so tough, so on top of everything, even when she'd told them all she was selling the hotel. But now, with Jake missing, she was falling apart.

'Here you go.' Wearing a pair of tracksuit pants and an oversized sweatshirt, Rose stepped back into the room with an armful of clothes. 'You're taller than Steph, but these should fit.' She dumped the pile on the table as Faith finished making the tea.

'Thanks.'

'Bathroom's down the hall.'

She changed in a hurry. A pair of leggings that came to just past her knees and a chequered pink shirt. Not her usual style, but dry. She pushed back her wet mop of hair and took a quick peek in the mirror. The girl looking back at her was barely recognisable, her face flushed, her eyes circled with black and riddled with guilt.

What are you doing here?

She stared at her for a moment longer, but it was a question she could no longer answer.

Back in the kitchen Rose was pacing the floor, tea cup in hand.

Faith's mug sat steaming on the table. She picked it up and blew across the rim. 'How long do you think before the police get here?' she asked.

'No idea.'

They sat quietly, staring into their cups. Faith studied the bouquet of flowers on the china as she shifted from one foot to the other. She didn't want to talk just for the sake of it, but she did want to try to make Rose feel better. 'I'm sure he'll be fine. They all will.' Tired platitudes seemed to be all she could come up with.

'We may as well sit, I suppose.'

She followed Rose's lead and dragged out a chair. Sipping tea was at least a time filler. The rain beat down on the tin roof of the old farmhouse like one of those never-ending drum solos that go on for far too long in the middle of a rock concert.

'Do you have any brothers or sisters, Faith?' Rose's question dragged her back to the dim lighting of the country kitchen.

'No.' That dull ache she'd had since she was small began to gnaw. 'I'm an only child,' she said, 'like Stephanie.'

The colour leached from Rose's cheeks. She placed her cup on the table and stared at it, glassy eyed. 'I had another daughter,' she said, vaguely. 'Before Stephanie.'

Faith's scalp prickled. This was not happening.

'I was seventeen. Couldn't get out of Birralong quick enough.' She paused, shook her head ever so slightly. 'Got myself pregnant before I even left town, but I didn't find out until I'd landed in Sydney. I was too ashamed to come back home. Thought I could just have the baby, give it away and get on with what I wanted to do – see the world. But then when she was born, when I saw her . . .'

Rain buffeted the weatherboards. Faith wanted to jump up and run out into it and get as far away as possible, but she also wanted the story. Her story. She sat perfectly still, her eyes fixed on Rose, waiting.

'She was so beautiful,' Rose said, her voice like shattering glass. 'They only let me hold her for a few minutes. But I gave her a name.'

Eliza.

Faith closed her eyes, willing herself not to cry.

'Eliza.' A small smile softened the brittle shell of Rose's face. 'Giving her up was the hardest thing I've ever had to do.' Her voice fell quiet, almost to a whisper. 'It was like a death.'

Faith looked over to the woman who had given birth to her. Sorrow was etched into the creases around her eyes. Pain lingered behind every word. Rosemary Barnes hadn't given away her child; she'd given her up. Given her up and never stopped grieving.

Grieving for me.

Faith shuffled forward and reached across the table. Her mother's hand was warm and comfortable beneath her own.

Tell her, tell her now.

But where would she start? What could she say?

Footsteps sounded in the hallway and they sprang apart.

Rose pressed the heels of both hands against her cheeks. Her breath hitched. 'Nobody knows,' she said quickly. She stood and greeted the group of people who had arrived to help.

Faith sat alone at the kitchen table, the room fading around her, a fog of voices and movement. The words she'd been fumbling for were lost.

Chapter Fifteen

Rose

ALL AROUND HER THE HOUSE WAS BEING TURNED INTO A command centre. Walkie-talkies, maps, torches and an assortment of paraphernalia lay scattered across the table and in boxes on the floor. Men and women – some friends, some acquaintances – moved from place to place like worker ants, each focusing on a specific task so that they seemed part of one larger organism. Rose stood in the middle of it all in a trance. Once she'd eaten a hash cookie that one of the backpackers had offered, and she had that same feeling now – the chatter and movement fading in and out, one minute ear-splittingly loud, the next minute no more than a murmur, her body here in the kitchen but not here, her mind a merry-go-round of faces and sounds and colours. She felt herself swaying and dragged herself out of la-la land. Jake's disappearance had already sent her into some sort of nostalgic time warp that had left her spilling her secrets to Faith. Once this was over she'd be having a quiet word and begging the girl to keep her lips firmly sealed.

'The search-and-rescue team is on its way, Mrs O'Shea, but it could take a while.' The sergeant gave her an apologetic look. 'Hopefully we'll have found him by then.'

She tried to move her mouth, but no smile came. A group of helpers from neighbouring properties had already set off on horseback and on bikes, but in this weather it was doubtful they'd get far. Over the sergeant's shoulder the clock on the wall read 5.54. Outside the day was shutting down. In just over an hour it would be dark. Would they keep up the search or call it off until morning? It was hard to say, and Rose was too afraid to ask. Surely they wouldn't leave a child out there all night?

They can't.

They simply can't.

Thinking about it certainly wasn't helping. She needed to make herself useful. Keep busy. Faith bustled backwards and forwards delivering mugs of tea and coffee, making small talk and doing whatever she could to help. Things here seemed to be under control. With a swarm of people in the place the bathroom would be getting a workout. Dodging the officers who had arrived and stationed themselves at the table, Rose made her way down the hall. The laundry was outside, so she collected the wet pile of clothes from the floor and dumped them into the bath, mopping the water up with a hand towel and giving the vanity a once over. The loo paper was getting low. She tossed the almost empty roll into the bin beside the sink but missed her target. Leaning down to shove it into place, her eye landed on a silver foil packet, a white plastic stick poking out from the wrapper. Gingerly, she picked it from the bin and slid the stick out. A solid pink plus sign was right there, as bold as brass in the window. She sat back on her heels. It was all starting to make sense. Stephanie had been feeling ill when she arrived at The Crossroads the other day. She'd been listless, more tired than usual, blaming it on the stress of the situation with Bryce. But as Rose looked down at the evidence in her hand she realised the truth.

She frowned into the mirror.

Why didn't she tell me?

Was it because she was afraid to tell Bryce? Or he did know and he didn't like it? Either way, it wasn't good.

The front door banged, and the sound of more arrivals rang down the hallway. Rose slipped the test back into the foil and returned it to the bin. She grabbed a new toilet roll from the cupboard, finishing the job she'd started. Her earlier queasiness reappeared as she made her way to the kitchen. Not only was her grandson missing but her daughter – her newly pregnant daughter – was out there in the rain searching for him while her husband was being carted off for an emergency operation. Could it get any worse?

She knew the answer. Yes, it could get a whole lot worse.

'You make sure they're all right, Michael O'Shea,' she muttered. 'Or I really will make you pay.'

Stephanie

'THE OLD WINDMILL!' SHE YELLED TO CAM. COULD HE EVEN hear her? They hadn't bothered with saddles, both of them more than capable of riding bareback at speed. Water poured from the brim of her hat as she dipped her head and pushed Bandit forward. Maisie followed, keeping slightly behind to start with, but they pushed the horses on and gathered momentum until they were riding side by side.

The deluge had turned the paddocks into watercourses. A solemn mob of cattle crowded beneath a lone stringy bark. Last week they would have been sheltering from the blistering sun – now it would be a miracle if they survived the rains. But it didn't matter anymore. All that mattered was finding her boy. Part of her wanted to strike out on her own, for she and Cam to split up and search different areas of the property, but they both knew that in these conditions it would be too risky. Better to stick together. Teamwork – that's how they would find Jake.

Jake.

Every fibre in her body pined for him. She had always known she would do anything to protect him, but her maternal love had never been so sorely tested. Had her own mother felt like this about her when she was a child? Of course. Even if she hadn't always shown it. The bond between a mother and her baby was like no other. Just last week she'd seen a video on Facebook about how a baby responds to its mother when in utero. How when the mother's heart is injured, stem cells from the foetus migrate to the damaged spot to heal the wound. Is that what the tiny baby growing inside her was doing right now? Protecting its mother's heart?

She lifted a hand to her face to wipe the water from her eyes. Tears or rain? Probably both. Bandit thundered along beneath her, sending plumes of water flying, mud splattering up onto her shins. The steady beat of his hooves, dull as it was on the sodden ground, was soothing, and she centred all her concentration onto just that.

Thump, thump, thump, thump.

Through one paddock and the next they made their way towards the spot where Bryce had last seen Jake. Even though he'd gone by the time Bryce had regained consciousness, it was all they had. When they reached the final gate Cam jumped down from Maisie's back to open it, and gave Stephanie a grim nod as he hoisted himself up again and they rode on for the final leg. One more stretch, one more impossibly long tract of land and there it was – the old windmill. Cold needles of dread pricked at the tissue beneath her skin. At the best of times the ancient structure looked forlorn, its spokes bent and broken, but now in the leaden light it looked like some sort of mechanical monster, its limbs fractured and deformed.

Cam let go of the horse's reins and jumped down to survey the creek bed. Stephanie followed suit, leaving Bandit to stand beside Maisie in the rain, and ran to the lip of the ravine. What she saw snatched the air from her lungs. What had been a barren gorge the last time she'd seen it was now a raging torrent that jumped and licked at the rock walls like a savage beast. If Jake had followed the creek, stuck to the edge of it too closely, he could have been dragged under as the water surged. She pushed a hand hard against her mouth, forcing back the vinegary taste at the back of her throat.

A firm grip steadied her. 'Let's head this way,' Cam shouted, pointing towards the northern border of the property. 'He might have headed for the boundary fence.'

She nodded mutely. Her brain had turned to mush. She couldn't think, could barely breathe. All she could do was lift herself onto the horse and follow Cam's lead. His pace had slowed, she noticed, and as he rode he turned his head from side to side, searching. Robotically she copied him, like one of those clowns she used to love at the carnivals when she was a kid, their hideous painted mouths wide and open, necks swivelling from side to side while you tried to get the ball into the slot with the highest score. Jake loved them too. Had won himself a Wile E Coyote toy at the rodeo just last year.

Jake. Where are you?

'Jake! Jake! Jake!' She began to scream his name, over and over in time with the fall of Bandit's feet on the earth. 'Jake. Jake!' She called until her throat was raw, her eyes burning, until Cam reached out and touched her arm, signalled for her to pull to a stop.

'Steph, we *are* going to find him, but you have to hold it together, okay?'

He didn't have a child; he didn't know how it felt to be on the brink of losing everything. A fresh round of sobs tore at her chest until she was hunched forward clinging to Bandit's neck, her face buried in his mane. He was warm, despite the incessant rain; a solid, warm body of flesh and muscle. She took in the scent of him, the smell of earth and wood and grass, and somehow it grounded her, brought her back. Pushing herself upright, she looked across at Cam. She could do this. They were *going* to find him.

A flash of colour jagged at the corner of her eye as she picked up the reins. She swivelled around, peering hard. Lying in the mud next to the gate was Jake's bike, its fluoro-green paintwork washed ridiculously clean. In an instant she was off the horse and flying towards it, dropping to her knees, righting the bike as if the movement of it would reveal Jake, safe and sound beside it. But there was no Jake, just the bike, intact, the engine dead.

Cam reached her side and they shared a frantic look before whirling around, searching. And now it was Cam calling her son's name, repeating it over and over, hands cupped to his mouth as he hollered.

Please be here, please be here, please be here.

She repeated the phrase over and over in her head as she ran, first in one direction, away from where the bike had been dumped and then back again before striking off in the opposite direction, all the time hearing her son's name ring out behind her, all the time begging silently that he would be okay.

In five minutes or ten or fifty – she couldn't tell – her lungs heaving, she stopped, doubled over, hands on her knees. He wasn't here. His bike was here, but not Jake. Someone was beside her. Cam. His hand on her back, concern in his eyes as she turned to look at him.

'Are you okay?'

Of course she wasn't okay. But she nodded just the same, knowing what he was asking.

A crackle erupted from inside her coat. The walkie-talkie. They'd found him! They'd found him and they were messaging to tell her he was all right. She tugged at the clips on her Drizabone, ripped it open with a single frantic yank and dragged the device from the inside pocket.

More crackling, then a voice. 'Steph, Steph can you hear me?'

She pushed the button in hard. 'Mum, I'm here. Have you found him?'

Another crackle. A pause that went on for far too long.

'No, love, we haven't.' Everything inside her shrivelled. 'I just wanted to let you know the rescue team has arrived and people have come in to help. They've been divided up into groups to search the entire property. They're heading out now.'

She stared vacantly at the machine in her hand as if it were a strange, ancient artefact she'd never laid eyes on before.

'Steph. Stephanie, are you there?'

Cam reached over and took it from her, watching her closely as he spoke. 'I'm here, Rose, we got that. We've covered the area to the south out as far as the old windmill and headed along the creek towards the boundary fence. Jake's bike is here. Not damaged at all. I think it's run out of fuel and he's headed off on foot. We'll keep looking.'

'Is Stephanie all right?' Even in her daze she could hear the worry in her mother's voice through the static of the machine.

Did she look as crazy and out of control as she felt?

Cam pushed his thumb against the button. 'She's fine,' he said, deliberately, looking straight at Stephanie. 'We'll keep in touch.'

'Cameron,' Rose said, catching him before he clicked off. 'We're going to run out of daylight soon.'

Stephanie didn't hear his mumbled reply as she looked out across the saturated paddocks. Rain had already shadowed the afternoon light but her mother was right: the day was fading. She was seized by a fresh wave of panic. 'Come on, we have to keep going,' she urged Cam, turning back to the horses.

'Steph, wait.'

Wait? Was he crazy? Soon it was going to be dark and her boy, her five-year-old baby boy who had only just begun to live his life, was out there somewhere alone – and Cam wanted her to wait? She wheeled around, ready to attack.

'Is there somewhere Jake might go to find shelter, a ridge, a hollow, a tree – anywhere?' His question pulled her up short.

What the hell was he talking about?

'He's a switched-on kid,' Cam reasoned. 'Once the rain started he would know he'd have to get out of it. But where would he go?'

Cam was right. Her son was smart. Farm smart. He knew the land, and both Bryce and she had taught him about safety. She walked herself through the list of things they'd told him. Never go off alone without letting someone know where you are – obviously that didn't apply in this situation. If you ever get lost follow the sun – no sun to follow today, so also useless. If it looks like a storm find shelter and stay there until the rain passes. Find shelter. Where would he go to find shelter?

'The bunker.' A tiny sliver of hope gleamed for the first time since they'd started out.

'The ammo bunker?'

Stephanie pointed along the fence line. 'It's down this way.'

'Would he know how to get to it?' Cam looked doubtful.

'I don't know, but it's worth a try.'

They made a dash to the horses. The rain showed no sign of easing and the light was thinning – soon there would be no chance of finding him before sunrise tomorrow, which meant he would be out here all night. Her stomach lurched. She forced herself through it, dragged her mind back to Bandit, to the man riding loyally beside her. He and Jake had once been such great mates. Uncle had been a role Cam had played happily. Even though he proclaimed himself a contented bachelor, he'd make a great dad one day. Just like his brother.

Bryce.

The memory of him, prostrate, his body broken, crushed her already fragile heart.

Was he okay?

Had they kept him sedated for the trip to minimise the pain?

Probably. She hoped so – that way he wouldn't be conscious enough to worry about Jake. She was doing enough of that for both of them. *I'm going to find him,* she'd promised as they'd trundled Bryce towards the ambulance. And she was. The alternative wasn't even imaginable.

The grey afternoon had dulled to a grimy twilight. Earth, trees, fences, horizon – everything around them was muted by the rain, edges softened so that one thing smudged into the next. Beside and below them the creek churned its way through the gorge, growling and spitting and throwing itself against the rock walls, vicious and unpredictable. If the downpour continued and the water rose and spilled over the banks, there was a chance the bunker could flood. And if Jake was down there . . .

The scrub and rocks that marked the entrance to the abandoned army depot appeared like a mirage in the distance. Ammunition had been stored there during the war, but now it was nothing more than a collection of snake holes and rabbit warrens, the ammo that the American troops had hidden long since found and destroyed. Apart from the occasional bullet or random stick of mouldy dynamite, the space was empty. Stephanie had never actually been down into it – not after the horror stories Bryce and Cam had told her about the thick black dark, the putrid smell and the scurry of unseen animals they remembered from when they were kids. The pair had been banned by their father from going in there, but of course it hadn't stopped them. Jake had told her about poking around down there one day with Bryce, who had given him the same warning he'd been given as a boy.

But surely Jake knew enough to ignore the warning this time around.

Please let him be here, please let him be here.

She swung herself down from Bandit's back once more. This was it – in a few minutes she'd be riding home with her son.

Cam joined her and they stared at the bank of prickly acacia and weeds guarding the entrance. A pile of rocks had been put in place long ago to block access to the bunker, but a few of them looked like they'd been moved. Not much, but enough that someone could crawl inside. Someone small. The glimmer of hope she'd been harbouring shone brighter. She flicked her eyes to Cam and without a word they shoved aside the remaining pile of rubble.

Rivulets of water were seeping into the passageway, turning it into a quagmire. She tried not to think about the mud devouring her feet, about the thorns clawing at her arms, about the cloying darkness as she scrambled through the tunnel. She'd had to toss off her hat to fit through the narrow entrance, and even though Cam was ahead of her clearing the way, strands of what she suspected were cobwebs clung to her cheeks. On a normal day she would have shrieked hysterically but today was not a normal day. Even though she couldn't see a thing she kept her eyes fixed straight ahead, her hands moving one after the other behind Cam's feet.

'Jake,' she heard him call and she was so glad because any form of speech was long gone. 'Jakey boy, are you here, matey? It's Uncle Cam, and Mummy, we've come to get you.' His voice, smothered as it was by the dense walls of the corridor, sounded so reassuring Stephanie almost smiled. They were going to find him, she could feel it, he was here.

A few more shuffles forward and they were out into the more open rectangular space of the bunker. While there still wasn't enough head room to stand, they could at least crouch. A shaft of light sliced through the darkness. She turned towards it – the flashlight from Cam's phone. He'd stopped calling out now and the echo of their combined panting filled the chamber.

She tried desperately to steady her breathing as she followed the glow from the phone. Cam held it as high as his arm would reach without scraping against the ceiling and began circling, shining the beam into each corner. Stephanie blinked as she followed its path, willing her eyes to adjust to the eerie brightness, willing them to see something. Cam had almost reached the three-sixty mark when she grabbed his arm.

'Stop.' She pointed. 'Over there.'

He shifted the angle of the phone back a fraction.

Stephanie sprang up, ignored the sharp pain that stabbed at her skull when her head collided with the solid roof of rock, then stumbled, falling onto her hands and knees again in an effort to move more quickly. One lunge forward, another, then a third and she was there by his side.

'Jake, Jake . . .' She repeated his name over and over as she gathered him into her arms, and curled him to her body. 'Jake.' Relief loosened her limbs, unfastened the chains of despair shackling her body. Her little boy. He was here. She'd found him.

'Jake,' she said again, easing back to look down at his beautiful face. Scratches marred his papery cheeks. In the dim, ghostly light she could see where the thorns had left trails of blood on his hands. His curls were flat and his eyes – his impish, chocolate bud eyes – were closed. 'Jake.' Squeezing him a little more tightly, she registered how limp and cold he was, how weighty he felt, how, despite her pleas for him to speak, he lay there, his little chest labouring with a sickening wheeze.

'Jake,' she heard herself whisper.

And then Cam reached out, his hands like tentacles around her child. He was trying to take Jake from her, take her son, but she shook him off and turned away, clinging to the small, still body in her arms.

Faith

IT WAS DARK OUT THERE. SO DARK. A BLACKNESS FAITH COULD hardly comprehend. Not after spending her entire life beneath the glow of city lights. The rain had eased a little, sounding more like a percussionist tapping away on a set of bongos now than a lunatic booming away on a bass. But it was still there, still falling and there was still no sign of the search party.

A few more recruits had arrived and headed out to help, and a few of those who had left only an hour ago had returned with dripping clothes, eyes roaming the floor, looking anywhere other than at Rose.

Behind her, in the kitchen, the surge of action and noise the rescue team had brought with it had dropped to a sullen quiet. There'd been a stand-up argument when the guy coordinating the search had suggested they might have to call it off until morning. Rose had gone nuts. Nuts enough that the commander had quickly binned the idea and, with the weather looking slightly less intimidating, had even called in a request for a helicopter.

If only the rain would stop they'd have a much better chance of finding him.

Faith had kept to herself for the past few hours. She had the illogical feeling that if she spoke too much, or if Rose happened to look at her too closely, she might become suspicious. It was a crazy notion, of course, but she just couldn't shake it, so it was better to keep her distance. If things hadn't turned out the way they had today she would have been holed up in her room back at The Crossroads, waiting out her final night in Birralong before getting on a plane tomorrow and getting the hell out of the place.

Is that what you really want?

To leave without telling Rose that the daughter she gave up was alive and happy? Wouldn't it be kinder to reveal the truth and give both herself and her birth mother – the whole BM thing seemed so flippant now – closure? She didn't know Rose well, of course, but she knew she was a good person, a woman who had lived with an unbearable loss for the past thirty-one years. And Faith had the power to ease that loss. Tomorrow was her birthday. The day Rose had given her up – to an amazing couple who had blessed her with a beautiful life, one for which she was, despite her lingering anger, extremely grateful.

She stared out into the night, the truth crystallising as she looked through the shadowy outline of herself in the window pane. Faith Montgomery and Eliza Barnes were the same person. Not two different people but one, whole, complicated, messy self. Her life had been a gift and, tomorrow, presuming Jake was found alive and well, she would give Rose a gift in return.

A loud crackle on the two-way startled the room into silence.

Faith turned, moved closer, her fingers pinching the bottom of her shirt as she zoned in on the commander's voice.

'Where are you?'

A pause.

'Is he okay?'

Another pause.

'Will we send someone out?'

Headphones muted the replies. The throng of people who had gathered at the house moved as one, circling the makeshift control desk. Rose stood at the centre, shoulders drooping, chin tucked to her sternum, watching the man as he spoke.

The commander looked up finally, the hint of a smile shifting across his face. 'They've found him.'

Rose leaped up, cheering and punching the air. 'They've found him,' she chorused, 'they've found him.'

An explosion of squeals, laughter and tears flooded the room as arms flew around shoulders and bodies pulled against each other in a rush of joy. Faith was swept up in it, clutching onto people she didn't know, joining in the rowdiest, most celebratory group hug she'd ever experienced.

'Sh, sh.' The commander held up his hand and the partying came to an abrupt end.

Faith watched his expression change as he listened to the voice on the other end of the radio. All around her smiles dimmed as the group became a stony faced bunch of statues. Sergeant Minter placed the walkie-talkie on the table and picked up his phone. 'He's in a bad way,' he said, beginning to dial. 'We'll need a doctor.'

But he was alive, right? That was the main thing.

The gathering resumed its chatter, more guarded now that Jake's condition was unclear.

Faith zeroed back in on Rose who had once again seated herself by the commander's side, her short-lived euphoria now tethered on a tight leash, the flame of hope that had brightened her eyes extinguished. Surely the world could not be this cruel, surely Jake would be okay.

Faith prayed silently. Please let him be okay.

For Rose's sake, please let him be okay.

Chapter Sixteen

Rose

WATCHING THE PROGRESS OF THE MINUTE HAND AS IT MADE its way around the circle was the only thing that was keeping her sane. In ten more ticks it would be nine-thirty; forty minutes since Cameron had called to say they'd found him. He was barely conscious and was wheezing, but he was alive. Standing by the window, hands clasped, she could still see Jake as a toddler, his little chest heaving as he struggled for air. But that had been well over two years ago and since then his asthma seemed to have all but disappeared. Still, considering what he'd just been through, another attack wasn't all that much of a surprise.

The cautious quiet that had descended on the house while the search was on had been replaced by the casual murmur of voices as people exchanged survival stories from their own families. Anybody who had lived in the bush for any length of time had an arsenal of them – tall tales and true about running out of fuel on dusty backroads, wrangling rogue snakes, altercations with giant kangaroos and, as always happened when the conversation turned to mysterious outback events, stories of the min-min lights, the strange unaccounted-for illuminations that seemed to follow you when you were driving – invariably alone – at night. Rose let the comforting soundtrack drift on around her as she kept her eyes on the clock and waited.

Why were they taking so long? Every ounce of her was on edge, every muscle as tight as a butcher's knot. Just when she was about to internally combust with the anticipation, a thin thread of light appeared in the distance. She bent forward, rubbing at the window pane to get a clearer view.

Watching closely as the light gradually grew brighter, she saw two solid forms materialise and make their way closer and closer to the house. 'They're here!' she shouted, flushing the tension from her shoulders as she waved her arms madly. 'It's them, they're back.'

Her feet couldn't get her to the door quick enough. Flinging it open, she ran out into the night, leaving the commotion her announcement had triggered far behind. The rain had lightened to a stubborn drizzle and she blinked it away, squelching through puddles towards the soggy trio, who were now only a few metres away. Jake was propped up like a rag doll in front of Cam on the horse's back and as Rose pushed open the gate she could see how deathly white his cheeks were, how precariously he was resting against his uncle's larger frame. For a moment she thought the worst. A tremor ran through her but she shook it away. He was alive, he was going to be okay. Another few steps and she was at their sides, reaching for her grandson.

'Here,' she said, 'I'll take him.'

'Watch his right wrist,' Cam said. 'I think it's broken.'

She lifted her arms and pulled Jake gently down from the horse. He'd always been slight but right now he felt weightless, a tepid bundle of skin and bone, so jelly-like it was hard to get a grip on him. 'It's all right, Jakey boy, Nanny's got you,' she whispered into his ear as she held him close, one arm under his bent knees, the other nursing his head and shoulders.

Stephanie was there beside her in an instant. 'He needs a doctor, Mum.'

'I know, love. Let's get you both inside.'

Others had followed Rose out and were taking the horses from Cameron and leading them back to their yards. Despite the number of people and the flurry of movement, she was conscious of nothing more than the boy in her arms, of the rapid in and out of his chest as he struggled for breath.

'I'll grab his inhaler and some clothes.' Stephanie shot through the door. Rose headed for the lounge room and lay Jake down against the back of the couch. Cuts and bruises marred his face and arms. The wrist Cameron had said could be broken was tomato-red, bruises staining the swollen flesh. Oh, what the poor little mite must have been through out there on his own.

'Here,' Stephanie said, thrusting a towel at her mother. 'We need to get him dry.'

Together they stripped off his sopping clothes and gave him a gentle wipe-down before pulling a pair of tracksuit pants up his legs and poking his arms and head into a wind cheater. He was lucid enough to whine and grumble at the pushing and pulling. It was a good sign and Rose almost smiled. 'Come on now, little man, let's get you toasty warm.' She took a blanket from whoever handed it to her and wrapped it around Jake while Stephanie readied the inhaler.

'Bear, I need you to have a puff of this,' she said quietly to her son.

Rose looked across at her. She was still soaking wet, and although it wasn't cold, her teeth were chattering. There were a few scrapes and scratches on her arms and hands but nothing major. Her eyes dropped lower to Stephanie's stomach, but there was no visible bump.

Jake whimpered. Rose gave him back her full attention and held him tighter. 'Come on, Jakey, just have a puff, it'll help you feel better.' The medication wasn't going to erase his shock or fix his broken bones, but it would allow him to breathe more easily and then they could deal with his other injuries. His eyes flickered and he mumbled something about Daddy.

'We're going to see Daddy soon,' Stephanie said, her voice like spring sunshine. 'Once we get you all fixed up, we'll go see him, okay? But you have to do this first.'

Rose felt the slightest nod of Jake's head against her chest as Stephanie managed to wrangle the inhaler into his mouth and get him to take one puff and then a second.

'That should help.' Steph shuffled back but never once took her eyes from her son's face. 'Is there an ambulance on its way?'

A clipped voice piped up from behind. 'No luck with the flying doctor, I'm afraid,' Sergeant Minter said. 'Still too risky for them to fly in this weather.'

'I can take him in to the hospital.' Cam stepped forward, dried off now and changed into a set of his brother's clothes. 'It's eased off enough to drive. Probably quicker than waiting for the doctor to come out here.'

Rose and Stephanie, sitting on either side of Jake, looked down at the boy simultaneously. His eyes were closed but his breathing had definitely evened out. He looked like a wreck and that wrist would have to be x-rayed. It probably should be on ice right now, but there was no way he was going to tolerate any more.

'That's a good idea.' Stephanie leaned over and kissed Jake's forehead. 'I'll just go and get changed.'

The room began to clear. Faith appeared with mugs of steaming tea. Cam took a seat opposite Rose. As much as she didn't really want to think anymore about her grandson being out there alone she had a desperate need to know what had happened and how they had found him. She summoned up the courage to ask and as Cam told her the story a wave of pride welled up inside her. As young as he was and as frightened as he must have been, Jake had tried to get help for his father and then, even when he lost his way he'd managed to find himself some shelter. She looked down at him and brushed a hand softly across his temples. He looked positively angelic lying there beside her, black lashes feathering his cheeks, which, now he was warmer, were two soft petals of pink. It had been a close call but he'd pulled through. He was safe.

'Thank you, Cameron,' Rose said to the man sitting quietly across from her, watching his nephew.

'No need to thank me. I'm just glad he's okay.'

'I'm ready.' Stephanie marched back into the room, her still-damp hair pulled back, her wet clothes exchanged for a clean, dry pair of jeans, T-shirt and cotton hoodie jacket. She didn't look like a woman who had been out searching for her missing son for the past five hours – she was completely focused on the next part of her agenda. No wonder Jake was so tough. He was his mother's son.

Stephanie leaned down and took Jake into her arms. 'Come on, Old Bear.' His head flopped against his mother's shoulder as she nestled him into the blanket.

'Would you like me to come?' Rose asked, already standing.

'Might be better if you wrap things up here,' Stephanie said, moving towards the door. 'I'll give you a call from the hospital and let you know how we go.'

A twinge of disappointment gripped Rose's belly. Her daughter had always been so fiercely independent, so determined to do things for herself. It was a wonderful trait, of course, but sometimes, as a mother, Rose just wanted to be needed.

'Okay,' she said, feigning a smile. 'That's okay.'

'Mum,' Stephanie said weakly. She laid a hand on Rose's shoulder. 'I'm going to need you around when they both come home.'

'I'll be here,' Rose was trying hard not to crack. 'You look after yourself too, love.' She pulled her into a quick embrace.

'I will. We'll be fine.' She nodded to Cam and the two of them made for the door.

Rose sighed so deeply she was momentarily dizzy. Giving herself a quick shake she looked across to where Faith sat, staring into space on the lounge chair. 'You look like you could do with a sleep, young lady.'

Faith roused. 'No, I'm good. I'll help you clean up.'

'No, you won't.' Now that the crisis had passed Rose was back into boss mode. 'You've done more than enough. There's not much left to do, just get rid of the last of these misfits and then I'll be going to catch a few winks myself. No arguments. Down the hall on the right. See you in the morning.'

Faith yawned, right on cue. 'Sorry,' she said, lifting a hand too late to try to stifle the sound. 'Well, let me know if you need anything. I'm so glad he's okay.' She gave Rose a brief but beautiful smile before following instructions and drifting off down the hallway.

Rose watched her go, saw the tired sway of her hips as she staggered off to bed. The girl really was something. When Rose had initially asked her to come along to help she hadn't been thinking clearly – what use was a born-and-bred city girl going to be in a situation like this? But Faith had been more than helpful, looking after all the volunteers and making sure Rose was fed and watered. So much so that she'd let her guard slip. That was a faux pas she would have to rectify in the morning.

Tomorrow. Despair swelled inside her like a rising tide. A new day would mean this horrible one was over, that Jake and Stephanie – and Bryce – her family, were all safe and sound. It wasn't the day itself that was the problem, but the date. The date she dreaded when it rolled around each year. The day she always tried to spend alone.

October 27.

Eliza's birthday.

Stephanie

COCOONED INSIDE A BLANKET IN THE BACK SEAT OF CAM'S car, Jake asleep and burrowed into her side, Stephanie could feel the adrenaline that had been pumping through her body begin to ebb. It was a strange sort of sensation, one of floating and being dragged under at the same time, of leaving her body and looking down on herself but also withdrawing inward, disappearing. Neither of those was an option right now, not until Jake was seen by a doctor. She allowed herself a slight wriggle to shake the fuzziness away, wary of jostling him too much, before letting her mind drift back over the events of the past twelve hours. She'd had no qualms about bringing Jake out to the farm to go riding with his dad – the two of them had been going out on the bikes together for over a year and nothing had ever gone wrong. The fact that the rain had started after Jake had gone missing was equally freakish. No one was to blame – and at the end of the day, while broken bones weren't ideal, both of her boys were still alive and would recover in a relatively short space of time.

Now that it was over, there was still the prickly issue of her relationship with Bryce.

For a few short seconds, when she'd seen him lying unmoving on the kitchen floor, she'd had a flash of what her life would be like without him. It was a life she couldn't picture and didn't want to consider. But she also knew that things could not go on as they had been.

When had all their problems even started? Cam's visit to Strathmore had undoubtedly sent Bryce into a downward spiral, added to the pressure of the drought itself. But for years now he'd been retreating into his shell and she had let him. She'd made excuses for him, left him to his isolation, been too cowardly to call him on his behaviour. She did what she'd always done – been the one to back down and childishly wish it would all go away. Too often she'd allowed him to be the one to make the decisions, pretended to go along with them even when everything inside her was raging against her own complacency.

Instinctively she rested a palm against her stomach. This baby was a prime example. She'd given in to his insistence that they wait even though deep down it had rankled. What had they been waiting for? The drought to end? Drought was a part of life out here. This one would end and then a few years down the track there'd be another. They would survive, second child or not. And yet she had convinced herself that Bryce was right. About so many things. Once Bryce had recovered they would sit down and have a chat – a long one – about their life together and how they were going to move forward. Part of that would be telling him about the baby, of course, but a bigger part would be insisting they make decisions together. No more emotional bullying from him, and for her no more conceding to his demands.

The car jolted as it hit a pothole.

Jake startled and moaned. She held him tight.

'Sorry,' Cam said, glancing at her in the rear-view mirror.

'That's okay.' She smiled at him even though he wouldn't see it. 'Thanks for everything you've done, Cam. He'd still be out there if it wasn't for you.'

'You're the one who remembered the bunker,' he said softly. 'The way you just kept going was amazing.'

'I'm his mother. I wasn't coming back without him.'

'He's a very lucky little boy.' He turned around quickly, before moving his eyes back to the road. 'In more ways than one.'

Cam was right: Jake was lucky. But so was she. A sudden burst of happiness made her buoyant and she touched her cheek to Jake's forehead. 'You ever think about settling down, having kids?'

For a good long minute the only sound was the swish of the car tyres along the slushy track of road. Either Cam hadn't heard her question or didn't want to talk. She let it go and closed her eyes, listening to the soothing hum of the engine as the car carried them slowly but ever closer to the hospital.

'I never used to think about it much,' he said, and it took her a few seconds to realise he was, after all, answering her question. 'But the older I get, the more I miss that sense of family. I've pretty much lost the one I had, so yeah, I think I would like to have one of my own one day.'

'You'd be a great dad.' Even though it had been three years since they'd had any contact she knew how much he loved Jake. 'And for the record, you haven't lost your family.'

She could see his small sad smile in profile. He didn't say anything else, but that was okay. They'd said enough.

———

The hospital had been notified of their impending arrival and a doctor was ready and waiting. Cam remained at her side, a steady presence helping her to calm Jake down when they wanted to examine him, waiting while they did the x-rays and reported that yes, the wrist was broken, the cut above his elbow would need stitching and they would like to keep him in for the night under observation. She wanted to take him home and snuggle up in bed with him and go to sleep for a good few days, but he did need to be properly checked over. Whatever sedative they gave him when they began to stitch him up seemed to be doing the trick as Jake drifted in and out of a woozy sleep, a sloppy grin on his face.

'I'll have whatever he's having,' Cam laughed as he walked into the examination room, two takeaway cups in hand.

She managed a tired smile, but when she held the cup to her lips the bitter coffee aroma made her insides writhe. Dropping caffeine from her diet wasn't an issue with her last pregnancy, her body's reaction immediately relegating it to the banned-substance list. It looked like this time around was going to be the same.

Cam gave her a puzzled look as she deposited the cup on the floor.

'I haven't eaten much, she covered 'Coffee doesn't really agree with me on an empty stomach. Sorry.'

'Don't apologise,' he said. 'The last thing we need is to have to put you in the bed next to our boy here.'

She gave him a rueful grin. 'Don't tempt me.'

They sat quietly while Jake was sewn up, his arm bandaged – it would take a few days for the swelling to go down before it could be plastered – and settled into bed. Once his eyes were closed she turned to Cam. 'Would you mind . . .'

'Waiting with him while you go see Bryce?'

She nodded.

'My pleasure.' He moved aside, making room for her to exit the tiny cubicle. 'Oh, and Steph,' he called as she was almost out the door. 'Tell him I said hi.'

The last time he'd said those words, back at Strathmore when he'd arrived with his proposal in hand, they had been laced with sarcasm. Now, any trace of it was gone. They were brothers, and in the end, that was all that mattered.

'I will.'

———

The image of Bryce lying in the hospital bed hit her hard. He was an up-at-dawn-no-naps-required kind of guy. Seeing him hooked up to a drip, eyes closed, his skin the colour of day-old dishwater reminded her of exactly what he'd been through. He looked so helpless. So vulnerable. She moved quietly, at once trying not disturb him but hoping he would wake. Tiptoeing to his bedside, she placed a hand over his where it rested on top of the sheets, leaned down and kissed his forehead. The cloying smell of antiseptic almost made her gag but she held her face close to his and inhaled that unmistakeable smell that was peculiarly Bryce. She straightened back up and he opened his eyes.

'Hi there,' she murmured, letting her fingers drift through his hair.

'Hi yourself.' He sounded drunk.

'They got you on the good stuff?'

He nodded. Then, as if suddenly remembering, his eyes popped. 'Jake,' he rasped.

The sound of her son's name coming from the only other person in the world who understood how impossible it would have been to have lost him made her crumble. She lowered herself into the chair by the bed.

'Steph?' He tried to push himself upright but immediately collapsed. As she lifted her eyes to his and saw his terror she realised her reaction seemed to be confirming the worst.

'He's okay.' She managed to push the two words out almost coherently before regrouping and starting again. 'He has a fractured wrist and a cut on his arm, a few scratches and bumps, but otherwise,' she took a breath, 'he's okay.'

Bryce slumped back against the pillow, closing his eyes briefly before opening them again.

She watched his face, saw the fear fade.

'It was only going to be a quick ride, before the rain came . . .'

She nodded. 'We found him in the bunker,' she said, needing to share the experience with him, only with him. 'His bike had run out of fuel, I think. He must have remembered where the bunker was and taken shelter in it when the rain started.'

His mouth lifted into a small smile, probably the best he could do under the influence of the drugs. He frowned then, his eyes narrowing. 'We?'

Stephanie dug her teeth into her bottom lip. He wasn't too zonked out to pick up on what she'd said. She'd imagined his reaction to the search on the way up in the elevator, had pictured him being so overwhelmed with gratitude that he would welcome Cam back into the bosom of the family. Now that she was about to relate the story she wasn't so sure.

'Cam was with me.' Their hands were entwined and she kept her eyes on the lumpy mountains of their knuckles. 'I called him and asked him to help me look, since he knows the place inside out. We took the horses. The weather was too horrendous to do anything else.' A shiver ran through her at the memory of the rain trickling through the gap between her neck and the collar of her coat, at the treacle-thick darkness of the night and the airless claustrophobia of the tunnel. She pushed her way through it now just as she had then. 'We found the bike when it was still light but by the time we got him out of the bunker it was pitch black. He was wheezing when we found him; he'd had an asthma attack and he had all these cuts and I couldn't get him to talk to me.' She could hear herself babbling but she couldn't stop. Being here with Bryce and finally knowing that they were both okay seemed to have unlocked all the fears she'd been harbouring and sent them shrieking from her like a pack of feral pigs. This wasn't how it was supposed to be. She was supposed to be calmly relaying the events of the day in an orderly fashion to her injured husband; she was supposed to be the one in control.

'Hey,' Bryce shifted his hand slightly beneath hers and the movement, along with his voice, was enough to shake her out of her borderline hysteria. 'You said it yourself, he's fine. It's good Cam came to help.'

'He drove us in to the hospital. He's down in casualty with Jake now. They're keeping him for a couple of hours just to make sure.'

He smiled again, a surer thing this time. 'Are you okay?'

Was she? Was she okay? She was dizzy, but that was probably just the stress of everything that had happened, along with the lack of food. She'd eaten so little, there was nothing in her stomach to throw up, but then that probably wasn't a good thing for the baby.

The baby.

'I'm pregnant.' It came out of her mouth as quickly as the two words had entered her head. 'About seven weeks, I think. So, I'm feeling a bit green, like last time, but otherwise I'm fine.'

She held her breath, relaxing her hold on Bryce's hand ever so slightly while she watched his face.

'A baby,' he said, his expression as blank as the wall behind him. But as she kept her eyes on his she saw them light up. 'That's good, Steph,' he said, 'really, really good.' His head lolled slightly to one side as he struggled to stay awake.

'Go to sleep, babe,' she said. 'We can talk later.'

'Love you,' he murmured.

She let go of his hand and brushed a stray curl from his forehead, just as she'd done with their son a few hours before. 'I love you too.'

Faith

IT WAS STILL DARK WHEN SHE WOKE. CRACKING OPEN ONE eyelid, she reached down beside the bed and felt for her phone: 5.34am. What was she even doing awake? She flopped back, wriggling her way under the covers. The bed was comfy, if a little on the small side. It had been eons since she'd slept in a single bed. Maybe if she closed her eyes again she could lull herself back to sleep. The house was quiet. Quiet meant the rain must have stopped. She lay still, listening.

Nothing.

Thank God.

It had already eased off by the time Cam and Stephanie took Jake to hospital, so with some luck it had now stopped altogether.

Cam.

She snuggled further into the doona. Lying here in the boy's bed, she couldn't shake the memory of Cam carrying Jake to the car and placing him into the back seat beside Stephanie, tucking a blanket around them both and closing the door gently. The tail lights flared red as he drove away through the still-falling rain and she'd wished she'd been sitting beside him. Wished that things were different, that she hadn't lied to him.

But it was too late for that now.

Her eyes flew open.

Today was her birthday.

———

Night was becoming dawn as she tiptoed into the kitchen. She'd never been a morning person, but there was something to be said for being up at 'sparrow's fart' as her father liked to call it. He said things like that just to push her buttons. It worked. There had always been this push–pull thing between them, but the bottom line was he would do anything for her. And she for him. She was his princess and even though she would never – ever – admit it, he was her knight in shining armour, the measure every man she met would have to live up to before the relationship progressed any further than 'nice meeting you'. They might not share the same blood but he'd been a wonderful father.

Good old Brian. He and Stella would be arriving home in just a few hours to 'surprise' her on her birthday. With everything that had happened in the past twenty-four hours she'd completely forgotten about catching that plane back to Sydney. She'd have to call Poppy and explain, get her to cover for her until she could think of a plausible story.

Or tell the truth.

Now there was a novel idea. The truth was, now that the anger had subsided and she was left with the facts: Rose hadn't been able to keep her, and her parents had desperately wanted a child.

A noise drew her attention and she peered out the window to see Rose sitting on the porch. She was staring into the distance, her coppery hair resting loosely on her shoulders, no glasses, her face wan. And Faith knew why.

A weird trembling sensation began in her stomach as she made her way outside. She let the door close quietly and pulled up a chair

'Hi,' she said, looking straight across the yard. Anywhere but at her birth mother.

'Good morning. You're up early.'

A soft, sherbet light was falling across the paddocks. Everything looked fresh and clean after the rain. The gentlest wisp of a breeze brushed along her arms and she shivered. 'Any news?'

Rose nodded, a smile melting across her lips. 'Jake's been stitched up. His wrist is broken but they can't plaster it for a few days. They kept him overnight but Steph's pretty sure they'll be letting him go this morning.'

'That's great.' She hushed out a long, slow breath, like air being released from a balloon you didn't know was ready to burst.

'And Bryce had his leg operated on. Did a pretty good job of smashing it up, evidently. Going to be a while before he's back on both feet. But he's tough. He'll be fine.'

'You're all pretty tough, if you ask me,' Faith laughed. 'I don't know how you do it.'

'You do what you have to do,' Rose said, the small spark in her eyes dying. She turned, suddenly serious. 'I said some things yesterday, to you, that I shouldn't have. About my past.'

Faith's mouth went dry as she anticipated Rose's next words.

'About me having another child. I don't know what got into me. The stress of it all, I suppose. But I'd appreciate it if you could keep the information to yourself.'

'Of course.'

This is it Faith, tell her.

'Funny thing is . . .' Rose paused, and although she wasn't looking directly at her Faith could tell she was trying to hold herself together. 'It's her birthday today. She'd be thirty-one.'

Tell her.

Fear twisted deep down inside her, as if her organs were being wrung, tighter and tighter. She wrapped her arms across her stomach, dug her nails into the curve of her waist. This wasn't about her. She could do this. She inhaled, letting the breath fill every crevice in her body as she turned to look directly at Rose.

'It's my birthday today,' she said, deliberately calm. 'And my middle name is Rosemary.' Now that she'd started to say it all out loud it was easier than she'd expected. 'I'm thirty-one. My parents, Stella and Brian, adopted me.'

Rose's mouth fell open. There was a quiver in her jaw and a matching one in her voice when she finally spoke. 'Are you . . .'

'I'm your daughter.' And then, because she wanted to make sure that Rose understood, 'I'm Eliza.' She picked up her phone and clicked on the photos, scrolling through the pictures until she reached the screenshot she'd taken of her birth certificate. 'This is my original birth certificate.' Rose took the phone. All the information was there – her original surname, Barnes, her given names – Eliza Catherine and her mother's full name and age – Rosemary Patricia Barnes, aged eighteen. And, of course, the date: 27 October 1984. It was all there. She watched Rose's face, trying to gauge her reaction. It was hard to read. She was staring, dry eyed at the photo, her cheeks hollow, her mouth ajar. What if this wasn't such a good idea, after all? What if she hadn't really ever wanted to know?

But when Rose finally raised her head a look of pure happiness shone on her face. Tears spilled down her cheeks and within seconds the ones Faith had been trying so desperately not to shed fell hard and fast. Without either of them saying a word they were both on their feet, clinging to each other, crying together, strangers who were intimately connected, a mother and daughter who were yet to know each other.

'You're so beautiful,' Rose whispered when they drew apart, keeping one hand on each of Faith's arms as if she might slip away if she let her go. 'You had a whole head of black hair when you were born. And now look at you.' She reached up and touched the wispy blonde hairs around Faith's ears.

Faith lifted a hand to her head, thinking back to the dark-haired baby in the photograph. It was certainly a transformation. Perhaps her father . . .

'But how did you find me?' Rose dropped her hands and folded them into a double fist in front of her, squeezed her fingers together.

'The letter. I found the letter you wrote to me.'

'You found it?'

Faith nodded.

'When?'

'A couple of weeks before I replied to your ad.' She was ashamed of it now, her duplicity, but Rose didn't seem to care about that particular detail.

'So your parents didn't tell you that you were adopted?'

'No.' Faith gasped, the hurt she'd felt at the discovery still smarting. 'I don't know why, but they didn't.'

'My caseworker let me write that letter.' Rose spoke quietly, almost to herself. 'She promised me she would pass it along, with the photo and the tag. She shouldn't have – it was highly irregular – but the laws were about to change anyway, to allow open adoptions. I was so distraught, and I wanted you to understand. Marilyn took pity on me, said she would give it to the people who adopted you.' She paused, closed her eyes briefly and opened them again. 'Your parents.'

Faith tried to smile. Strangely enough, it was easier than speaking.

'Are your parents . . . what are they like?'

'Weirdly, everyone says I look like my . . . my mum.' Faith winced. Maybe that wasn't the most tactful thing to say. She forged on. 'She's blonde too – more grey now, though.' She took the phone from Rose, scrolling through until she found a photo of the three of them at her father's sixty-fifth birthday dinner. 'This is a few years old,' she said, a gush of warmth flushing her skin as she passed it back, 'but it's a nice one.'

'Wow. You actually do look a little like her,' Rose said. 'They look lovely. Really lovely.'

'They are.' She meant it, her parents really were amazing people. 'I've been very lucky.' Shame sat like a swollen seed in the pit of her stomach. 'I'm sorry I came here the way I did, under false pretences.'

'Don't be.' Rose patted her hand. 'You got a shock. You were scared. It's completely understandable.'

Is it?

A magpie plopped to the ground in front of the porch, stabbing at the muddy lawn and clamping his beak around a fat, brown worm before gobbling it down. He turned and looked at Faith, and then he flapped his wings and flew away. A phone rang from inside the house. Everything was so normal.

'That'll be Steph,' Rose said, springing from her seat and diving for the door.

Faith stayed put, happy to have a few moments to herself. She'd done it. Not exactly in the way she had planned, but all things considered it hadn't gone too badly. The world hadn't ended. There was one question still unanswered, the matter of her father, but it could wait.

'Jake's being discharged.' There was a spring in Rose's step and she came back outside. 'Steph wants to stay in town close to the hospital so they can be with Bryce. I'll just go and pack a few things for them and then we'll have to get going.'

So that was it.

She stood, a little wobbly on her feet, but before she could take a step, Rose grabbed her hand. 'Happy birthday, Faith,' she said, her smile watermelon wide. 'We have a lot of catching up to do.'

Chapter Seventeen

Rose

THE FINAL TRAY OF SAUSAGE ROLLS WAS IN THE OVEN AND the timer was set for twenty-five minutes. Everybody loved them, which always made Rose laugh, since she got the recipe from the back of the frozen pastry pack. That was her little secret, though, and not one that was going to have any earth-shattering consequences. Not like some others she'd kept.

Had it really been six weeks since her world had changed so drastically? She squirted a good amount of detergent into the sink and wriggled her fingers into a pair of pink rubber gloves. So much had happened since then and she still couldn't believe the girls had managed to pull this shindig together. Stephanie had wanted to do something to help the local farmers, a sort of thank-you for everybody's efforts when Jake went missing, and now that they didn't need the cash for The Crossroads, doing a fundraising event for Aussie Helpers had been a worthy alternative. Of course, it hadn't put a plug in the inevitable gossip once Rose's news about Faith got out, but what did it matter? After all, the people it would have impacted the most – her mother and father and Mick – were all dead. She scrubbed absent-mindedly at a handful of dirty cutlery. Had she made the wrong choice? Should she have been brave enough to bring Eliza home with her from Sydney, live her life as a single mother? They might not have gone so far as disowning her, but she knew for a fact that her mother wouldn't have coped, and Rose couldn't have borne the disappointment in her father's eyes. It might have been the mid-eighties but her parents were both totally old school when it came to morals. Even if they had accepted the baby, the whole course of Rose's life would have changed. Chances are she wouldn't have married Mick, Stephanie wouldn't have been born, Jake wouldn't exist. It was pointless to wonder, really, and when all was said and done, Eliza – no, Faith – had been raised in a loving family and that was all a mother could wish for her child. The knowledge didn't stop the pang of sorrow that jabbed at her heart. She'd missed so much. But she had so much to be thankful for.

Stephanie had been a real trooper about it all, embraced the whole sister thing – and Faith – as if it was something she'd been waiting for all her life. In a sense it was. All through her childhood she'd begged for a sibling, and a few times Rose almost gave in and tried again. But the memory of those dark weeks and months after Stephanie's birth was too much. Having another child had dredged up so many painful memories and even though Mick didn't know why she'd been so miserable, had believed it to be normal post-baby blues, he had gone along with her decision to stop at one. She'd even suspected he was happy with it – liked the idea of having just the one little girl he could dote on and spoil rotten.

Wash-up finished, she wiped a cloth around the sink. Summoning the courage to tell Dave he had another daughter had been harder than she'd imagined. She'd skirted around it more than once in the days following Faith's revelation. She was covered in dirt, weeding the veggie garden at Strathmore when he'd walked outside after a planning meeting with Stephanie and Faith, unable to put a cork in his excitement.

'Those girls are both bloody champions, 'he said. 'I couldn't be prouder of them if they were my own flesh and blood.'

She froze, trowel mid-air. She'd promised both girls she would tell Dave the truth – soon – and here he was, handing her the perfect opportunity. Stripping off her canvas gloves, she pulled at the corner of her tee shirt and dabbed at her eyes. Dave was standing opposite her, red-faced and mopping his brow with a handkerchief. Her breath stuttering, her mouth as dry as week-old bread, she stared at him, trying to form the words. Why was this so difficult?

Old habits die hard, Rosemary.

Yes, Mum, they do, but it's time they were buried.

Decision made, she stood and accepted the glass of cordial he held out towards her. Taking a mouthful, she let the sweet orange syrup coat her tongue. She looked across at him. He still had that same goofy smile he'd had as a boy. The boy who, on one fateful night, had claimed her virginity and unknowingly fathered her child. She took a deep breath and clamped her fingers around the glass to stop them trembling. It was now or never.

'About that,' she said.

Dave gulped his drink and smacked his lips together. 'About what?'

'About the girls.' She could hear herself – she sounded surprisingly calm. It spurred her on. 'You have good reason to be proud. One of them *is* yours.'

He stared back at her, eyebrows prickling like a pair of hairy caterpillars.

'Dave.' She said his name gently, as if to buffer him from the blow. 'Faith is *your* daughter.'

He lowered his glass and for a minute she thought he might drop it altogether. His mouth fell open. His eyes were still that striking shade of blue that had attracted Rose to him in the first place – so similar to their daughter's. Why hadn't she seen it when Faith walked through the door? 'You mean that night we . . .'

Rose nodded. The night they'd both conveniently neglected to acknowledge. 'In your car, the night of my farewell party.'

'Why didn't you tell me?'

'I didn't know until I got to Sydney and even then I was in denial.' She shook her head, disgusted with her younger self's cowardice. 'By the time I faced up to it I was four months gone. I was too scared to come home. But after I'd had the baby I . . .' Her voice faltered and she swallowed hard to regain her composure. Would the pain and the shame of it ever go away? 'I was too scared to go anywhere else. So, I came back to Birralong, put it all behind me. It was the only thing I could do.'

'And I'd already left town.'

'Yes, you had. So, nobody was any the wiser. I never told a soul.'

Silence settled in between them, purring like a lost cat that had just found a new home.

'Well,' Dave coughed out a laugh. 'Can't say I was expecting that. Although it does make more sense now, the way you were all jittery with me when I first came back.' He jerked his eyes to hers. Rose could almost see the lightbulb flickering in his head. 'Does Faith know?'

'Yes. But she promised not to say anything until I talked to you.'

'Which explains why she's been looking at me so strangely.'

'I'm sorry, Dave. I should have told you sooner.' It was a terrible thing, to be ashamed of yourself, but it was a feeling she was so familiar with, like a scar that faded but never quite disappeared.

The sound of laughter rang from inside the house. Steph and Faith making up for lost time. It seemed an age before either of them moved. 'Well, we've both got things to do,' Dave had said, finally. 'But maybe we can sit down and have a proper talk about it all tomorrow, eh?'

'Of course.'

Shell-shocked he'd stumbled off to his car, leaving Rose alone in the garden feeling completely disoriented, like she'd just stepped off a train after a long journey – while she knew where she'd been she didn't have a clue where she was going.

———

'Crikey.' Dave stepped through the door, arms laden, surveying the platters of food cooling in various locations around the huge expanse of the kitchen. 'You've got enough here to feed an army.' He laughed as he stacked another box on the industrial-sized bench.

Rose shook that difficult conversation from her mind. Back to the task at hand. 'Well, we're going to have what amounts to an army battalion in that hall come seven o'clock tonight.' She wrung out the dishcloth and hung it over the tap.

'What time are Faith's parents due?'

Rose turned to look at him, blank faced. Over the last few weeks she'd started to think of herself as Faith's mother, and on the odd occasion when she and Dave were both in their daughter's presence, had begun to acknowledge to herself that he was her father.

She bit down on her lip as she pondered the imminent arrival of Stella and Brian Montgomery, Faith's actual parents.

He clapped a hand to her back. 'You've got nothing to worry about, Rosie. They'll love you.'

She wasn't so sure. From what Faith had told her about Stella and Brian, they sounded a bit on the posh side and posh wasn't exactly her middle name. Or any of her other names, for that matter. Faith had talked to them via Skype and explained the whole thing. Apparently they'd managed to get their heads around the news, but knowing the facts and confronting them in the flesh were two completely different things.

Rose was worried that it would all be too much.

'They'll love you too,' she said to Dave, hand on his shoulder, covering her own uncertainty, 'once they find out about you, that is.' The poor buggers were in for another shock.

The oven bell dinged. 'I'd better get the sausage rolls out or they'll burn to a crisp.' Before she made it back to the bench a hand appeared from over her shoulder, snatching a sausage roll from the tray.

'Ouch, they're friggin' hot.' Cleo dropped the pilfered pastry onto the floor but bent over just as fast and scooped it up. 'Five-second rule,' she said, shoving it into her mouth whole.

'I hope you burn your tongue,' Rose scolded.

'I'll leave you girls to it. They need some more chairs and tables put out in the hall.' Dave mumbled and shuffled off, but not before Rose noticed the way his cheeks had turned scarlet at Cleo's arrival.

Rose turned to give her friend the eye.

'What?' Cleo said. 'Have I got grub all over my face?' She brushed a hand across her mouth.

'Don't think I haven't noticed,' Rose said, one eyebrow raised.

'Noticed what?'

'The goggle eyes you and Dave Ryan have been making at each other for the past few weeks.'

'I haven't got a clue what you're talking about,' Cleo grumbled but Rose could tell it was all for show.

'Don't give me that, of course you do. And just for the record,' she dipped her head, gave Cleo a cheeky smirk. 'I think you two would make a very nice couple.'

'Really?'

Rose nodded, throwing a clean tea towel across the last of the pastries while they cooled.

'And you honestly wouldn't mind?' Cleo, uncharacteristically sheepish, blinked and rubbed her palms up and down her hips.

'Why would I mind? I told you, Dave and I both agreed after that one night fling that we were better off as friends. But you two,' she waved a finger towards the door where Dave had last been seen high-tailing it out of the kitchen, 'you have a definite thing going on.'

Cleo scrunched up her face, her nose wrinkling. 'It's a bit weird, though, isn't it, after you and he have . . . you know.'

'Yes, I do know, but that's beside the point.' Rose gave a wicked laugh. 'And take it from me, you won't be disappointed once you get him in the sack.'

'Rosemary O'Shea, you are positively evil.' Cleo grabbed her by the arm in a sideways hug. 'Which is why I love you so much.'

'I love you too.' She paused, guilt shrinking her insides as she took in the genuine joy on her oldest friend's face. 'Which is why I have to tell you something right this minute.' For some reason telling Cleo the entire story about the baby she'd given up had turned out to be as impossible now as it had thirty-one years ago. She'd given her all the details except the niggly matter of paternity, which she'd attributed, when Rose had filled her in the day after Faith's revelation, to a clandestine liaison in Sydney. Facing up to the whole truth felt like something akin to bolting stark naked down the main street of Birralong screaming, 'This is who I really am' at the top of her lungs.

'Have to tell me what?' Cleo eyed her suspiciously.

It was time to strip off the tatty undergarments of her past and start running. She held Cleo by the shoulders and looked her straight in the eye. 'Dave is Faith's father,' she burst out. 'I had sex with him in the back of his station wagon the night before I left for Sydney.'

The smile on Cleo's face vanished. Rose could see the wobble in her jaw as she tried to keep herself under control. 'All these years and you never told me.'

'I never told anyone,' Rose said, forcing herself not to look away, 'I couldn't.' She waited a few seconds to let her words sink in. She took hold of Cleo's hand, willed her to understand. 'But I wish I had.'

'I would have been there for you, Rosie.' Cleo's voice wavered.

'I know you would have. I just . . . I couldn't face it. I wanted to put the whole thing behind me and telling anyone – even you – would have made it real.' Rose hung her head, pressed a hand hard against her chest in an effort to stop the ache. A tear ran down her face and dripped from her cheek. What a fool she'd been, lying to the people she loved the most.

Cleo took a step closer and Rose lifted her chin. Their hug was tentative at first, arms resting lightly on each other's backs, but when Rose felt her friend's grip tighten she reciprocated. They stood together for a good minute or two, their tears healing any damage her lie of omission might have done. Eventually Cleo fidgeted out of the embrace. 'We are sitting down with a bottle of wine very soon, Rosemary O'Shea, and you are going to tell me the whole story.'

'Righto,' Rose sniffed. She felt suddenly lighter. If she didn't know her two feet were firmly planted on the ground she could swear she'd just floated up into the never-never.

Cleo, never one to miss an opportunity, pulled her back down to earth. 'So, even with all that history, you're really sure it's still all right for me to go for it with Dave?'

'Absolutely.' Rose gave her a naughty wink. 'Leave it with me.'

Cleo laughed. It was good to see her so happy. Now that her father was in the nursing home her life was a little easier. There was still the drought to contend with and the banker wolves to keep at bay, but things had greened up a bit since the last lot of rain and the bureau had predicted a few more falls in the coming weeks. If things kept improving, Tim planned to go back to school and apply for a mechanic apprenticeship. All in all, things were looking up.

'So, did you book that trip of yours?' Cleo asked, unpacking the boxes of groceries Dave had delivered.

'Yes,' she said uncertainly. 'But I've taken out extra insurance in case I need to cancel.'

'Oh bollocks. You will not be cancelling. Stephanie is doing fine and you will be back well and truly before she's due. Between her and Dave the pub will be in good hands. All you need to do is get yourself on that plane and have a bloody good time.'

Rose sighed. She wasn't so sure. Even though she and Stephanie were now officially partners in the pub, along with Dave, who had convinced her to sell him a share, it seemed wrong to just take herself off on an overseas jaunt. Sure, she could justify it as a business trip, since she was going to be brushing up on her culinary skills, but she couldn't shake the feeling that she was being self-indulgent. And, if she was honest with herself, it was a little scary finally getting to do something that had always been just a fantasy. No, not scary, bloody terrifying.

Stephanie poked her head through the door. She was heading into her second trimester and was starting to look more like her old self again. Her hair was out and shining, her skin flawless, her smile bright and open. 'Need any help in here?' she called.

'All good love.'

Steph smiled and stepped back out, the swinging door rebounding noisily.

Rose whipped off her apron and straightened out her T-shirt. Fessing up to Cleo had completely wiped the even more nerve-wracking prospect of meeting Faith's parents from her mind. She looked down at her casual clothes. 'They'll be here soon,' she sighed. 'I should have worn something more elegant.'

'Bullshit,' Cleo said. 'You look beautiful just as you are.'

Rose's eyes began to well but she blinked the tears away. She'd done more crying in the past two months than she'd done in her entire life. There was nothing to cry about. She was about to meet the two people who had raised her child and given her pretty much everything she could have wished for; she had not one but two beautiful daughters who got on like a house on fire; her financial problems had been solved, in a roundabout way thanks to her departed mother-in-law; and she was about to embark on a trip she had only ever dreamed about – the first, she hoped, of many.

Life, after all, was damned good.

Stephanie

'ARE THEY HERE?' BRYCE NODDED TOWARDS THE FOYER.

She pulled up a seat. 'Not yet. Mum's got herself in a state about meeting them.' She was excited to meet Faith's parents but the same word couldn't be applied to her mother.

'Still feels a bit weird.'

'Yeah, but good-weird.'

Rose had broken the news soon after she and Jake had returned from the hospital that first day. She'd tucked Jake into their shared bed at The Crossroads, wanting to gnaw off her arm she was so hungry, and made her way downstairs. As soon as she entered the kitchen she knew something was up. A thick silence clouded the room. Rose was pretending to organise the pantry, moving jars of sauce and packets of pasta from one place to another and then back again. Faith was absently scrubbing the cooktop. The smell of bleach was so strong Stephanie's eyes began to burn. She looked from the woman lurking in the half closed cupboard to the one visibly hiding by the sink.

'What's going on?'

Rose reacted first, closing the pantry door with a bang that made all them all jump, and moving into the middle of the room. She nodded vaguely towards a chair. 'Sit down for a minute, love.'

If Stephanie didn't already feel sick with hunger, the strained look on her mother's face, would have done the trick. What was this about? Jake and Bryce were both safe, if a little worse for wear. What else could be this important? 'Mum, what it is?'

Faith joined them and all three sat heavily at the table. Rose bowed her head, hands clasped in front of her and for one larger than life moment it seemed her mother was about to say grace. Instead of launching into prayer, Rose flicked her eyes to Faith who gave a barely perceptible nod. 'When I was a young girl,' Rose started; her eyes were damp, her voice as raw, 'I got myself into . . .' she pressed her lips together and shook her head. 'I fell pregnant.' Stephanie listened to the rest of the story in ever deepening confusion until Rose ripped her from it with the words 'and Faith is my daughter'.

But I'm your daughter.

None of this made sense. She blinked her eyes once, twice, more times than a rational person should, and looked across at Faith. 'You're my sister?'

The girl with the white blonde hair and lilac eyes attempted a smile. Sisters. The idea was so foreign. She looked back to Rose for help.

'I should have told you sooner, Steph, should have told your father too, but it was so . . .'

Stephanie leaned across the table and took her mother's hand. The residue of yesterday's fear – the fear of losing her child – still lurked like a poisonous fog in the dark corners of her brain. Rose had been her rock. Not just in the last twenty-four hours, but for her whole life. Now she had the chance to return the favour. 'It's all right, Mum,' she said, 'I understand.'

A chair scraped against the floor, drawing Stephanie's attention back to Faith. Her sister was smiling, her long, thin fingers stretched out toward her across the table, searching. Stephanie reached out to her until their hands overlapped, the bond between them secured.

'There's something else you need to know.' Rose had managed to corral her emotions enough to continue.

God, what else could there be? Wasn't the fact that her sister had suddenly appeared enough?

'David Ryan is Faith's father.'

Stephanie released Faith's hand and sat back into the chair as this latest piece of information hit her like the first squall of a southerly buster. David Ryan, the bloke she'd caught in her mother's bed, the bloke her mother claimed was just an old friend, *he* was her half-sister's father? Faith was bug eyed, watching her reaction. Stephanie stared back at her. Surely this whole thing was a hallucination, some kind of post-traumatic stress attack. Or a joke. She started to laugh, but it died on her lips when she saw that neither her mother nor Faith was joining in. The three of them sat perfectly still, settling into their new reality; fresh, silent tears shimmering on cheeks.

Yes, finding out she had an older sister had been quite the revelation. Bryce was having a hard time getting his head around the whole thing, but at least he liked Faith.

Stephanie dragged her attention back to her husband. 'How are you feeling?'

'Not too bad.' He shifted his plastered leg to make himself more comfortable. 'Feel like a bit of a goose wearing shorts, though.'

'I don't think anyone's going to mind. There's not exactly a dress code, and we all know Rocco is going to turn up in thongs, boardies and a singlet.'

'True.'

He brushed a stray hair back from her face and the touch of his fingers left her skin tingling. 'You look hot. I hope you're not over-doing it.'

'I'll take that to mean, "Wow, you look *hot*."' She smiled but put a curb on her teasing when she saw he was serious. 'Don't worry, babe, I'm taking it easy. Not lifting anything and not rushing around too much. I promise.' For some miraculous reason the morning sickness this time around hadn't been as intense or as dragged out as it had with Jake. She was hoping that was a good omen for the rest of her pregnancy, that she'd get through it without complications. But she certainly wasn't taking any risks.

'You do look the other kind of hot too. More than.' He leaned over and gently kissed her cheek, giving her hand a squeeze. 'Just you wait until I get this plaster off.'

'I'm ready when you are.' That was an understatement. It had been six very long weeks since the accident and her hormones were ready to party.

'Mind if I join you two lovebirds?'

She looked up to find Cam shuffling from one foot to the other. 'Of course not.' She sensed a smidgen of hesitation from Bryce but after Cam had visited him in hospital the two of them seemed to have come to a truce.

'Speaking of lovebirds,' Bryce said, cocking his head towards the doorway, 'Your missus is about to have her two worlds collide.'

'She's hardly my missus,' Cam argued.

'Not ready to meet the in-laws yet, eh?'

Bryce giving his brother stick almost made it feel like old times. Stephanie had managed to wheedle the truth out of Faith about what had happened between her and Cam, and then she may, or may not, have done some matchmaking over the weeks that followed. By the sappy look on her brother-in-law's face, it seemed to have worked. But where would they go from here?

'It's a shame she's heading back to Sydney,' Stephanie said, her eyes drawing a direct line from Faith to Cam.

'Yes and no,' he hedged.

Maybe her instincts weren't so on point. 'What does that mean?'

'That means,' Cam began, stroking the stubble on his chin, 'I might be heading that way myself.'

'To Sydney?' Was that a hint of disappointment in Bryce's voice?

Cam nodded and dropped his hands into his pockets. He didn't quite meet his brother's eyes. 'I've decided this mining gig isn't really my style. There's a job down there I'm interested in. I'm going to check it out.'

'More like a girl you're interested in,' Bryce scoffed.

'That too.' Try as he might Cam couldn't hide how pleased he was with himself.

'I knew it!' Stephanie jumped to her feet and threw her arms around Cam's neck. Everything was falling into place.

Jake came hurtling towards them and Bryce held up a hand, signalling for him to slow down. His feet got the message before his mouth. 'Mum, Mum, look, Tim signed my cast.'

'Hey, take it easy, my man. What have I told you about running around like a lunatic?'

This time Jake heeded his father's warning. He quietened down and held out his arm, the plaster cast grubby and chewed around the edges, covered in a rainbow of signatures.

'Here,' he pointed.

Stephanie tried to decipher the freshly inked name squished along the elbow end of his cast. 'Timbo,' she read out. 'I'm amazed he could even fit that in.' Cleo's son was Jake's latest man-crush.

'He said I can hang out with him later.' He planted a wet kiss on his mother's face before racing away again.

'Poor Tim,' Bryce said, a look of mock horror on his face.

There was so much movement in the hall. Bodies coming and going, tables being decorated with green and gold ribbons, the dance floor being set up – the band tuning up their instruments. So many people had helped organise the event, donated raffle prizes and supplies and time to make sure it was a success. It was good to be doing something positive. The drought was far from over, but watching the way a community could come together like this was what living in a place like Birralong was all about. Stephanie wasn't one to boast but she allowed herself a quiet, fleeting moment of pride.

'I meant to ask,' Cam said, pulling her back into the conversation, 'what does it feel like to be a part-owner in The Crossroads?'

'It feels good.' She gave the two men a broad, easy smile. 'More than good.'

'If you're angling for free beer, mate, think again,' Bryce quipped. 'Steph's the restaurant manager. Dave's the bar manager so you'll have to suck up to him for discount booze.'

'I'm also the accountant,' she said, wryly, 'and there won't be any family discounts.'

A ripple of joy ran through her as they sat together and discussed the new family venture. She sent yet another silent thank-you up to her grandmother for inadvertently saving the pub. Her mother had flat-out refused to take any money for the renovations. Bryce had shocked them all when he suggested they buy a share in the place, along with Dave, who had already been trying to persuade Rose to take him on as a partner – a financial one. It was a win–win–win agreement: her mother now had the funds and freedom to travel whenever she wanted but still had a home and job to come back to; Dave got to come back to Birralong and feel useful again; Stephanie got to help run the pub and organise package tours that included visits to a bunch of other places in the area. Excluding Strathmore. As long as she still had time to help Bryce on the farm and be there for Jake – and the new baby – she'd be happy.

Cam stood. 'I'll catch you in a bit.'

She watched him walk towards the doorway, to where Jake and his buddies were playing hide and seek. A squeal of familiar laughter rang through the air. Judging by the noise, her son had been found. He was back to his old self, his cuts healed, cast almost ready to come off, and the nightmares that had cracked her heart in two as she cuddled him and tried to soothe him so often in those first few weeks had just about vanished.

She reached out and grabbed Bryce's hand, holding on tight to stem the unexpected wave of emotion that was threatening to bowl her over, but was too late to stop a single happy tear from falling.

'Damned hormones,' she said.

He pulled a hanky from his pocket and handed it across, with a knowing smile.

It wasn't the hormones, of course. But that was okay.

More than.

Faith

'SO, THE FLIGHT WASN'T TOO BAD?'

'A bit rocky at the end, but otherwise all right.'

The feigned casualness in her father's voice was an exact replica of her own. She'd already asked that question and he had already answered it. She checked the rear-vision mirror of Rose's car. Stella was in the back, clutching her handbag, looking terrified. Not quite as terrified as when Faith had contacted them via Skype to tell them where she was and why. The way she'd launched into them both hadn't been her finest moment.

'I'm in Birralong, Mum,' she'd hissed at Stella's blurry image on her laptop screen. 'Ring any bells?'

She watched her mother's eyes dim as the cogs began to turn in her brain and then heard the sharp intake of air as they snapped into place. Stella's hand flew to her mouth. Brian, who had drifted in and out of the background like a clueless extra in a low budget soap opera, reappeared, kneeling by his wife's side. He leant towards their home computer, so close Faith could only see the pulsing vein in his forehead. 'What's going on?'

Ignoring Stella's quiet sobs, Faith continued her attack. 'What's going on, Dad, is that I'm in a country town in Queensland where I've just met my birth mother.'

Brian sunk back onto his haunches. 'Oh.'

She watched her father's tanned holiday face turn a ghastly shade of white, the colour blanch from his lips. He looked like an old man. A sad, lost old man. Stella was now back in the picture, all of her holiday *joie de vivre* gone, along with her excitement at being home for her daughter's birthday.

'You found the letter,' she said timidly.

Seeing her two elderly parents looking completely shattered brought Faith to her senses. She recalled Rose's anguish, remembered Poppy's words about how crushing it would be to find out you could never have your own child, and her anger paled.

'Yes.' She started to tremble. 'Why didn't you tell me?'

Stella dusted a handkerchief across her eyes. 'We always intended to, but the time never seemed right, and once five and then ten and then fifteen and twenty years passed, telling you the truth seemed, well, unnecessary.'

Tears welled in her father's eyes. 'It was because we loved you so much, Faith,' he said, his voice cracking. 'It wasn't the best way to handle it, in hindsight. But everything we did for you was done out of love.' He didn't give in to tears easily. Faith had seen him cry before – at her grandfather's funeral, when Tippy their labrador had to be put down, and he'd been a little milky-eyed at her graduation – but now he was so genuinely fragile. 'Please forgive us, Faithy.'

She watched as he rested his head against Stella's and they cried together. Unable to form any words, Faith nodded. Of course. Of course she would forgive them. They were her parents. 'I love you, too.'

It had taken a few more conversations to clear the air and there was still a fair amount of smog to get through. That, Faith hoped, would happen tonight. To their credit, both her parents had jumped at the chance to come up for the fundraising bash, which they knew meant coming face to face with Rosemary Barnes.

'Pretty warm,' her dad said, pulling at the collar on his polo shirt.

You could always trust Brian to settle on the weather as a reliable topic of conversation. They had a running joke in their household that he should have been a meteorologist. Faith smiled at him. 'You'd be used to this sort of climate after your stint in the Mediterranean, wouldn't you?'

'Nowhere near this dry.'

He was right. Even with the small amount of rain that had fallen, tufts of green had started to appear across the dried-out paddocks. And it wasn't just the land that was looking more hopeful. People around town had broader smiles on their faces and there was already talk of re-stocking. The rampant optimism was contagious and she was happy to listen, happy to learn. Happy to be here. Birralong was pretty cruisy. The people were friendly, the pace relaxed and the landscape had its own special magic that sometimes left her tongue-tied.

'How are all the plans for the party tonight?' Stella piped up from the back. Trivia was her usual modus operandi, her way of avoiding the actual situation at hand and going for something much safer. But that was okay.

'Really good, brilliant.' She answered her mother with exaggerated enthusiasm and spent the rest of the drive into town raving about pretty much everyone involved in the planning and execution of the event. Rambling was a great way to fill a void. She managed to prattle on all the way to the Community Centre, where she pulled up and turned off the engine.

Nobody moved. Or spoke. If it wasn't for the heat inside the car that started to build as soon as the airconditioning was cut Faith had the feeling they might have sat there procrastinating for the rest of the day, but if she'd learned anything from this whole crazy experience it was that denial did nothing but damage. 'So, let's do this.' She jumped out of the car before anyone – including herself – could think of a reason not to, waited on the footpath until her parents joined her, and led the way inside.

In the hall, tables were being unfolded and set up, chairs arranged, tablecloths laid and balloons inflated. One popped just as they stepped inside and Stella almost hit the ceiling. 'Sorry,' she said, with a giggle.

Her mother never giggled. 'It's okay, Mum, she's not going to eat you alive or anything.' She took her arm. 'You'll really like her.'

Well, I think you will.

Her mind drifted back to the first time she had met Rose, how brusque she'd been, how un-Stella like. But she knew now that there was a lot of bravado and that underneath Rose was really quite the pussycat. A pussycat who was just as petrified as her parents about the impending meeting.

'Hi, there.' Stephanie bounced towards them from the storeroom, a huge box full of decorations in her arms. A riot of green and gold streamers spilled over the sides and she was having a hard time keeping them all contained. Faith was in awe of her sister. For all the crap she'd gone through, including horrendous morning sickness, she looked stunning – her skin shone and her long chestnut hair was to die for. There was a pink blush to her cheeks now and the frown lines she'd been sporting when Faith met her had completely disappeared.

'Mum, Dad,' Faith began the first round of introductions, 'this is Stephanie, my half-sister.' She felt her mother flinch but she carried on. 'Steph, this is Stella and Brian.' Stephanie deposited the box on the floor, stepped forward and threw her arms around each of them in turn, telling them how happy she was to meet them and how exciting it was that they'd made the trip. They tried to mould their startled expressions into something more like pleasure, but really, they just looked like they'd been given a mutual electric shock.

Faith held back her laughter.

'Mum's in the kitchen,' Stephanie said. 'I'll let her know you're here. Better get on with the finishing touches.' She picked up the box again, stuck her head around the corner and called to Rose before throwing them another huge grin. 'I'll catch up with you a bit later.'

'She seems lovely,' Stella murmured. Poor Mum. She was having a hard time getting her head around all of this. Her hair, normally neatly coiffed, had flopped with the heat and perspiration had broken out across her cheeks, dotting the usually unblemished surface of her foundation. The sooner they got this meeting over and done with the sooner they could all have a drink and relax.

For her part Faith was feeling surprisingly calm. The worst of it was over, after all. The three of them fidgeted nervously, tweaking their smiles, and then Rose appeared. In her tie-dyed navy T-shirt and frayed knee-length cargos, a purple paisley scarf wrapped around her loose bun, she could almost have passed for Faith's older sister. She'd been helping out at Strathmore these last few weeks while Bryce was recuperating and her skin was a light copper that blended perfectly with her auburn hair. Faith's eyes flicked from Rose to Stella and back again. You couldn't find two women more different from each other and yet they had one undeniable thing in common.

'Well, are you going to do the honours?' Rose asked abruptly. She was wringing her hands together, obviously more on edge than her directness suggested. But that was Rose.

'I was getting to it.' Faith placed one hand on Stella's arm and the other on Rose's. 'Stella, this is Rosemary Barnes, my birth mother . . . and Rose, this is Stella and Brian Montgomery, my mum and dad.' She had to step back and out of the way as the two women threw themselves into each other's arms. It was impossible to tell who was sobbing the loudest. All around them people froze, wooden smiles on their faces as they tried to work out what the hell was happening. A few of them knew who Faith was, but she'd kept news of her parents' arrival quiet. It was a family affair. She waited, tiny wings beating against the walls of her stomach while her two mothers – two! – clung to each other. This was their moment, not hers. At some point they released their grip on each other to include Brian in the embrace.

'Thank you,' Rose said finally, sucking back her tears. 'Thank you so much for taking such good care of her. Faith has told me what wonderful parents you are and that's all that I wished for.'

'And thank you.' Stella looked across at Faith, remarkably composed, and gave her a soft smile. 'We were truly blessed.'

Faith's lips quivered. The past two months had been the craziest, most emotional period of her life – and this meeting marked the end. The way she'd chosen to go about finding her birth mother might not have been the smartest, but now that they were all here, together, it didn't really matter.

They spent the next ten minutes chatting politely before Rose apologised and returned to the kitchen with Stella in tow to help with the salads. Faith dragged Brian to the bar that had been set up on the verandah outside. Not that it was open yet, but some pre-dinner drinks were definitely in order.

She poured her father a beer just as Dave sidled up. He had a strange, tortured look on his face.

Brian looked on, confused. 'What's going on?'

She took a fortifying breath. 'Dad,' she said, 'this is David Ryan.' She looked at Dave and he nodded, seemingly okay with what he knew she was about to reveal. 'He's my biological father.'

The two men stared at each other. Her father's welcoming smile died on his lips, his mouth flat-lining. She'd told her parents bits and pieces of the story but they'd never asked about her paternity and she'd decided they had enough to deal with until she could see them face to face. Springing this on them as soon as they arrived wasn't really ideal.

'Well, this is a surprise,' Brian said. There was a shudder in his jaw but he was doing a good job of keeping it in check.

Dave lifted his hand. 'Good to meet you.' He shook his head. 'I've only recently found out myself.'

Faith's heart ached at the look of utter confusion on her father's face. 'It's a long story, Dad.' She took his arm and led him around to the other side of the bar, pulled two beers out of the ice-filled esky and popped the lids. 'How about you two go debrief on the verandah.' She handed them each a bottle and watched them wander away. Turned out she'd hit the jackpot all round in the parent department.

'The bar's open, I see.'

She smiled at the sound of Cam's voice. 'Not really, but I might be persuaded to sneak you a drink.'

'What's the asking price?'

She leaned towards him as she answered. 'A dance.' She straightened back up and laughed as his face dropped. 'I even wore my dancing shoes.' Stepping around to the customer side of the bar she tapped her feet lightly on the floor showing off the new western boots Stephanie had bought her as a belated birthday present, a soft caramel leather with emerald stitching.

He grinned. 'Very fancy. Not sure there'll be too many places to wear them in the city.'

Faith had explained the real reason for her aborted hasty departure a few weeks back and it had taken him a while to thaw, but gradually the spark had reignited. A flame was burning pretty fiercely now as they stood against the bar, elbows touching. 'Oh, I don't know,' she said, 'they might look good with a smart black suit.'

'Any ideas what you're going to do when you get back to Sydney?' He was looking down at the opened bottle she'd placed in his hand.

'Not really,' Faith shrugged. 'I'm looking into starting up the online tourism thing with Steph, but that won't pay my bills. Hunt around for a new job, I suppose.'

'If you have some free time I could do with a tour.'

Faith arched an eyebrow.

'I've got a job interview down there next week.'

'Have you now?' Trying to hide her glee was futile. 'Well, I suppose a tour could be arranged. For the right fee.'

'Geez, you're all about the fees, aren't you?' He said, pretending to sound wounded. 'What is it this time? Another dance?'

'No.' She edged closer. 'A kiss.'

When their lips met, it was gentle and light but carried the promise of so much more, like the first warm day at the end of a long, cold winter.

Her phone buzzed in her pocket. She gave him an apologetic nod and fished it out, smiling into the phone. 'Any news?'

'Yes. There is news.' Poppy sounded tense. 'The news is that I am in labour right now and if you don't get your arse back here to meet this ... ugh ... this baby ...' She growled so loudly Faith had to hold the phone away from her ear. 'I will officially fire you as godmother.'

'Oh, Pops.' Her chest tightened. She dropped her head and ran a hand roughly through her hair. If only she could be in two places at once. She'd missed a fair chunk of her best friend's pregnancy and she couldn't wait to get back home and see her and the new baby. 'I'll be back first thing on Monday, I promise. Now get off the phone and have that baby and call me as soon as it's born.'

She ended the call but kept her eyes fixed on the phone cupped in her hand, a photo of The Crossroads the new screensaver. It would be good to get back to her real life but some time soon she would come back to Birralong. It was her second home now, and Rose and Stephanie, Bryce and Jake were her second family.

Cam bumped his shoulder against hers. She looked up to his curious gaze.

'All good,' she smiled.

And it was absolutely, positively true.

Acknowledgements

WRITING CAN BE A LONELY PURSUIT BUT NO BOOK MAKES IT to publication without the input of a whole lot of wonderful people.

This book is a work of fiction and none of the characters are based on anyone in particular. Birralong is (very) loosely based on the township of Hughenden, Queensland, where I spent an amazing time seeing the town and some of its outlying properties. Huge thanks to everyone who welcomed me so warmly in Hughenden, in particular Tracey Edwards super-librarian and all round fabulous person. Tracey, this book would never have existed without your invitation to visit – I am eternally in your debt. Thanks also to Bronwyn and Greg McNamara, Suzie and Billy Payne, Eva Luther and Deb Viney for allowing me into your homes and onto your properties. Also to Juanita and Andrew Holden for sharing your stories. And to everyone in Hughenden for your generosity and hospitality. I hope to get back there one day.

To my gorgeous friend, Sonia May, thank you for sharing details about your adoption and steering me in the right direction. Thanks to David Fisher for your help on the restoration rules and regulations for heritage buildings.

My trusty writing buddies, there as always – Monique, Terri, Annabel, Angella, Sharon, Perla, Wanda, Kerry, Kay and Bron – thank you for your feedback on various chapters. Special thanks to Krystina, Rae and my favourite reader, Carrie, for your brilliant feedback and guidance.

Another huge bunch of thanks to my amazing publisher Vanessa Radnidge who always listens, consoles and encourages. You are the best! Thanks to Kate Stevens, my wonderful editor for always making my pages better and to Claire de Medici for your astute edit. And to everyone at Hachette Australia for continuing to believe in my writing.

Thanks also to everyone who has read my books – I hope you enjoy this one!

In what has been the most difficult year of my life, I would like to thank my close friends and family for pulling me through. Erica, Denise, Tanya, Kerry, Donna, Rhonda, Allison and Toni. And our beautiful Kath, who is no doubt up there partying. Cheers Lovey! Thanks to my mum, Gwen, sister Lynne and brothers Peter and Gary for cheering me on. To Deb for your continuing friendship, despite the distance. To my girls – Freya, Amelia and Georgia – for your constant love and support. As always, to John: your unwavering belief leaves me without words.

Pamela Cook is a city girl with a country lifestyle and too many horses. Her rural fiction novels feature feisty women, tangled family relationships and a healthy dose of romance. Her first novel, *Blackwattle Lake*, was published in 2012 after being selected for the Queensland Writers' Centre/Hachette Manuscript Development Program. *Blackwattle Lake* was followed by *Essie's Way* (2013) and *Close to Home* (2015). *The Crossroads* is Pamela's fourth novel. When she's not writing she wastes as much time as possible riding her handsome quarter horse, Morocco.

Pamela loves to connect with readers both in person and online. You will often find her lurking in one of these places:

www.facebook.com/PamelaCookAuthor
@PamelaCookAU

You can find out more about Pamela and download reading group notes from her website:

www.pamelacook.com.au

About Room to Read

PAMELA COOK IS A COMMITTED WRITER AMBASSADOR FOR Room to Read, an innovative global non-profit organisation which seeks to transform the lives of millions of children in ten developing countries through its holistic literacy and girls' education programs.

Working in collaboration with local communities, partner organisations and governments, Room to Read focuses its efforts on developing reading skills in primary school–aged children because literacy is the foundation for all future learning. Since it was founded in 2000, Room to Read has impacted the lives of over nine million children by establishing school libraries, publishing original children's books in more than twenty-five local languages, constructing child-friendly classrooms, and supporting educators with training and resources to teach reading, writing and active listening.

Room to Read is changing children's lives in Bangladesh, Cambodia, India, Laos, Nepal, South Africa, Sri Lanka, Tanzania, Vietnam and Zambia.

As Pamela says, 'Having visited Room to Read schools in rural India, I have seen firsthand how life-changing their programs really are. Where you happen to be born should not determine whether or not you receive an education. I truly believe that world change starts with educated children and that's why I support Room to Read.'

For more information visit www.roomtoread.org

Room to Read®

Stories that make you feel

Books with Heart is an online place to chat about the authors
and the books that have captured your heart . . .
and to find new ones to do the same.

Join the conversation:
(f) /BooksWithHeartANZ • (y) @BooksWithHeart

··
Discover new books for **FREE** every month
··

Search: Books with Heart

Search: Books with Heart sampler

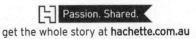
get the whole story at hachette.com.au